The Opal Miner's Daughter

Drawing from her earlier life as a rural midwife, Fiona McArthur shares her love of working with women, families and health professionals in her books. In her compassionate, pacey fiction, her love of the Australian landscape meshes beautifully with warm, funny, multigenerational characters as she highlights challenges for rural and remote families, and the strength shared between women. Happy endings are a must.

Fiona is the author of the non-fiction book *Aussie Midwives*, and lives on a farm with her husband in northern New South Wales. She was awarded the NSW Excellence in Midwifery Award in 2015 and the Australian Ruby Award for Contemporary Romantic Fiction in 2020.

Find her at FionaMcArthurAuthor.com

Also by the author

Red Sand Sunrise
The Homestead Girls
Heart of the Sky
The Baby Doctor
Mother's Day
The Desert Midwife
Aussie Midwives
The Bush Telegraph
The Farmer's Friend

FIONA McARTHUR

The Opal Miner's Daughter

MICHAEL JOSEPH
an imprint of
PENGUIN BOOKS

MICHAEL JOSEPH

UK | USA | Canada | Ireland | Australia
India | New Zealand | South Africa | China

Michael Joseph is part of the Penguin Random House group of companies
whose addresses can be found at global.penguinrandomhouse.com.

Penguin
Random House
Australia

First published by Michael Joseph, 2022

Cover photography: woman by Jarvier Pardina/Shutterstock;
opal by Somjit Chomran/Shutterstock
Cover design by Louisa Maggio Design
Typeset in Sabon by Midland Typesetters, Australia

Printed and bound in Australia by Griffin Press, part of Ovato, an accredited
ISO AS/NZS 14001 Environmental Management Systems printer

A catalogue record for this
book is available from the
National Library of Australia

ISBN 978 1 76104 068 9

penguin.com.au

*We at Penguin Random House Australia acknowledge that Aboriginal and
Torres Strait Islander peoples are the Traditional Custodians and the first storytellers
of the lands on which we live and work. We honour Aboriginal and Torres Strait
Islander peoples' continuous connection to Country, waters, skies and communities.
We celebrate Aboriginal and Torres Strait Islander stories, traditions and living
cultures; and we pay our respects to Elders past and present.*

To the dreamers and those who chase their dreams –
I hope you dream big
xx Fi

'. . . an ethereal connection to see bright sparkles shining from the cool dull clay stone . . . an explosion of the spectrum . . .'
– Opal Queen Kelly Tishler on opals, Lightning Ridge

Prologue

Adelaide

'So, how'd you end up in Lightning Ridge?'

Adelaide Brand peered over her sunglasses at the chatty white-haired woman behind the counter of the fuel station. Nosy, she wondered, or was it a case of small-town curiosity about strangers? Or was she just being friendly?

Adelaide had been buying diesel every couple of days for the last fortnight since she'd moved to the Ridge, but the times she'd called in here there'd been other customers. Her old Lister generator proved thirsty but reliable, and as an opal miner she needed lights to see by underground.

She nodded at the kind eyes and experienced a flicker of kindred interest. 'I'm addicted to the opals. A new fascination. You?'

'Oh, I followed a miner fifty years ago.' The woman brushed a sticky strand of white hair away with a callused hand. 'We roughed it off the grid for ten freakin' years. But like a lot of the business owners in town, I decided there's more comfort in trade than in digging.'

She laughed loudly, her crooked teeth and sunburst wrinkles affable and uncomplicated. Her stark white hair looked quite beautiful, even tied back off her neck with an old shoelace. She stood about twenty centimetres shorter and maybe ten years older, say mid-seventies, than Adelaide, who was tall at a hundred and eighty centimetres.

Her new acquaintance's aged appearance could be a premature result of the outback's tough sunlight, or it could be a personal lack of interest in slowing the imprint of time on her face. Adelaide suspected both.

The woman had a great smile, though, and Adelaide liked her. 'I retired from nursing but enjoy being busy.'

'Husband?' The EFTPOS skipped as Adelaide's new acquaintance tapped in the amount with a firm hand.

'We're still married, we just live in different parts of the country. Tyler's not interested in opals, or being a tourist. He much prefers armchair travelling and the city.' *To spending time with me*, she added silently.

'Ha. Go you on adventuring, then.' The proprietor nodded at the small world outside the window. 'Some men like their routines, stayin' home. I reckon most get more settled as they get older.' She gestured with her fingers up the wide street towards town. 'That's why the business part of the Ridge is mostly run by women.'

She handed back the credit card after a long look at the name on it. 'Nice to meet you, Adelaide.' She gave a quick nod of hello. 'I'm Desiree, here weekdays till five. See me for fuel and small equipment breakdowns.' She waggled her brows. 'They call me the engine whisperer.'

In her seventies? 'Nice to meet you, Desiree. And call me Del.'

'We have a Friday-night ladies' get-together out the back.' Desiree jerked her head sideways to indicate the rear of the building. 'As soon as my shop door's closed for the night. Feel free to drop in. It's BYO.'

Somewhere deep in Adelaide's belly, a cold cube of sadness, one she tried to ignore, seemed to warm and soften. 'Thanks. I might do that if my own company gets old.'

Desiree snorted. 'Oh, we all get old, Miss Del. Come tonight if you want.' She paused for a moment, then said, 'Have you got yourself some decent gloves now?' Her gaze slid non-judgementally over the healing scabs on Adelaide's hands.

'I do. Leather ones.' Very expensive driving gloves that Tyler had given her once for the small Virago motorbike she'd moved on from – last decade's crisis.

The gloves, soft plum kid, were not designed for scrabbling in rock, but were soft and supple under the hardy gloves she wore on top. She'd had her daughter post them out and they'd arrived two days ago.

Now Riley had her postal address, which was fine because Adelaide was settled. She'd needed to make sure the family knew she was alive. Didn't want a police hunt for her rotting corpse.

Desiree rocked back on her heels. 'Whose claim are you working?'

'Cooper's. It's mine now.' Her own opal mine. Still couldn't believe it.

'The old Wayfarers Inn?' Desiree's scarce brows lifted. 'Good choice. Some nice colour pulled out of there.'

'Good to know.' And it was. Once she'd decided on the Ridge, Adelaide had paid a broker to find the best claim up for lease, preferably with some form of dwelling, but you never knew the spin involved in the final sale.

The tiny, quirky shack had once been a gin joint and stables, with a twenty-year mining lease inside the acre of fencing. The bargain had only used a fifth of her inheritance from her mother, which left a decent chunk in her personal savings.

There was something incredibly satisfying about owning a shack with fabulous sunsets and endless bush views. And no neighbours. Even more satisfying was leasing the rocky patch of soil inside the fence, which meant she had her very own mine to climb down and dig in.

'See you.' Adelaide lifted a hand in farewell to Desiree and turned, walking out to her battered troop carrier, which also had been a bargain. The bed popped up from the roof, making it ridiculously painful to climb in and out of – no way would Tyler try it – but she'd felt safe up there when travelling. She'd done some solo travelling before settling on the Ridge. Tyler had predicted she'd be back home in a week wanting to sell the uncomfortable vehicle again. She hadn't. And Rocky, her troopy, could manage any road conditions she might come across. It was her lack of four-wheel-driving skills she worried about. She was booked in for an off-road day course with an ex-paramedic in Walgett tomorrow. The woman had been recommended by the previous owners of the Wayfarers Inn when she'd inquired. She couldn't wait.

Her phone rang. Good timing. The service was iffy out at the inn. She knew without checking the screen that it wouldn't be Tyler. He'd be at the gym now. It was her daughter's smiling picture that appeared. 'Riley, darling. How are you?'

'Mother. I'm good. Trying to clear my patients before holidays. How're the gloves working?'

4

'Wonderful. Much better for my soft hands. Thank you.'

'You're welcome.' She heard the smile in her voice. 'Our hands aren't supposed to be tough. I can't believe you're using a pick-axe underground.' But as well as amusement, did she detect a hint of admiration? Warmth spread as her daughter's voice softened. 'As for posting, well plenty of times you posted care packages when I was at school.'

Inside Adelaide that ice cube melted a little more and began to puddle into liquid. There had been distance and silence from her daughter when she'd left Tyler behind, but it seemed Riley was over that. Or moving on. She was good at that.

Riley was usually in a hurry, so she'd better not hold her up. 'It's not like you to call when you're at work.' Her daughter led a very busy professional life. 'Two phone calls in one week?'

'One of my patients cancelled last minute with the flu, so I've got time. Dad said some certificates came for you.' The smile was back in her voice. 'You been doing courses again?'

Lord, yes, she had. 'Once I leased the mine, I needed to be a legal miner,' she explained. 'They're my certificates for Mine Property Manager and Environmental Mine Operator. I have the digital versions on my phone.'

Riley laughed. 'So cool. All this because you got bored after your retirement party? I never did ask you. Why opal mining?'

Adelaide thought about the path she'd taken to get here. And the fact that her daughter, or her husband for that matter, indeed never had asked why. 'It was that place I wandered into on Wentworth Avenue in Sydney, Gemmology House. It was like a museum, with a stone facade, tall columns and arched windows.'

'A building sent you mining?'

She thought about the treasures in those walls. 'Maybe. Inside, they had those gahnite crystals, you know those sharp, deep-green crystals, the ones Grandma gave us when we visited them at Wilcannia?' She'd been delighted to recognise the gahnite. 'Just seeing those cabinets of precious stones and gems and our gahnite made it special.'

'Wow.' Riley did sound intrigued. 'That's interesting.'

Yes, it was. Hence Adelaide's enrolment in the practical gem-mology course, and about four others. 'Well, that was the start. I'd never thought of gems as raw and mysterious until I saw the opals. I'm afraid I have an opal obsession, now.'

In the classes and display cases, she'd discovered the shifting brilliant colours of the black opal, the dark base underlying the spray and sparkle of colour giving the gem such rainbow intensity. The kaleidoscope had fascinated her. Sometimes she thought she could see a whole universe in those colours, pulling her in.

'Opals are pretty,' Riley said.

Adelaide sniffed teasingly. 'Opals aren't pretty. They're magnifi-cent, mysterious, marvellous. And bloody hard work to mine for.'

'I stand corrected.' Riley laughed, and it was so nice to hear her voice. 'Any passion is a good passion. Go you, Mum.'

'I love them,' she said simply, aware that Riley might not want to hear more. Tyler hadn't, so she had stopped enthusing to him.

'You sound happy, Mum.'

'I am.' It was time to change the subject, though, before Riley asked when she was coming home. 'How's Josh?'

'Fine.' Her daughter's tone turned a little flat. 'We're spending some time together over my holidays. There's a couple of charity dos he wants me to go to, and we have dinner with his parents next week.'

'That will be nice.' Not, but she wouldn't say it. Josh was more boring than Tyler's television. A subtle tone pulsed in the distance on Riley's end.

'I've got a call coming in, I'd better go. Talk soon, Mum.'

'Bye, darling.' But she was already gone.

Adelaide walked to her vehicle and started the engine, thinking about the gemmology courses. The birth of excitement, and Tyler, her husband, the ex-business executive, refusing to come. By the time she'd completed that night class, after he'd patted her hand and said new interests were good, she knew she'd found a passion. By the last course, she'd been completely captivated and wishing she'd found these studies forty years ago.

That was when she decided to come to the Ridge. The home of the black opal. She'd asked Tyler to go on a road trip with her – just to see – but he'd raised one cultured brow and with a laugh said, 'Why on earth would we want to do that?'

Adelaide suspected he'd not thought for a minute that she'd go on her own. Or if she did, that she might dabble for a weekend or two at the most. Until Adelaide had packed up and left two months ago to travel. He'd been horrified then – was still horrified – but not enough to follow her.

Instead of growing bored and lonely, she'd travelled and learned something quirky and fun every day. She'd met new people and enjoyed new places. When she took over the inn a month ago she'd learned a lot more. Her new home had solar panels and batteries. Gutters and a rain tank that never caught rain and needed filling with bore water from the tanker, which luckily, came out when needed. She'd learned to work a gas fridge and a turn-of-the-century wood stove and she'd tweaked her cooking skills to match her kitchen. That too had been tricky but satisfying.

Then there was mining opal with two fifteen-metre shafts down a steel ladder to a central underground room and two short side tunnels. Her cabin/inn/shack stood five kilometres out of town, still close enough to pick up supplies or catch up with new friends, one of whom she may have just found in Desiree.

And the neighbours, some definitely working under aliases or nicknames to avoid the law, were far enough away that she didn't hear the parties or have many uninvited guests. She had some, but they were friendly, non-judgemental and live-and-let-live. One thing she could say about those uninvited, two-legged guests was they were never boring.

She also doubted they filled out their census.

Chapter One

Riley

'Eighteen starlit nights with you.' Joshua Bouvier's big brown eyes were determined. He was pleased with himself, and pleased with the very expensive 'surprise' cruise tickets he'd just presented to Riley.

In that moment, not-as-tall-as-her, handsome, impeccably dressed Josh looked like his extremely well-off stockbroker father.

'And . . . while we're away, I have a very special question to ask.' This he said archly as he patted his pocket. Good grief. Did he have words written on paper in there, or heaven forbid, a velvet box?

In her Macquarie Street consulting room, Dr Riley Brand's stomach fell. *Not the M word*, she prayed. *Please, not the M word.* She'd thought they might go away for a weekend here and there through her holidays, spend some time together, some apart, general fun and relaxation on leave.

Now, with Josh sitting across from her desk in her lunch hour with his eyes unwavering – his plans laid out – she felt guilty. Trapped. And she felt the overwhelming need to run. Like she always did when a relationship threatened to become more than a dinner date and a useful plus-one arrangement.

He wanted to discuss commitment and she wanted out of anything serious that interfered with her scheduled career advancement. He'd also want the big one – kids – and she still had no rush of anticipation at the thought. She'd begun to doubt she ever would.

Familiar guilt wormed its way through her because her clients were searching for the elusive dream of parenthood, and here she was flapping away the idea with her ringless fingers. Her mother said it's because she hadn't found the right man yet. But Riley wasn't sure she'd ever do what her own mother had: put her life on hold until everyone was finished leaning on her. It's one of the reasons she didn't feel she'd ever be as good a mum as her mother. She was pulled out of her thoughts when Josh continued.

'I've been watching the weather. It looks perfect for the Top End. Lazing on the deck through the Kimberleys, jumping into the zodiacs through the gorges, helicopter rides into the sunset – together . . .' He drew out the last word, his smile confident. 'You'll love it.'

She probably would, but not with him. And certainly not with the M word possibly hanging around. 'Sounds amazing.' She tried for an apologetic smile, but could only manage a closed-lip one. 'I can't. I know we *were* going to spend time together . . .' Because she hadn't really decided until the 'special question' reference. And then there was the eighteen loooong days together with no breaks . . . That was certainly enough for Riley to decide against.

It was time to edge backwards out of this relationship.

She tried again. 'I'm sorry, Josh. I've decided to drive to Lightning Ridge and convince my mother to come home to Dad. The cruise is out.'

'Don't be silly.' Josh's hand brushed in a you're-pulling-my-leg wave. 'You can see Adelaide when we come back. I'll come with you. After we do this.'

If it wasn't so ludicrous, she'd laugh. Take Josh on a road trip to the outback? With sub-standard coffee for him to complain about and constant whining about everything else? No, good grief no. 'I'll need the four weeks. Mum will take some convincing,' she said with finality. But she might go insane twiddling her thumbs for that long.

Josh stared at her. 'You could take extra leave? Do both. We're booked for this cruise, Riley.' He didn't look so sure now, finally seeing the real picture, as opposed to the promising one in his head.

She'd laid the rules down early in the piece. They were exclusive but not permanent. Friends with benefits. Though to be fair, her schedule had played constant havoc with the benefits.

Riley pointed at her computer and the open appointment schedule. 'I've only got four weeks of leave. My appointments are already fully booked for that first week back.'

Josh snapped down the brochure. 'Can't you phone Adelaide?' That was the first whine. 'Convince her from afar.' The second. He did that when he didn't get his way. Truly most annoying.

Riley wanted to crack her neck from the strain of being gentle. 'Mother will take more convincing than a phone call,' she said.

With his eyes stormy and a hint of impatience in his voice, Josh muttered, 'Why doesn't your dad sort this out? He's the one left behind in Sydney. Dumped for a mining claim out west by his wife.'

Yes, her dad had been ditched. The dad she'd always thought of as her hero. And he probably deserved desertion because he hadn't found his feet after retirement as fast as Mum had. He'd fallen down the rabbit hole of Netflix, current affairs and the gym since he'd finished work, but Mum's absence had gone on long enough. Riley had the feeling both her parents were acting out of pride now. 'He's reluctant to look needy.'

Josh screwed up his face. 'I still can't believe your mother's roughing it on a mining lease. Grubbing in dirt off the grid.' That was patent disbelief, Josh thinking, *How the heck could she run a coffee machine without electricity?* No doubt about that.

He sniffed and Riley's eyes narrowed. She might complain about her parents, but he'd better not. Riley could read Josh like the screen in front of her. He'd just realised she wouldn't change her mind on the cruise. He knew she could be inflexible when she cared enough to make a statement.

That entitlement Josh suffered from had bruised. Everything was supposed to fall into place the way he wanted it to, because it was him. Josh. The only child. The golden child.

And what had she been thinking?

Sitting here looking at this man across the desk from her, Riley suspected she'd drifted close to disaster through laziness. Because Josh being there had been easy and she'd assumed that lack of intent went both ways. She'd been too busy to notice the change in him. Well, it was time to stop now, and take notice.

She glanced at her watch. 'Josh, I really appreciate all the organisation that's gone into this and I can see you were really looking forward to it —'

'It's one-sided. Isn't it?' Josh interrupted. 'This whole relation-ship.' He threw his hands up. 'You're really not going?'

'You're a great guy, Josh.'

He blew out a big breath. He even rustled the papers on her desk with the gale he sent. She could smell the peppermint he'd sucked before he'd come in to see her. 'I don't like saying it, Riley,' there was a hint of sternness in his voice now, 'but maybe we need a break.' He paused and gave her a look, as if he expected her to be devastated.

He just didn't get it. Gently, she said, 'Not a break, we're breaking up, Josh. You deserve someone much more invested in doing the things you want to do. Invested in the future with you. I'm not.' That might have been a tad blunt, but Riley felt she needed to be to get the message across.

Josh gaped, spun, then turned again before he opened the door, but she kept her mouth firmly closed and finally he left. He shut the door after himself with exquisite politeness. She wished he'd slammed it.

A rush of feelings hurtled through Riley all at once. Guilt. Shame. But yes, the biggest was relief.

Riley held off calling in her first patient of the afternoon. She was often too fanatically on time with her appointment schedule, anyway. Instead, she stared at the printed advertisement for a locum doctor in Lightning Ridge that she'd seen last night.

Her gaze slid to the uterus-shaped stress ball on her desk and she picked it up and squeezed the womb until her French-tipped nails dug into her palms.

'Lightning Ridge? Of all the back-of-beyond places. Really, Mum?' Riley said into the room, blowing out her breath so hard the same papers Josh had jiggled earlier moved again.

'You left me holding the abandoned baby, which is what Dad's been since you went. He needs you. And you need him.' She looked again at the vacancy in this month's *Medical Practitioner's Review*.

She squeezed the ball, then breathed. Squeezed. Breathed. Tasted the idea that had floated when she first saw it. Since she'd posted her mother's soft leather gloves last week, Riley had been mulling her options. A locum stint would give her an excuse to go. She'd have four whole weeks to convince Mum to return.

She squeezed the foam, and settled. She had four weeks already booked for leave, so getting away would be easy. It would be her first vacation in years. Talk about a change from Josh's luxury cruise along the Kimberley Coast. Instead, she'd be working in a mining town in north-western New South Wales as a GP with male and female patients.

It would take time to convince Mum to come home from her new love of prospecting. Or mining, or whatever you called living rough in a desert and scrambling through rocks for the elusive opal.

The question was, could Riley practise general medicine for four weeks? Could she work in a mullock-strewn whistle stop of rough blokes, miners and grey-nomad escapees like her mother?

There was only one way to find out. At least she'd be close to the leased opal-mining claim and shack, without crowding her mum. Or herself. The stint would give them a chance to talk sensibly. That would be more subtle than Riley trying the conversation via email or phone again, because that hadn't worked. Maybe she'd wait a week after arriving, then just seed the idea of her mum coming home. Hmm.

Did her mum even have running water to nurture a thought seed? Thankfully, the locum placement came with 'digs'. It was a mining town, but she guessed that was a pun for accommodation and not a plot to fossick in. She'd have water and electricity, and hopefully, she'd have the internet.

Stop being a wimp, she told herself. Of course, she could manage. A small voice whispered that Josh would say she wouldn't last. Her spine straightened at that. Josh had no idea of the stock she came from. That her great-grandpa had raised cattle out near Wilcannia and her great-gran had been droving beside him in flood and drought.

It was funny how generations changed. Went to the city. Went soft. The four-week stint would give her the chance to brush up on medical skills she hadn't touched for ten years. She looked at her manicured hands and thought of wrinkled scrotums. Then she laughed again at herself as she looked around at her swanky office. There were no men here. She'd been an obstetrician and gynaecologist for more than a decade. The last five years had focused on infertility – factors increasing the chances of falling pregnant and those that prevented pregnancy – so examining male body parts wasn't part of her brief, except for prescribing tests. Although, there had been surrogacy and donor-gametes studies, and she did have amazing transgender and LGBTQIA+ community clients among her success stories.

Riley squeezed the foam uterus in her hand again. She could do this. And she had an idea for something extra, if the hiring GP agreed. It would be a fast dip into something crazily different and then dip back out again. She'd have to work. She couldn't do kicking her heels on a rock-strewn opal claim while taking time to convince her mum to come home. She knew her mother when she was set on something. Riley was like that herself.

She picked up the phone and put a call through to the professor, her business partner, who was also at lunch, no doubt immersed in a medical journal.

'Grace?' she launched as soon as the call was picked up. 'While I go out and see my mother, I'm thinking of an outreach clinic for remote families, in my break. What do you think?'

'Lightning Ridge? Yes!' Grace gave an enthusiastic response. Her partner had been interested in that concept for a while.

'So, I could offer a few days of an infertility clinic in tandem with the locum GP position for the four weeks?' The idea grew rapidly attractive with Grace's interest.

Grace was always to the point. 'Logistics?'

'I could ask the onsite doctor's surgery if they could take care of the clinic appointments and admin. Surely they'd have a practice nurse for the hands-on stuff. I could do everything else myself, but I'll check.'

They both agreed there would be remote women who could use Riley's skillset within a few hours' travel of Lightning Ridge, instead of coming all the way to the capital cities. If the practice manager at Lightning Ridge was happy to donate a few afternoons, Riley could do the rest.

'I'll set up a flow chart for future referral from out that way, too. Assuming there's a need. It'll smooth the speedbumps for remote families.'

'We'll find the women,' Grace said. 'You get the locum position and I'll put the word out.' The call ended.

Riley scanned Google Maps on her desktop computer, drumming the fingers of her thankfully ringless left hand. Hmm. It would take eight hours and thirty minutes of driving from

Sydney, seven hundred and twenty-five kilometres from her home in Mosman to the Ridge. At least it was tarred road all the way.

Road trip.

'Jeez, Mum,' she groaned aloud, but there was only her designer-decorated consulting room to hear. 'Your retirement was supposed to be relaxing for everyone. Why there?'

Chapter Two

Riley

The following week, Riley turned off the Castlereagh Highway past a blue-painted cement mixer and a large sign that read, 'LIGHTNING RIDGE'. It seemed the town didn't want anyone to miss the turn-off.

Driving into the settlement wasn't what she'd expected. She'd expected mounds of white gravel and barren hills, and there was some of that, but mostly she got posters and signs, on poles and rocks, and up trees, advertising opals and accommodation and tours. The place was way more tourist orientated than she'd realised. Right now, she needed a sign to the service station, but then a familiar-shaped building appeared right past the first caravan park on the outskirts. The caravan park with the vehicle perched high up in a branch.

Interesting place.

She'd fuelled up in Moree three hours ago, a town she had been surprised to find vast green parks in. So far, she'd enjoyed the drive – her convertible didn't get to stretch its legs much – and she'd savoured the silence. Dad had declined to come when she'd offered to take him, so she hadn't had to have the radio on. Plus, there was the peace of not having Josh looking for the next oat-milk, extra-hot latte to complain about, which had made the silence heavenly.

She had to admit, though, that there had been that strangeness of isolation, with so much openness to the landscape and the long, straight roads as she drove. As if there'd be no use rushing when there were hours to go. A strange, odd concept for Riley. It had been too many years since she'd been on her own for an extended period and at least childhood since she'd driven west into the sunset. That had been with her mother when they'd visited her grandparents towards Broken Hill.

She hoped Josh would find someone else very soon because he'd already said he'd be back after her 'break' to discuss their 'issues'. That problem floated like a muddy mirage on the horizon . . . to worry about later. For now, she had to fuel up and find her new workplace. She'd look for her mum after that because the medical centre expected her at five pm, and it was almost that now.

Riley climbed out at the large, high-roofed fuel station and stretched her stiff body, using the part of her Pilates repertoire that eased her shoulders. A prickle on her neck, one she'd always felt under scrutiny, made her swivel to the cashier section. An older woman with white hair nodded at her through a streaked window with a faint smile on her face. Riley nodded, turned back and topped up her car.

Once she'd recapped and locked the vehicle, possibly not necessary in a small town but old habits died hard, she strode to the door of the shop. She was pleased to see the handwash dispenser, which she made use of to rid her fingers of the petrol smell and greasy pump-handle smudge. And to stay safe, too, of course.

'You the doc arriving today?'

Riley lifted her head and stared at the woman. At one hundred and eighty centimetres tall with a cap of red hair she stood out, she knew that, but she hadn't sent a description. She'd anticipated that news of a fertility expert would travel fast in small towns, but this was ridiculous. 'Were you expecting me?'

'You don't look like a tourist or a miner. Plus, there's a line of women waiting for you to get here.'

Riley rubbed her left brow. It was still a little itchy from the permanent make-up tattoo she'd had done two weeks ago. Something one of her more fashion-conscious friends had encouraged, and even Josh had thought worthy since most of the time she understated her make-up, but which she still wasn't sure about. The woman in front had barely any eyebrows at all, and what was there was white. Somehow, that made Riley feel guilty that she'd given in to vanity, which was a strange thing to think about.

'I guess that's good,' she said to the woman.

'Good for them. You'll be doing ten-hour days to get through them in four weeks.'

This was spooky, and a lesson in the bush telegraph. 'Does everyone know I'm coming today and how long for?'

'Those who care.'

'And you care?' Riley asked.

'Because my daughter cares.'

Ah. The professor had sent the word out far and further than far, and she had been told that the need was greater than either of them had anticipated. Riley might not have to deal with scrotums, after all. 'Thanks for the heads-up.' She dipped her chin. 'Riley Brand.'

The woman inclined her own head. 'I'm Desiree. You got a mother out here?'

Seriously? What was that word? Piloerection. Yup, Riley had the hair waving about again on her neck. 'And if I do?'

'I guess her name's Brand, too.' She looked Riley up and down. 'About your height, strawberry-blonde? Same walk.'

Riley relaxed. Not creepy at all. 'Well, I know where to come when I get a chance to look for her.'

'Does she know you're coming? Doesn't seem like she does, from the look of you.'

'It's a surprise,' Riley said. Did it matter if she gave anything away? The woman was omniscient.

'I won't give her address without her say-so, but it's Friday, she might come after six tonight for ladies' night. Or she might not. If you wanna try your luck, come round the back here after then. It's BYO. You're welcome to come and see.'

The 'Outback Practice at Lightning', The Ridge Medical Centre, could almost see Desiree's service station from where it sat on Harlequin Street. Amusingly, the acronym OPAL made up the first four letters. Riley hadn't noticed that when she applied for the locum, but out the front of the centre it was loud and clear in big letters.

It was two minutes to five on Friday, so just before the surgery closed for the weekend. She'd meet the current practice manager and any other doctors she'd be working with, she guessed.

A dusty, used-to-be-white four-door utility pulled up in a rush in front of her on the wide gravel shoulder of the road. *There are plenty of parking spots, unlike Sydney,* she thought, as she stepped out of the way.

They seemed in a hurry. Two men around her height, one bald, one grey-haired, both mid-fifties and smelling of sweat and beer, climbed out towing a third. The third was young, maybe twenty, and not quite conscious. He gurgled a bit, like someone gargling on mouth wash, when they let his head droop, and the acid stink of vomit floated in a personal cloud.

Riley leaned forward and opened the door for them as they strong-armed the middle fellow through. Nobody said thanks. She followed them.

The slight young woman at the desk, wearing what looked like a grey tent, saw the men and stood. Her thin pixie face pulled tight in anxiety, and she pressed a bell on the desk and stepped back against the wall, her cheeks pale as she clutched her chest.

Two seconds later a door opened and a Germanic-looking god, possibly Thor or the Aussie actor playing him, bigger than these guys by six inches anyway, squeezed his shoulders through the frame and approached. With wild blond hair and cool blue eyes, Thor oozed an impressive Viking vibe.

'What happened?' he asked, no Eastern European accent. That was pure Aussie drawl.

Riley had to smile. Seriously? The guy should have a straw poking out the side of his mouth he sounded so laidback, but she suspected he knew she was there, too. Something told her he was no stranger to situational awareness.

The younger man gargled again.

Grey hair said, 'Toby hit the turps, then had a fit. Choked on his vomit.'

The bald man growled, 'In my car.'

Thor nodded. 'Goose. Put him on his side on the obs-room bed.' The man gestured and the young girl slid along the wall to a closed door, opened it and glanced in. What she saw must have reassured her, because she pushed the door wider and then scuttled back behind her desk.

The two men did as they were told, dumped their charge, and shouldered out again.

'Thanks, boys. You can go. I'll ring Greta.'

There was barely a noise, they left so fast.

Thor gestured for the girl to close the front doors with an excellent circular hand-signal. 'And lock it. We're done for the day.' Then he threw over his shoulder, 'You can come too, Dr Brand.'

Riley raised her brows, smiled at the girl, and followed. What was it with this town and no introductions? The door shut behind her.

Chapter Three

Melinda

Melinda Grace Lowenthal returned her shaking fingers to where her heart fluttered like feathered wings inside her chest. The flapping sensation felt as if a stupid bird was trying to get out. She really needed to get over this panic thing. The surgery wall behind her desk felt hard and cold against her back as she pressed into it. Trying to hide. Escape. Be safe.

She was so sick of this overpowering terror state when that happened. She'd thought she was getting better – it had been months – but when the two men had rushed into the room with Toby just now, it had been so much like when the men had held up the bank that she'd panicked.

If it hadn't been for Dr Konrad at the hospital that night, she didn't think she'd have been able to face the next weeks of flash-backs. He'd warned her, said she was strong, told her she wasn't alone. Eventually, they'd caught the gang of armed thieves – they'd been hitting small towns all over the state – but she couldn't make herself go back to the bank to work.

He'd sent the nurse to see her every day in her little rented room behind the pub while she got over the shock and the few bruises she'd collected. And set her up with ten sessions with the visiting psychologist at the Wellness Centre for the PTSD. Then, he'd offered her the job as receptionist – if she wanted it – a month later. Because she couldn't work at the bank, she couldn't afford her rent, and he'd suggested she take the accommodation behind the surgery in one of the tiny units. Very quietly she'd said, 'Yes, please.'

She trusted Dr Konrad to keep her safe. She shouldn't have panicked today. And now they were gone. Just ordinary men, back out to the street.

As she locked the doors, the face of the woman – Dr Brand – came back to her. They'd been expecting her. Red hair and green eyes. She narrowed her own to bring the memory clearer.

Tall and city-looking, the woman had radiated calm and confidence like the nurse at the health centre had. Melinda had a feeling she'd also be kind and strong. Anyone who helped families have babies would be a good listener.

Some of the tension left her shoulders. It would be much easier to have another woman here. Someone to share the worries she hadn't been able to tell Dr Konrad, even though her reticence made her feel guilty. Melinda shied away from that thought and slotted the link tab, making sure the chain was across the door to the frame.

The sound of someone gagging drifted through the door. Poor Toby was having a rough trot. She knew what that was like. She liked Toby. Liked his mum, too. She hadn't liked his dad so much, but he'd left Greta now – off to find gold instead of opal. Not that Mr Harris had been anything but nice to her. Just a big, rough man, and too close in build to the armed men. She just couldn't feel comfortable with rough-looking men, like the two who'd just left.

She slumped into her chair. She had to get over this panic thing.

Chapter Four

Konrad

Konrad decided that Dr Riley Brand looked like her web photo. Tall, a styled cap of ruby-red hair that fell in a straight line under her ears, green eyes bigger and brighter than he'd expected. She screamed up-market Sydney specialist. And she was hot.

Toby burped and gagged and Konrad grimaced. This wasn't the introduction he'd hoped for. But at least she'd followed him in. Hopefully, she wouldn't turn right back around and leave. And with more luck, she'd be useful. He desperately needed useful.

Konrad listened to the lungs of his patient but couldn't hear any signs of aspiration. He pulled the stethoscope buds out of his ears and let the rest hang from his neck. They'd been lucky.

He looked her over again. She really was fabulously tall, sleekly fit and toned. Maybe a runner. Svelte and sexy. Not that he had time for things like sex. Sweet heaven, he hadn't had time to think about a relationship, he just wanted a business partner to take half the work. He wished he could ask his mum and dad to come and locum here, but it would be too heartbreaking for them.

Maybe his sister? Without looking up, Konrad said, 'You are Dr Brand?' It was a question, but he didn't doubt it.

Konrad supposed he should have been more respectful with their new locum instead of just dragging her in. The woman was a consultant obstetrician and an expert on infertility, after all, but he'd had a day of dealing with idiots. Mostly men. Most who should have known better. Now Toby was trying to kill himself again.

'I am she.' The irony clear. 'You could ask the woman at the service station. She seemed to know my identity without introduction.'

Konrad shone a light into Toby's pupils. Slow but adequate pupil reaction. 'Desiree. Desiree knows everyyything. And her daughter is one of the three dozen women hoping to see you, in between my patients.' And hadn't that been a surprise? An unexpected need in the community and beyond. Even if he sounded cynical, he was impressed.

He looked across at his new work mate. She radiated an oasis of serenity, despite Toby's rushed arrival. He cheered silently. 'Welcome to Lightning Ridge. I'm Konrad Grey.'

She nodded without commenting. He liked that for some obscure reason.

He gestured to the examination couch. 'Toby's a recently diag-nosed epileptic with issues taking his medication. Since his first seizure six months ago, when we sent him to Sydney for assess-ment, he's had five grand-mal seizures. He lost his apprenticeship in carpentry soon after and became clinically depressed. When he drinks alcohol it all goes downhill because he doesn't take his medication or he throws it up.'

Konrad considered his next words, the personal distress they caused, but they needed to be said. 'Toby has tried to end his life twice because he hates the idea of the seizures so much.'

Her face showed polite interest, but he just caught the flinch. Yep, most medical professionals had had their brush with suicidal patients. 'Should he be in Lightning Ridge?' Her tone sounded mild but her eyes interrogated – so he wasn't fooled. She could be a hard case. Good.

'Should any of us be here?'

She gave a small shrug. 'I'm only here for four weeks.'

He studied her. Yeah, so had he been, two years ago. 'I hope you manage to get away.' But he didn't mean it. The place grew on you.

As he talked, he rearranged Toby's limbs so that he wouldn't fall off the narrow examination table and checked that his airway remained open to breathe. Then he buckled the thick elastic seatbelt around Toby's armpits. He'd made the band because Toby had almost fallen off the bed once during a seizure and Konrad didn't have bedrails or people to stand around and watch patients while he sorted everything else.

He realised Dr Brand had crossed to the sink, washed her hands and pulled on a pair of nitrile gloves. He saw her scan the room and move to the syringes and needles, where she assembled a set for drawing blood.

She held up the syringe. 'I assume you want to do AED levels.'

At least she knew about anti-epileptic drug levels. From the fertility clinic site he'd read, she'd been a gyno for the last ten years. Though, of course, there must be epileptic women of child-bearing age. 'Yes, please.' He glanced at his watch. 'Might have time for them to go out with the pathology bag if we're quick.'

He gathered the tubes and started writing Toby's details onto the tiny labels – he knew them by heart – while she drew the blood. Hands steady, no hesitation, she drew blood until it filled the syringe, then she removed it. After taping a cotton ball over Toby's needle site, she began filling the vials he'd written on.

Toby snored.

When she was finished, she said, 'Do you think he aspirated?'

'Chest sounds clear. We'll find out soon enough if he gets pneumonia. I think it was more that they had his airway compromised.'

'Better than the other.' She disposed of the sharps and syringe and washed her hands, before she turned back to face him, one slender hip leaning against the sink. 'Why was your receptionist up against the wall?'

She was observant. 'Bad experience in the past,' he told her. 'Not with those guys. She couldn't find work that made her feel safe, so I installed a buzzer out the front and promised to come if she pushed it.' Which was no big deal for him but a massive deal for Melinda.

'I was supposed to meet the practice manager?'

'That would be Melinda.'

'And the rest of the doctors?'

'That would be me.'

'Accommodation?'

'Out back. Motel-room style. Set of six. Three are empty. There's a shared kitchen lounge, and Melinda has a room, too.' And wasn't that going to be a fun threesome. Konrad, Riley and Melinda.

Toby groaned as he began waking up, then he gargled.

'Pass me that bucket over there, please.' Even he heard the hint of urgency. 'The black one.'

She handed him the garden-variety black-handled bucket and he pushed it under Toby's cheek. Once Toby had finished emptying his stomach, with much noise and stink, she handed him a wad of tissues and he noticed she had gloves on again. Guess he'd have to order in twice the usual supplies while she was here. But really, that was the least of his worries right now.

'Give me the bucket.' Her fine long nose wrinkled but her voice stayed steady. She had a strong stomach as well. Handier and handier. She took the bucket, glanced in it and winced. 'Toilet?'

'Over there.' He gestured with his head, still mopping up. 'You can go out that door. The other door in there goes back out to the waiting room. Can you ask Melinda to come in, please? I'll get her to print out the form from last time, and then run the bloods over to the clinic and the bag can go with their pathology at six.'

She nodded as she left, taking her horrid cargo with her, much to his relief, and he heard her speak to Melinda.

The next four weeks were going to be very interesting.

Chapter Five

Riley

Riley emptied the bucket, swallowed back the urge to lose her own stomach contents, and pressed the flush. Once the mess was gone, she felt better and rinsed the receptacle in the sluice sink.

Good grief. Where was the practice nurse? Maybe they didn't have one? Now that would be a whole new learning curve. It would also be inefficient for consultations without being able to skim off some of the associated tasks. It would cut down the number of patients she could see if she had to take her own bloods, do her own urine tests and sterilise her own equipment.

She glanced around the clean unisex toilet and sluice area. There was no need to jump to conclusions just yet. The nurse had probably gone home early.

Riley carried the rinsed bucket back to the observation room, put it on the floor, stripped off her gloves and washed her hands again.

Toby was awake. Sitting up on the side of the examination table, he sipped water. Thor – no, Konrad – stood beside him, ready to catch him if he took a dive for the floor.

Dr Grey – yes, that was better – was saying, 'You do the right thing and your condition will do the right thing. You drink booze, you end up here making our new doc empty your spew bucket.'

Riley held up her hands. 'And I resign from that. I nearly added my own.'

Toby's eyes widened and he smiled shyly. He had a nice smile; unexpected, self-mocking. Then he blew out a disgusted, and disgusting, breath and both Konrad and Riley almost fainted from the fumes. 'Okay. I get it. But my fiancée just dumped me. Told me she doesn't want to be with a guy who has fits. After I bought the engagement ring. And everyone in town knows I'm a loser who has spectacular seizures.'

'I'm sorry, Toby.' Konrad's eyes seemed strangely haunted, which seemed oddly unprofessional and Riley wondered at his obvious distress hearing that statement.

'Take your meds, avoid alcohol and your episodes will decrease,' Konrad said. 'I'm also sorry about Sheila, and the ring.' Riley liked the way he acknowledged he'd heard Toby. 'Maybe it's better to find out now that she hasn't got your back?'

That was a bit harsh. Riley raised her brows at Dr Grey before she spoke to Toby. 'Is there anyone else in town with epilepsy?'

'How would I know?' This came out as a depressed mumble.

'I quote, "everyone in town knows about me". So, do you know of anyone else? Anybody born with, or had a head injury that gave them seizures?'

He looked at her. 'No.' And she could see the self-pity and exasperation of others who didn't understand in that one word.

She turned to Konrad, who was watching her sceptically. 'Do you? Don't want their names – just if you know any?'

33

He dug his big fingers into a blond flop of hair in a left-handed swipe. It made him look oddly boyish. 'A couple of kids in high school and one primary school kid. One woman your age. There must be more. The two other doctors in town would have patients.'

'That's what I thought.' She looked at Toby. 'You'll be sleeping a lot today, but when you're awake, look up this website.' She wrote on a piece of paper and handed it to Toby. 'You've probably seen it already, but look again. Helping others will help you get back on track. They've got a couple of comic-slash-cartoons on it about epilepsy now. Lots of info. Maybe one afternoon a week you can add to their blog, talk about your week and be a resource for others, even ask the local school if you can help.'

The young man squinted at her, but he almost smiled. 'And stop feeling sorry for myself?'

Riley spread her hands. 'One life, that's all you get. Up to you.' She met his gaze. 'I'm new here, but I'm not cleaning up your vomit again if it's from alcohol. Deal?'

Melinda was gone when Konrad opened the door to Toby's mum, who'd come to get him. Through the observation room, Riley could see the back of the petite woman as she shook Konrad's hand and slung an arm around Toby's shoulders. 'Come on, darling.'

Konrad had explained that his mum ran the café and Toby listlessly mined for opal for a boss.

'I'll see you Monday, Toby. First appointment after lunch,' Konrad added, and the boy nodded.

Stories within stories, Riley thought as she stripped the sheet and bundled it into a skip in the corner. No. She wasn't going to empty the skip. If they didn't have someone delegated to that, then Konrad could do it.

She washed her hands again, picked up her handbag from where she'd put it in the corner and left the rank room. She needed an open window.

In the waiting room, Konrad turned off the background music, which was of course country. An amusing reminder that she'd left the city. His voice self-mocking, he said, 'So how was that for a first date?'

'The black bucket was a highlight,' she quipped.

'We aim for the full experience.'

'I can see that.' They studied each other, both taking their time, assessing. It couldn't really be classed as a power struggle, more a sizing-up. With that one appraisal, Riley suspected he wouldn't give in if he didn't agree on something she wanted, but she had no problem with that. He had no idea how tenacious she could be.

He said, 'You sure you wanna do this?'

'Life is for living.'

'You're big on that.'

Yes, but she'd forgotten it lately. Which was a disagreeable thought, so she went back to the patient. 'I know someone with issues like Toby and being involved in supporting others helped her.'

'Toby's the son of a miner but never enjoyed mining. It's "be tough or be taken" here.'

'Good to know.' She glanced around, then pointed to a closed door. 'Is that my consulting room?'

'Go for it.'

When she opened the door, the room held two chairs jammed opposite her desk and an examination table tucked behind a drab brown curtain against the wall. 'Lucky I didn't bring a cat to swing,' she joked.

'Indeed.' He did that one-brow-lift thing.

'Fine.' She glanced at her watch. 'And accommodation?' She'd almost said digs.

'This way, Dr Brand.' He opened a back door and waited for her to precede him outside. 'I'll close the surgery properly later,' he said, gesturing towards the rooms behind them.

'Call me Riley,' she told him, thinking now was a good time to ask. 'Is there no practice nurse?'

'Nope. We're self-sufficient here.'

She sighed out a discreet breath. Right, then. Hopefully, most instruments and equipment were disposable, and as long as the chores were equal she could handle that. She suspected Konrad was very capable, although she wasn't sure how she came to that assumption.

He crossed a small patch of dry stubbled grass and pointed to a motel-style door, one of six, and wrestled two keys off a big ring of janglers and handed her one. 'This is for your room. It has a door front and back. Around the other side is where you park your car outside your unit.' Then he handed her another key. 'This is for the shared lounge and full kitchen.' He pointed to a door next to hers. 'Greta comes in once a week to heavy clean and she'll change your sheets unless you do it yourself.'

As if that wasn't a hint. She could manage to change her own sheets.

'We share the big fridge, kitchen and lounge. We clean our own mess. Wi-fi password, all lower case, is "digadoctor".'

She snorted. 'Your inspiration on the password?'

'Not guilty.'

'It all sounds like fun.'

He raised his one brow again. 'Oh, it is.'

She'd done something to annoy him, she realised, but she'd had a big day and didn't really care. 'I'll get organised, then.'

'Dr Brand.' His voice stopped her.

'Riley,' she repeated as she turned back.

'Thank you for your help in there. It's good to know you aren't squeamish or too much of a princess.'

Seriously? 'Good to know you aren't, either.'

He looked struck with that. 'Touché,' he said and smiled, and just for a second there she melted and smiled back at him. Then she remembered: four weeks. There was no time for benefits.

'Do I get to my car from the front street through that way?'

'Go back through the clinic and I'll lock up after you. Do you want to eat in or out? Because if you're eating out, the only takeaway shuts in twenty minutes, but the supermarket shuts at seven.'

Opening the door to her accommodation from the back was like opening a door to a cave. It was all dark, except for the small windows behind the closed blinds she could see ahead. Only a spear of late-afternoon light around the far door pierced the gloom.

Entering from the lane and the parking space where she'd left her car, Riley switched on the light and saw plain, clean and tight quarters. To her right was a circa-1970s-tiled bathroom with shower, toilet and pink vanity, all sparkling clean. Past that was a bed with a floral comforter, not a grungy quilt that others might have had sex on – so not the greasy hotel she'd feared – and fat pillows in crisp white cotton. Shiny sink, jug, microwave and mini-fridge for the tiny kitchenette area, and the exit door was just past that, one she opened onto the patch of grass leading back to the surgery rear door.

This was all she needed and bless the lovely housekeeper for her pristine work. She didn't even need to share the next-door common room for anything – this would be fine and perfectly suitable for hibernation between maternal-rescue missions and work for the next few weeks.

It was almost six pm. Should she look for her mum? Did she want to do ladies' night with Desiree? Who, according to Konrad, knew everything. Or did she want to kick back and have take-away? Maybe she could carry takeaway to Desiree's? It *was* BYO, she'd said.

Riley wasn't sure she wanted to surprise her mum amongst a bunch of women. Although, how many could there be in such a small town? Otherwise, she would have to wait for her mother to give Desiree permission to share her address.

The passive option didn't sit well, and she'd driven all this way, after all. If she dropped in around six-thirty, most of the guests would have arrived and she could meet and greet and leave quickly if her mum wasn't there.

Riley ran into Konrad as she locked up after changing clothes, now dressed in a blue crinkle-free silk-look sleeveless shirt and jeans with her Ariat tooled western boots. He still wore his work clothes. His once-over had been appreciative as he looked down at her – not many men could do that, look down on her. Many were appreciative, which she didn't care about, but his height made her aware. *Just his height?* she mocked herself. She wasn't sure what she thought of that awareness, but her cheeks did warm up. Darn it.

'Going out?'

'Off to Desiree's ladies' night. I'm looking for my mother. She has a *claim* and lives in a *camp*.' She'd looked up what the off-grid homes were called, and there was no reason not to share that.

'Curiouser and curiouser.' His brow rose. 'Enjoy your night with the ladies,' he said, a flicker of amusement in his eyes. 'At least it's not far to Desiree's.'

They both looked down the slight hill to the intersection and the lights of the service centre.

Chapter Six

Adelaide

It was Adelaide's second Friday-night visit behind the Lightning Ridge Service Station and this time she came in loose trousers and a bright top. With make-up. Last week, she'd dressed down in blue jeans and a cheap work shirt, not wanting to be the city woman overdressing. Of course, she'd learned that nobody cared what she wore as long as she was happy in it. So she dressed for her and it felt good to spruce up.

The first night had been an eye-opener with the words 'eclectic women' not touching the sides of the experience. There were only seven of them including her, but the personalities were so big it felt like more.

Gerry-with-the-pacemaker ran the local arts-and-craft emporium with an extra jewellery section, mostly opal. In her late fifties and shimmering in bright floral fabric, Geraldine had what she called 'a ticking determination to enjoy life' and promote artistic expression in others.

Her partner, Elsa, tall, thin and understatedly elegant, performed stand-up comedy with chameleon flair, including the routine she'd shared of a well-known politician. Elsa flew out every month for a week in Melbourne, where she had a long-standing gig at a prestigious comedy club.

Everyone was supposed to bring one joke this week and perform it before the end of the night. Homework. Adelaide, who hadn't told a successful joke in her life – just not her style – had searched the internet and come up with one, possibly two, which amused her enough to share. She hoped everyone would have forgotten, though.

Greta Harris was small, blonde and busty, a self-confessed clean freak and champion of the underdog. Adelaide had spotted Greta's OCD a mile off, which Greta admitted to, as well as being the proud third-generation proprietor of the local café. Everyone knew the chance of exposure to germs from Greta's establishment was more remote than the town was from Sydney.

Greta's café had become Adelaide's favourite place to eat on the occasions she came in from her claim. Greta also cleaned once a week for one of the local docs because he'd saved her son, and Adelaide imagined she'd be able to eat off those floors, too.

In the handful of weeks that she'd been here, Adelaide had discovered that on the surface Lightning Ridge was a town where perhaps more than a few of the inhabitants had changed their names. But under that first impression, reality proved that the women held most of the administrative and retail/trade/service jobs, while the men focused on the chance to strike it rich. Though she had met a few third-generation women miners, too.

Easygoing was the norm for the residents, and strangely, Adelaide felt at home and comfortable whether she was working by herself on her claim or strolling through town for supplies.

The delightful thing about the Ridge being nobody judged. You could go barefoot and bearded or polished to the nines, everyone smiled and nodded and wished you a good day.

At Desiree's soirée, the women who attended could hold their heads up amongst the most confident of nurses she'd met over the last fifteen years. Even 'impressive individuals' did not begin to describe the awe Adelaide held them in.

The two first cousins, Silvia and Selena, had inherited the rivalry of their fathers. One ran the only pub and the other managed the local bowling club, just down the road from each other.

Desiree was the biggest hoot. A proud single woman who could engine-whisper struggling machinery if you brought it to her thriving fuel depot and left it overnight. And Desiree knew . . . well . . . everything about everybody.

Around six-thirty, Adelaide pushed open Desiree's back gate and noted the familiar, already favourite faces, which really was a ridiculous emotion after only one previous visit. She'd accepted the gift to have the Friday-night ladies to look forward to after picking and chipping her way through the dirt all week. Searching for the elusive sparkle of shifting colour was hard work but surprisingly rewarding – that hint of bright promise, if she was lucky, emerald-green or sapphire-blue flashes that jumped out at you when the gem was wet. She loved that moment when out of the dull clay, suddenly rainbows shifted and shone as she turned the chunk in her hand.

Opal hunting had become exhausting, addictive, dirty work, with broken nails, blisters and bolts of pure delight. She wasn't making money, yet. She had thought vaguely of getting a part-time job, but she was having too much fun working for herself.

In her two-roomed tin shed, her mastery of the secrets of solar power and off-grid living wavered between pride that she could manage things and a hedonistic wish for more mod cons, a little more company and certainly less ever-settling dust.

Carrying her small esky holding soft cheese, biscuits and a bowl of tasty pasta from Greta's café, plus two cans of gin and tonic, Adelaide raised a hand at the assembled ladies. She pushed a chair closer to the small table and put her own offerings beside the assembled snacks.

Before she could sit, Desiree cooeed and gestured her over to the outdoor bar she had set up under an awning.

'Got news.' At the words, the hubbub died down and everyone turned to listen. Desiree waved her grease-ingrained but best-as-she-could cleaned hand. 'Not you lot. Go about your business.'

Catcalls of, 'Not fair, we'll find out anyway,' made Adelaide smile. 'Hey, Desiree,' she said. 'How was your week?'

Desiree's eyes sparkled and Adelaide had come to recognise that meant she had an excellent piece of gossip to share. Adelaide's generator chewed a lot of fuel, so she and Desiree met often.

'You know I've got a daughter?'

'You've mentioned her,' Adelaide said.

'She can't fall pregnant. But there's one of those outreach clinics in town for the next four weeks. A fertility doc is coming.'

Adelaide's neck prickled. 'And?' A little blip of excitement, not dread, fluttered under her rib cage, so that was good.

'A tall bird, who looks a lot like you, bought petrol today. She's working at the OPAL Docs for a month. She might come tonight. Did you want me to give her your address if she doesn't?'

Riley was here.

'Of course. Yes. Was anyone else in the car?' Had Tyler come? She wasn't sure she was prepared for the guilt of deserting Tyler, but she couldn't help the tiny spurt of hope.

'Nope. She was on her own.'

Oh. She buried the disappointment. Nevertheless, it would be fun to show Riley her new life. And the air between her daughter and her needed clearing anyway. 'It'll be lovely to see her.'

Desiree raised her brows and nodded across the room. 'Lucky, that.'

Adelaide turned.

Standing elegantly at the door, with a confidently inquiring look on her face, was her daughter. She hadn't seen Adelaide yet, because she was speaking to Greta, who'd crossed to ask if she needed help. In that moment before they both looked her way, Adelaide felt a rush of pride. Riley was such a lovely-looking woman, graceful in her jeans, boots and silk shirt. She always had a knack for picking the perfect outfit.

Her only child had always seemed to know exactly what she wanted and how to get it, which was probably why Adelaide sometimes felt slow and dowdy next to her. Or that could have been the private school Tyler had insisted Riley board at for her senior-school years.

Riley saw her and the brief flash of delight on her daughter's face made Adelaide's own smile flash out.

'Mother,' she said softly, but Adelaide heard her. Or felt her. With long strides, Riley crossed the room and took Adelaide's hands in hers, then pulled her in for a warm hug, before she stepped back.

So many expressions crossed Riley's face that Adelaide couldn't guess them all. 'I've found you.' She inclined her head to Desiree. 'Thanks to this lady here.'

'Desiree knows everything,' Adelaide said with a laugh, savouring the reality of her daughter's fingers in hers. It was okay that she'd been found. It wasn't like she'd been hiding . . . had she?

'I've already heard that about Desiree.'

Desiree's eyes sparkled. 'And that would be Doc Konrad.' The woman was obviously chuffed that she'd been spoken of.

'You talking about my favourite man?' Greta had followed Riley, and now Gerry and Elsa joined them, followed by Selina and Silvia until a small team was huddled along Desiree's bar.

Adelaide stepped back from her daughter and gestured to the others. 'Riley. You've met Desiree, this is Greta from the café, Silvia and Selina from the two watering holes in town, and these two lovely ladies are Gerry and Elsa, who run the art store.'

Elsa said, 'Hope you can come up with a joke off the cuff. Everyone had to bring one tonight.'

Adelaide felt her daughter's amusement and saw the raised brows as she looked at her mother. 'Do you have a joke, Mum?'

'I do,' she said primly.

'I'm proud of you.' It could have been a joke on its own, but there was a thread of appreciation in those words, as if her daughter was proud of many things about her mother. Why hadn't she noticed that before?

Chapter Seven

Riley

By the time she'd spent an hour with the Friday-night ladies, groaned over the best pasta alfredo she'd tasted and sat on a plastic chair beside an old AMPOL oil drum, Riley knew her mother had found kindred spirits. And she wondered if she had any right, or inclination, to try to extricate the happy miner and return her to the trendy but boring marital fold in Sydney.

Maybe she should have just motored up for the weekend to talk to her mother instead of rearranging a month of her life to try to impose her will. Why had she done that? Because she always rushed everywhere? Made snap decisions? Thought she knew best for everyone else?

Or was it worse than this? Was it conceit? Indifference to her mother's right to choose what she wanted in her life? Selfishness because Riley didn't want to deal with her father herself? None of those traits were flattering and she'd have to think on them later and decide how many were unpleasant truths that needed adjustment.

Her mum didn't need anyone imposing their will on her. She looked the happiest Riley had seen her since she'd left work.

Happier, in fact, than when she'd been at work. Her mum deserved this freedom, and of course Riley could see the lure of being beholden to no one.

'Old-joke time.' Elsa's elegantly fingered hands clasped as if in entreaty, and suddenly she was larger than life. Nobody had turned on the outdoor security light, but it was as if Elsa had dialled up her own internal spotlight to illuminate her charisma. 'I'll start, just to give you an idea.'

She smiled at Gerry. 'For the artists among us . . . "If it ain't baroque, don't fix it."' Everyone groaned. 'No? How about "Earth without art is just . . . Eh."'

Riley slid a look at Gerry's face, her eyes resting indulgently on Elsa. When Riley looked at her mum, Adelaide had pulled a piece of paper out of her pocket and was studying it intently, as if to reassure herself she'd memorised it.

Her mum hated jokes. Riley thought back in time. No. She didn't hate them, she'd had trouble laughing at them and Dad said she was terrible at telling them because she always forgot the ending. It was a family joke, and she wondered if the family – she and Dad – had been a little cruel in perpetrating that myth. In fact, Mum's shortcomings on humour, and on a lot of things, had been the source of much shared amusement between her dad and her.

For the first time, she wondered if her mum had found their amusement funny at all.

'Right, then.' Desiree stood. It was her turn. 'You know Gladys?' Everyone nodded. 'She hates putting petrol in her car. So,' she shrugged, 'I usually do it. This morning,' she held out her hand as if holding a fuel nozzle, then shook her head as if bemused. 'Suddenly, I got really emotional.' Her lips turned down with theatrical sadness and her voice drooped in woe. 'Don't know why.' She spread her hands as if asking everyone if they knew. 'I just started filling up.'

She waited two beats and looked around. Everyone laughed. Even Adelaide snorted. Riley grinned. *Okay. Mum got that one.*

'My turn.' Greta stood. 'I was thinking,' she said, then gave a small pause, capturing the audience easily. These guys were good. 'I'm sick of cooking. I might change the name of the restaurant to the Karma Café.' She gave another pause, as if thinking. 'No main meals – just desserts.'

Desiree hooted.

Selina jerked her thumb at her cousin. 'If you go to her bar, you should dress as a tennis ball.'

Silvia frowned at her. 'Because . . .?'

'Only way you'll get served.'

This time Desiree honked like a goose, and everyone laughed more at her now than the joke.

Silvia jerked her head at Selena. 'And her club should be called the Light Brigade. She sure knows how to charge.'

Riley's mum actually giggled. She was looking relaxed and happy, and she hadn't even started her second G & T.

'My turn.' She looked at Riley and a little of the amusement seemed to fade. 'I'm no good at telling jokes.'

Elsa waved a hand. 'Of course you are, and you'll be an expert by the time we finish with you.' Everyone laughed.

Adelaide lifted her head to her new friends, but she avoided looking in Riley's direction. 'What did the nurse say when she found the rectal thermometer in her pocket?' Adelaide looked around, schooling her face to confusion as if she really couldn't remember. Then she patted her empty pocket and said thought-fully, 'Some arsehole has my pen.'

Desiree nearly fell off her chair, she laughed so hard. Riley was right there with her in shock. Her mum didn't ever swear. Adelaide watched Elsa, who grinned and applauded.

'Beautiful delivery. See! You tell great jokes.'

Adelaide blushed with delight.

The next morning, Saturday, the sun had almost risen by the time Riley climbed out of her surprisingly comfortable bed in her room cave. It had been a long drive here yesterday, and she hadn't made it home from ladies' night until ten-thirty. Who knew a party of unknown women could talk and laugh so much?

She had a ten am appointment with her mum at the shack, though 'appointment' was too definite a word, and Riley had said she'd bring breakfast. But she wanted a run first. It was still doable. She had just enough time to blow away the cobwebs of driving and Sydney . . . and Josh.

Whenever she'd travelled overseas, Riley had tried to start her visit anywhere with a run in the morning to check out the sur-rounding areas. It would work here, too. The place had roads.

Dressed now, she came out of the back door past her parked car. The long driveway ran from the rear of the accommodation behind the surgery and past the front consulting rooms to the road. The breeze brushed cool against her cheeks until she'd popped out into the slight downhill road leading to the servo.

To the right the sky glowed an orange pre-sunrise, but to the left the moon was full over the skeletons of the old mine site coming up. A mine right in town? She'd seen a man in there yesterday with a fuel drum, so she assumed they still used the equipment. A huge yellow crane-looking thing, that she suspected drilled holes in the earth, was mounted over the ground. At the front of the yard, rusted skeletons of vehicles from the past crouched in the weeds.

As she jogged past, she noted an old blue truck, a totally rusted ute and piles of mining machinery in the dawn light. Her feet crunched on the pinkish gravel shifting under her soles, and in the trees all around her the different birds cheeped and called in the background. *Cheep, trill, warble.* It was the only sound apart from her slapping feet, in fact, which made her glance around. She wasn't used to lack of noise. No traffic. The air crisp and clean, unpolluted by car fumes and dirty alleys. No voices or music. No people.

She passed tall gums, a palm tree she hadn't expected in western New South Wales, and sprays of bougainvillea on walls and fences and up trees. The vine's vibrant cerise flowers glittered even in the dim light. She'd have to come back when the sun was shining to see the best colour.

To her left the light was changing, the moon strung in pink-and-blue pastels of sky now, and opposite the dawn was a brilliant watermelon pink threaded with power lines. She turned right past Desiree's fuel station and up the main street, past the Historical Society hut and cottage hospital, and wondered briefly how long it would have taken to get to Lightning Ridge from Sydney a hundred years ago.

She passed a very stylish and gated opal store, an opal and fossil centre, and a church with a strange car door on the front fence. Amusingly, the sun chose that moment to rise and the odd orange car door and the church seemed to glow like gold in the morning brilliance.

On the sides of buildings, the bright and clever murals splashed across walls were like unexpected flowers amongst the store fronts. Occasional ramshackle dwellings were signposted as built early last century.

The wide main street could hold three lanes on each side, but she saw one car in the first ten minutes and the driver looked as though he'd had a big night as the vehicle crawled past.

Ten minutes later, she passed another glorious display of bougainvillea, this time backed by the purple flowers of jacaranda trees, the colours pulsating as the day brightened. She saw one of the other medical centres in town and turned into a street where oddly the city fathers seemed to have run amok with red pavers.

She glimpsed the sign for the artesian baths, so she turned that way, away from the closed shops and another medical centre. The road was open in the distance and she picked up her pace as she passed the small hospital and ambulance station. There was also a fire station. The houses began to spread out and she spotted a path through thinning trees up ahead.

Once she reached the artesian baths, a fenced area with an arched entrance behind which steam rose, the road was open, but she'd done enough for halfway and she turned to jog back. She passed the hospital again on the other side of the road and the morning light brightened to normal golden sunlight. The moon was a hand's breadth from the horizon and she ran towards it. Back to the OPAL Medical Centre along Harlequin Street.

Back towards the man running ahead of her. At least he wouldn't see her. She didn't know how she knew, but there was no mistaking her temporary boss. It seemed they'd both done a loop in opposite directions.

Lithe and powerful, his long, muscular legs were eating the distance effortlessly, and she wondered if he competed in events. She felt the stirring of awareness for an intriguing man that she didn't need to complicate her life with. *Nope*, she told herself. She could do this for a month and then go home. But it was a nice view from the rear.

She mentally snapped his picture – there was no harm in looking – and followed him at a distance back to the units.

After a quick and surprisingly powerful shower, dressed in her jeans and boots again, Riley stopped at Greta's takeaway to order two bacon-and-egg rolls and strong cappuccinos.

Greta fired herself out from behind the formica counter and threw her arms around Riley's waist. 'My Toby says you were there and helped him. I didn't know, last night.' She stepped back and smiled up at her. 'Thank you.'

Riley's mind whirled. Ah, Toby, whose mum owned a café. She'd missed that. 'You're welcome. Dr Grey did most of the work.'

'That man is a saint.'

Um no. Riley did not believe that. She'd seen him notice unsaintly parts of her when she'd been dressed to go out last night. But she inclined her head. 'He seems like a very caring doctor.'

Greta nearly nodded her head off. 'He is. He saved my Toby.' She sighed and added softly, 'Though he couldn't save his own brother.'

Riley stilled as the words sank in, but Greta stepped back and turned to disappear behind the counter. She picked up a pen. 'What can I make for you?'

Riley gave her order and Greta scribbled away. When it had been added and cash exchanged Riley asked, 'Is there something I should know about Dr Grey?'

'No. It's his story to tell, but it was a sad thing.' Avoiding Riley's raised brows, she spoke to the cash register. 'You taking this out to your mum?'

'Yes. If I find her.'

Greta laughed. 'You will.' She waved her hand at the wall. 'Study that.' Then she bustled away.

Riley shrugged and turned to the big hand-drawn map on the wall and compared it with the folded paper one her mum had given her last night. Lines went everywhere. The names made her smile. Borehead Road. Potch Street. New Chum Terrace. Well, she guessed that was what she was. A new chum. Which was fine because she wasn't planning to become an old chum.

This map had the café drawn on it, which was helpful for orientating her mum's drawing. She'd been holding it upside down. Ah, *there* was the way to Mum's camp, Three Mile Road. Her mum might be able to tell jokes, but she couldn't draw maps to save herself.

Considering everything had looked like the middle of the desert yesterday as she'd driven in, with barely any trees, Riley hoped she wouldn't miss the turn-off. At least now she knew which way was up on the map.

In less time than Riley thought it would have taken to fry an egg, her order was ready. The package came in a soft-sided thermal carry bag with flamingos dancing in vibrant pink.

'You can drop this back, or even bring it next Friday night when you come to Desiree's. It'll keep the rolls warm. I put some fruit cake in there for your mum as well.' She handed over a cardboard coffee carry tray. 'Say hi to her for me.'

'Thanks, Greta.' Riley waved the bag at her. 'I'm sure I'll see you soon.'

Riley stepped from the café straight into the path of what felt like a brick outhouse with wide shoulders quite capable of absorbing the impact of a tall woman. His hands came out and steadied her as she hit his chest, and heat spread and tingled through her as the masculine scent of some divine aftershave, something mossy-green and ginger maybe, had her breathing in deeply.

The chest under her cheek rumbled. 'Good morning.'

She knew that voice.

Desperately trying not to scald him with the coffee, stab him with her keys or drop the flamingos, Riley allowed herself to be steadied.

'Good morning.' She looked up. And up.

'Konrad,' he said, as if she'd forgotten.

'Konrad. Thanks for the steady.' She stepped carefully back out of those very capable hands, still juggling her load, and he was quick to let go.

He continued to look down at her and his eyes sparkled with humour. She didn't see anything funny. He looked at the two cups in the holder, the keys between her fingers and her carry bag. 'I'm guessing you found your mother,' he said.

'Last night at Desiree's. I'm hoping to find her again.'

'Ah. Going bush. Or in this case, boulders. Good luck.'

'Hopefully, I won't need it.'

'Me too. There's patchy telephone reception out of town.' He tapped a finger to his hairline in salute and left her as he strode away towards the newsagents. Riley glanced down at the coffee in her hand and turned to her car.

The coffee was getting cold, and apparently Mum didn't have a microwave.

The old Wayfarers Inn was almost five kilometres out of town. Riley had looked up its history last night on Google. The building had been used as a tiny posting house in the late 1800s and early 1900s, and had been falling down in the real estate pics in the twentieth century. Hopefully, Mum had it in better nick now.

This morning, the rail to tie horses still stood outside, though the end posts leaned like the drunks that had probably slept on their mounts as they wandered home.

Riley spun slowly, looking behind her and to the side. To the left, the red-and-white gravelly dirt stretched as far as the eye could see with white mullock heaps and occasionally a shanty type of building, tufts of brown grass and bare spindly shrubs that she doubted were alive. Straight ahead, below the plateau the inn stood on, a vista of trees spread to the skyline, and there'd be a good view of the sunset from here. There were no other dwellings that way she could see.

Turning back to the shack, she approached the front verandah and noted the rusty scallops of iron clinging like fingernails to the sagging roof. The verandah sat flush to the ground, where pale crushed gravel had been smoothed to create paths through the red earth and under the roof. Spindly wooden chairs dozed on either side of the door. There was only a single step to enter.

It was two minutes to ten and the door creaked and squeaked as she reached it. Her mother's smiling face was open and welcoming, too.

'Riley. Come in.' The door groaned wider and her mum stood back against the dim interior drying her fingers on a small, smudged hand towel. Dressed in scuffed dusty jeans and a torn checked shirt, she looked shabby but gratified to see her. 'I got side-tracked on the claim and only just made it back to the house to wash my hands for ten.'

She wore dirt in a swipe across her cheek but looked content and composed. It really felt so great to see her. 'I've missed you the last couple of months.' The words slipped out of Riley's mouth and surprised both of them. Riley murmured, 'I have coffee, which is probably not hot by now, and some food from Greta.'

'Yum. I'm starving.' When Riley didn't step past, her mum turned and gestured. 'Come through. It's a small shack but has what I need.'

Inside the dim room, the windows were wood-framed eyes in the front and a porthole in the other. The curtains were old but clean, yet barely allowed the day illumination in. An old, black metal fuel stove took up half the back wall and sat under a stone chimney – which expanded outside and away from the roof – which sat beside the sink and iron taps. To the left of the Aga was a side window. The floor clunked as she walked over wooden boards.

'No lights?'

'I don't use them unless I need them, with the solar-power batteries halfway through their life. I was lucky that the place came with a bank of batteries and enough solar to do what I need at night. The stove gives me hot water and an oven, and it means the kettle is always boiled. I have a generator, too, but I mainly use that for the mine.'

She still couldn't believe her tuckshop mother had a mine. 'Neat.' What else could she say?

Adelaide laughed. 'I'm sure you don't think so, but the novelty hasn't worn off for me.' She gestured to her bed, which was made up as a day lounge in the corner. The covers were bright and the pillows plumped. 'It's comfy and it keeps me warm at night. It's October, so I haven't done summer here yet. We'll see what I think of it when it's as hot inside as it is outside.'

Hmm, Riley thought. Her mother had no immediate plans to leave for home, it seemed. 'I hear it makes the high forties. You reckon you'll be here for the summer, then?' And that was the gist of it.

Adelaide paused, studied Riley's face and inclined her head. 'I think so. Yes.'

'As I said, you look happy.'

'Thank you. Do you think your father is?'

'Happy? He says he's missing you, but he's always plugged into the television or at the gym, so he seems his normal self.' Thinking about it now, she'd say her dad was more established than happy.

Her mother didn't look surprised. Maybe a little disappointed but philosophical. She didn't say anything else, so Riley shifted her shoulders and looked down at the food in her hands. 'Inside or out to have this?'

If they stayed inside, the small table covered by a red checked tablecloth was buried by a scattering of rocks and some odd-looking equipment and books. It didn't leave much room to put down the food.

Adelaide pursed her lips. 'Let's go outside. I have a nook out there.'

'And a freaking mine shaft.' Riley shook her head. 'Lead on, Mother.' She waved her full hands and followed Adelaide out the front door again and along the white gravel path. The path ran past the end of the shack and under a trellised wooden shade. In the far corner of the yard stood a contraption with a winder over a covered hole – sort of like a well with a bucket. And there was another hole with a ladder popping out of the top. So, there were two mine shafts? Everything around the area was utilitarian. Shovels, picks, wheelbarrow and work equipment, but the shaded table was tidy, just two reference books stacked neatly, a pretty crystal centrepiece, and two more spindly wooden chairs backed by cactus and coloured stones.

'Two shafts not one? Are there two mines?'

'One mine. You need two shafts if you're tunnelling. One as a safety measure and spare exit and to winch the rocks removed from the tunnel and bring them to the surface.'

'Sounds like a lot of work. But this spot here is pretty.' And it was. But it was also dusty and stark. Riley didn't voice that addendum.

Adelaide took the coffee tray from her. 'There's not a lot of pretty around here, but it does fascinate me.'

Her mother sniffed the coffee, smiled a little dreamily as she held her cup and then waved at the shaft in the corner of the fenced yard. 'And my lease is right here. I'd say I'm addicted. Caught up in the whole,' she air-quoted, '"it could be today" for that elusive find.'

'Sounds like you're into it. Each to their own.' And she was coming to see her mother had made her own interests. 'I'm guessing it beats the heck out of not going anywhere and watching the telly.' She didn't add, *with Dad.*

They both settled into the smooth wood of the chairs and a small silence lay between them. Greased paper crackled as they unwrapped food and coffee steam rose into the still morning air. 'Your father is a good man. There's a lot of history in forty years of marriage between us, and of course I still love him. But he's decided he's happy to sit, work out at the gym, talk to old business cronies and be content. Which is fine if that's what he wants.'

'And . . .?'

Adelaide met Riley's eyes. 'Once I'd finished work, I realised quickly it's not enough for me. Staying home was driving me insane with boredom and it was discover an interest or take up shopping, gambling or food. I chose adventure.'

Good choice, then. Adventure with a vengeance. 'I think I get that. You've always been a doer. It's certainly a no-frills living style, though. I have to say.' She shrugged again. 'I'm impressed that you make it work.'

Riley stared at a sprawling pile of split wood for the fuel stove, shook her head and glanced down at her mother's work-roughened hands. 'You manage the solar power and whole living-off-the-grid thing as if it's nothing.' She looked at her own French polish and soft palms. 'I'm impressed and super-proud of you. I don't think I could do it.'

Her mum turned her face away to look towards the hills. The skin of her neck turned pink. 'That's sweet, thank you. But I come from pioneer stock and so do you. You could do this if you wanted to, but it's not for everyone.'

'Including Dad?'

'I haven't given up hope.' Mum waved that away. 'Anyway, I'm very proud of what you do, Riley. You help people achieve dreams of a family that they've almost lost hope of. You have years of work ahead of you. I didn't.'

Adelaide scrunched her empty food wrappings with a shrug. 'By the time I found my passion for nursing, it was almost time for the new guard in my profession. Clever young things and computer nursing. After retirement, I needed a new adventure and I consider myself very fortunate that I found a pastime as absorbing as this.'

Pastime? As in passing time until what? Old age? Death? Riley couldn't help herself, even though she knew she sounded like a child. 'Are you ever coming back?'

'Of course. If summer gets too hot. With the idea of returning here in spring, if your father is happy to have a part-time wife. I'm sure when the middle of summer hits I'll be back to air-conditioning and beaches. The best of both worlds.'

Adelaide turned her face away again to look over the old paling fence and the dirt, rock and distant horizons beyond it. After a long pause she said, 'But of course that's up to your father to agree to us leading separate lives for part of the year.'

That was a worry. 'Do you miss Dad at all?' Riley asked.

'Of course, I do.' Riley heard the crack in her mother's voice and winced to have caused her pain. 'I do, but he's set in his ways. He worries about things that worrying won't change. He judges the people on the news. Judges the people in the supermarket. And he judges me if I don't straighten up the milk in a line in the fridge.'

Riley winced again. 'The last time I visited I noticed he did that.'

Her mother laughed, and surprisingly, it was a real laugh. 'Which is fine, I can handle that, I'm getting older and have my funny ways as well. And sometimes, it's hard to keep excitement and vitality between two people if you've been married for a lifetime. I need my moment to play.'

'I guess we all have those,' Riley said, thinking about Josh's coffee perfectionism and her own strict time management. And the way meeting Konrad made her question how much fun she was having.

Her mum gave her that *I-love-you-darling* smile, which suddenly she couldn't imagine not being able to see. She was so glad she came.

'Sometimes it's lonely here, but then Desiree makes me laugh when I go for fuel. Or I find a glimmer of opal when I don't expect it. I see a change in the pattern of the rock or the suggestion of a seam in the shaft.' She lifted her eyes to Riley's and her face broke into a mischievous grin that shone with delight. 'You should see me with a pick and a helmet when I think I've found something.'

That animation dropped twenty years off her mother's face and Riley couldn't wish her anywhere else.

Her mum spread her arms. 'At least here I know I'm alive. I wasn't so sure I was in Sydney until I found this whole, wonderful world of elusive colour.' Her mother's face crinkled into fine amused wrinkles deepened already by the sun.

'You look happy.' Riley was repeating herself, so she sat back and put down her cup. Wasn't that what she wanted, to have her mother happy? Of course it was. 'I get that's from being here. Maybe I understand more clearly now than I ever have. Dad needs to come out and see how amazing you are, even if he runs home afterwards.'

And she needed to make that happen. Which was why she was here. Sort of.

Chapter Eight

Adelaide

Adelaide looked across the table to the puzzling woman who was her daughter and felt a stab of remorse. She wasn't trying to lessen her daughter's respect for her father – that was the last thing she wanted – but she needed Riley to understand that she had a life to live and didn't need her daughter's mediation to be saved from Lightning Ridge.

She wasn't stupid. She knew why Riley was here – interference!

Hopefully, Riley would see that Adelaide's decisions and choices made her a better mother, and even wife, if her husband came to his senses and decided to broaden his mind. But she couldn't just sit and wait for that to happen. Tyler's choices were his own, and hers were hers. Neither were Riley's to manage.

'How's it all going with you and Josh? I thought you had holidays and some flash events planned for this month?'

Riley looked away and Adelaide sat back. How very interesting and hopeful. She'd always thought Josh lacked backbone.

'It's all been cancelled. We've decided to go our separate ways, and I came here.' From her daughter's tone, Adelaide suspected Riley had decided more than Josh had.

'The professor's happy because of that infertility outreach clinic we've been talking about for a long time now.' Riley shrugged her elegant shoulders. 'As for Josh . . . we had too little in common. Maybe I'm too much like you. I became worried about his intentions on a surprise cruise he organised.'

'A surprise cruise with intentions?'

'He mentioned a special question he was going to ask and patted his pocket. I may have bolted, at great pace, at the thought.'

Excellent, Adelaide thought, and tried not to laugh. 'His proposal wouldn't excite you?'

'No. More like make me want to skid backwards. Fast.'

Adelaide couldn't help it, she laughed. 'You are your mother's daughter after all. It took your father three attempts for me to marry him.'

Riley looked shocked. Oh yes, Tyler wasn't perfect, but Riley had always had such a great rapport with him. They were so close. Dad's little girl. Dad's little dux of the school. Dad's amazing young doctor daughter.

Adelaide had been a late-to-the-profession part-time nurse once she'd finished being her daughter's perfect mother. And wife to the corporate executive. At least until Riley had left for boarding school.

Keeping the home fires going and working her shifts around Riley and Tyler on weekends had been fulfilling. But Riley had been gone for a lot of years now and it didn't look like grandkids would appear soon. If ever. Thank goodness she'd left home after retirement when she did or she'd be working out in the gym, too. She used enough muscles now without paying fees for it.

Time for a change of subject. 'Tell me about your job here? You said a month?'

Riley shrugged. 'My first day is Monday. Though I had a taste yesterday. With Toby.'

'Greta's son? She mentioned last night that he'd had an episode. I don't know the families that well, just the ladies, but I understand he was diagnosed with epilepsy earlier this year.'

'Yes. I'm thinking his depression is more of an issue. Dr Grey said he'd already tried to harm himself.'

'What's he like? I haven't met him.'

'Toby?' Her daughter glanced at her watch, avoiding her gaze. Which amused Adelaide because there was nowhere to rush to here.

The patient mother. That was her. Being entertained by Riley underestimating her. 'I'm sure he's a nice boy if Greta is his mum.' It wasn't like Riley to be flippant, or dodge answering questions. 'No, I meant your new boss.'

'Ah, Konrad Grey.' Riley paused as if she was searching for a description. 'He's like the town. Resilient. Can probably deal with anything. Likely has hidden depths and secrets. But the surgery has no practice nurse, only a young, PTSD-affected office manager receptionist and he picks up all the slack.'

Yes, Adelaide had heard quite a bit about the doctor's hidden depths. 'Greta thinks the sun shines out of him. And I'm pretty sure Desiree agrees with her.'

Riley nodded. 'Hmm. He's a big man, good-looking to some, I imagine, so I'm not surprised that the ladies are impressed.'

There was something in that, Adelaide was sure. 'You don't think he's handsome . . . or impressive?' she prodded.

Riley's new avoidance technique turned her to look over the wire fence, as though fascinated by the tailing. 'I met the man yesterday. He seems like a good doctor, though I doubt he'd suffer fools . . . He's not hard on the eyes.'

Ooh, Adelaide thought. That was big praise from Riley. Words that were even more delightfully droll.

Her daughter turned back to look at her. 'Greta said something about a tragedy he had. Do you know anything about that?'

All Adelaide's humour fled. Tragedy. Loss happened to many. 'No. Sorry. But maybe you'll be able to find out in the next few weeks. I'm still a little stunned that you've left Sydney for that long.' And she was. Happy, but astonished.

Riley shrugged. 'This seemed a way to be useful as well as spend some time with you. I'm sure it'll be good for my soul to be a GP for a stint.'

And wasn't that out of character for her city-bred daughter and the Macquarie Street practice she'd worked so hard to attain.

Riley looked away again and Adelaide laughed. 'I'm sure, darling, that you'll be able to manage anything that can happen here. I have great faith in you.'

'Thanks, Mum.' Her daughter's tone held dryness. 'Seeing as it's your fault I'm here.'

Adelaide laughed out loud, and this time she had to wipe a stray tear from her eye. 'Excuse me? It's your fault you're here. You were the one who decided to stage "an intervention".'

Riley froze and then snorted a laugh, too. 'True. Maybe it wasn't my brightest idea.' She sighed ruefully. 'But the work will be a change. Now that I'm obligated, I'll meet those commitments.' She tilted her head. 'I'm beginning to think spending the next couple of weeks here and seeing you as often as I can is going to be more fun than I deserve.'

Adelaide's heart felt as if it grew in her chest. 'Thank you, darling. Me too. And you'll have your consultations. Desiree tells me there's a cohort of women who've been desperate for help here.'

Riley widened her eyes and nodded. 'The response was a little overwhelming. I may end up coming back if I can't get a reasonable pathway set up while I'm here. I'm scheduled for general practice appointments in the mornings and fertility clinic on Monday and Tuesday afternoons if I can get them all done. I might have to write off every afternoon for the clinics if Dr Grey will agree. We'll see how I go.'

Chapter Nine

Konrad

Konrad opened the rear surgery door on Monday morning half an hour before he needed to. It had nothing to do with being in a position of power before his new locum came in. He had results to look up. People to contact. Coffee to make.

He'd spent more time than he should have over the weekend thinking about Dr Riley Brand and her grass-green eyes. Probably just because for two years now he hadn't seen much green grass.

Okay. He'd be the first to admit that the elegant, medically qualified stunner had all the right subtle curves and charisma and might have knocked him for six, but that didn't mean he was going to do anything about it. He doubted she was a bump-pelvises-in-the-motel-room kinda girl.

Nope. This was not in his game plan. And not in hers, he would bet. But it would be very interesting to see how she went today when the old boys started coming in. He had no doubt they would. They'd have all heard about a hot lady doc arriving and would dredge up whatever innuendo-laden illness they could think of to check her out. His mouth quirked up. Miners were curious. Cheeky. And inventive.

He suspected with Riley being an obstetrician that she'd be about as comfortable with men's tackle as he was when a few of Desiree's ladies had come for their pap smears last year. Judging by the cackles from the waiting room, he'd known they'd all had a few drinks before their appointments. Bunch of stirrers.

Still, last year's craziness and Riley's impending male-patient explosion made him smile.

When she'd asked if she could run women's health and infertility appointments a couple of times a week, he'd agreed because he hadn't thought she'd be able to fill the spots. And nobody else had applied for the locum role. He'd thought complacently that it would be no problem if she agreed to take normal surgery appointments when the vacancies were there.

Vacancies? What a joke. Melinda said she had a waiting list of women and every Monday and Tuesday afternoon filled for the next month. And that was without Dr Brand needing follow-up appointments for her new patients, which she would. And word of mouth would add more.

Which left him nonplussed. How had he not realised that so many women were in need of specialist gynaecological services? None had mentioned it to him and he had women patients. As did the other doctors in town. He and his new locum needed to have a conversation, where she could offer ways for him to be more proactive with referrals. To help him figure out the right questions for those women who were too shy to ask for help.

Then again, just how long was he staying here at the Ridge?

More to the point, how long would it take to ease the pain and guilt that had sat like acid in his stomach, acid that ate at him since William had taken his life in the minefields a month after Konrad arrived to check up on him? Trying to make up for his missed cues on his brother by watching over Toby and the like wasn't working as well as he'd hoped.

He slapped the switch of the kettle and pulled down his mug from the cupboard. 'TRUST ME. I'M A DOCTOR,' it read. Melinda had bought it for him, tongue-in-cheek, and that was when he knew she'd turned the corner.

Maybe someone would see what a sweetie she was and fall in love with her? Argh. He needed to stop trying to fix people's lives. Just fix the coffee.

So he did. It tasted like crap, as always, but at least it was strong enough to kick him alert. No doubt this soul searching was because of Toby's mental state last Friday, if he was honest with himself. And hadn't his new locum managed well? He liked her confidence, her lack of drama. All of her, really.

And there he was back to thinking about Dr Riley Brand. It was funny how one blink in his mind's eye had her in his focus. In technicolour, 3D. She was different to his usual locums that's all, he reasoned. The last few octogenarians had been nearer to the grave than retirement. He'd been worried more about them not dying out here than them doing their work. And some had been scarily old-fashioned in their treatments. He doubted Riley did anything old-fashioned.

The back door opened and he looked across to the movement. His new colleague stepped in wearing smooth black trousers – designer label, if you took in the way they sculpted her belly and thighs and accentuated her long legs – and finished perfectly at the toe of her black boots. His trousers were always too short – a curse of being so tall. And hadn't her boots been brown on Friday?

'You brought two pairs of fashion boots to Lightning Ridge?' he said by way of a greeting.

'Good morning, Dr Grey.' Her too-dark-for-red-hair brows rose. 'The boots are what you observe?'

Oh, he observed lots of things. The way the white silk top caressed the curves and fanned her long neck. He observed and then he wondered about silk and the heat. If she didn't mind sweating, then he didn't mind it sticking to her.

'You're early.'

'I'm organised.' She carried a two-handled square bag the size of a large shopping basket.

'Coffee?' He stepped out of the kitchen doorway as she headed straight for him.

She strode past him to the kitchen, wrinkled her nose at his cup, and marched towards the bench. 'I'll make my own before I start, thank you.' She glanced at the tin of cheap coffee on the sink. 'Did you want one of mine?'

She lifted a compact white coffee maker onto the bench. It wasn't expensive, a chain-store brand, but it had its own milk-froth attachment. *Will you look at that*, he thought, his cheeks holding firm to suppress his smile.

She withdrew a bag of ground coffee, organic of course, and a yellow coffee mug. Hers read, 'I LIKE MY EGGS FERTILISED'.

His lips compressed in a battle to stop them twitching. He lost. 'Nice cup,' he said.

She looked at his, then snorted, which was sort of endearing for a posh chick. 'Yours too.'

71

'It's from Melinda. So, you came from Sydney, you wear designer threads, and you brought your own coffee machine to Lightning Ridge?'

'Got it in one. May I say, you dress like a hobo, don't have a practice nurse and drink cheap powdered coffee. Go you.'

Ouch. There was nothing wrong with his coffee or his clothes. They both did the job. 'I had a practice nurse. She moved east last month and it's a little hard to come across registered nurses out here.'

'Would you hire one if you found a suitable one?' She tilted her head for his answer as she packed the portafilter coffee dispenser, tamped it, swiped the edges with her finger and twisted the connection into the machine with muscle memory. She removed the boxy milk container and filled a finger height with milk she brought out of the bag. Skinny, of course. He hated skim milk.

His previous practice nurse, Charlotte, used to perform so many tasks at the surgery, making his day easier by taking on the injections and dressings and tidy-ups. 'Yes,' he said. He needed to tear his eyes away. Be professional. 'Melinda said you've got a full schedule Monday and Tuesday for the women's clinic. Did you want to slip another afternoon or three in there for your clinic?'

'Thanks. And yes, if that's okay with you. I'm just as confounded at the response. Don't you have any female doctors in town?'

To his shock, Konrad realised that he hadn't considered it before. 'No. And apparently, we men are useless at asking the right questions because I had no idea there was such a need.'

'Not all are from here. We advertised in a four-hundred-kilometre radius. Any further and they'd be better going straight to Sydney, Brisbane or Adelaide.'

Four hundred kilometres. Outback families who wanted kids and couldn't fall pregnant. The thought left him hollow with the idea that they'd been forgotten. Okay, then. That decided things for him. She could have all the afternoons she needed.

Chapter Ten

Riley

Riley's first patient of the day, Cyrus Pinkerton, was a large, hairy, unwashed behemoth covered in ink. The black-headed snake tattooed up the side of his neck seemed to shimmer as it disappeared into his ear. *That was different*, Riley thought, forcing her eyes away from the red flicking tongue. She indicated the stronger of the two client chairs. 'Please take a seat. I'm Dr Brand. How can I help you, Mr Pinkerton?'

'Call me Cyrus.'

First-name basis, oh goodie. 'How can I help you, Cyrus?'

The man showed a semi-populated mouth of yellow teeth. 'I've got an itch.'

Oh boy. 'I'm sorry to hear that. Where?' She suspected she knew.

Cyrus's chins wobbled as he grinned and all the teeth that were present came out to play. 'Me balls.'

Yup. It had to be. 'That must be uncomfortable.'

'It is.' He nodded enthusiastically, totally amused by his own wit. 'I spend the day scratching.'

She lifted the blood-pressure cuff and gestured for him to give her his arm. 'I'll just take your blood pressure while you're explaining.'

He frowned but obediently held out the massive limb. 'Nothing wrong with me blood pressure.'

'Won't hurt to check, then.' She could imagine some social excesses would have impacted on this enlarged body. 'Is your itch something new or have you had it for a long time?'

'Long time.' He gave the matter some thought. 'Ages.'

It could be a simple heat rash, eczema or a sexually transmitted disease. 'And in the past, what's helped?'

Cyrus gave her another cavernous toothy grin. 'Scratching helps.'

Riley sighed inwardly. 'Have you tried ointments or powders. Talcum powder?'

He leaned back and the spring tubing from the sphygmomanometer cuff stretched as he skewed, almost as if she'd thrown a pink pair of lace panties at his face and he had to scramble away. 'I'm not smelling like no baby's bum.'

Of course, but it was okay to scratch for years. 'I was thinking something scentless like zinc powder. But we'll see.' She released the compression in the blood-pressure cuff and unwrapped it from his arm. His blood pressure was far too elevated and on the way to stroke territory.

'You have very high blood pressure. I'll order some blood tests before you go and start you on an antihypertensive tablet until your tests come back. I'll also make an appointment for a specialist in Moree whom you'll need to see.'

'I didn't come for no tablets.'

She smiled calmly. 'Then why did you come if you've had your itch for years?'

He had no answer.

She stood and gestured. 'How about you head behind the curtains over there, drop your trousers and your underwear and lie down on the bed. There's a sheet if you're shy.'

'I'm not shy and I don't wear underwear.' He waited for a response, but she kept her face neutral.

'Then I'll just type this in until you're ready.'

He strolled over behind the curtains and pulled them back. Once the rustle of clothing began, she picked up the phone and dialled Konrad's room.

'Do you normally have a nurse with you if you examine a female patient?'

'Of course. Since the nurse left, I have Melinda come in.'

'Excellent. I'd like you to step into my room for a moment and do the same for me.'

He laughed. 'You've got Cyrus and his itch, haven't you?'

The rest of the morning ran on a similar vein, but finding and offering relief for the array of symptoms had its own rewards. Riley had forgotten how many men suffered from heat rash, indigestion, haemorrhoids and liver disease. There were a few suspicious prostate problems she referred to Konrad as well.

Most of the men hadn't had a doctor's appointment in years, but they had a bevy of them coming up in their future now. She doled out prescriptions, helpful suggestions, blood tests and further investigation for those who needed them, and remained calmly professional for the ones who had tripped in for a laugh.

The novelty of a female doctor would wane soon. Very soon, she hoped.

She also saw Selena, one of the cousins from the Friday-night ladies who needed further tests for some suspicious bleeding down below. From past experience, Riley went straight ahead and booked her for investigative surgery with a colleague she knew who worked at Moree, less than three hours away, the following week.

Riley's fertility clinic afternoon began with Desiree's only daughter, Olivia. Riley guessed Desiree had fronted receptionist Melinda the first day the appointments were announced to have her daughter lead the list.

Olivia presented as determined as her mum, if her strong hand-shake was anything to go by. Height-wise she came to Riley's shoulder, a blonde like Desiree, but she was twice as wide around. That wouldn't help her fertility, but it wasn't the only problem if the answers on the questionnaire were correct.

Olivia clutched the hand of an equally round man. Riley assumed he was her husband, a teacher at the local primary school. She welcomed them into the small space with a friendly wave of her hand. It was squashy and she hoped the rickety chairs would hold. One had held Cyrus, after all.

'I'm Riley Brand. I'm an obstetrician and gynaecologist with a special interest in ways to enhance fertility for those who aren't having success falling pregnant.'

They nodded. It was her usual intro and she didn't see why it wouldn't work at the Ridge. 'I've been working specifically in women's health and fertility in Sydney for the last ten years,' she said. 'Thanks so much for sending the information forms back. I've read them all and have some questions, but before that, it's good to meet you both in person.' She sat back. Now it was their turn to talk. 'Tell me how I can help.'

'We want babies,' Olivia said with the same dry forthrightness her mother showed, and Riley smiled. Olivia fluttered her fingers at the man beside her. 'This is my husband, Aiden. I wasn't sure if he needed to be here or not, so let us know when he can go.'

'I'm glad you're here,' she said to Aiden. 'It's best to have both partners present for the first visit.' Riley tilted her head. 'You're both teachers, right?' When they nodded she continued. 'As people who educate others, you know it's easier to discuss information if two people can share and discuss. How long have you been married?'

'Nine years,' Aiden replied. His eyes warmed as he glanced at his wife. 'She's a wild woman, but I'm the luckiest bloke in town.'

Olivia didn't smile. 'Except I can't give him children.'

From across the desk, Riley could see the flicker in Olivia's eyes, but the woman made a show of wiping her mouth to hide the emotion.

And there it is, Riley thought. Grief, heartbreak and frustration in the desire to become a parent. Helping people like this was why she loved her job. She'd started the journey after a friend's marriage had disintegrated when they couldn't have children. She'd seen the heartbreak for two people she'd cared about and vowed she'd find ways to help others. That anguish was why she was tenacious. That and guilt. From her own miscarriage she'd told nobody about at the same time as her friend's divorce.

Some people couldn't ever fall pregnant and she'd wished hers gone. And it had. Her obstetric career had started as penance and had become an obsession. It was the reason she worked long hours and kept at the forefront of research.

'You're here. First step taken. And you're not alone. One in six Australian couples experience delays in falling pregnant. The object is finding which part of the conception pathway is causing the glitch.'

The couple opposite her seemed to relax slightly and she felt her own tension ease. Rapport was important and they were nervous. 'There are three main reasons for not falling pregnant. Production of sperm or eggs. Structure or function of the male or female reproductive systems. And/or a hormonal or immune condition in both men and women.'

Aiden said, 'You're good at explaining. I like a methodical approach.'

Riley nodded. 'It's how it was explained to me and I've stuck with it.' She looked at Olivia, who'd gained a frown line that scored her forehead.

'What you're saying is lots of tests.'

'Yes. And there are tests for males and for females. For you, I'll order a combination of blood tests, one of which measures your egg count. Then there's an ultrasound scan to help identify any specific issues such as polycystic ovary syndrome or endometriosis. Plus, we'll check that ovulation is occurring each month.' She lifted her hand in question. 'Did you know they have sticks like pregnancy test sticks just for ovulation?'

Olivia rolled her eyes. 'Not in Lightning Ridge, they don't.'

'You might be surprised.' Riley tilted her head. Thought about that. 'And if not, we'll get them in.' Judging by her waiting list, they were going to need them.

Aiden leaned forward. 'I've read about some apps for fertility.'

Olivia rolled her eyes again. 'He loves his apps.'

'I'm with Aiden,' Riley said. 'You're going to love yours, too. They're super-easy and pinpoint the best time to fall pregnant with incredible accuracy. I'll give you the printed instructions before you leave.'

Olivia raised her eyebrows at her husband. 'We might need a date night to figure it all out.'

'Any time.' He waggled his brows. His wife blushed but didn't look uninterested. Which was terrific because mutual attraction helped so much. Der.

'Working together is the secret. But Aiden gets his tests, too.'

Aiden nodded. 'Sperm count?'

'It's the most important male fertility test because it measures the number of sperm in a sample as well as their motility – swimming ability and morphology. Basic shape, size and structure. After a woman's age as a factor, male infertility is the second-biggest factor in a couple's inability to conceive.'

Both winced, but unfortunately, there was more to come. They hadn't heard the tough stuff yet.

'Plus, we have the lifestyle changes.' She let that hang, and finally Olivia sighed and said what needed to be said.

'You mean I have to lose weight?' It was spoken as a question, but Olivia sank lower in her chair as the words emerged.

This was possibly a long-standing issue and Riley sympathised.

Many of her patients had extra weight as a dilemma and there was no easy fix.

'You don't need to be a bean pole. In fact, too little body fat is just as fraught with issues. But you need a plan and you need to start.'

Olivia glanced at her husband and then back at Riley.

Good. It would take the two of them working together – or at least it would be much easier. 'See what you can do in the next two weeks with finding foods you can substitute for added-sugar ones. If you can eliminate sugar and bread before your next appointment, that's all I ask. That's a tough short-term goal that will give you progress. Remember that a BMI over thirty-five will impact your chances of falling pregnant in a definite way.' Olivia's BMI sat over forty-two.

Riley looked at Aiden. 'It's always easier to follow a change in lifestyle if you have a buddy and you guys strike me as quite the team.'

Aiden nodded. 'I got it. No sugar. No bread.' He didn't look too worried. 'Best-shot scenario. We can do that.'

Riley had the feeling they'd be fine. 'Changing habits is challenging, but so is what you're both going through.' She turned to Olivia. 'Back to apps. Weight-program apps can be a great tool. There are free ones and the big company ones. It's what fits you. But if you fill them in every day, until I see you again, I think you'll benefit the most.'

'We can do that.'

Excellent. 'I think you'll be surprised. Apps work for a lot of people. Start today and see over the next two weeks before your next appointment.' She glanced down at the completed questionnaires. 'Neither of you smokes, so that's one less issue to surmount. Smoking is another factor in infertility.'

She handed the pre-printed forms she'd collected for the pathology tests and ultrasounds. The appointment took forty minutes as they discussed the frequency of sex versus optimal sperm counts, positions for prime fertility and she answered questions about the apps that she had downloaded on her electronic tablet that she used for explaining.

Before they finished the visit, Riley ended with what sometimes was the trickiest lifestyle change.

Both admitted to moderate alcohol intake and daily wine and spirits. She'd felt the barrier when they'd first touched on obesity and had put this discussion away until the last. 'If possible, for the next couple of months, I'd like you both to avoid alcohol completely.'

She heard the words sink to the floor like an unwanted guest. They lay there, miserably.

'There goes the five o'clock wine club.' Not quite so much amusement this time from Aiden, but Olivia sagged a little in her chair and smiled.

'I thought you'd say that, but I didn't know Aiden was included. If I fell pregnant, I'd have to stop anyway.' She shifted uncomfortably in her chair. 'I do binge-snack after wine, so I guess that will help with the weight loss.'

'It certainly will.'

'And it's very important that Aiden stops as well?'

'Yes. Apart from making it easier on you, drinking alcohol can reduce both men's and women's fertility. Even drinking lightly can reduce the chance of pregnancy. Heavy drinking increases the time it takes to get pregnant and reduces the chances of having a healthy baby.'

Aiden's downturned mouth indicated he was sadly resigned to the inevitable.

'I suggest trying a joint stroll at the same time as you would have sat down for your sundowners. Then when you come back home for your healthy dinner, you can enjoy your iced water in pretty wineglasses.'

They looked at each other. 'We can try,' Aiden said, before he looked over the top of his glasses at her. 'Do you enjoy alcohol, Doctor?'

'I do,' she admitted, 'but not frequently. Too many nights on call or when I might need to drive. But I do like a good Western Australian shiraz. And a gin and tonic on a hot day.'

'So at least you understand.' Aiden blew out a breath.

'I do.' And Riley did. She was asking a lot. 'But you have choices.'

'No, he doesn't. No wine. No sugar. No bread. Until we come back.'

Aiden blinked and Olivia stood up ready to tackle the changes.

'Let's get this show on the road,' the militant mama said.

Chapter Eleven

Melinda

Melinda watched each couple as they emerged from Dr Brand's surgery. They all had something in common. Hope. It shone from their eyes, their straighter spines and the way they lifted their chins. It was in the quick glances they shared as they came out that said, 'We did a good thing coming here today.'

And while she arranged the next appointment, shook her head and said, 'No cost. Dr Brand is bulk-billing,' she ached inside. She wanted to see the magic behind the closed door. She had a fertility problem of sorts. She needed to tell someone and if she waited for a vacant appointment it might be too late.

So, she did what Dr Konrad told her to do if she ever needed to fit someone urgent in. She made the appointment for the next morning before the day started. She typed in her own name: *Melinda Lowenthal. Age twenty. Consultation Dr Brand. Eight-fifteen.*

If she had a chance, she'd mention it to the doctor before the appointment arrived, but when the door opened and Dr Brand appeared and called out the next patient's name, Melinda put her head down in embarrassment.

Melinda forced her chin back up. She saw the doctor stand back to allow the couple to enter, and as she always did, she glanced across to her and smiled.

It would be fine. The doctor hadn't had a break yet. No morning tea. No lunch. No drink at all. Melinda made eye contact with the doctor and mimed a coffee and a knock. She received a quick nod of appreciation and Melinda's chest eased. It was good she could do something for the doctor. She had some of Toby's mum's fruitcake left over from her own lunch, and she'd add that as well.

Chapter Twelve

Konrad

Konrad glanced at the clock and then at the closed door of Riley's consulting room. It was nearly six pm. He'd caught up on all the files he needed to sort, any pathology results were checked, and patients he needed to phone had been spoken to. It had been a big day.

But it had been bigger for Riley. She had her last patient in there now. Melinda said she'd had no breaks and appeared only briefly before the next hope-to-be-a-parent was ushered in.

He'd seen Melinda take her a coffee at two. He hadn't caught sight of Riley since she'd passed him when he was leaving for lunch. That had been well after the amusing incident with Cyrus and his itch.

He heard voices, the door opened, and a smiling couple came out. He didn't know this pair. He hadn't known many of the couples in the waiting room, so he suspected they'd come from other towns.

Riley followed them out and damned if she didn't look as fresh and immaculate as she had this morning. He glanced down at his jeans. Guess he looked the same, too, but without the designer start.

'I'll see you in two weeks,' Riley said to the departing couple. They waved and Riley turned to face him. She cocked a brow as if to say, *Did you want something?*

He shook his head and waited until the couple closed the front door behind them. He stepped over and locked it. Melinda had been gone for an hour. He turned back to face his colleague and she looked as if she'd given herself permission to sag just a fraction.

'I have a takeaway roast-beef dinner if you're interested. I ordered extra-large in case you wanted to stop and eat with me in the common room.' He gestured with his head towards the units out back. 'But if you'd rather do something else'—he shrugged— 'I'll just keep it for tomorrow.'

She blew out a breath. 'Ten minutes. I need to shower and change. Do you have anything alcoholic?'

'The last bloke left a bottle of gin and some tonic. I could mix them.'

'Sold.'

Ten minutes and she was back. Crikey, that was a first. A woman with speed shower skills. And she looked good enough to eat. Well, he was hungry and that blue shirt she'd worn on Friday night looked mighty fine as it smoothed over her . . .

Stop. This is a professional colleague, he reminded himself.

He busied himself with the G & T, even sliced a lemon wedge he'd kept from his last fish and chips – he hoped it wasn't fishy – and ice cubes. It wasn't his tipple, but it sat nicely next to his beer as she smiled her thanks.

He handed her the glass. She took it, sipped, and blew out a sigh like she'd just untied a balloon full of air. Except the air balloon didn't rush in a wail around their head, just the scent of toothpaste drifted his way. 'I've died and gone to heaven.'

'You've died and gone to Lightning Ridge.'

She snorted. 'I've certainly met the locals today.'

He had to grin at that. 'Anybody live up to Cyrus?'

Her eyes met his in a can-you-believe-that-guy look that had him grinning back. 'One of a kind, that man. But he has lots of little brothers in the 'hood.'

'We call it the "Ridge". I owe you. I've been trying to get some of these blokes in for check-ups for a year now. You drew them in on your first day.'

She smiled and it was the first relaxed one he'd seen. 'Lucky I ordered all the tests, then. Your pathology service is in for a busy week or four.'

She was funny. And smart. And gorgeous, and he needed to stop thinking like this. 'How did your fertility clinic go?'

'There's certainly a need. And some have almost left it too late.' She stared pensively at her glass. 'I'd never thought much about the tyranny of distance. Those away from the cities do suffer from lack of access to specialists.'

'Too true.'

She shook her head and the shiny cap of red swished around her ears. 'And I should have.' She looked at him. 'I have roots in the outback. My grandparents ran a station out past Wilcannia. I've gone soft and self-absorbed in Sydney.'

'Whoa.' He looked at her drink. 'Your glass is still almost full. It's too early for gin-soaked moping.'

She laughed and took another sip, then closed her eyes with a puff of pleasure, which he assumed meant she savoured the cold sliding down.

His gaze wandered to her long, elegant throat as she swallowed. And he dragged his eyes away just as quickly to the benchtop oven, where their dinners were electronically being timed and reheated. 'That's a lot of introspection for someone who's had barely a minute to herself all day. You should eat.'

She too glanced to where the aroma of roast beef rose with the steam from the oven. 'I should.'

'Tired?'

She pulled a mocking face. 'A little. Not too much. Obstetricians are used to long days and nights on little sleep.'

'Do you still do that? Answer call-outs to save mums and babies?'

'Not often, not now. Though I'm hands on when one of my clients gives birth and that can be an all-nighter.'

He finished his beer, decided not to have another one in the interests of keeping his hands off her, unless she asked of course, and moved to divide up the meal Greta had sent over for them. He slipped on his tartan oven mitt and pulled the loaded foil tray from the oven.

She raised her brows. 'Nice glove. Does it have an apron to match?'

'It comes with a kilt, which of course I wear commando.' He allowed a little of his interest in her through to his voice. 'But I only show that to close friends.'

He was flirting? He never flirted. Or not recently. But there was something about her that made his mouth want to run on in a way it hadn't for almost two years now. He dipped his gaze to the tray that sat on the bench in front of him. 'Hope you're hungry. You must have made an impression on Greta because this is a generous serving.'

'My mother knows her. And Toby mentioned that I'd helped you on Friday.'

'Ah, that explains it.' He dished out piles of roast beef and vegetables until her plate began to heap.

'Stop.' She lifted her hand as he went to add another roast potato to her plate. 'I can't eat all that.'

He took two pieces back. 'It'll be in the oven if you want more. Greta's potatoes are to die for.'

'I can see that. Did Toby come in today?'

'Yes, he did. After lunch. Sheepish and sober.'

'I'm glad he turned up. How was he?'

'Not too bad. He'd looked at that site you suggested. We talked about the schools and mentoring. The results of the blood tests made me suggest a different anti-epileptic medication.'

She nodded. 'Any news on the girlfriend?'

'I'd say it'd take a lot for Toby to forget she said what she did.'

'Maybe he needs a new girl?' She looked thoughtful and he wondered what the heck she was thinking.

No, he wanted to tell her. He'd learned that tragic lesson too well. It was the second relationship failure that had killed his brother. It had started the drinking again and exacerbated the depression. Pain sliced through him with remembered guilt and the room, and the woman in it, receded into a grey mist. What followed had devasted Konrad, his sister Bella – William's twin – and his parents. His ears buzzed and he could see the white, cold hand of his dead brother reaching out for help.

He hadn't been there in time.

He should have picked up on that before the end.

He shook his head and the buzzing stopped.

His vision returned to the plate in front of him and he straightened his shoulders. Glad he had his back to her, he turned and carried her plate to the small table. He was still disconnected, though, on auto pilot. 'Sit. Eat.'

'Woof,' she said.

That made him blink. He'd really zoned out. He looked at her questioning eyes and grounded himself. 'Sorry. I had a flashback to something.' He replayed her words and huffed out a strange noise. 'You're no dog,' he told her.

'That's good to know. But on the topic, I was thinking about Toby and Melinda. She tells me she doesn't have a boyfriend.'

Bloody hell. Konrad screwed up his face. 'Melinda's not been out with anyone since . . .' He paused. Really, it was Melinda's story to tell. He finished with, '. . . her bad experience.'

'From my brief meet, I didn't think Toby would be a bad experience. He's not mean to girls, he's not that kind of guy. As long as she can handle the epileptic part.'

He put his own plate down on the table a little too hard, and it landed loudly. Before he sat down, he met her eyes and held her gaze. Once he had her attention, he shook his head decisively. 'No. Do not meddle in Toby's life. Or anyone's life out here.' It came out a little harsher than he'd intended, but he couldn't help adding, 'Or Melinda's, either. They're both damaged and fragile. Just . . . leave them be.'

Chapter Thirteen

Riley

The man opposite her sat with unexpected speed but managed to look dangerous while he did it. It seemed Toby and Melinda weren't the only ones who were damaged, if that little fade-out and overreaction were anything to go by.

Where did that come from? Riley studied his strong profile as he glanced across to check the oven – or to avoid her eyes. Instead of firing up, she sat back in her chair and studied him as he reached for the salt.

One of her girlfriends had come back from Afghanistan with swings like that. 'Do I detect a knee-jerk reaction to my comment?' she asked.

'I don't think so.' His features had taken on a calm and stillness that tried to lie about his thoughts, but she wasn't fooled.

Emotions vibrated off him, raising her spidey senses. She poked. 'No past trauma activated by my comment?'

'No.'

'Then you're just really anti-matchmaking?'

He didn't look at her. Instead he picked up his knife and fork and gestured at her with the tines. 'Let's go with the latter. Enjoy your dinner.'

'And stop asking questions?'

'Don't meddle.' He flickered her a flat glance and took a mouthful of food.

Riley was curious but not finished. Sadly, it seemed she was a meddler. What was solving infertility issues if not meddling in lives? But she nodded and sliced into a crisp golden roast vegetable.

Oh yes, the potatoes were to die for.

He'd placed gravy in the middle of the table, still in its plastic dish. Aromatic steam rose, so she generously doused her beef and vegetables. Her mouth flooded with anticipation. It was just like her mum's. The scent of the meal rose in a fragrant wave of food scents and she appreciated her good fortune after the big day.

She wasn't a cook, never had been, and if she could eat out every night she'd be happy. 'You can certainly reheat potatoes with the best of them.' She paused on the thought while she took another gravy-soaked slice of beef. 'This'—she chewed and swallowed—'is delicious,' she said between mouthfuls, and his stern face relaxed.

'Greta's the best cook in town.'

'And she's Toby's mother. Who would love to see him happy,' she said, more to tease him than to open the conversation again.

Now why would you want to tease him? an inner voice questioned, but before she could think about it, he spoke.

'New subject.'

Riley savoured another slice of beef behind her held-in smile, and swallowed. 'I saw my mother's claim on Saturday,' she told him. 'About five kilometres out of town. She's living in an off-grid solar-powered shambles of a place that used to be some sort of inn.'

He looked up, interest making his blue eyes a shade lighter and warmer. 'The Wayfarers Inn?'

Was that what her mum said? Or was it Greta? It sounded right. 'Yes, I think so.'

He nodded and his eyes returned to his plate for more food. She did too. Now that she'd dropped Toby as a subject, it was quite companionable. They were both ravenous, apparently.

'I saw that for sale a couple of months ago,' he said when he'd finished his forkful. 'I was even tempted to buy it myself.'

Why on earth? 'You can run a doctor's surgery off grid?' She was still stupidly keen to tease, it seemed.

'Heaven forbid. Imagine the steriliser, and the immunisation fridge.' They both smiled at the thought.

He shrugged those massive shoulders. 'But I could escape there. Sometimes it's hard to get away from being on call twenty-four hours a day.'

She was hearing him. They had that much in common. 'It's the same with my practice when a longed-for baby is due. It made Josh frustrated when I was waiting for a labour to come on.' Now why would she bring up Josh when he was goneski? To hint to Konrad Grey that she was seeing someone? Or to remind herself not to get involved?

He stilled then lifted his head. 'Yet the rewards outweigh the disadvantages?' He didn't ask about Josh and she buried a tiny disappointment that he hadn't thought it worth mentioning.

'Absolutely. I love to meddle.' She smiled at his frown. 'And what's solving infertility issues if not meddling in lives?' she repeated

94

her earlier musing for him out loud. 'It's very satisfying to see the results.' Even she heard the enthusiasm in her voice. It was good to be reminded. 'There's something immensely rewarding about helping a couple realise their dream to become parents. There's a myriad of technologies available now and I can help with most of them.'

He put his knife and fork together and pushed away his empty plate. 'Solving fertility challenges is a worthy profession.'

She was a little in awe of his ability to devour such an enormous plateful with such speed and economy. She still had half of hers to go, but she paused long enough to wave her hand at him. 'As is providing medical support in places like this.' She waved her hand towards the door.

'Places like what?' He cocked an eyebrow. 'You putting the place down?'

'Of course not. I know nothing about Lightning Ridge.' Had she sounded snobby? Waved with disrespect? She hadn't intended to. 'I meant, what you're doing so well out here is worthwhile. For people like Toby. And Cyrus. A long way from specialists and with a nurse-led multi-purpose centre hospital as your only backup.'

'Our hospital nurses are extremely competent. Lives are saved out here. And there's always the RFDS.'

He did seem to be spoiling for a fight. 'They'd have to be. But you know what I mean. Desiree and Greta think you're a hero for staying here.' She wasn't sure why she felt the need to push his buttons, but there was something stimulating about trying to work out how this guy ticked and why he remained in Lightning Ridge.

'Nobody is a hero if they're doing a job they care about.' His voice sounded calm, detached and cool. Cold, really. Yup. She'd annoyed him. How fun. 'We both know that.'

He stood, lifted his plate and put it on the sink. 'See you tomorrow for day two.' His lips were a firm white line. Tight. Tense. Ticked off.

What the . . .?

But she let him go with a shrug. 'Thanks for the meal. I appreciate it. I'll make sure I'm more organised for food tomorrow. Maybe you'll share my order-in.'

'Probably not. I've got plans for tomorrow night. I've got some calls to make. Good night.' He jerked his head in a goodbye salute and walked out the door.

Huh. She'd really annoyed him. Or whatever he'd been lost in had killed his good mood. So much for dinner and a casual chat. She shrugged as the door shut behind him and finished another bite. She had some phone calls to make, too, and tomorrow would be another long day.

With more not-so-delicate digging into the dour Doctor Grey.

Chapter Fourteen

Konrad

Konrad closed the door softly when he wanted to slam it, even though it wasn't Riley's fault. He was too touchy about others meddling in people's lives.

Hell, he could even understand her desire to interfere. But she hadn't seen first-hand what could happen. She hadn't been responsible for causing such heartache that someone chose not to live. His own someone. He'd only introduced the girl to his brother, thinking they might have interests in common. They'd hit it off and then imploded and William had killed himself.

He couldn't even protect the people he loved. And that meant his parents and his sister both suffered guilt and grief because he'd failed. There was no way he was going to encourage anyone to intrude in the lives of others and risk someone else.

Pushing open his unit door, he went into the dark and stood there for a moment, centring himself. It was crazy how much Riley could get under his skin and not just in irritation. Which might have been why he'd overreacted? Because she was right, he realised. He had overreacted.

His mobile phone vibrated and flashed in his pocket, and as he pulled it out the flash strobed the dark room. He switched on the room light and blew out a breath. It was Greta's number. She'd want to know how they'd enjoyed the meal, he realised with a smile.

'Konrad,' he said and threw his keys on the table.

'It's Greta.' Her voice was laden with something that had his gut coiling in dread. 'Toby didn't come home for dinner. Since that girl broke off their engagement, he's been too quiet.' She cleared her throat noisily and he knew she was trying to hold back tears. 'Have you seen him?'

'I saw him today, in the surgery. He seemed fine. He's probably found someone to talk to.' Hopefully not gone for a drink again.

'Maybe, but I'm worried. It's that same gut feeling I had the last time he did something bad. And he's taken the car even though he knows he shouldn't drive.'

Konrad's fingers tightened around the phone and his gut twisted more. Poor Greta. She was most likely alone and stressed. She needed reassurance. Calm. And Toby needed to get out of the car. He compressed his lips to keep his voice level. 'I'm sure he's fine, Greta, but you need company until he comes home. Ring Desiree to come sit with you. I'll drive around to look for him. Ring me if he turns up and I'll do the same.'

'You'll let me know if you find . . .' Her voice trailed off. 'Find him, I mean.' Her voice broke and Konrad winced.

'I'm sure he's fine, Greta,' he repeated.

But he wasn't sure. Toby had had a wall up today. Did the young fool think he had nothing to live for? Like Konrad's brother, William, had done?

That wasn't going to happen.

He grabbed his keys back off the bench, pulled out his emergency medical bag hoping like hell he wouldn't need it, and flicked off the light. As he closed the door to his unit behind him, the next opened, and she appeared.

Riley stepped out, her hand reaching up to stop him mid-stride. 'I hope I didn't upset you,' she said.

He didn't have time for this. There were real problems, not imagined ones, to sort. 'Toby's missing and his mother's worried.' He grimaced, remembered Greta's words. 'She said she feels the same foreboding, like when he tried to hurt himself last time.'

Her hand fell and she slipped in beside him as he headed for his car. 'You want me to come with you?'

He didn't look at her. 'Not really.'

She laughed. 'Yet . . . if you did need medical help, a second person would be better?' It was still a question, so he had a choice.

His hands tightened on the handle of his medical bag. 'Sure. Jump in. I'm just planning to drive around town.'

Chapter Fifteen

Riley

Riley climbed into the front seat of the late-model Range Rover Sport, a tough but luxurious option for driving out west. *Nice*, she thought, and inhaled the redolent scent of leather and the subtle wisp of Konrad's delightful aftershave. By the time she'd closed her door, he had the car moving and she clipped in her seatbelt. Obviously, that speed of take-off was an indication of his stress. She'd have to be blind not to see his ramped-up concern, so she said nothing.

Long, strong fingers had a white-knuckled grip on the wheel and his focus on the twin beams of light in front of him meant he was ignoring her presence beside him. Well, he had said he didn't want her to come. Her mouth quirked. That was a first. She'd never had popularity problems before, but as her mother would say in one of her drier moments, 'It's not all about you, Riley.' Thank goodness for Mum's level head or Dad would have turned her into the princess Konrad had been afraid of. Yes, this wasn't about her. It was about Greta and Toby.

'What happened the last time Toby tried to harm himself?' she asked gently.

Konrad didn't shift his eyes from the road and she realised he was scanning corners and dark areas along the few streets. 'He overdosed on paracetamol. He was bloody lucky he didn't wipe out his liver, but we got there and pumped his stomach early.'

'Nasty thing, Panadol overdose. Aren't there studies on anti-epileptics exacerbating Panadol toxicity?'

'There are indeed.' That earned her a quick glance. 'That's not something I would have thought an obstetrician and fertility expert would be interested in.'

'I read my research papers.' Her voice stayed mild. He probably hadn't intended that as a slight. 'And as I've said, I had a client not dealing well with her epilepsy, either. How's his liver?'

'Still healthy, thankfully, though I always add liver-function tests to his usual blood tests. The time before that he had to be talked off the edge of one of the deeper mine shafts.'

Two failed attempts could mean he was seeking to be seen rather than dead. 'Attention seeking?'

'I don't think so. Both were poor management of the attempts rather than execution. Greta is onto him.'

Tragic as well, she thought. 'Where are we heading?'

'First a quick trip around town to make sure he's not in one of the drinking holes. Or drunk against a wall.'

'Do you want me to ring the pub and ask?' She pulled out her phone.

'There are only two places in town. I'll duck in and ask if they've seen him.' He scrubbed his face, obviously thinking. 'You could ring the Club in the Scrub out at Grawin to see if he's there. It's open till eight. It's fifty minutes of driving out of town and not worth the run if he hasn't shown his face.'

She huffed out a laugh. 'Club in the Scrub? Sounds interesting. Must go out there one day.'

'Good food. Great people. No frills.' He glanced at her, his brows raised.

'What?' She sniffed, pretending to be offended. 'I can do no frills.'

He didn't say anything, but his hands loosened on the wheel and his face didn't look quite so set. If she could make him take a breath, then she was willing to be the butt of the joke.

The car pulled in smoothly. 'Here's Diggers Rest. I'll be back in a sec. Could you ring Greta and see if she's heard anything yet. The number's the same as the café.' He was out before she could agree. So, she looked for Greta's number in her phone, which she'd saved for takeaways, and touched the number. The call was answered straightaway.

'It's Riley. I'm in Konrad's car. He asked me to check if you've heard anything. He's dropping into the pub to check.'

'No. Desiree's here and she's ringing around, too.'

'Okay. You can phone this number or Konrad's if you need to contact us. Talk soon.'

She tapped the number for 'Club in the Scrub' after looking it up on Google – the things you could find – and the proprietor denied seeing Toby for a few days now.

Konrad's door opened and he slid behind the wheel. 'They haven't seen him.' He pulled out onto the deserted street. 'We'll try the bowling club.'

'Greta's heard nothing, Desiree's ringing around and he's not been seen at the Club in the Scrub for a couple of days.'

'That one was a long shot. His ex's mother works in the kitchen out there.'

Five hundred metres up the road, he stopped again and jumped out.

He was back less than a minute later. 'Nope. Not there.'

'So, where to now?'

'I'm thinking the old church site. There are lots of mine shafts out there.'

Ouch, Riley thought. 'Morbid much.'

'He asked his girlfriend to marry him at the edge of the spot where it used to stand. The building itself came down in a tornado.'

'Not a place of good vibes, perhaps?'

'It's a pile of tin. There's a bench seat there for sunset. He was very proud of himself for being romantic for the proposal.' The dread was back lacing Konrad's voice. And she had to wonder why he felt so emotionally and personally responsible for Toby.

'Don't underrate romance,' she said, but that was more of a reflex comment on his. She was thinking about Toby. Sure, he was a young, likeable patient, anyone would care, but this seemed . . . more. She wondered how much of a chance there really was that they'd find Toby's broken body at the bottom of a mine shaft.

She peered into the dark on her side of the car. Did they find people at the bottom of shafts? Probably not. She shuddered, suddenly feeling a little emotional herself.

They left the outskirts of town and turned into the track that would eventually take them past her mother's claim. 'So,' she wondered out loud, 'the church site's out towards the old Wayfarers Inn?'

He glanced at her, gave a quick nod, then his eyes were back on the road. 'Near your mother's place. It might be worthwhile stopping to ask her if she saw a car go past this afternoon. Toby left me at two pm, so we can discount anything before then. This road's not often used.'

'Sure. I can do that.' She glanced at his stern profile. 'You want to meet Mum, or are you in too much of a hurry?'

He gave her another nod. 'I'll hop out and say hi and maybe recognise a description if any local cars have gone past.'

Her brow furrowed. Riley wasn't sure how she felt about the fact that not many cars went past her mum's place. It must be more isolated than she'd thought. She'd assumed there'd be a heap more claims right along the road as neighbours.

She stared ahead into the circle of the headlights. 'But Wayfarers was an inn, right? This track must've been on some sort of travel route before the customers hit the opal fields?'

'It was.' He shook his head. 'Down the hill will take you to the Castlereagh Highway. The main road was rerouted onto Bill O'Brien Way, which takes you into the Ridge now. The old road's a rough track these days.'

He swerved suddenly to avoid a loping kangaroo and his left arm came out in front of her as if to stop her flying through the windscreen.

Her brows went up. 'I have my seatbelt.'

'Yeah.' His hand lifted briefly again from the wheel as if to say, 'ignore me'. 'Habit. Younger sister and brother, twins, both menaces for not doing up their seatbelts.' His voice sounded tight and he'd stiffened all over, as if regretting he'd moved. Or spoken.

The darkness lightened and her mother's shack came into view, the light spilling out from the windows in golden beams onto the track. Riley watched as his tense shoulders relaxed a fraction at the sight.

Curiouser and curiouser. 'I'll get out first, shall I? She might get a bit jumpy at night when people pull up.'

'Sure.'

'A minute will be enough.' Riley slipped from the car and slammed the door noisily so her mum could hear that someone was there.

She called out, 'Hello, Mum? You there? It's Riley.'

The creaking front door opened and her mother's head came into view, looking far too relaxed at the idea of somebody coming after dark to her isolated house. Dad had always said that Mum had big brass ones. Riley had agreed, but this was proof.

Konrad stepped up beside her. 'Hello, Mrs Brand. I'm Konrad Grey. Nice to meet you.' He held out his hand and her mother shook it. They both let go. 'I know it's late, but we're looking for Toby, Greta's son. He hasn't turned up at home and his mum's worried. We thought he might have come out to the old church-yard and wondered if you saw any cars go past this afternoon?'

'Greta's boy? I did see one car driving around about four o'clock? One of those little Jumbuck utes. A blue one. I haven't seen it come back.'

Konrad blew out a breath. 'That's the one.' He met Riley's eyes and she saw the flare of worry in his before he looked away towards the disappearing track. 'We'd better go.' He glanced back at her. 'Or you can wait here and I'll pick you up in a while.'

She turned to look at him. 'Not happening.' As if. 'You might need help.'

'Of course.' He looked at her mother. 'I'm learning she's stubborn.'

'You look like you're glad. Do you want me to come too? I'm a nurse.'

Riley answered for him. 'We'll drop back in on the way back, Mum, to let you know if it's a false alarm. Or I'll call you.'

Her mother nodded, worry creasing her face. Lots of creases. Her mum had wrinkles. Riley froze for a moment as the reality hit home. Her mum was getting older. That would be her thirty years in the future. Yet despite that worry, she showed an air of serenity that Riley felt she'd never noticed before, and one she personally had missed out on.

Her mum said, 'I hope everything is okay.'

Riley waited for Konrad to answer, but he said nothing, so she responded with a frown at him. 'Toby's probably having some alone time. I'm sure we'll find him, Mum.'

It seemed none of them drew comfort from that suggestion. She and Konrad returned to the car. Silence hung in the vehicle as they pulled back onto the road.

'You're really worried that he's attempted suicide, aren't you?' she asked.

'Aren't you?' His voice was clipped.

She was trying not to. There were other reasons people took off by themselves. 'I've only met him once and it seems like he's got a really supportive family.'

'Support of families doesn't always keep people safe. Sometimes they can cause more problems.'

That there, that was personal experience, she was sure of it. 'You've lived through this personally, haven't you?' she said, though she felt she already knew the answer. Then she remembered Greta's cryptic comment about Konrad and his brother.

'Yes.'

The face that turned to her could have been carved from one of those gravel boulders outside her mother's house. She waited. He didn't say more, but she had learned over the years that if she just waited a person out, then who knew.

After a long, long, long pause, he said, 'My brother, William.'

She slid her hand across to his muscled, jean-clad thigh and touched him. He flinched, and below her fingers the muscles were taut. She squeezed in sympathy once then took her hand away. She was pretty sure it wasn't welcome. 'I'm sorry. Was this the younger one who didn't put his seatbelt on?' Somehow, she knew it was.

'Yes.'

'I'm sorry, Konrad. That's heartbreaking. I hope for Toby's sake, and yours, that Toby's fine.'

He didn't say anything. The car slowed. 'We'll find out shortly,' he said eventually.

Konrad angled the car over some deep potholes and along a two-rut track that she barely felt under the excellent suspension. In the swing of the headlights, she noted an ancient and bent sign that read, 'SITE OF OLD CHURCH'. Less than fifty feet further along the track, a large gravel parking area opened out into a scatter of tin and broken building materials.

There, in the corner next to some mullock heaps of rubble, sat a small blue utility.

No lights. No movement. No sounds.

Chapter Sixteen

Konrad

Konrad blew out a breath that felt like it started in his well-worn leather boots. Hell. Bloody hell.

He didn't want to get out!

He left the headlights shining over where he knew some of the shafts were hidden and pushed open the door, reaching for the flashlight he carried in the pocket of the car as he swung out. 'There's a flashlight on your side, too,' he told Riley. 'Just in the door pocket. Watch, carefully, where you walk. Shafts can be knocked uncovered and they're deep.'

'Great, thanks. I'll be careful.'

He heard her door open. He shouldn't have brought her. It was dangerously uneven in the rough gravel and there were too many places for accidents. Especially in the dark. 'Use your torch on the ground in front of you. Please don't be a pain and fall down any mines.'

'I love you too.' She actually laughed. 'I'm a big girl.'

His breath stuck in his chest for a second, and then his shoulders relaxed. She was a big girl; he liked tall, athletic women, but he wasn't thinking about that now. 'Maybe I could have said that better.'

Then he pushed her from his mind and called out, 'Toby?' his voice ringing out over the open gravel and the night. It echoed back in. *Toby, Toby*, in diminishing vibrations. He tried again. 'Toby?' *Toby, Toby.*

There was no other answer, until pebbles rattled and he swung his torch towards the sound. He would have killed for the full moon to be up, it would have been handy for the nooks and crannies of the landscape. But, it was as dark as a shaft out here despite his lights.

'Over here.' A tired, dispirited reply had them both spinning to the left. A large boulder and the figure slumped there materialised into view, like an actor with two stage lights trained on him.

Riley's ribbon of light was the first to fall.

Konrad tilted his beam out of Toby's face and blew out a breath heavily laced with mind-shocking relief while his emotions seesawed from exhilaration to instinctive anger that wanted to rise instead and fill the painful void.

He felt Riley's hand on his shoulder, as if she sensed his mood swing, and she stepped forward before he'd even blinked.

'Hey there, Toby,' she said, her voice calm and conversational. 'Your mum was worried, and seeing as my mum lives out this way, Konrad and I drove around to see if you were here.'

Silence greeted her words, but she just kept walking towards him, her torchlight covering the ground in front of her feet as Konrad had told her. Slow, unthreatening, totally at ease, and he marvelled a little.

The silence of the night stretched around them like black elastic, pulling and pulsing with an eerie detachment, but it was menacing nevertheless. As if bad things could still happen. He followed her.

Finally, with a huff of what sounded like disgust, Toby muttered, 'I wasn't planning on killing myself.' He directed his ire to the ground, but then he slid a glance at Konrad and their gazes met in the uncertain light.

'Glad to hear that, mate.' Good, his voice was working, thank heaven, and his shoulders felt like someone had lifted a tree off them, but his gut still roiled.

'I'll let your mum know. Do you want to come back and meet Riley's mother? We could give yours a chance to settle down before you get home?'

He saw Riley's start of surprise, but she'd wanted to come, so she may as well be useful to get over the awkwardness.

He saw her head nod in agreement in the diffused light as she walked over and sat on the boulder next to Toby. Of course, she'd take that in her stride. 'Knowing my mum, she'll have managed to bake something in the ten minutes since we saw her that tastes amazing, despite being off grid.' Her voice floated in the night air, calm and conversational. There was no angst or anger like he could feel still churning within him from the fear of it all.

Toby had straightened, but he didn't look at her. 'Does she jump to conclusions like my mother?'

'She's cool, and a good cook like yours.' He saw Riley bump Toby's shoulder with hers. 'Whatcha doing out here?'

Konrad had wanted the answer to that badly but hadn't been able to figure out a way to ask diplomatically. Typical. If she wasn't so feminine, he'd call her a bull at a gate.

'Throwing the engagement ring over the edge.'

He saw her head incline in the shadows. Non-judgemental. Supportive without doing anything special. It was a skill. Then she looked at Toby, up close, studying his face in the dim light. 'Was it satisfying?'

'No.' He shifted fully upright and huffed out another one of those weary sighs. 'It was a damn waste of money. I should have hocked it.'

Riley laughed and finally Konrad could feel the dissipation of excess emotion in his shoulders and gut. He'd bet Toby felt better, too. It was hard to believe, but Toby would be fine.

Riley stood. 'Wanna follow us or stay?'

Konrad started forward. He didn't want to leave Toby out here to rethink his options.

Toby jerked too. 'You trust me to stay out here and not jump into a mine shaft?'

His gaze slid to Konrad, who'd stopped, and he forced himself to mimic Riley's easy manner. His shrug was a little stiff. 'You said you weren't planning to kill yourself. Were you lying?'

'No.'

'Up to you, then. Come on, Riley.' Though it had been her idea to leave, he didn't want to stuff up any of her good work. Suddenly, he was bone-freakin'-weary and wanted to get away from the desolation of the place.

They walked away from Toby, who'd stood with obvious reluctance and had clenched his hands, and Konrad suspected he wasn't sure what to do. He turned back. 'Come meet Riley's mum. I suspect she's just like our new doc.'

Toby blew out a breath and took a step. Then another. 'Sure, why not. You ring my mother so she can calm down. I should have told Mum why I was coming out here. She would have said hock the ring.'

Chapter Seventeen

Adelaide

Not long after Riley and her interesting boss had left in a ball of unseen but throat-scratching dust, Adelaide's mobile phone rang. She'd just slipped a tray into the oven and she put the mitt down to answer it.

'Hey, Adelaide. It's Desiree. You see any cars passing your shack today? This afternoon? Going either way?'

'Yes, I have.' Great minds think alike, obviously. And it just proved Desiree knew everything. 'I can tell you what I just told Riley and Konrad. A blue ute went through about four pm. They've gone to see some old church site and I'm waiting for them to return.'

'Ah.' She heard Desiree relay that information to someone else. 'Okay. Phone us if you see the ute again or when they come back. I'm at Greta's. If Riley doesn't stop in, at least phone us to say they've come back.'

'I imagine they'll stop.'

'Great, thanks. Talk soon.' And Desiree hung up.

Adelaide slipped the phone back into her pocket as she thanked the telephone gods for service. She thought about the caring of the women here, pushed the front door open and went outside to wait. She wasn't going to envisage anything bad happening to Toby. She believed you could draw disaster by constantly dreading it. When things happened, that was time enough for angst. It shouldn't take them long to check and come back. Maybe they'd bring Toby, too? At least she had food.

Adelaide held up the front of her shack with her body. Technically she was standing on the verandah, but she was on the ground, so maybe it was more apt to think of it as a floorless porch that needed support instead of the grand-sounding verandah. She smiled at the whimsy as she leaned her shoulder against the doorframe of her rough little inn. *It really didn't wobble too much*, she thought, as she fixed her eyes on the dark road.

There was nothing to hear. Nothing to see. Nowhere to be.

She breathed in the cooler night air, stepped forward from under the overhanging tin and tilted her head back to admire the sweep of the Milky Way as it crossed the sky above in a ribbon of scattered stars in the still, moonless sky. The full moon would rise soon, but for the moment, she had sparkles on velvet. Intricate constellations and the Southern Cross, reminding her again why she loved it out here so much.

She breathed deeply, her chest rising and falling in rhythm. That sky was a gift she'd never tire of, day or night. She'd turned into quite a cloud chaser since she'd settled in, snapping shots of the changing skyscape on her good camera. Toasting the sunset colours. Snapping the pastels of the pre-dawn. Trying to capture the Milky Way on her tripod in long exposures at night.

The quiet of solitude had seeped into her, making her savour the sounds of birds and wind, and distant thunder when it was around, or the rattle of gravel when a car went past, sticks or stones shifting from a ground creature when storms were absent.

It was so different to the clattering cacophony of the city with its sirens and neighbours and the constant sound of their own television in the background since her husband had retired. It had been the TV that had driven her away. Though she also had disliked the cars roaring up and down the street, now that her neighbour's three sons had grown into driver's licences and muscle cars.

Lucky she'd escaped. She'd been turning into a cranky old retiree glaring out of her lounge-room window. Well, not quite that bad, but who knew what would have happened. She'd just known she needed a change. Desperately.

There were no cars here now. None. Not even the one she waited for.

She'd thrown together a batch of cheese-topped scones in case they dropped in and were hungry after burning off all that adrenaline. The kettle hissed steam on the wood stove.

Her nose lifted and sniffed as the scrumptious aroma of crisping cheese tendrilled in a tease to follow her outside. If they didn't eat tonight, she'd be right for lunch tomorrow, but if they did come back and all was well, they'd need food and tea.

Unless the worst had happened. *No. Not that.*

To distract herself, she thought about the man who'd come with her daughter and a smile tilted the corner of her mouth. For people who hadn't known each other four days ago, there was a rapport there. A sizzle of awareness that she could feel, even if they were ignoring it. And from the brief few minutes she'd seen him, she suspected that Konrad Grey had plenty of backbone. He was no pampered wimp that her daughter could shove around as she felt like it, someone to use for a dinner date or social event and drop at her will. No, not Konrad. What fun.

Not that there'd be a future in it. She couldn't see Riley leaving the city, certainly not in exchange for Lightning Ridge, and Desiree said Konrad was settled here. But he just might convince her daughter there was more than that boring relationship she'd just left before she did something stupid and allowed Josh back into her life. *Please.*

Josh wasn't a bad man. He'd inherited his wealth and he loved to spoil her daughter. He just wasn't the right man for Riley. She knew that her daughter couldn't benefit from someone agreeing to her every request and comment. She'd be restless in a year. Adelaide had been irked in the first hour she'd met Josh and she didn't understand what Riley saw there.

Now, Konrad? He was a different kettle of fish. Konrad wasn't a 'yes' man. In fact, he looked to be more of a 'no' man and that thought made her smile wider. 'No' was the one word that fired her daughter up. If someone said it couldn't be done, then Riley was right in there pushing the envelope.

She suspected there was a whole post office of 'NO' envelopes where Konrad Grey was concerned. It was extraordinary how she'd made that impression from just a few minutes. She might be totally off, but she didn't think so. Sex-on-a-stick Viking. Lovely big shoulders, taller than Riley, which was very nice, and blue eyes to go with his too-long blond hair. He reminded her of one of the superhero Aussie actors . . . oh, what was his name?

Adelaide huffed at the unexpected delight of having Riley around. She'd missed her daughter. And there hadn't been enough occasional drop-ins in Sydney when they'd both worked.

Maybe she should invite Tyler out to see his daughter while Riley was here. It might be an added incentive. And wasn't that typical. She had to entice the man who'd married her with the one thing he loved more than his television.

His daughter.

Chapter Eighteen

Riley

In the cabin of the luxury all-terrain vehicle, Riley waited for Konrad to say something.

He didn't.

The headlights pierced the night and illuminated the potholes and white mounds of mine tailings each side of the dirt road. The silence felt as if it sucked the oxygen out of the air between them.

She was actually worried about him, which was odd. She wondered how much time she had before they reached her mother's shack. Five minutes? About three of those minutes after they'd left, Toby's headlights had appeared behind them, and with the extra light she noted the pulse beating on the side of Konrad's throat. He was screaming stress. Stiffly still. Silent.

'Huh,' she said as if surprised. 'I'd imagine you'd be feeling more relaxed. From where I'm sitting, it doesn't look like it.'

He didn't answer.

She tried again. The guy was hard work, but she was persistent. 'Are you okay?'

'I'm fine.' Said flatly. Well, didn't that make her think of that French movie with Meg Ryan.

'When you say that it makes my bum twitch.' Not quite the right words from the movie, but she'd never said 'arse' in her life. It wasn't one of her words. Or her mother's word, but she'd said it. Her mouth curved at the memory of her mum's joke.

Still no answer from Konrad. Distress continued to roll off the guy in waves.

'You don't look fine,' she pressed.

His gaze swung her way again, and thanks to Toby's head-lights she could see the frown. He blew out a breath. 'Delightful as your bum is, you can keep your twitches to yourself.' It was a poor attempt at humour, but at least it was an attempt. She'd give him that.

She snorted and then laughed. She had no idea why the guy cracked her up because what he said wasn't that funny. Still, an odd thought intruded; she'd never raised a laugh when Josh tried to joke.

'Okay, I'm being serious now. You don't seem as delighted as I am that Toby's behind us in his car and not down the bottom of a mine shaft.'

He flinched. His gaze lifted to the rear-view mirror and back again to the road in front. Toby's headlights threw the strong lines of his immobile face into sharp relief like a chiselled statue in pain from haemorrhoids. She smiled in the dark at her idiocy.

'I. Am. Delighted.' He enunciated each word. 'But I don't need to talk about it.' When she didn't offer any comment, he said, 'However,' his tone dry, as if he needed to meet expectations, 'I will thank you for coming with me.'

'Feel free. And after that . . .' she decided to use the opening, 'I think you need to talk about it. I think you're back in the past with the loss of your brother.'

He straightened and yep, it was possible for him to look even grimmer than before. 'I thought you were an obstetrician, not a psychologist.' The words held more than a tinge of bite.

She ignored them and softened her voice. 'How long ago did William die?' The words swung like threads of strong and sticky spiderwebs between them, stretching towards him, as if floating on an unexpected breeze, reaching out and not so easily brushed away.

She heard the creak of the steering wheel and noted the movement of his fingers as they tightened on the wheel. That was one tight grip; she hoped he wasn't imagining her throat. She got the feeling he didn't let many people into his thoughts.

'No.' The word shot out of him, heavy with finality. Then more quietly, he said, 'Don't make me regret telling you about my brother.'

The soft words belied the strong emotion behind them. A signal to stop. As if . . . because he needed this.

She turned fully to face him. 'Regret away. I'm thinking that if you didn't need to talk about William, you wouldn't have mentioned him.'

'You're wrong.'

'I don't think I am.'

His foot came off the accelerator and his head turned. She could see the narrow eyes glaring at her. 'I'm beginning to see that you think you're never wrong.'

She ignored that comment, though she looked away so he wouldn't see her lips twitch. At least he was looking less despondent and more energised than a few minutes ago. 'How long ago did William die?'

This time the expelled breath was noisy and disgusted at her persistence. 'Eighteen months. Okay?'

Less than two years? No wonder. The wound was so fresh. 'That's not long, and of course you're grieving.'

'Thank you, Captain Obvious.' That pulse beat again in his throat. Toby's attempts had hit him hard, she realised, so she lowered her voice. 'What happened with William has nothing to do with Toby. You can't be responsible for someone else's life choices.'

'Or end-of-life choices.' Something dark and chock-full with self-loathing shadowed the words. 'You know nothing.'

'I'd like to.' He really was suffering, and it made something deep in her stomach feel cold, clenched, an ache that she wanted to soothe. She saw the lights from her mother's house up ahead. 'But I can wait.'

He muttered something under his breath that she thought might have been, 'Lucky me.'

Chapter Nineteen

Adelaide

Adelaide saw the lights as a halo in the distance and jerked her shoulder from the rough post to stand straight. Then she caught the glow of a second pair of lights and sagged with an expelled breath. Unconsciously, her hand went to her pocket and her fingers closed around her phone as if communicating with Toby's mother. Thank goodness.

But she'd better wait to call in case it wasn't Toby.

Konrad's car stopped in front of her shack and Riley's eyes sought her out and she tipped her chin. That was a good sign. More tension eased out of her shoulders.

The other car came into view, slowed and stopped just behind Konrad's big vehicle, then the engine shut off. This was the little blue utility she'd seen earlier, and yes, there was a young man at the wheel. Excellent.

She waited, not wanting to crowd anybody, as Riley climbed out and came towards her, while Konrad strode towards the other vehicle and the young man.

So, that was Toby. The boy was about twenty, a foot shorter

than Konrad, but then most people would be. The man had to be six foot six. Toby's hair was blond, like his mother's, and she could see the same sweetness of face as in Greta.

She'd heard a lot about this young fellow, starting from his unusual introduction to her daughter, to the stresses of being depressed about his illness from his mother. He looked ordinary, if a little bit sheepish, but he moved with Konrad towards her with his back straight. And when their eyes met, he lifted his chin and offered her a tentative smile.

Her heart melted. Toby's young face seemed creased with the worries of the world, so she added extra warmth to her voice. 'Hello, Toby. It's so nice to meet you. I know your mother from Desiree's Friday-night ladies' gathering.'

Understanding crossed his face and his smile looked more natural this time. 'You're one of those ladies.'

She grinned wickedly at him. 'I am.' She waved her arm to include them all, because the others were standing back, and she suspected that Riley had relied on her ability to help Toby feel less self-conscious, to bring him here. She'd do what she could. 'Come inside and have a cup of tea or coffee and some hot cheese scones.'

She caught Toby's glance flick back to Riley and Riley laughed. 'I told you she'd make something. Unlike my cooking, it will melt in your mouth.'

All except Konrad bundled past the old wooden door, and it creaked and groaned as if with excitement as each body pushed past the rusty hinges. Having so many people in her shack wasn't something she was used to since arriving here.

'I'll phone Greta,' Konrad said.

A couple of minutes later he came in and the room seemed even smaller.

Adelaide had set the table, after moving the clutter that had stopped her and Riley eating there the other day, and it looked homey and hospitable even with the crowd. It made her proud of her little abode.

She'd put all the lights on, which she'd pay for later when the solar batteries died and everything went off, but that was okay. This was an occasion. A release of tension. A celebration of life.

The thought sobered her, and she handed out the cracked plates that had come with the inn. She really needed to take a run back to Sydney and make the place more civilised with the possessions Tyler would never use. She offered the mugs of tea that all had agreed on and finally sat back in the plush chair that was the only comfortable seat in the house. The others sat on her three rickety kitchen chairs and ate and drank with very little conversation.

Finally, after glancing at the other two, Toby said, 'This is nice.' He took another scone at Adelaide's encouraging nod. 'I was starving. Haven't had anything to eat since breakfast.'

'Well, if there's any left, you can take them home.' She tilted her head. 'Though I'm not sure. Do you live with your mum, or do you have your own place?'

His head went down. 'With Mum.'

'In that case, don't tell me if your mother thinks I could've done better with the scones.'

Toby smiled, and this time it was a natural boyish delight. He really was a lovely boy. 'Mum hasn't got a mean bone in her body.'

She was thinking, *I don't believe you have, either.* 'Now, Toby, if you get bored in the next couple of weeks, maybe you can help me. I heard you're pretty good with woodwork. If you or one of your friends needs some casual labouring, there are a few jobs around here I could use a second pair of hands for. Twenty dollars an hour. No rush – mostly future projects – just if you think of someone or want to do it yourself, phone me when you're ready.'

His eyes met hers and he inclined his head. 'Thank you. I'll call tomorrow and see what you need.'

The guests ate quickly and she couldn't help noticing the new awkwardness between Konrad and Riley. Riley kept sliding glances that made Adelaide wonder if they'd had words, but she couldn't see how that could happen when they'd just been looking for the boy. Both should have been relieved, not silently bickering. Which was an odd thought for her to have but matched their vibe perfectly.

Still, Riley's chin was up and she had more colour in her cheeks than usual, and that made her maternal brain engage. Just what was her daughter up to? Maybe pulling Konrad's tail, because somehow, she doubted it would be the other way around.

She was unsurprised when ten minutes later they were all ready to go. Adelaide shook hands with the men, Toby's callused ones first as he was leading. Konrad's hands were big, firm with thanks. A nice man.

'Thank you,' he said, and she knew he meant for making it easier for Toby to lose some of his tension.

'My pleasure.' She leaned forward and kissed Riley's cheek. 'See you Friday if not before.'

Riley kissed her back. 'Look forward to it.' They were going to Desiree's together.

Then they were all gone and her little shack echoed with vacant space and emptiness as she tidied up used cups and plates that she'd refused to let anyone help with. Soon she had it all back to normal. Straightened. Lots of space. Silent.

But the solitude sat serenely and Adelaide smiled.

Chapter Twenty

Konrad

Konrad turned on the ignition and the vehicle burbled softly to life. Without looking at Riley he said, 'Your mother is a sensible woman.'

She laughed. She had a great laugh. It sounded good after the tension of the night. 'And I'm not?'

He could hear the amusement in her words, so she wasn't offended by his grouchiness, made him wonder what she got out of yanking his chain. He decided not to bite, even though she was already irritating him. And he'd started the conversation.

Konrad put the car into gear and pulled out slowly, letting the dust settle from Toby's departure. Hopefully, ahead, Toby wouldn't feel like he was following them home with his tail between his legs. Or be too embarrassed to keep Konrad as his GP. He still worried about Toby, but he didn't say that out loud.

Instead, he said, 'I'm sure someone in your field is always sensible. But I meant your mother made Toby feel comfortable and that was useful.' Then he replayed that comment. It wasn't just Adelaide Brand who'd been great. Riley had been excellent, too.

And she'd offered to come with him, so he wasn't being fair in judging her harshly. He was usually fair, so why did she make him behave unfairly?

'I apologise.' He felt her shift beside him and she said, 'Wow,' very quietly. Ha. He'd surprised her. Good. But it only made him feel marginally better.

He needed to explain. Give credit where it was due. 'You did well at the quarry. I couldn't think what to say and you got it right.' It had been a big day and a major worry until he'd seen Toby on the rock in the dark. And she'd saved the situation from some awkwardness. He could see that now, looking back.

There was a pause and then she said simply, 'Thank you.'

Her light acceptance helped his shoulders ease. Maybe they could just ride home in silence now.

'Why do I get the impression that you blame yourself for your brother's death?'

He sucked in a shocked wheeze of air and felt his hands tighten involuntarily on the steering wheel. This woman. 'For pity's sake, Riley,' he managed very quietly between his clenched teeth, 'let it go.'

She turned to look out the window on her side. Said nothing. For kilometres.

Now, she'd shifted to watch him. For the last few minutes, she hadn't taken her eyes away.

'Stop staring,' he grumbled.

When she didn't react, he lifted his chin. 'I'm not responding.'

Crikey, she had him behaving like a toddler. In his periphery, he saw her settle deeper into the seat, but she didn't turn her head.

He huffed out a breath. 'Because I do blame myself for not seeing it coming.'

To his surprise, but not his chagrin, not at all, she remained silent.

As if driven by he-knew-not-what, the words slipped out. 'I was the last to see him alive. I should have done more. I let him, my parents and my sister down.'

There it was. The ugly truth. And the survivor's guilt.

He knew that it had chewed away at him for the last year and a half. That the guilt had kept him huddled inside his private shell in Lightning Ridge. And he knew that he was trying to create a place inside himself he could shut it all away and never see it again.

It had been working until Toby tried to take his life. And then tonight when Greta had phoned, the fear and guilt had buried him like a tunnel collapse out on the opal fields. Which made him realise that okay, maybe he wasn't doing any good by locking it all away.

'Does staying here help?'

Was she reading his thoughts? He looked at her from beneath lowered brows. 'I moved here to be near him. There was a job opening.'

'I'm sure. Remote GPs are like gold.' Her tone was dry. 'Or more like big black opals, around here.'

'Funny girl.' He resisted the urge to turn down the instrument lights because he felt her scrutiny still.

She was silent for a few blessed minutes while he berated himself for bringing her along.

'What did your parents say when you stayed out here?' she asked after a while.

'Are you always this nosy?' He couldn't help the snarky tone of the question.

'Hmm.' She seemed to think about that, but he doubted she needed to. 'Yep. Pretty much. Maybe it's the nature of my work.' Another silence. He was not encouraging her, even if he was, just mildly, interested.

'Maybe it's because my uncle was an investigative reporter and I spent a lot of time with him when I was at uni.'

Oh, yeah, he thought, *that makes sense*.

'Or maybe,' she continued and he heard the smile in her voice. Despite himself, his pulse rate picked up. 'I'm just interested in what makes you tick.'

Well, then. That was a little more interesting. Was it a mutual awareness? 'Yeah. Nosy,' was all he said. Maybe he could turn that around. 'So, have you got any siblings?'

'Nope. I'm the only offspring. The golden child, my dad calls me.'

'Why am I not surprised.' He slanted a glance at her. 'What does your sensible mother call you?'

'My mother loves me as I am.'

He laughed. She hadn't answered the question, which meant that Adelaide did not call her the 'golden child'.

'That's better,' she said, and his mirth stopped. 'You were in a hole. It makes for poor company, you know.'

'So sorry.'

She ignored his sarcasm. 'I'm guessing'—her voice was softer than he'd heard it; great, now she pitied him—'that after you stayed out here to hide, you were knocked for six when Toby tried to kill himself?'

His foot lifted off the accelerator and slowed the vehicle with the brake. 'Stop.' And he was fairly proud of the lack of emotion in the word. So, he added another one. 'Now.'

They both heard the finality in those two stark words. Perhaps that was too much to hope for, because she shrugged and opened that infuriatingly active mouth again. 'I'll just say – final words – that I'm glad we found Toby.'

He increased his speed and drove the last kilometre back home as fast as he safely could.

When they stopped, she simply slid out of the car and into her unit and closed the door.

Konrad locked his car and stood silent in the night, breathing in the air, letting the emotion seep out of him once he was alone. After a minute, he lifted his head and moved towards his unit.

The worst thing was he doubted his locum would let the conversation drop. And he'd have to see her again first thing tomorrow morning. Just under four weeks to go. That didn't fill him with the relief he craved.

Chapter Twenty-one

Riley

Riley closed the door and the lock clicked. Not that she imagined Konrad was going to come in and push a pillow over her head while she slept, but he might sleepwalk and do it.

'And you would deserve it,' she murmured mockingly. She had no idea why she hadn't been able to shut up, and, she suspected an apology would just work him up more.

On the positive side, Toby looked reasonably stable, though he still needed a friend. As far as she was concerned, there was nothing wrong with the idea of Melinda and Toby comparing emotional wounds. She just had to make sure she didn't encourage that anywhere around Konrad.

She glanced at her watch. Despite it feeling like midnight, it was only nine pm, early enough to phone her night-owl business partner to confirm the logistics for the patient pathway. She sat down at the little table and chairs and fished her phone from her bag. As far as the outreach fertility clinic today had gone, it had been a success.

If she didn't sway her mother to return to Dad – and that was less of a goal now that she had her head out of her interfering-daughter backside over Mum's choices – the clinic was a worthwhile reason to be here.

Her thoughts swerved like that veering kangaroo they'd seen, to the hunky guy with too much baggage, possibly undressing, next door. Undressing. Undressed. Naked.

Who knew she'd find her libido in outback New South Wales? Even though it wasn't helpful right now. Not at all.

Riley straightened her shoulders and pressed the 'call' button.

Riley woke before six, again with time enough to go for a run before work. She threw on long tights and a loose T-shirt and pulled on her running shoes. Pushing her phone and keys into stretchy pockets, she slipped out the door into the cool pre-dawn. The air smelled fresh and sweet with flowers and gums, and she eased the door closed quietly behind her.

She'd head towards her mother's track, go halfway and turn back; it would feel good to stretch out. She kept her shoulders and arms relaxed, not over-striding, aiming for light on her feet and breathing with a steady rhythm.

As she did so the morning embraced her, curling wisps of calm to free her mind until all she concentrated on was the cool breeze, inhaling the pink-and-purple glow of the sunrise, and enjoying the deserted gravel road opening up before her.

The pastel colours of dawn softened the corrugated iron and repurposed oddments disguised as mailboxes and signage that popped up in the oddest places. The gentle light tinted the white gravel a pale pink and poked fingers of gold into the shadows of the occasional trees.

The quiet crunch of her feet as they sprung up from the gravel road rhythmically melded with the call of the hidden birds as they woke. Once a dog barked noisily in one of the camp yards she passed, but an irate voice told it to be 'quiet' in no uncertain terms. She smiled and let the jarring noise glide away as she did.

After fifteen minutes, she turned and retraced her steps. She wanted to be back in time for work. Halfway home the dog barked again, with the same result from its owner, so maybe she'd try another route to miss it next time. But as she neared her accommodation, the slide of sweat and strength in her muscles felt good and strong, and her previously whirring mind had shifted to calm and focus.

The sun breached the horizon as she turned into the alley where her accommodation lay tucked away. Another runner closed in from the opposite direction. They had chosen opposite directions. She raised her brows and took him in – the tall, packed-muscle lean length of him, the strong legs pumping as he sprinted up the hill, the all-male splendour of his powerful thighs and biceps covering the ground between them like a big, blond jungle cat in the middle of suburbia . . . And we're back to him.

The calm she'd just worked on wavered like a candle in the wind and she cupped it with her mind. *Steady.* She lifted her hand to Konrad and turned away to slip inside with the door shut so she didn't stare.

Riley turned up half an hour early so she could be in her room when Konrad came in. Melinda was already there and she held out a coffee, just how Riley liked it, in Riley's special cup.

'You rock as a receptionist,' Riley said. Melinda smiled shyly as Riley took the cup and went past her into her tiny room.

When she turned on the computer and opened her patient-appointment screen, her first patient of the day, surprisingly, was Melinda. Melinda, who had not been an appointment when she'd scrolled forward yesterday morning but now was scheduled fifteen minutes before Riley was due to start. She guessed that made sense because Melinda would have to man the desk when the patients started arriving. She sipped appreciatively at the coffee. Good tactic.

She stood up again and moved to her door. Konrad still wasn't in. Maybe he was avoiding her, too. She smiled grimly at that thought but replaced it with a more welcoming one when she turned to the receptionist.

She curled her fingers. 'Come in. Let's get you seen before anyone else arrives.' Riley assumed that was the idea.

Melinda's cheeks turned pink, and with her head down she brushed past Riley into the office.

Riley shut the door and waited for Melinda to sit down before she settled behind her desk to study the young woman. If she had to guess at the other woman's emotions, she'd say twitchy but determined. 'How can I help?'

Melinda's eyes were wide, stressed, and her hands shook, even though she'd clasped them together. Riley wasn't sure if this was something new or something permanent since whatever bad thing had happened to her.

Melinda broke the silence and her voice came out strained and squeaky. 'Did Dr Konrad tell you I was held up at the bank I worked at?'

Ah. PTSD. Riley kept her face neutral. 'No, he didn't. I'm sorry that happened to you, Melinda.' She raised her brows. 'Melinda or Mel? I should have asked sooner.'

She looked shyly pleased. 'You can call me Mel.'

'Right, then, Mel. He said you had a bad experience and that he'd tried to provide an environment for you that felt safe.'

'And he did. But after the event, I had a one-night stand with an acquaintance. One I hadn't intended sleeping with. From what I've read, I think it's because I wanted to be held.' Melinda took a big breath and her shoulders slumped. 'Anyway. It was a dumb choice, and I think I'm pregnant.'

Hence the baggy clothes, Riley realised. She should have suspected that. The hold-up mustn't have been as long ago as Riley had assumed.

Before she could say anything, Melinda drew a shuddery breath as if preparing to speak. Not that Riley planned to say anything until she was asked. Konrad might not believe it, but she did know when to shut up.

'Well.' Melinda screwed up her face. 'I haven't done anything to confirm that, but I'm pretty fat and getting fatter around my belly. I haven't had a period for about six months.' She stopped as if running out of breath and sucked in more air. 'And my belly is moving.'

The last was spoken in a matter-of-fact tone of voice that said Melinda might just have reached a mindset of resignation if not acceptance that this was a baby moving.

Oh, you sweetie. 'So, do you think this pregnancy is from the person you slept with? And you're not with that person now?'

'He left town, which is good. I didn't really like him as much as I thought I would. And I haven't had any other experiences.'

Ah. 'I understand.' And that made it even more unfair. 'I'm sorry this happened to you and had such consequences.'

'I don't think anything else is wrong . . . except a baby.' Her eyes widened and Riley suspected that Melinda might not have said the 'baby' word out loud before now.

'From what you've said, that's a possibility.' She tried to see her shape beneath the baggy clothes, but she really couldn't tell. 'Will you slip out to the toilet and bring back a urine specimen in a cup?'

Before she'd finished the question, Melinda pulled a Vegemite jar from her bag and handed it over.

Riley's mouth twitched. 'I guess sitting out there as the receptionist, you know all about these things.'

'Yeah.' She didn't elaborate.

Riley stood and took the jar. 'How about you hop up on the couch behind that screen over there and I'll have a feel of your tummy? You can stay dressed if you pull back your top so I can actually get to your belly. There's a clean sheet.'

Melinda nodded and Riley took the jar to the corner sink, opened it and found a pregnancy test strip. She checked her watch, dipped the test into the urine and washed her hands. Then she crossed back to the curtain and opened it gently.

Her eyes widened. She had not expected a belly like that. The pregnancy test was redundant. 'Oh my, Melinda.' Riley shook her head. 'You really have a magnificent belly. In fact, it looks like you're hiding a basketball in there.'

'Baby?' A question.

'Baby.' No doubt.

Melinda glanced down, and when Riley smiled the girl smiled

back. 'I guess I won't be alone when the baby's born. That's one thing.'

'No, you won't. Your life is about to change. In a good way. I hear babies grow on you.'

'They grow in you, too,' Melinda murmured, but they were the most positive words Riley had heard from her yet.

'Indeed they do. Let's confirm you're a healthy young woman and your passenger is healthy, and then we'll need to work out just where you're having this baby, because,' she raised her brows, 'I doubt you have that long to wait.'

By the time Riley had finished examining Melinda's belly and taken her blood pressure – and they'd listened to the foetal heart rate, much to Melinda's awe – Riley determined that Melinda's baby was due in the next four weeks. When she correlated that with the date of the bank hold-up, it tied in with her own assessment of foetal size. She took blood for the usual antenatal tests but doubted there'd be much they could do with the results before the baby was born.

'It seems you're designed to have babies, Melinda. Your belly is the perfect size for your dates, the baby is moving well and has a normal foetal heart rate. He or she is engaged in your pelvis facing the right way, ready for exit when the time comes. Still, we'll do an ultrasound as soon as I can arrange one.' And find out how far she'd have to travel to get one.

Melinda's glazed and rounded eyes hinted she was still digesting the news of her pregnancy and this was real. Riley watched silently until Melinda blinked and then stood up.

'I'd better get back to the desk,' she said. 'People will be arriving.'

'It's a big shock. You sure you're okay to work?' Though goodness knew what they'd do if she said no.

Melinda's chin came up. 'I'm not going to sit in my room by myself and stare at the wall.'

And there was a woman with a new purpose. Riley liked this young woman. Very much. 'I'll do the paperwork and we'll send these,' she held up the vials of blood, 'with the next lot of blood from my patients this morning. You okay with that?'

Melinda nodded as she edged towards the door.

'One more thing. Will you tell Dr Konrad the news or would you like me to?'

Melinda re-donned her rabbit-in-headlight expression. 'I haven't been able to tell him. Can you? I haven't told anyone. I guess I'll have to, now, but I dread the questions.'

Just who did she have on her side? 'Have you relatives in town?'

'No. My pop – my mum's dad – died last year. I lived with him.' Her head dipped at remembered sadness.

'I'm sorry for your loss.'

Melinda inclined her head with dignity. 'Mum's in Sydney somewhere, but I don't know where. After he died, I moved to the pub.' Her voice was soft. Not sorry for herself, but philosophical, as if a hard life had always been normal.

She added, 'Mrs Harris, that's Greta from the café, Toby's mum, she's good to me. After Pop died, Desiree said I could come to the Friday-night ladies for company, but I couldn't do that.' She seemed to shrink at the idea. 'They're funny, but all of them together make me nervous.'

'They're nice ladies.' And if Melinda was going to stay in Lightning Ridge, she'd need some mothering. 'Maybe you could rethink that. Some experienced ladies who've had children might be nice to chat with. But perhaps it's best if you get used to the whole idea of a baby first.'

She waited until Melinda looked up from her hands. 'Thank you for trusting me with this, Melinda. Believe me, it's much better this way than going into labour and having to explain it all. Nobody wants to tell a long story while their belly's tightening every three minutes.'

Melinda nodded, looking struck by the thought. 'You're right. I'm glad you're here.'

Riley nodded and watched the receptionist open the door and slip out. She spent the next few minutes typing up the patient notes and then picked up her phone.

Chapter Twenty-two

Melinda

Melinda edged out into the reception area, and as her gaze flicked around the room, she saw two couples had arrived. She needed to concentrate on them. On doing her job. She could feel the heat in her cheeks from the embarrassment of her own silliness with not doing something about her pregnancy earlier.

Oh, my stars. I really am going to have a baby, she thought. *And soon.*

She'd known. She'd just refused to believe it. And now she hoped she could keep her job. Though she'd have to take some time off, obviously. But after that? Surely, she could have a baby and still work? Women did that. Which also meant she would still have a place to live. She should've thought about all this before. She'd relied too much on Dr Konrad's kindness.

And look how she'd repaid him. Guilt swamped her. She'd been a coward.

'Excuse me.'

Melinda jumped, blinked and looked up at the two women

who'd come over to the desk. Flustered, she said, 'I'm sorry. You're here for Dr Brand? What were your names?'

She bent to the computer screen and highlighted each arrival, taking a moment to appreciate their circumstances. These people couldn't have a baby and she'd just 'got' one. It put a different slant on her own 'misfortune'.

Yesterday, she'd come to realise that many of the couples arrived early due to the long distances they had travelled. They made sure they arrived on time because they were absolutely busting to get help. Which meant that Dr Brand never had a moment when someone wasn't waiting because most of the visits went over time and into the next appointment slot. Yet the doctor saw them all. She never rushed, projected calm and kindness and unhurried interest. Like this morning with her.

Both women sat, satisfied, and Melinda heard the phone buzz in Dr Konrad's office. Dr Brand ringing him about her.

Her cheeks heated again. It was a poor way to repay him for all his help, not able to tell him herself. Now she'd have to face him.

Chapter Twenty-three

Konrad

Konrad studied the receiver before he picked up his phone. He knew who it was. He'd recovered from his annoyance last night, so that wasn't the reason he hesitated. Now it was about today.

He still felt blindsided by the sight of the goddess running towards him this morning. Blindsided enough to have the technicolour picture lodged in his brain far too clearly – as in every curve and delightful muscle as clear as a digital photo on his phone – and making his body respond. Dry mouth, pounding heart, and not from the run. At least he hadn't been crass enough to take a picture.

He couldn't help the wry smile at his own idiocy, and he could hear it in the drawl he answered with. 'Dr Brand?'

'Can you come to my room, please.' Something odd hovered in her voice. 'When you're free, of course.'

He glanced at her highlighted list of patients already checked in as waiting. His own hadn't arrived yet. He'd better do it now, then.

Though, he thought as he stood, *why couldn't she come to me?* Yet, he opened his door and crossed the small waiting area that was slowly filling with couples, knocked on her open door and went in.

'You rang?' His Lurch impersonation made her lips stretch in appreciation.

She huffed a laugh, which made him feel good. He had no idea why it would do that. 'Not you too?' she asked. 'I loved that show.'

And suddenly, he was relaxed, like he should have been earlier. 'Problem?' he asked, his tone professional, and the question hung in the air between them.

She tilted her head to the open door. 'Privacy?'

He closed the door without taking his gaze off her face. It snicked shut behind him. Something was up, and he hoped she wasn't leaving. Purely for logistical locum reasons, of course.

'Melinda came to see me this morning.'

That came out of left field, but it was something he'd wanted to ask about. 'I saw on the schedule that's where she was. Is she okay?'

Riley's expression looked odd: distant yet compassionate. 'She's well. And her estimated date of birth is in five weeks.'

'She's pregnant?' He felt the breath puff out of him as his legs slowly bowed to a seat in the client's chair in front of the desk. How had he not noticed? Konrad scrubbed at the back of his head. And why hadn't Melinda told him?

As if she'd heard his thoughts, Riley said, 'She asked me to tell you.'

That stung. Despite all his attempts to provide a safe environment and protect Melinda, she'd turned to this stranger, this woman, who'd been here less than four days. Another person who didn't trust him with their worries? Like his brother. Not only did he not notice a woman was nearly eight months pregnant, but obviously his management skills were lacking in rapport with his staff.

'She's feeling foolish for the delay. For not finding out earlier.'

How could he have missed it? 'She didn't say anything to me.'

'She got bigger. Until she couldn't ignore it. It was easier for her to ask me, a stranger.' Riley said. His own words coming from her.

'I didn't even know she had a boyfriend.' Did he see anything?

'A regretted one-night stand after the hold-up.'

That made him sit forward. 'Ah, damn.'

'Yes. Absolutely,' she agreed, still in that compassionate tone that was starting to irk him. 'But she hasn't told anyone about the baby. I suspect that it went past the point where she could say something to you without feeling like she should have told you earlier.'

'That's crazy.' But it wasn't. Guilt made you do weird things. 'I can't believe I didn't see that my receptionist was very pregnant.'

She made an odd sound in her throat. 'It's my specialty and I didn't see it.'

Oh. Okay. He felt better . . . marginally. All this would take time to process, but at least his brain was functioning again. He began thinking about all those ghastly baggy clothes that had been there from the start. Clothes he'd thought were a product of Melinda wanting to hide from danger. 'Poor Melinda.'

'I'm impressed,' she told him. 'I knew you'd get there.'

His irritation spiked. 'What's that supposed to mean?' Here was someone he could be annoyed with. Someone not Melinda and who, without a doubt, got under his skin.

'It must be hard to swallow. She told the outsider and not you.' And the woman across the desk took the wind out of his sails again. He was sick of underestimating her.

'Right.' He thought about that. 'Five weeks? We're going to be out of a receptionist soon as well. Have you got the answer to that?' He could feel his smile and he made it bigger. 'You're the busy one with the overfull schedule.'

'Something will work out.' She sat back in her chair and glanced at her screen. No doubt someone else had arrived. 'But now you know.' She stood and he did too. 'We both have patients waiting. I'll follow up with you on her future care later.'

Yep. She had him moving like a puppet when he was the boss, but now wasn't the time to sort that. He would though.

He turned back as he opened the door, a sensible thought pushing through the annoyed ones. 'Thank you.' And he meant it. Regardless, it was good that Melinda had someone she could confide in.

As he crossed to his office, he glanced at Melinda. 'Everything will be fine,' he said quietly, gently, and she smiled back, tentative at first and then with obvious relief.

Though he had no idea how it would all work out.

Chapter Twenty-four

Adelaide

'Friday comes around so fast,' Adelaide murmured. She'd been doing that a lot – thinking out loud. She shrugged as she climbed into her big, old four-wheel drive and her muscles creaked from the day of kneeling and digging. Yet it had been exciting. A tiny seam in the shaft had held streaks of colour. The last bucket of cloudy rock she'd washed had shone in the sunlight when she'd come back to the surface.

She wasn't really waiting for Fridays. When she'd been a nurse, weekends and weekdays had all run together with shiftwork, but knowing the days of the week was good for a change. And never having to do night shift again was fabulous.

'Retirement is wonderful,' she said to the red-eyed bush fly crawling across the windshield on the inside of her vehicle. She absolutely was not talking to herself. 'I'm not responsible for any wellbeing except my own and I'm doing something I love.'

The words echoed and the fly didn't comment. It just buzzed past her nose out the window and she was alone again.

The loneliness was a little confronting sometimes. Her nursing job had meant she'd been part of a vibrant team full of banter and support and new ideas, which she missed and of course was why she was excited about going out tonight to be with others. Plus, the bonus of having her daughter in town to share the fun with made her more conscious of being alone.

She'd rung her husband – it seemed that she still had one – and Tyler had been quite interested in visiting now that Riley was here. She'd said she'd have room if he had wanted to come visit, although if she was honest, the idea was unsettling because she enjoyed having her house to herself. Or was it because she didn't want Tyler to say her shack was lacking? No, not that. It was her choice not to be swayed to view her little home in a negative way.

It would be good, she told herself. They'd talk, which they needed to do.

She used to love lying in bed at night talking with Tyler, murmuring in the dark, mostly about Riley, or current affairs, or a deal he'd brokered at work. But mostly, they would hold hands while they talked. Yes, she really missed that.

Still, it was Friday, and soon she'd collect Riley from behind the doctors' surgery and have a chance to stickybeak at her daughter's accommodation. And she did look forward to that takeaway pasta for two.

When Adelaide arrived, her daughter had her fingers on the latch drawing the unit door shut. Darn. There went her chance to have a peek.

'Ready,' Riley said, and something must have shown in Adelaide's face because Riley keyed open the door again. 'Come in.

Check out my cave. You had that same look when you visited me at boarding school.'

Had she? Probably.

This tiny unit looked compact, clean and dark – and similar to the school dorm. Still, it had more mod cons than Adelaide had, but she couldn't see her daughter satisfied. 'Is it okay for you?'

Riley waved her hand as if flicking water off her fingers. 'It's fine. I'm that busy through the day I'm happy for a quiet place to put my head at night. And I'm running five kays in the mornings, which is great.'

The adjacent door opened and Konrad appeared in a thin cloud of aftershave sporting wet hair, as if he too was off somewhere.

Adelaide decided if she was twenty years younger, he might have increased her heart rate. He wore a pale-blue checked button-up shirt that sat splendidly across his shoulders, sleeves rolled up to his elbows, forearms all sinew and power when his hand lifted in a wave of greeting.

Adelaide glanced at her daughter and caught the slightly glazed look in her eyes, which made amusement tickle under her ribs. She knew it. There was definite attraction there.

He smiled at both of them and it was something to behold. The man loomed even bigger, but it might have been because he was moving towards them.

'Hello, Konrad,' she said. 'Nice to see you again.'

'You, too, Adelaide.'

An awkward silence ensued. Adelaide tilted her head and watched the two of them trying to avoid each other's eyes. Her lips twitched.

Finally, Konrad said, 'You ladies going out for a wild night at Desiree's?'

Riley nodded but didn't answer, so Adelaide responded with, 'We are.'

She caught a flicker pass between the two younger people and felt like a third wheel until Konrad said, 'Your daughter deserves a wine after that big week.'

'Indeed. And you?' Adelaide piped up cheerily again, though she thought her daughter needed to say something.

'I'm off to the Club in the Scrub. I've got an appointment.'

Riley nodded as if she understood, then she pulled her room door shut. 'Have a good weekend.'

Konrad murmured, 'You too,' and strode away in the opposite direction to his car. What was with the 'have a good weekend'? They'd surely bump into each other in the next two days? They lived three metres apart.

These were all curious things she'd like to know. 'Was your week busier than you expected?' Adelaide asked as she turned towards her car.

'Crazy busy. And next week will be worse.' Riley stopped and looked at her. 'Don't suppose you'd be interested in a couple of weeks' work as the practice nurse/receptionist?'

Adelaide raised her brows. 'I'm retired.'

Riley huffed out a laugh. 'Yep, I know, but you're still a registered nurse. Or even a half-day for my afternoon appointments? Our receptionist is having a baby in about four weeks, long story. It'll be tricky if we can't find a replacement with all the extra patients I have coming in.'

Adelaide didn't hate the idea of working. Not full time, but maybe some hours after lunch when it was getting hot outside. 'I'll think about it, but ask me again if Konrad doesn't find anyone while you're here.'

Chapter Twenty-five

Riley

When they arrived at Desiree's ladies' night, the discussion centred on Melinda's unexpected pregnancy. Currently, a verbal sparring match was all about what the ladies could do to help her.

'Who's Melinda?' Adelaide's sotto voce question took Riley by surprise, as her mother had been in the Ridge longer than she had. Still, she hadn't met Konrad either before Monday night.

'Our medical receptionist.'

'Ah, yes, that one.' Adelaide nodded while Riley wondered how Desiree, who knew everything, had found out. Despite how that osmosis had occurred, the ladies were in the process of organising a baby shower. Riley didn't even know if Melinda wanted a fuss – somehow, she doubted the young woman would have thought of asking others for help and good wishes. Riley felt slightly uneasy, even though the gesture was meant kindly. She knew it wasn't her fault that the news had spread and had to assume that Melinda had mentioned it to one of the women.

'She'll need nappies,' Greta said. 'I'll buy the nappies. And one of those little hanging nappy holders. With those fluffy little over-pants that keep the dampness from wetting clothes.'

'They use disposables nowadays.' Desiree shook her head. She shot a look at Riley. 'Ask the obstetrician. Disposables, right, Riley?'

Oh heck, why me, she thought. 'Many do.'

Greta looked downhearted and Riley added quickly, 'I'm pretty sure they all have cloth nappies for when they run out, though.'

'I thought she'd need them,' Greta said complacently. 'And six double-O singlets.'

'We've put our hand up to give the going-home-from-hospital outfit for the baby and a pair of fine muslin wraps,' Gerry said and Elsa nodded. 'One of the girls down in Walgett makes those wraps in pastels, with Peter Rabbit on them. They're beautiful and you can get matching outfits. We sell a lot of those in the shop. I hear if you wrap a baby's arms in muslin they settle more quickly.' She too looked at Riley. 'Do you agree with that?'

How had she become the expert on baby clothes and wrappings? She was the pregnancy and birth doctor. However, she had heard that about the wraps. 'It sounds great.'

She could feel her mother's amused glance at her. Riley had skipped the maternal urge. Or it was hiding. Mostly, she wanted to help those she could see were hurting and felt her delight with success in little pink and blue bundles belonging to others.

Desiree screwed up her face in thought. 'I've got a huge old pram out the back that my daughter said she'd never use. She wants one of those new ones if she ever falls pregnant.' She sent a sidelong glance at Riley before she went on. 'I'll polish the chrome till it shines like new and put one of those baby mattresses in it and pretty sheets and stuff. The kid can sleep in it when Melinda goes back to work.'

Everyone was very excited about that one.

'How about if I do the nighties, undies and bathroom bag.' Riley wanted to get away from the baby stuff. 'The hospital-bag thing.'

The ladies stopped and looked at her. They were smiling and she felt her cheeks warm. What? Of course, she'd help too. Did they think she wouldn't?

'That's a great idea,' Desiree said as she nodded.

Her mother straightened beside her. 'And I'd like to kit out a baby travel bag, for when she goes out with the baby. With a thermometer and baby creams and change mat. I've seen what mums put in there. Plus, a pretty growsuit as a spare change of clothes.' Adelaide looked at Desiree. 'She can hang it on the back of your pram.'

Everyone nodded.

'So, when are we going to do this if she has four weeks to go?' Silvia asked. 'She could go early.'

'The sooner the better,' Desiree said. 'Greta's taking her to the hospital at Moree tomorrow morning. For the ultrasound. Greta will tell us if she buys stuff there.'

Gerry said, 'We've got beautiful hand-painted invitation cards. Elsa and I could do the invites. Melinda can keep her "baby shower invite" card for her baby album. We'll hand out the rest and drop one in for Dr Konrad at the surgery.'

'What about next Saturday afternoon?' Selina suggested. 'It gives us a week to shop or order in. And time for Melinda to get used to the idea. I'll close off a section at the club and we can decorate and put on a spread.' She winked at her cousin. 'We can share the costs for food and drink seeing as I charge like a bull.'

'That's fair,' Silvia said. She winked back. 'I'll wear yellow, so I get served.'

'Reckon she'll stay living in that little unit at the back of the doctor's surgery?' Desiree asked Riley, who'd been watching the by-play and division of required essentials with something akin to awe. She'd never seen anything like it. These women had hidden talents and hearts as big as boulder opals. It was strange how she'd begun to feel more connected to them than she had to many she'd worked with for years in Sydney.

Riley answered Desiree, but knew everyone had stopped, listening for her answer. 'I can't see Konrad asking her to leave. There are still three empty units in case he needs one for another locum, so until she wants to move, I'd assume she'd stay there.' Which was interesting when she thought about the extent of Konrad Grey's kindness and his support for Melinda, as well.

This town was not the rough and tough place it had seemed at first.

The ladies sorted the rest of the details, poured another drink, and settled into a discussion on the latest local business to be bought by a tree changer from the city. Desiree said it was two young girls who were starting a clothes shop. They hadn't arrived yet, apparently, and Riley wondered how Desiree knew so many details. The thought made her shake her head.

Her mother pulled out her phone and stood. 'It's your father,' she said and stepped away to answer the call.

Chapter Twenty-six

Konrad

On Saturday morning, Konrad let himself into the first spare unit at the end of the block of six he'd bought from the previous doctor when he'd decided to stay. Inside the light was dim, the furnishings old-fashioned. And the kitchenette consisted only of a microwave and jug.

He stepped out again and pulled a face. Unlocking the next unit, he went inside and opened the connecting door. Then he went back outside and stood further away to study the two open doors and nodded. That could work.

When he'd first come to town, he'd vaguely considered opening the doors between the units to make two or three bigger units. One for him and one for the locums. But if he stayed here – which wasn't something he was sure about now, for some reason – he'd probably buy out of town on some land and build a house, to get away from the surgery.

Maybe he was moving forward finally.

One of the further doors opened and Riley glided into the daylight dressed in a long, loose blue T-shirt and black tights that hugged her like two loving hands. She had legs to die for.

'Morning, Konrad.' She sashayed his way, her jogging shoes silent on the grass. 'Whatcha doin'?'

The slang made his mouth twitch. Not something he thought the proper Dr Brand would say, and he guessed they were on friendly terms now, though he had no idea what he'd done to earn it.

To his surprise, he shared, 'I was thinking I might paint the empty unit on the end, open the connecting door and get it fitted out as a flat. I'd get Toby to help me. He's handy with wood and a paintbrush if I keep him off the ladder.' He looked away from her suddenly intense eyes and shrugged. 'In case Melinda needs more room when the baby comes.'

'Interesting,' she murmured.

He gestured to the eaves. 'Could run a verandah along the front of all the units to an outside sitting area and somewhere out of the rain when opening the door.' That would work, instead of the patchy grass that was there now between the rear of the surgery and the units.

'You're happy if she stays here even if she can't work for a while?'

His brows drew together. Huh? 'Of course. I don't understand.' Was he out of the loop again? 'Has she said she wants to go somewhere else?'

'No.' She held up a hand as if to stop him thinking that. 'Not at all. I'm glad she has a secure place to live. You're a nice man.'

He shook his head, brushing the praise aside. 'Anybody would do the same.' For goodness' sake. 'As far as I know, Mel has no relatives except her unsupportive mum in Sydney, and very few friends. She's better here where she's safe until she wants to leave. And the renovations won't go astray.'

'Nice man,' she said again. 'Though I wouldn't say she hasn't got any friends. The Friday-night ladies are putting on a baby shower next Saturday. You're invited.'

'That's good to hear.' He wasn't surprised. The women did pull good deeds when needed and he'd seen it time and again. But him at a girls' party? 'Do I have to? Can't I just donate for a present? Do men even go to baby showers?'

'No idea.' She laughed. 'I've never been to one and it wasn't on my bucket list.'

That amused him and he couldn't help his bark of laughter. 'You mean you don't feel your biological clock ticking? A non-maternal fertility expert?' How funny.

She lifted her chin. 'Spare me. Would you say that to a man? I wish it would tick faster so people would stop asking me when I'm having children.'

'No rush, then?'

'No rush, ever.'

Oh. Okay, then. Different, but . . . 'Me either. Each to their own.'

'If only people really thought that.' She shrugged. 'It's not my problem, though. See you later.' She turned and jogged off towards the road.

He watched her backside, shaking his head. He needed to get out more. He needed to try harder at being that nice man she thought him to be and take his eyes off her backside.

Chapter Twenty-seven

Riley

At least Konrad hadn't looked surprised when she said she wasn't maternal. Though he had looked amused. Maybe she should start carting clocks around to throw at people who queried her maternal instincts.

No, she wasn't clucky. Never had been. Yes, she liked kids. But other people's kids, not her own. He hadn't asked any of those questions, thank goodness.

She had quite a few friends in Sydney, male and female, who'd decided against parenthood. She did feel sorry for her mum, who'd said she'd love to cuddle grandchildren. Still, she was sure Melinda would let her cuddle her baby when it came. Perfect.

Her feet smacked the bitumen road more firmly than usual as her thoughts pinged back to Konrad, standing outside the little motel units considering renovations for Melinda. What a caring guy. He'd said any renos would be advantageous later, though she wondered at the resale prospects in Lightning Ridge.

Then she found herself wondering how long the works would take and if the workmen would intrude on her quiet times. She was such a selfish person. Except in her work. She was happy to give there. Nobody's perfect, she figured.

When she turned onto the gravel the road opened out in front of her, and the dog didn't bark this time; maybe it was getting used to her jogging past. Her thoughts went to the couples she'd seen through the week. So many women and men dwelling in angst for unfulfilled dreams. She'd unearthed – which was ironic for a mining town – a variety of reasons so far for the infertilities. She suspected two of the women she'd seen would need to look at staying a couple of weeks in Sydney for full testing and possible surgery.

A follicle-stimulating hormone should work for several others, and lifestyle changes might achieve more than her clients expected for a number of them. She could do good here in the brief time she stayed. And that was enough to satisfy her.

Chapter Twenty-eight

Melinda

At eight o'clock on Saturday morning, Melinda straightened her back as she stood outside her front door waiting for Greta. She didn't use that door often because she didn't have a car to park there. Maybe she'd have to get one. Her fingers smoothed the maternity top she'd been given yesterday as it hung over her belly. Greta had 'whipped it up'.

This wasn't a disguising tent in dark colours like she'd been wearing for the last few months. It was a bold statement in a pretty lemon that showed the ball of her belly and her popping-out belly button. The shirt said she had a baby in her belly and was putting him or her out there for everyone to see. She wasn't sure how she felt about that, but she'd spent a lot of time looking at herself in the mirror this morning and mostly she'd left the mirror with a smile.

She'd had to wear it over an elastic-waisted skirt, the waist band pulled down under her belly, because apart from 'the tents' not much else fitted her and Greta had said she should wear two pieces so they could look at her tummy for the ultrasound.

They had to leave at eight. It would take nearly three hours to get to Moree for their eleven o'clock appointment at the hospital.

Dr Brand wanted the ultrasound done sooner rather than later and was ringing to get the results this afternoon from the radiology department. The nearest town, Walgett, was only an hour away from Lightning Ridge, but they didn't do ultrasounds on weekends.

After the ultrasound, Melinda had an appointment at the hospital antenatal clinic. Then they were going shopping!

Melinda had her driver's licence, but she hadn't driven for ages and certainly hadn't been to the shops in another town. Not since her grandfather was sick and her mother came and took Pop's Holden. Maybe she needed to rethink transport issues with the baby coming. She might need a car if the baby got sick? She'd been saving her wages apart from her tiny rent from the start. Why not – she had nothing to spend it on – so she could afford to buy and run a vehicle.

What if she couldn't live at the back of the doctor's surgery? Like when she'd had to move after leaving the bank? The panic started in her throat and she pushed it down. Not now. It was a worry for later. But maybe she'd wait for the car.

Greta pulled up and Melinda noticed someone else was in the front beside her. Toby jumped out and held the door for her.

'I'm getting off here,' he said. 'I've got a day's work.'

'Oh. I'm glad for you.' She'd hated that Toby's boss in Moree had fired him after that first fit and he'd had to come home. Toby hadn't worked except for occasional stints with some men on the claims, which he didn't enjoy, and two days with Riley's mum last week.

She slid past Toby and into the front seat of Greta's little Toyota. She'd gone to school with Toby and he'd always been kind.

She stretched to pull the seatbelt around her belly, but it was harder to reach around than she thought, and the next thing she knew, Toby had caught it and pulled it for her. He handed her the catch with one of his sweet smiles. He was staring at her belly in her new shirt.

'An ultrasound sounds very cool. Wave to your baby for me,' he said, which was possibly the nicest thing anyone had said to her so far this pregnancy. She blushed and nodded, too awkward to thank him. He closed her door and stepped back and they pulled away.

Greta steered the car towards the road out of town.

Melinda glanced shyly at her driver. 'It's good that Toby has some work.'

Greta nodded as she watched the road. 'Yes. He needs it. It makes him feel useful.' The pain she tried to hide resonated in Greta's voice, and Melinda wanted to touch her shoulder in sympathy. It had been a tough six months for Toby and his mum.

'Have you ever seen an ultrasound?' Greta filled the silence with her question and Melinda jumped.

'No. Have you?'

'Just the one I had with Toby twenty years ago.' She laughed. 'I bet they're different now.'

Melinda's cheeks heated. Her voice sounded hesitant as she said, 'You're welcome to come in with me, if you'd like? They said I could bring someone.' She didn't want to go in alone and had wanted to ask.

Greta's face split happily. 'If that's okay with you, I'd love to see the baby.'

Inside, something defrosted in Melinda. The cold spot of lone-liness she'd felt when she'd hidden her secret away from everyone. Her hand slid down to rest on her belly. 'Thank you.' She chewed her lip. 'I'm a little bit nervous.'

'That's natural,' Greta said sagely. She turned her head for a second. 'You still glad you asked me to tell Desiree?'

'Yes.' More tension slid from her. 'Desiree will make sure everyone knows and nobody will ask questions.' She hadn't wanted to have surprised conversations with people. This way her baby could just happen.

Greta went on. 'The ladies would like to have a baby shower for you next Saturday. Would you mind?'

They did? Melinda sucked in a breath. 'Why?'

'Why wouldn't we? A baby is exciting, especially when it has a nice mummy like you. You'll be a wonderful mother.'

The road ahead disappeared into a blur as Melinda's eyes misted. Would she? She didn't know. She just knew it wasn't her baby's fault how it came into being. And she wanted to be a good mother. Except she didn't know how. She didn't have a good mother to copy. But Greta was a good mother, so perhaps she could copy her. 'Thank you.'

'You know the ladies like to have something to look forward to. We thought we'd have it at the club. Selina wanted to have it there. Though Silvia offered too.'

Melinda had no idea how much she'd need for a party. 'Will it cost much?'

Greta shook her head emphatically. 'Nothing for you. And everyone is sharing the costs as a gift for you and your baby. Have you talked to Dr Konrad about when you're stopping work?'

Stopping? Did she have to? Where would she get money? 'No?' Her forehead crinkled. She just thought she'd stop when she went into labour. 'Do you have to stop work before the baby?'

Greta's face crinkled up. She had a lovely, kind smile, and Melinda relaxed. It was so good to talk about all this with someone. Which was why she'd told Greta and asked her to let the other ladies know. She needed to work things out. Initially, she had pushed away all thoughts of the future, but now that she'd found out for sure, well, Greta would help her discover what she needed to know.

Greta said, 'I guess if you're feeling okay you could keep working, but you need to think about labour. And how to tell when you need to go to the hospital. Have you read up on having babies?'

Not yet. She'd tried to find some information on her phone, but then she'd backed away at the overload. 'I only found out for sure this week.'

'The antenatal clinic today will help. Then ask that nice Dr Brand. I'm sure she'll suggest the best thing to do. Or talk to someone else who's had a baby in town.'

Everyone Melinda knew was older or didn't have kids. She'd met a few patients with babies, but she didn't know them well.

Greta frowned. 'That's funny. I don't know anybody with a baby. Do you?'

When they drove into Moree, Melinda was busting to go to the toilet. She hadn't been silly enough to drink too much water with the long distance, but as her pop would say, 'her back teeth were floating.'

Greta seemed to know where she was going and when she ushered Melinda to the reception desk in the X-ray department there was only a man there waiting. With a shock, Melinda realised the person doing the ultrasound wasn't the lady she'd expected but a man.

She stopped and Greta put her hand on her arm. 'It's okay,' she said quietly.

He was young, didn't look much older than Toby, and was slightly built so not threatening, but still Melinda swung her gaze to Greta with a stutter of panic.

'Melinda would like me to come in with her when she has her ultrasound.' Greta's tone was calm but firm. It plainly said, Greta was coming in with her or it wasn't going to happen. Melinda's breath eased out a fraction.

When the man said, 'Of course,' she relaxed some more. 'I'm Noah. Dr Brand rang and said you were coming. We usually only do emergencies on a Saturday. Are you dying to go to the toilet?'

Melinda nodded. He pushed his lips together in a sort of grimace. She thought it might have been sympathy. 'Good. That makes it easier to see the baby because ultrasounds work with sound waves that help create a picture of your baby. The fluid in your bladder makes the pictures clearer.' He pointed with his hand. 'This way.'

Ten minutes later, Melinda didn't even remember that the sonographer was male. With Greta's hand squeezing hers, they both watched the screen in front of them, avidly. They'd seen the baby's spine, curves of legs and arms, the circle of the head and the moving parts of the baby's heart. Each heart chamber valve was pointed out as the pulsing noise came through loud. Even clearer than in Dr Brand's rooms yesterday.

In Melinda's chest, it seemed a whole flock of birds was flapping as excitement swirled and her baby kicked, making her gasp. Her free hand slid down and on the screen they saw the movement of tiny legs. 'Oh my,' she whispered. This was real. This was her baby. A perfect tiny human inside her belly.

'Do you want to know if you have a boy or a girl?' the sonographer asked.

Melinda blinked, tearing her eyes away from the screen to Greta's face.

'You're the mum.' Greta shrugged. 'You get to choose.'

Melinda thought about having time to deal with the sex of the baby before the birth. Did it matter? She decided that it didn't. 'No. I'll wait. As long as it's healthy, that's all I care about.'

The sonographer nodded without looking at her. 'Not many people say no.' His eyes were on the screen, calculating and checking things. 'I've done the measurements of the head, abdomen and length of femur,' he told her. 'The placental flow looks excellent. That means nutrients and oxygen are moving between you and the baby normally. The heart chambers look normal. And the overall measurements are consistent with a foetus of thirty-five weeks. The machine's date is the same as your due date.' He sat back. 'Is there anything else you'd like to see?' He handed her two printed snapshots from the ultrasound. A little grey face stared out with a long nose like hers. The second was a full body one that showed the spine and limbs.

She clutched the photos, her fingers shaking. Her mind felt fuller than her bladder. Her baby was real.

Chapter Twenty-nine

Konrad

Toby had been quiet since he arrived, Konrad thought as he walked down to the units. He glanced again at the young man beside him. He appeared in good spirits, especially when he mentioned seeing how pregnant Melinda was.

'I think she's so brave having the baby.'

Konrad nodded. He thought about Riley's comment regarding Melinda and Toby supporting each other, but he remembered his brother and backed away fast. If it was meant to be it would happen without anyone's intervention.

'It's good of your mum to take her to Moree.'

Toby's expression lifted. 'Mum likes to shop. She doesn't get much chance. Reckon they'll go to the department store and buy baby things. She couldn't talk about anything else this morning.'

The ripples of caring that had started around town since Melinda's pregnancy had been outed made him proud to be a part of this community. The Friday ladies, Greta and Toby. He guessed he was a part of that, too. It helped restore his faith in human kindness that he realised he'd lost since Melinda's trauma and Toby's suicide attempts after being sacked from his job.

'It's an exciting day for Melinda,' he said. 'Now let's get in and have a look at these units. I need your advice.'

He tried not to react to Toby's astonished pleasure at his throw-away comment.

Two hours later, Konrad watched Toby finish undercoating the long wall inside the first unit. He'd finished the long wall in the second.

They'd found two tins of pale peppermint from the last surgery renovations, and after he and Toby had sugar-soaped the walls, they'd got straight into painting a white undercoat over the dull grey that was there.

The weather today had grown hot and dry enough to make the walls ready for the next coat almost as soon as they'd finished the first application. When they were finished they'd have to do the skirting boards.

Konrad hated painting low, but it was going faster than he'd expected. And both units were looking great with the door open between them, the furniture out, all the curtains removed, windows open and the light flooding in.

Riley reappeared like a daffodil in spring. She'd been in her consulting room for a couple of hours now catching up on diagnostic results from her week of patients, and his thoughts flicked back to this morning when she'd come back from her run and jogged past him. He could still see her T-shirt sticking like a second skin, and she had smelled of woman and exercise and maybe contentment.

Something he hadn't expected. She'd waved and disappeared for a while, before reappearing post-shower in a yellow frock, before slipping into the office. She had to be finished now because she pulled the surgery back door shut and he heard it lock.

She drifted their way, long and lean and sexy in her floaty dress. 'Can I look in at what you've done?'

'Sure.' He waved her past and she disappeared into the two units while he and Toby stood outside debating what to tackle next.

When she came back out, her face was soft. 'It's brighter already. Nice work, boys. I promised Mum I'd come for brunch or I would've offered to give you a hand.'

He eyed her dress. 'I'd like to see that. You don't look the reno type.'

Her back straightened, which pushed her breasts out and deepened her cleavage, but he didn't think she'd intended that. 'I come from tough stock. You have no idea of my hidden depths.'

'No. I. Don't.' Even he could hear his slow words saying he'd like to.

Toby looked between them and then away. She lowered her brows at Konrad and he held up a hand. 'Just teasing.' His voice dropped. 'And curious.'

She shrugged. 'Bad luck. I'm starving.' A smile for Toby, not for him. 'I'll see if she has more scones for you, Toby. I might be able to bring some back seeing as your mum's gone to Moree with Melinda.' As she strode away with purpose, he tore his eyes off the dress that showed her luscious legs to perfection.

'The bathroom's tricky,' Toby said.

Bathroom? He blinked. Renovations. Right.

Toby went on. 'Though I've seen modules that could fit in there if we pulled the fittings out, but you'd want to pick the right one.'

'You're saying we could tear it out but it's risky?'

'Maybe.' Toby shrugged, looking worried. 'Not guaranteeing I'd be able to make it work properly afterwards, though, and she'll need a bathroom.'

'Me either. How about I phone the Construction Girls?'

'I think that's a good idea,' Toby said, his relief palpable.

Konrad liked that Toby knew his limitations and wasn't afraid to share them. The local carpentry and repair company, run by one of his female patients, was known for efficient renos. He would have suggested them as employers to Toby, but after taking over from a company who'd kept losing their male workers to opal lust, they were a fully female-run business and now frighteningly efficient girls' club.

'We'll look at it for after Mel moves in if she wants it. Maybe they could come this weekend and check it out or next week for a working bee out of hours and get the structural changes done,' Konrad said. And they could see Toby at work as well, but he wasn't raising hopes by saying that. Still, you never knew.

He took out his phone and punched in the number.

Chapter Thirty

Adelaide

Adelaide swept her gaze to the clock for the hundredth time this morning. Riley would be here soon. And she wasn't the only one.

Tyler was coming today!

He said he'd leave at four am to beat the peak-hour traffic. Peak out of Sydney. There was no busy traffic at the Ridge. It seemed funny to think of traffic out here.

Her breathing quickened again. She still didn't know how she felt about Tyler arriving, but most of all she didn't know where he'd sleep. It felt like a first date, which was ridiculous when they'd been married for forty years, but it had been more than two months since she'd seen him. What if he was different or thought she was?

His imminent arrival left her a little excited, a little horrified, and a lot worried that he'd hate her shack – and the new her – and that the lifetime of marriage between them would deteriorate into a depressing and devastating divorce.

She'd never intended that – didn't want it – but she wasn't going back to being a handmaiden, either.

She looked across at her day bed, which was certainly a single-person sleeper. That wasn't going to work. She'd just have to make up a bed on the floor for him and see how he went. If it was too rough, then he could go to the caravan park. It wasn't like the onsite vans were booked out.

She'd been cleaning all morning and the old stove glowed with a black shine she could see her face in. She'd baked a pie for lunch and scrubbed the bathroom and outhouse within an inch of their tiny lives.

She still didn't know what she was going to do to amuse him. She'd told him there was no TV. She hoped he hadn't forgotten. In the best-case scenario, she could educate her city husband about opal mining.

The sound of Riley's car outside made her put down the cleaning spray. She'd done enough shining of the table. At least her daughter would be able to eat inside because the little kitchen table was immaculate now.

The *whoosh* of Riley's car door as it shut sent her to the front to let her in. 'Hello, darling. It's lovely to see you.' Her little girl looked gorgeous and possibly more carefree than she'd seemed in ages, which was an extra delight.

'Hey, Mother dearest.' She leaned forward and pressed her cool lips against her cheek. 'Coffee is here.'

Adelaide marvelled again how everything had turned out unexpectedly when she'd decided to do this crazy thing and move here. Suddenly, she felt closer to her daughter than she had in years, had found new friends and an exciting new pastime. She didn't want to diminish her work as a hobby because it felt like her new passion. If only Tyler could see that.

Would her husband understand what all her decisions were about? Would he be interested enough to stay for a while? Or would he turn around and never come back? She'd just have to wait and see. She'd instigated that change. There'd been risk, but she had opened the way for a new beginning. For the moment, Riley was here.

She'd have to buy a couple of those gorgeous painted reusable cups Gerry and Elsa had in the shop for takeaway and give them to Riley. Or even better, send Riley to buy her own. She really was changing.

'Coffee smells good,' she said as the disposable cups were settled on the table.

Riley pointed to the bench. 'So do the bacon muffins I can see. Can I take some for Toby when I go?'

'Of course.'

Even she heard the vagueness in the agreement. Her brain stretched – between Riley's arrival and Tyler on his way – making it hard to concentrate.

'You okay? You look distracted.' Riley's gaze had sharpened as Adelaide stood absent-mindedly in the middle of the room and she snapped out of her rambling thoughts.

'I'll tell you later. Let's eat.'

Her daughter nodded. 'I'm starving.'

Adelaide tilted her head and grinned. 'Since when are you starving?' She'd had trouble all those early years of high school getting Riley to eat enough. As a teen, Riley had been stick thin.

Her daughter shrugged. 'I don't know. Something about this place, I guess. I do my run then come back and eat a huge cereal breakfast. At night I could eat a horse. I'm really enjoying food.'

'Maybe it's because you're missing lunch with your full schedule?'

She shrugged. 'I've never eaten lunch. It's all very odd. Hopefully, I won't turn out to be twice my size by the time I go home.'

Adelaide pulled the cracked plates from the shelf. At least Tyler was bringing her favourite dinner set when he came. She still hadn't told Riley – she suspected because she didn't know how to answer the questions she knew her daughter would ask.

Instead, she said, 'I'm sure that won't happen. Did you see Konrad this morning?'

'Yes.' Riley took a plate and added a large savoury muffin onto it, which she quickly sank her teeth into and then chewed as if it was the best thing she'd tasted for years.

That was still odd, Adelaide mused, as she pushed the plate of muffins closer to her daughter.

When she'd finished the bite she said, 'Actually, I'm pretty impressed with him.'

More than yesterday? 'I noticed that.' Adelaide raised her brows in amusement.

Riley rolled her eyes, like the teen she'd just been thinking of. 'I don't mean like that.' She swallowed. 'I meant with what he's doing today. He and Toby are painting the two flats to join into one for Melinda and the baby. For when she comes home from hospital. I was impressed he thought of it. It's unexpectedly kind.'

'And generous.'

Riley's face softened. That too was something she didn't often see. 'Generous, indeed. There're some lovely people in this town. They make me want to do more for others.'

She thought of Friday night's spirited discussions on helping Melinda. 'Me too,' Adelaide agreed.

'Good.' Riley wiped her hands, eyes sharper with purpose. 'Come be practice nurse and receptionist for us when Melinda goes on leave.'

'I might not be able to. Your father's coming today.' It was out. Her daughter did not look surprised.

'Ah. I wondered.' Which meant Riley had suspected he would come. And then the question she'd been dreading landed. 'How do you feel about that?'

She needed to be honest. And maybe she needed to verbalise the whirlwind that spun in her brain. 'I don't know.' She met her daughter's eyes. 'A part of me is excited. The other part of me is hoping that he won't rain on my parade. Not that it rains out here.' She looked down at her hands as they turned the paper cup on the table. 'I have no idea what he's going to do because there's no television.' She glared through to the outside world. 'And I'm not getting one.'

Riley laughed. 'You should cross your arms when you say that.'

Adelaide pulled a face. She let the pent-up emotion blow out in a breath, and felt it release and drop her shoulders. She'd been so tight she hadn't noticed . . . although she bet Riley had.

Her daughter went on. 'What do you think he expects when he gets here?'

Adelaide brushed the hair that had come loose from her ponytail away from the corner of her eyes. 'I have no idea.'

'It doesn't matter, really. Keeping Dad amused isn't your problem. It's just Dad being Dad.' She looked around the house. 'Your little shack is sparkling as much as it can. Have you been wearing your arms out?'

She'd been at it for hours, which was crazy, of course. 'Yes.'

'What time is he arriving?'

'Twelvish.'

Riley lifted her wrist to see the time. 'Hmm. Soon.' She picked up her coffee and took two long sips. 'I'd better finish my coffee and go.'

Adelaide's stomach dropped. Darn. She'd planned for Riley to run interference for potential recriminations.

Her daughter slanted a wicked glance her way. 'If you'll bag a few more of those evil bacon delights, I'll be on my way.'

'I thought you'd be here for when your dad arrived?' She tried to keep her voice calm as she made a large paper bag of food to go. Konrad would eat some, too.

'No way José. This is between you guys.'

Typical. 'Says she who drove all the way out here to con me into going home.'

Riley had the grace to look sheepish. 'Well, yes. My bad. But you guys have stuff to sort out.' Her face brightened. 'And I might try my hand at house painting.'

She finished her coffee in one long swallow and crossed the room with her hand outstretched. 'I hope it works out.' She took the food bag. 'I love you. Still, I can see a little of each side and I really, really hope you can both meet at a happy medium.'

Helpful. Not. 'Thank you, darling.' Good grief, Riley was almost at the door. Suddenly, she desperately didn't want her to leave. 'Before you go, tell me about Melinda. When does she stop work?'

Riley paused and turned back. 'She hasn't talked about it with me, not sure about Konrad, but I don't think she's even thought about it yet.' Riley rattled her car keys, mulling. 'However, she's spending the day with Greta in Moree today getting an ultrasound, so a discussion will be happening.'

They both smiled at the idea of Greta in mother-hen mode. 'Greta will be sensibly informing her of all the little changes that will soon happen in her life. With some luck, I can have a good talk to Melinda this afternoon or tomorrow. Before we all get thrown back into the mayhem that is my fertility clinic on top of Konrad's general practice.'

Another topic. Excellent. 'How's all that going?' Adelaide felt inordinately proud of her daughter's work. And her choice to come here, even if it was to hide her true purpose.

Riley's eyes gleamed with pleasure. It was safe to say she had the bit well between her orthodontically corrected teeth. 'It's going well.' There was satisfaction in Riley's words. Deep satisfaction.

'I'm glad,' Adelaide said. 'I wondered if being away from the city would make it too difficult.'

'We'll need to outsource some aspects. But we can start addressing the problems here. I feel useful and can see how we can streamline even more. I feel'—her voice grew even more determined as she straightened the hem of her dress—'almost embarrassed that I haven't thought about these women before.'

'Not just you, Riley. Others could have as well. But you're here now.'

'It's too late for some.' She met Adelaide's eyes with a fierce green gaze. 'That's a crime when I have the resources to make things happen.' Her chin rose. 'It'll be different from now on. There's a fantastic opportunity to create a network of women who can touch the lives of those who don't normally ask for help.

Big changes to access and support for infertile couples. It's past the time it should have happened.'

In the passion and the words and the determination of her daughter's pronouncement, some of Adelaide's tension lessened. What she worried about was small stuff. Yes. Her worries were minor compared to infertile couples. She and Tyler had had lives that were satisfying in their own ways, even if not always together. They'd been so fortunate compared to the families Riley was talking about. And she could help while Melinda had her baby. Why would she hesitate to help her daughter in that vision?

Was it because she was now worried her husband would be bored without company? He'd just have to find something to do, as well. Adelaide relaxed and lifted her head to meet her daughter's regard.

'If you can't find a replacement, I'd love to come and help you while you're here.'

Chapter Thirty-one

Riley

Riley slapped the top of the steering wheel as she drove away. Woo hoo. She had a backup receptionist and practice nurse. Bless Mum. And with her mother's efficiency, Riley could see more women because she wouldn't have to deal with the phone calls as well.

Fingers crossed, Mum and Dad's reunion would go off well, too. Who knew all this would happen when she decided to come out here and pester her mother into going home? There had been unexpected complications and bonuses for sure. Maybe she had been stuck in a privileged rut in Sydney. She needed to see outside her own sphere, like her mum had made happen. Like her dad was about to find out.

She'd known he'd been thinking about coming to the Ridge because she'd called him and shared the reality about not expecting comfort or electricity. The thought made her chuckle. She'd even suggested he'd be happier at the caravan park and dropping in, to 'court' Mum, instead of dumping himself on her and expecting her to wait on him.

Somehow, though, Riley doubted that was going to happen. Mum had emancipated herself. He'd laughed and said he'd managed for himself for a while now, and that was a good thing. Dad had been spoiled for years as a company director with minions who followed his every order and Mum to keep him comfortable at home.

Riley snorted as she turned onto the main road. He hadn't seen the new Adelaide. The calm and assertive woman who enjoyed her own space and company. The off-grid opal miner. Riley did not even want to be a fly on the corrugated-tin wall. No sir. Too much information.

However, other walls were different. She would like to see what Konrad and Toby had achieved while she'd been away. Really, she wanted to see Konrad's face when she said she'd come to help paint. She suspected he didn't believe she could be useful in a practical way. True, she had no experience, but she could learn anything. She had a brain and a fit body. She'd barely need a step ladder in the low-ceilinged units.

'I'm back.' Riley knocked on the door of unit six and looked in at Konrad perched on the ladder, his backside facing her and his tanned muscles on show as he wielded the roller on the low ceiling. Lots of nice eye candy right there.

He rested the roller on the tray and turned his head. 'You're back fast?' Was there something in his tone that said he was glad to see her?

'Yep. My dad's arriving and I didn't want to be there for the reunion. Third wheel and all that.'

The wicked amusement in his eyes made her conscious of his height, him looking down, and her open-necked dress inviting a peek. 'Stop ogling.'

'I'm pretty sure you looked at my backside when you came in.'

'Busted.' How on earth had he seen that? 'I thought I'd ask if you guys wanted a hand?'

His brows rose. That was all the surprise she got. 'Can you paint skirting boards?'

She inclined her head. 'I can paint anything if you point me in the right direction.'

'Of course you can.' He looked thoughtful. 'Then again, I've watched you make coffee. You're OCD and will do a perfect job.'

He had her pegged. 'I'll be back in a minute, then.' She brushed her hands down her front, indicating the pretty material. 'I'll just get changed first.'

She felt the weight of his gaze and knew he liked what he saw. He liked this dress. She sincerely hoped she hadn't put it on because of that reason. A clothes change was a great idea. Maybe even a shirt with a priest's collar. 'How's Toby going? I brought him muffins.'

'We're having a little competition. I'd say he's slightly faster than I am on the walls, but I'm flogging him on the roof because he has to use a pole.'

She laughed. 'If I've got OCD, you've got male competitiveness.'

He didn't take his eyes off the ceiling as he recommenced his rolling. 'Indeed, I do.'

'Then I'll have to race you around the skirting boards.' He laughed and the ladder wobbled. She grinned and walked away to change, calling over her shoulder, 'Mum put enough muffins in there for you, too.'

*

By the time they'd spent two hours crawling around the floor painting skirting boards, Riley knew she wasn't going to beat Konrad in the painting race, but her boards were much tidier than his, which helped salve the disappointment.

The job was done. 'The peppermint looks amazing with the white,' she said, as she sat back and arched her back. Konrad was washing his brushes outside on the grass and turned her way. If she wasn't mistaken, his attention shifted to the pull of fabric across her body, which had her fighting the urge to stretch more and tease him. Lots of banter under the ladder this afternoon had stirred the pheromones.

'Toby's gone to the café to buy sandwiches,' he said as he came back in.

So, that left just the two of them in the unit. He dried his hands on a towel and strolled her way, then reached one large hand down to offer her a lift from the floor.

She could get up herself but reached out for his help, anyway. Strong masculine fingers were warm against hers, slightly damp from the brushes, and when he pulled her up he didn't let go as she stood. They were close. Chest to chest. Him that six inches taller, which was a lot further from eye height than she usually got from a man, and he was looking down at her with a dare that she recognised and made her lift her chin.

He said, 'You smell good.'

She didn't think so and resisted the urge to lift her arm. 'I smell like sweat.'

'You smell like flowers,' he said quietly as his eyes searched hers, before they drifted to her mouth, 'and muffins.' He glanced at their held hands. 'And paint.' His gaze travelled to her breasts, then up her neck, past her mouth, and held her eyes again. 'And woman.'

She'd felt every scorching sweep of that examination like a paint brush dipped in chocolate. Heat slid like a wave up her neck and she blinked to break the spell he'd spun. 'That doesn't sound too bad as far as smells go. You'—talking did help to ground her, she decided as she stepped back and pulled her fingers from his— 'smell like paint.'

He quirked an eyebrow as if he knew what she was feeling and not saying. 'I've been working hard longer than you this morning, but,' he sniffed under his arm, 'I still smell okay.'

Indeed he did. She moistened her lips. 'But your edges need work.' Her voice was softer than she wanted it to be. She may have put a step between them, but her eyes were caught again. Like his gravitational pull wouldn't let her leave his orbit. Her moon to his larger planet and just the two of them in the solar system.

Konrad leaned closer and took her hands, both of them, gathered loosely but held. She knew he wanted to kiss her. Knew because she wanted it, too. Which was right out there in crazyland, but somehow her vision was filled by the colours that shifted and darkened in his blue, blue eyes. 'You have a sapphire ring around the outside of your irises.'

The creases at the corner of his eyes crinkled in amusement. 'You have a forest-green smoky smudge around yours.'

'Must be all this painting that we're noticing edges.' She stepped back and he laughed.

'Running away, Dr Brand?' he teased. 'We should have dinner tonight. It's your turn to bring takeaway. Or we could go out, just for fun. An afternoon beer garden somewhere and dinner after.'

Shocked but not displeased at the idea, Riley tilted her head at him. 'Do they have places to go out in Lightning Ridge?'

'One pub. One club. Several restaurants. Or we could do the Club in the Scrub or have a picnic at sunset.'

'Right.' She laughed. 'We could go hunting for engagement rings at the old church site and give it back to Toby.' Actually, that wasn't funny. What a dumb thing to say. She saw the moment the laughter faded from his eyes.

'Or not.' He turned and scooped up her brushes and paint tin. 'I'll fix these if you want to clean up before the next round of skirting boards.'

He was a moody beast. 'Am I paint splashed?' She paused. 'Or dismissed?'

'Your choice.' He gave her his back as he walked to the door with her painting equipment.

After the break, they swept through the second coat of white at floor level and then moved the bed ensemble back into room six. The rest of the furniture had been distributed next door, which had seen the bed disappear and the room turned into a living area. They were careful not to touch the still-fragile walls, but the windows were open and the last coats of paint had nearly dried.

Toby left them standing in the connecting doorway between the units as he headed home, happy with his day's wages and possibly even happier with the result of the work.

'It looks really fresh.' Riley walked between the two rooms. 'Pale peppermint and white always look good together.'

'I'll get the carpets steam cleaned and new pulldown blinds. For the moment, I'll leave the curtain rods in case Melinda wants to put up her own curtains.' He shrugged as if it was nothing. 'I can always change them later if and when she moves out.'

A couple of young men had arrived earlier and taken the other queen bed.

'Where did the chest of drawers come from?'

Konrad lifted his shoulders again, his lips compressed. 'I swapped it for the other bed. At least it was a new mattress. One of my patients complained about a bad back yesterday.' He looked over the gorgeous piece of furniture. 'I didn't think the drawers would be that impressive.'

Stories within stories. Something bloomed inside her at his kindness and awkwardness with others seeing it. The feeling had been building since they'd painted together, sexual tension shimmering like a mist since he'd pulled her up from the floor and they'd had that staring contest over eye colour.

For a while after that they'd avoided each other, but the awkwardness had dissipated over lunch and Toby's presence had helped. Melinda wasn't expected for another few hours given the long drive she had to do today.

But now, the thrum of energy between them reverberated against her skin. Now that the job was done and there was just the two of them left, Riley felt as if her body had been plugged into a charger when she should have been tired.

'Do you like them?'

His gaze had settled on her. Visceral. More intense.

Slowly, she blinked and returned to the here and now, feeling the sticky heat on her skin from the day and the dryness in the air, and the closeness of Konrad. But the reference point in that conversation was lost. 'Do I like what?'

'The chest of drawers.' He laughed softly and she knew, just knew he could tell he was getting to her.

Right. Drawers. Concentrate. 'It's a great colour for the room with the light wood. Nice piece of furniture.' She eased her shoulders again.

His gaze shifted back to the tallboy. 'I'll ask if Bob needs linen to make up for the value difference. I have too much now, anyway.' He scratched the back of his head. 'We'll leave the rest of the furniture until Melinda decides what she wants. I'm for a shower and a beer. You interested?'

'In the shower or the beer?' It came out before she could stop it. So much inuendo and foolishness in six words. Her face flamed, but she lifted her chin. She'd meant it. But she could pretend she didn't.

'Definitely both,' he said and held out his hand.

She laughed. Not too shakily, but too loud. 'My bad. Just teasing. Meet you in the common room in twenty.'

Chapter Thirty-two

Konrad

Konrad watched Riley walk away. Again. He was doing that a lot, like a homing pigeon swooping in to roost. He laughed and shook his head. What was he going to do? Land on her bum and coo?

He wondered if she'd really been fleetingly interested in the shower concept, with or without beer, because he had no trouble imagining that scenario. Although, the showers in the units were small. He really should look at getting his own home with a big bathroom. And a huge shower.

But she'd be long gone by the time he'd make homeowner status, so being creative squashed together in a motel cubicle, naked, didn't sound too bad at all. Amusement tickled his throat and he scooped up the last of the rags and towels, and swiped droplets off the bathroom sink before heading for the door.

Today's work had been satisfying, even fun with Riley here. Though he'd been super-impressed with Toby's work ethic and knew they wouldn't have finished without his young friend. He had to do more for Toby to get him established in employment.

They needed to find someone to be his work buddy so that if something did happen, like Toby had a grand-mal seizure, that person would have his back and know what to do.

Where did you find someone like that? He'd think about it later, but for now, his thoughts were tied up with a tall red-headed fertility expert – he laughed; he needed to watch that – who could tempt and tease with the best of them.

Where could they go this afternoon?

Where would they go tonight after dinner? His room or hers?

Tomorrow was Sunday, offering a long, luxurious lie-in – for two? He snorted as he locked the doors. It was unlikely that she was going to climb into his bed, but a man could dream.

They ended up at Silvia's pub checking out the beer garden. Well, that's what Riley had said she wanted to do, so he went along with her.

There'd been raised eyebrows at the two single docs sipping drinks together, his light beer and her sparkling wine, but eventually the few locals in the beer garden ignored them. Newcomers waved in a friendly way and he realised he didn't do this often – get out and socialise with the locals. He just saw them in his rooms and stayed with his own company.

Today he concentrated on his escort, but sadly she was the one with the questions and of course she had no hesitation in firing them. Her determined chin rested on her palm, elbow on the table, green eyes on his like the curious cat she was. 'Where did you work before here?'

'Mostly southern Sydney, but later in Port Macquarie.'

She nodded. 'I know where that is. Halfway between Sydney and Brisbane on the coast.'

'You've been there?'

She shook her head. 'A client came from there to see me.'

'People travel a long way to see you, don't they?'

Her mouth curved on one side, softening her usually serious expression. 'Not as far as some of the ones I've met in the last week. But I'm not getting sidetracked. We can talk about my work later.' She waved away her life. 'Were you a GP in Port Macquarie?'

'Yep. Just for a bit, to help my dad cut his hours. I don't know how the docs with young families manage. Down there, they have to spread themselves around to be dad and husband, or wife and mother, as well as on-call GP. My sister's a GP and she said the same thing. We both came home to the parents when William was diagnosed with severe depression, to lighten the load. Then I followed him to the Ridge.'

She nodded in understanding. Of course, she'd understand. 'So, your parents still live there?'

'You're nosy.' When she didn't answer or look away he sighed. 'Still in Port Macquarie, yes.' He didn't want to talk about it any more. He waved his hand as if to push it away. 'You know what happened then.'

Well, she didn't, but that was as much as he was telling. It was time to change the subject. 'How did your parents go with the reunion this morning?'

She tapped her glass with her fingernail, her eyes wide. 'I haven't even given them a thought. Which is odd really, when that's why I'm here.'

'No doubt they'd be happy to hear that,' he said drily. 'You can be nosy.'

She laughed – it looked good on her, softening her eyes, rounding her hot mouth – and he slipped the question in while she was relaxed. 'Tell me about your boyfriend?'

He saw the shift in her eyes as she looked away and the tightening of her mouth. Her gaze came back to him. 'Josh?'

She sounded calm. Good. 'If that's his name, then yes.'

'Why?'

'I want to know if you're available, of course.' He savoured the startled opening of her mouth, the flush in her cheeks and the tiny nervous movement of her tongue. All places he wanted to explore, taste, savour later, which he considered for all of the long moment it took for her to answer.

Chapter Thirty-three

Riley

Riley watched the blue of Konrad's eyes grow bedroom dark and his mouth curl wickedly as if he was imagining . . . what?

He leaned forward until his head was close to hers, his breath fanning softly over her cheek. 'If you're a free agent, I'd very much like to take you to bed.' He waggled his brows. 'Not to sleep.'

He waited. She stared. Their eyes held.

Lordy, lordy.

Riley's heart rate took a skip and a jump at his words and deep in her belly something clawed and purred like a sleepy feline stretching. Her left hand slid down and dug into her thigh, kneading in time to the waves in her belly. He was certainly putting it out there. And she was feeling it. Everywhere.

'No strings?'

'No strings.'

Riley accepted the tingle along her nerve endings – a low buzz of danger and excitement, and yes, that would be lust. Something she hadn't taken much notice of for a long while in her busy world, but there was no denying the shimmer of energy between them at this moment. Strong energy. Hot. So hot she could barely breathe.

She straightened and sat back in her chair as if to break that awareness, but the connection just stretched like sticky, boiled toffee between them as she studied this outrageously outspoken, incredibly hot man.

Sapphire eyes bored into hers, devil dark and intense, yet the skin at the side of his eyes crinkled with amusement. He tipped his chin on an angle, shoulders back, sleeves rolled up to the elbow on those corded muscles and sinews of his truly wonderful arms. He lifted his hands in question, daring her. *Lordy, those arms.* She'd heard of boob-men and leg-men; maybe she was turning into an arm-girl.

The silence had gone on for too long. She moistened dry lips and looked down at her glass. Not at him. 'On one hand'—she tried for lightness, not sure she made it but giving it her all— 'I admire you for saying you don't want to break up relationships.'

Her gaze flicked up to his and she couldn't help her own amusement that they were talking about this out loud, though softly, in a public place, as if it was an item on the daily special menu they were considering.

She ran her finger around the top of the glass, pushing the rim into its soft pad, suddenly wishing the empty flute still held wine. 'On the other hand,' she waggled her fingers, 'I fear you have tickets on yourself.'

But she hadn't answered his question. His smile stayed lazy. One hand reached across the table and a long, strong finger slid down her thumb where it rested against the glass, while his hand curled around the pulse on her wrist. It held. Squeezed. Measured. 'There's only one way to find out.'

He was checking her heart rate. Well damn, that was a tell she couldn't hide. She'd always been drawn to honesty and her gut said this guy didn't tell lies. She hadn't slept with anyone except Josh in recent years. Lord knew how long ago that was, too, which explained the aversion to a stronger relationship with Josh if he didn't rock her boat.

Not that she'd been tempted to sleep with anyone else. Until now. Right now.

She tried to joke. 'What am I supposed to say? We're having a break so it's okay if I sleep with you?' Konrad had said not much sleeping would happen.

His gaze never left hers. 'Sounds good to me. Is it true?'

She inclined her head. 'We're having a break. Permanent, I imagine. He wants more than I do.'

'Welllll.' The word was long, drawn out. Yep, he was seriously attempting to seduce her into his bed, leaving her in no doubt that he wanted her. He drawled, 'I'm unattached and asking for a long afternoon. Into the night. Possibly extending to a leisurely Sunday morning in bed to finish off.'

He was arrogant, she'd give him that. 'Don't want much, do you.'

'All of it. Are you interested?'

Oh, lordy yes. Her face burned. 'Let's see how the rest of the afternoon pans out.'

And then, with a whoosh and a flash of heat, the stove in the kitchen of the pub caught on fire and somebody screamed.

Konrad was out of the chair before Riley even recognised the problem. As she pushed her own chair back, a sheet of flame, hotter than her cheeks that she'd thought scalding, climbed the kitchen wall, a fair distance from their table, yet heat blasted across the beer garden. On his dash, Konrad scooped up a fire extinguisher and headed for the flames.

Through the service window into the food-preparation area, she could see a man in the whites of a chef's uniform beating at his beard and shirt and trying to back out of the flame-filled kitchen.

Riley wasn't far behind Konrad as she scanned for the fire blanket. All restaurants had them. She found it just inside the door of the kitchen; lucky, because the heat pushed Konrad back as he discharged the extinguisher at the base of the flames to let the man past. Riley pulled the square of material from the bag and flicked it out to its full width.

As Konrad beat the flames back with the extinguisher, the cook slid along the rear wall, his shirt smouldering while his hands slapped his chest and beard.

Riley folded the blanket over her hands and wrapped it around him. 'Down and roll,' she said, and the man fell to the floor while she patted him to smother the flames.

'You're out,' she said and called behind her to the beer garden, 'Iced water in jugs, please.'

Patrons rushed to the bar and within a minute she had a jug of cold water, which she poured over the cook's hands, and a bar towel that she soaked. 'Put this on your face.' Two more jugs appeared. 'Now give me the towel. I'll do that. Hold your hands in the ice water.'

She took the towel from him, patting his face while he sucked in his breath as the water covered his fingers and wrists. The hands were the worst, already peeling red skin, but everything had happened so fast and the rapid first aid would help the long-term outcome.

Riley re-soaked the towel she held and replaced the cold material again over the tufts of his beard that hadn't burned away to leave red facial skin. It wasn't so bad here. His lips were red and his cheeks scalded, but it looked more first than second degree. She couldn't see any obvious full thickness burns. It was a shame about the eyelashes and brows, which were all gone. She hoped Konrad had kept his.

They'd have to watch this guy for shock until he could be transferred to hospital. She glanced over her shoulder, where Konrad had swiftly doused the fire and was handing the extinguisher to another man, who seemed to know what he was doing.

The sound of a siren drifted into the smoky room and she assumed someone had called the fire brigade or an ambulance. Both would be good.

Chapter Thirty-four

Adelaide

Adelaide heard the soft purr of her husband's car outside and her fingers tightened on her other wrist as she looked at her watch. A small spurt of laughter that was more nerves than amusement slipped out. One minute past twelve. That sounded like Tyler.

She opened the front door and leaned back against the door-frame, noting the dust on his pride and joy, which dulled the shiny black paint and coated the car windows and usually sparkling rims. He'd hate that.

She waited for him to alight. It always took him ages to climb out of a car. He'd be checking the kilometres travelled, the fuel status, that everything was tidy in the console and all the windows were fully closed before he switched it off.

When she'd first met Tyler Brand, she'd stood outside the car for minutes when they arrived at venues and finally, she'd learned to wait in the car. Rather than annoying her now, it amused her. It was just one of his foibles and she had a few of her own. She even had some new idiosyncrasies Tyler would have to put up with, if he wanted to stay with her here, for his visit.

The engine stopped. No, she wasn't going to rush down the path and meet him at the door of his precious Audi, another possession Tyler probably loved more than her. Good grief, she was defensive already, and he hadn't even got out. *Stop it*, she told herself.

The door opened and Adelaide straightened and smiled as she watched her husband of forty years uncoil. Unexpectedly, butterflies crept up her body from her feet to her chest as she took him in. A softness, and heat and the forgotten allure of the man, her man, tingled against her skin. His chiselled cheeks, full mouth and strong chin were the same. A little crinkled and wrinkled and creased, but Tyler looked trim and tanned and surprisingly casually dressed. His short dark hair was liberally sprinkled with grey at the temple and sides, but all in all he looked darn good.

He wore blue jeans, which she hadn't seen on him in thirty years at least, though they looked new and, like the white shirt and the brown boots, sported the look of Mr R.M. Williams. He was trying to fit in. The thought warmed her.

Their gazes met across the gravel between the road and the inn, and the recognition of a shared life sizzled between them. The silly protective barrier she'd put up softened and cracked as the connection of years reached out and brushed it away. That connection felt unexpected and strong. This was her Tyler, her gorgeous Tyler, whom she'd fallen in love with decades ago, despite the fact that somehow they'd lost their way.

They were both older and sillier, perhaps. They'd dug their respective heels in for the wrong reasons, not coming together for the right ones, and too much distance had grown between them.

'Oh, Ty,' she said softly, forgetting her vow to stay and crossing the raked gravel with her hand outstretched. 'It's so good to see you.'

Stopping in front of him, she lifted her hands and placed them on either side of his face and stared into his grey eyes.

For a moment, she thought she saw uncertainty and surely not anxiety, something she'd never seen in him before, and that brief glimpse was enough to propel her into his arms.

'Del.' His voice was deep, rumbly with emotion, another thing she rarely heard in her husband. 'I've missed you. It's very, very good to see you, too.'

She buried her nose in his chest. They were a similar height, with Tyler just a couple of centimetres taller. The familiar scent of his spicy aftershave made her eyes prickle, but no way was she letting tears out. She squeezed his waist, where her hands rested, feeling his solid muscles – his achingly familiar warmth – and then she stepped back.

'You must be tired from that drive. Come inside out of the heat.' But when she turned to walk away, his hand reached out and captured her fingers. Something he'd done years ago when they were still holding hands. She remembered this feeling of her hand in his. Another thing that had fallen away except at night. So sad, so silly, the loss of that.

'Wait,' he said quietly. 'Let me stand here for a minute and just look at your little shack and this place where you settled before we go in.' He tugged on her arm and his other hand curled around her hip until her back was against his chest, while he held her gently within the circle of his arms. His chin rested on her shoulder as they both looked towards the inn.

'I want to take it in.' She felt his chin move as he talked. 'You always were amazing when you tackled a project. Look at you managing all this.' His arm swept the gravel and the shack and the wheelbarrow full of implements. 'No neighbours, just a big sky, desert and dirt.' He shook his head again. 'I don't know if it's in me, but I want you to know, right at the beginning, I'm very, very proud of your determination to follow your dreams.'

This time, a tear did escape to run down her cheek, but it was okay, he couldn't see it. She leaned her head back into him and his hands tightened.

'Thank you. That means a lot. I'm glad you came out to see my Wayfarers.'

'Is there room at the inn for me?' She heard the teasing in his voice.

'We'll see.' She matched his tone. 'You may not want to stay when you see how basic it is.' And that was true.

'If it's good enough for my wife, I'm sure it's good enough for me.' He sounded stalwart, but she could hear the uncertainty.

She laughed. 'Come on, then. I'll show you the space on the floor that's yours.' She spun in his arms and caught the hopeful look that she was joking. She laughed again. She was giddy with him being here, and that was not what she expected to feel at all. 'You're not tied to anything. We'll just see what suits and work with that. There's always an onsite van at the park in town.'

She took his hand to lead him down the gravel – there was no garden path here – to the wonky verandah and the rusty tin roof.

He looked at her sideways. 'Do I have to take off my shoes?'

Adelaide mushed her lips together to hold in another silly giggle. 'No, dear. You'll surely end up with gravel in your soft, city feet.'

She pushed open the squeaky door, because the blinking thing liked to close itself all the time and even though the curtains were pulled back it was still dim inside when she pushed it wide. But, she decided, it felt cool and welcoming, and darn it, she was proud of her little shack. She stood back to let her husband go in front of her.

He shook his head, smiling. 'After you,' he said, so she went ahead but could feel him at her shoulder. It felt good. Right. Wonderful.

When he stood in the centre of her home, he turned a full circle, his eyes travelling over her books and chipped plates, her tiny kitchen nook, and finally the single day bed made up of cushions and quilts. 'My love,' he said, his voice intrigued, almost fasci-nated, to her relief. 'My wife is camping. But it looks so homey, I can see you here.'

At least he hadn't mocked her little world. And he'd called her his wife. His love. Still. 'It's better than camping. The sun gives me power and the stove runs on wood. Even if the rain doesn't often give me water, I'm off the grid.'

He tilted his head at her. 'I'm sure you have an answer for water?'

'Well, yes. I pay the man to come in and pump water into the tank. I've learned how to manage the solar and batteries and I'm a mean hand at gauging a wood-oven temperature.'

He was watching her, shaking his head in admiration. 'You're incredible. I've always known that, but it seems I needed reminding just how much.'

Adelaide soaked up the praise like a plant denied water, def-initely needy, and she tried to keep her face from too obviously showing her delight. Which was silly, too.

His gaze tangled with hers. 'I've missed you, Del.'

Thank God. 'I missed you, too.'

They stared at each other, with still too much distance between them, both physical and emotional, but it was a start.

'Do you ever get lonely?' He gestured to the empty doorway with one elegant hand.

Her gaze shifted to his fingers. She'd always loved his hands. His wedding ring caught the light. He still wore it. Good. 'Of course, sometimes. But I get immersed in what I'm doing. I love it here.' She grinned at him. 'I'm so pleased you came because I can't wait to show you it all.'

He rubbed his hands together, flirting with her. 'I can't wait to see.' Their eyes met and held. It seemed as though another brick in the wall between them had been pushed out.

'Would you like a drink?' she asked.

'What have you got?'

'Water.'

He laughed. 'Evian?' He was teasing her again.

'Better than that,' she joked back. 'Bore water. Though it might give you a belly ache if you drink too much.'

Over the next hour, apart from when Tyler raved about the bacon-and-egg pie she'd made for lunch, they chatted about people and changes in Sydney, and about Riley of course, but strangely, Riley didn't figure a lot in their conversation. It was as if they both knew the importance of connections between the two of them that didn't involve others.

Once they'd washed up – she'd nearly fallen over when Tyler picked up the tea towel and tidied the remains away – she showed him her finds.

'You mined this opal? From the walls, underground?' Tyler was holding a palm full of tiny pieces of opal, inexpertly cut and polished, but she kept learning new skills. If she found anything that looked really promising, she had someone else look at it for her. Desiree had put her onto Kelly.

'I did.' Pride swelled inside her. She had! 'I chip away at the grey wall until I see something with colour. A lovely woman, Kelly – she's a third-generation miner – cuts the promising stones for me. She came and showed me how to use the pick and look for seams and colour in the rock. How to take chunks of rock and rubble and winch them up to the surface to wash and screen them.'

'And you do all that by yourself?'

'I do.'

'Will you show me?' Tyler was keen to see the mine. Apparently, more than keen. Who knew this would happen?

'Of course.' She kept checking his face, but as far as she could tell he looked genuine.

She watched him walk all over the yard, studying the implements and piles of stones, and the second shaft where he examined the winch and bucket, before they actually went down into the mine. Tyler had been eager to see everything on her tiny block of land – more interested than she thought he'd be in the mechanics of opal hunting – and he was particularly struck by the shaft and tunnel in the backyard.

When the time came to venture underground, she made Tyler remove leather-soled boots and put on joggers. She didn't need him to slip off a rung of the ladder and land on her head.

'Do I really have to wear a helmet with a light?' he asked, as if she was babying him.

'Yes. You do. I'm not carrying you out if you hit your head on the roof. Plus, even though the generator gives light, it's possible for that to fail.'

'I don't even know how to work a generator,' he said.

'Neither did I, but I know now.' She waved her hand at the large machine under a sheet of tin. 'It guzzles fuel but runs the lights in the tunnel, so the fuel is worth it.'

Adelaide led the way down the ladder, swinging easily over the rim of the shaft and disappearing below ground, but she stopped when he didn't appear in the light above her. 'Are you coming?'

His foot emerged and then the second. With the light blocked out and his fingers tight on the rungs, he began to descend. Stiffly. Jerkily. He was obviously awkward and tense.

She finished her own descent and waited for him to arrive. He took his time, ensuring each foot was secure before bringing the next down. That was good. She didn't want accidents. The ladder wobbled a little, but it always did that.

From the bottom, she watched him. *Ooohhh. The old man still has a good backside on him*, she thought, and then almost immediately a negative inner voice said, *You're too ancient for this stuff*, which raised her hackles. Maybe she wasn't. She turned her face and grinned into the dim tunnel so he wouldn't see.

When Tyler reached the bottom, he turned around and looked up at the ladder and the ring of light. Then slowly, he circled the packed walls with posts holding up the ceiling. He noted the string of lights that crawled along the ceiling in two directions and disappeared around a corner. 'My wife is an opal miner,' he said slowly, then he seemed to clamp his mouth shut as if unable to say more.

'You knew that.' She took his hand. 'Come on, Tyler Brand. Come see my mine.'

He tugged her back. 'That's a very sexy thing.'

'Really?' She shook her head in amusement.

'You realise, of course, that if I kiss you here, nobody can see us?'

She laughed. 'Tease.'

He stepped closer. 'So? How about it?'

'How about what?' Who knew he had it in him? She leaned in and kissed him quickly. 'There. Let's go.'

'My turn.'

She laughed again, but when he leaned in, Tyler captured her face between his lovely hands, rubbed her nose gently with his and feathered his lips on hers, until he put some passion into it.

Whoa. She responded, probably out of shock, but then she disregarded the hows and whys and leaned in further and slid her hands into his hair until they were both lost in a kiss that she'd forgotten they even knew how to generate.

Chapter Thirty-five

Melinda

Riding back to Lightning Ridge in the passenger seat of Greta's little car, Melinda decided she'd possibly had the best day of her entire life.

After the wonder of the ultrasound and confirming the reality of the new life she would meet soon, Melinda was on a high. Then the friendly midwives at the antenatal appointment had given her a bag full of booklets and baby information. Although they'd mentioned labour and birth and breastfeeding – all concepts she hadn't wanted to think about – now at least she had a rough plan for the future.

After that, she and Greta had gone to lunch at a place called the Relaxing Café. And it had been, relaxing and scrumptious and a whole world she hadn't known existed. Well, she'd known cafés and experiences such as that existed but not for her, anyway. There had been only one problem – a small altercation with Greta when Melinda asked to be allowed to pay for the lunch. She worked, she had money, she'd argued, and since Greta wouldn't let her pay for the fuel, please, could she pay for lunch? Finally, Greta had agreed, but it had almost made Melinda cry.

After that, they went to the department store. And oh my. Melinda hadn't been to a store that big since before Pop had died. And it had been years before that. They had racks and racks of baby clothes, cots and sheets, prams and pilchers, nappies and fluffy white towels with hoods for the baby's head to stay warm. And women's clothes that Greta kept trying to drag her to but she resisted. Melinda could have stayed in the baby section all day.

Finally, Greta promised to bring her back next week when she had to return to the antenatal clinic. They could make a list to shop for after the baby shower.

Now they were on the way home. And she thought again how fortunate she'd been to have Greta come with her today. Melinda glanced across at her fairy godmother. 'I think I need to buy a car and learn to drive again, Greta.'

They'd turned onto the highway towards Lightning Ridge.

'That's an excellent idea. You'll want to have transport after your baby comes, I'd think.' Greta tilted her head before looking back at the road. 'Do you have your licence with you?'

'Yes.' Melinda's heart thumped. It was in her phone.

'Would you like to try now for a little while? We've got a couple of hours of driving ahead of us.'

Melinda looked at the countryside flashing past and the long strip of black tar out the front windshield. She could drive the car along the straight highway, just to get the feel back.

As if she'd heard her thoughts Greta said, 'It's an automatic. And there's barely anyone on the road. It's not the time for trucks or couriers.'

Melinda felt her eyes sting, again. They'd done that so many times today at the kindness from the woman opposite. 'How can you be so caring? You don't even know me that well.'

'Don't be silly. I've known you for years. You and Toby went to school together and he always said you were a thoughtful girl. I know enough.' Greta patted her shoulder, put on the indicator to turn and slowed the vehicle. 'If you're sure? Don't let me push you into doing something you don't feel comfortable doing. There's precious cargo in your belly.'

Melinda laughed a little shakily. 'I loved driving. Pop's car was an automatic.' Inside, a cowering part of Melinda that she'd let fester and spoil her since the hold-up broke up and drifted away.

'If you're not too worried for your car, I'd love to drive for a bit. Pop did say I was a good driver.' And maybe Toby would help her pick out a second-hand car before the baby was born.

She slid behind the wheel, Greta had pushed the seat back, and she tucked her tummy in, a smile of pure delight on her face. She would be responsible for keeping her helpless baby safe. Driving would be a part of that.

Chapter Thirty-six

Konrad

After the fire, and by the time they made it back to the OPAL Medical Centre, the playful mood and seduction plans had well and truly dissipated. Konrad wondered if they should still go out to dinner, or if, like him, Riley was feeling a bit of a need to kick back and not get dressed and be social again.

Ned from the pub had second-degree burns on ten per cent of his body, and they'd transferred him to the Multi-purpose Health Centre in Konrad's car to stabilise him. The ambulance had still been en route back from Moree with another patient, so they'd waited another hour until they were able to transfer him. The air ambulance had been retrieving others and couldn't respond for at least four hours.

They'd called in an extra nurse, and between the four of them they'd cannulated, given pain relief and dressed the seeping wounds to prepare Ned for transfer. He'd been reasonably comfortable by the time the ambulance arrived to transport him, and they'd seen him off, satisfied that their patient was stable.

Again, Konrad had been impressed with Riley's efficient first-aid treatment and calmness. It had been a long time since he'd been able to share responsibility during medical situations, and he hadn't realised how much he'd missed a worthy partner in the practice. Maybe his sister, Bella, could ask her friends if they were interested in working at Lightning Ridge. He couldn't see Bella here, but she must know other junior doctors.

As they turned in to park outside his unit, Greta's car pulled up. It was later than he'd thought, and then he saw Melinda driving. That made him stare.

Greta climbed out of the passenger side, looking happy as she walked around to the driver's side to open the door for Melinda. He could just hear Greta's voice. 'Your grandfather was right. You're an excellent driver.'

Melinda heaved herself out of the car and she was grinning too. Her young face beamed with delight and he felt his own mouth curve.

Quietly, to Riley, he said, 'I haven't seen Melinda look so happy, ever. Bless Greta.'

'Full marks to Mel for daring to drive.'

Their eyes caught and held, and a flicker of their connection earlier flashed between them. He shook his head. 'Go Greta.'

'She's a champion.' Riley watched them, happy like the parent of a clever child.

'Hey, Melinda, Greta,' he called. 'Did you have a good day?'

Melinda lifted her arm and waved. 'Best ever. I shopped.' She then gave Greta a hug, something he hadn't seen the girl close to ever doing to anyone, and they both moved to the rear of the car.

He crossed towards them. He'd guess there was a boot full. He'd better help; she was pregnant, after all. He shook his head at how his life was changing. Here he was connecting with people and their lives instead of brushing past – he was out of practice – but it looked like he was being force-fed links among his work colleagues.

He expected Riley to disappear, but she stayed by his side as he walked towards the women. Her voice full of warmth, she asked, 'How was your ultrasound, Mel?'

The young woman's face turned towards them and her cheeks glowed with joy. He watched Riley's features soften even more, her caring essence shining through. How had he missed it before? He'd guessed, of course, that she was someone who had empathy doing the job that she did, but he hadn't realised how attached she'd become to Melinda in so short a time.

An uncomfortable prickle of shame itched under his collar that he'd worked with Melinda for seven months and he hadn't tried to make any connection apart from ensuring that she was safe. It was different for men, he rationalised. It wasn't his fault.

Melinda was gushing when he returned to the conversation. 'We saw the little limbs move. And the face. I've got two photos.' She patted her handbag. 'The heartbeat was so strong and steady and the man said everything is perfect.'

'Mel seems to have had an amazing day with you,' Riley said to Greta.

'We both have.' The older woman's face radiated glee. 'Mel asked me to go into the ultrasound with her. It was so exciting.'

'That's wonderful.' Riley looked back to Melinda. 'What about the antenatal clinic?'

Her head bobbed up and down. 'They were lovely. They gave me all these books.' She waved vaguely to the back of the car. 'I have to go back next week. Greta said she'd take me.' Melinda looked at Greta. 'If I can get a car before then, I might take myself. Though they said I shouldn't drive myself in labour.'

Konrad's jaw dropped and he shut it quickly. 'You're buying a car?'

'If I can find one. Greta said Toby might help me find a good deal.' She lifted her chin. 'I've been saving.' Her eyes met his and the gratitude in them made him squirm. 'Thanks to you, I could save and still have somewhere to live.'

He shrugged uncomfortably and looked away. He suspected Riley was laughing at him, but the only giveaway an extra sparkle in her eyes.

He squirmed a little more. 'You're welcome. It suited us all.' He wondered if now was a good time to show her the peppermint room four doors down, while Greta was here. Somewhere in his thought process, he considered Greta's advice for furnishings and curtains. He looked at Riley and wished he could've asked her.

She raised her brows and jerked her head towards the unit and he chuckled silently. Of course, she got it. Darn woman. She understood too much. And what was with her calling Melinda 'Mel'?

He lifted his chin, preparing himself for more gratitude, which he knew he couldn't avoid regardless of how much he didn't want it. 'Actually, if you're not rushing away, Greta, maybe you and Melinda would like to come down and see what we've done to units five and six?'

Greta looked interested. She must have known because of Toby's day of work, but pretended she didn't. Melinda looked confused.

He shrugged. 'I thought when the baby came that you might like to move into a freshly painted unit. We're not using them, so if we open the door between two of the units you could have a larger space and make a little nursery.' His voice trailed away as his neck heated.

Melinda's face scrunched and slowly her eyes filled with tears.

He looked away quickly and started walking. 'Anyway, come have a look.' Darn. He turned back as a thought occurred to him. Why hadn't he considered it? 'Of course, you don't have to. There's no compulsion or onus on you to do anything, you know.' Would she feel she shouldn't leave if she wanted to? 'Obviously, you can leave whenever you like.'

He was rabbiting on awkwardly, wishing he knew how to stop.

Riley bumped him. 'You'll see,' she said to Melinda as she interrupted him.

He shut up. Yeah. He'd been digging a hole for himself.

They all trooped past the first four units and he unlocked the door of five and then six and stepped back.

'Toby and I,' he glanced at Riley, 'and Riley, did some painting this morning. We got rid of extra furniture and I thought maybe Greta could help you with a few ideas for curtains if you want.'

Melinda and Greta went inside and he glanced at Riley.

She was laughing at him. 'You're a big softy who hates thanks.'

His neck heated. 'So?'

She laughed aloud and leaned in to pat his shoulder. 'It's sweet.' She lifted her brows and said, 'I never would have guessed.'

Chapter Thirty-seven

Riley

He cracked her up and Riley savoured the slight pink on the skin at the open neck of Konrad's shirt – and other aspects of the hard muscles. There were a few curling hairs in that V that begged inspection, too.

She laughed softly, again, as he seriously squirmed at Melinda's gratitude until the girl ducked inside. Though he looked chuffed at the squeaks of delight and murmurs from Greta, as they opened and closed drawers and exclaimed at the paint colour.

Yes, she thought, *he's done a good job and made a young woman happy. The man is good people.* Though why she was feeling all gosh and darn, she had no idea. She barely knew these individuals. It had been a strange day with painting skirting boards and the drama of the fire, and now all the excitement with Melinda. And she'd hardly thought of her parents' interesting reconnection. She should phone her mother at some point.

Right now, all she wanted to do was sit somewhere quietly and chill. Just to close her eyes and relax. Strangely, she'd be happy to chill with Konrad. Maybe discuss the day and the people in it.

People she felt unusually interested in and wanted to be happy. How the heck had that come about?

It was curious how she felt she could relax with him. Earlier today, it had all been about who would jump whose bones, but not at this moment. With this guy, the more facets she noted the more she liked. It was such a rotten shame he didn't live in Sydney.

Melinda reappeared at the door and walked up to Konrad, tilted her head and wiped the back of her hand across her eyes. Then she gave him a swift, embarrassed, awkward-around-her-big-belly hug. 'Thank you. It looks beautiful. I'd love to move in when it's done. Greta said she's got just the material for the curtains.' She looked thoughtful, her brow furrowing. 'I should pay you twice as much for the rent, though.'

'No. You won't.'

Kind but not diplomatic, Riley thought with amusement, as she watched Melinda's jaw firm stubbornly. Riley had a thought about the financial ramifications and wondered if it would stretch Melinda's budget too far. Especially if she bought a car.

'Yes,' she insisted.

Greta laughed. 'She wouldn't let me pay for lunch, either.'

Konrad shook his head. 'Nobody lives here. We still have a spare unit. Until we need more accommodation, the unit would've been empty, anyway.'

It sort of made sense, Riley agreed, but she suspected Melinda wasn't happy.

'Then half as much again,' she persisted. 'As long as I can keep my job when the baby is born.'

He waved his hand in the general direction of the surgery. 'Yes, you have your job before and after. Bring the baby with you.'

Aww, the man is so sweet, Riley thought.

But Konrad hadn't finished. 'And no, you are not paying more. Though you can live in just one unit if you wish.'

So, Riley thought watching the standoff, *Dr Grey can be stubborn, too.* She watched him raise those brows and shrug innocently.

Finally, with narrow eyes, Melinda said, 'I'll figure something out.'

She would. This new Melinda who had catapulted herself from her sheltered cocoon after just one day away in the company of Greta. Who knew?

When all of the day's purchases were transferred from Greta's car boot to Melinda's old unit and Greta had driven away, Riley and Konrad were left staring at the departing tail-lights.

Konrad raised that one brow. 'What's the eyebrow for?' As if she didn't know. 'It looks very cool.' She'd always wanted to be able to do that. She suspected you needed to be born with the skill. She mocked herself at her whimsy.

'Now, where were we?' he said, his expression mischievous.

She shook her head. 'Not there.'

'We've had a busy couple of hours. Fancy a cup of tea?' he said.

'Soon. Though perhaps I need a Bex and a good lie-down,' she said, the old-fashioned saying popping up from goodness knows where. Maybe her paternal grandmother? Konrad was probably too young to understand it, but he laughed.

'It's been years since I heard that one. I'm thinking all our hot and sweaty sexual anticipation is on the backburner and we need time to draw breath.'

It was nice that he got that. 'I'm for the shower. I stink like smoke.'

She saw his eyes darken, and though he didn't say it, she could almost hear the suggestion that she use his bathroom with his help.

'By myself.' She laughed. 'I'll meet you back in the common room in half an hour. I have to dry my hair.'

'It's still Saturday night.'

'Indeed, the day's a pup.'

Her phone rang, a private number, often seen when hospitals rang, so she answered. 'Dr Riley Brand.'

'This is Dr Lee. I'm the reporting radiologist from Hunter New England Health. I have morphology results for Melinda Lowenthal's ultrasound today at Moree.'

Wow, she hadn't expected formal results until Monday. The sonographer had already phoned to say all was well. It was a pretty flash service for a weekend. Unless . . .

'Go ahead.' She'd missed his name while her mind sorted the reference. Riley glanced behind her, had Konrad gone, but he still stood there, watching her. When she widened her eyes at her caller, his brows rose. 'I'm sorry, what was your name again?'

When she repeated it out loud Konrad nodded that he knew the man. 'Go ahead.'

'I've sent the formal results through to your email. This is a courtesy call as I understand the patient is already thirty-five weeks' gestation.'

'She is.' Riley wasn't liking the sound of this. She'd taken too many of these phone calls.

'While the first scan appeared without anomalies,' Dr Lee paused, 'on further investigation, we'd like to reverse that result.

There appears to be a small abdominal opening and a gaseous shadow on the foetal abdomen suggestive of the coiled external intestine of a gastroschisis or omphalocele. The patient requires further ultrasound, in a higher level centre if possible, and probable referral to a neonatal surgeon.' More advanced equipment would make it more definitive.

'I see.' Too clearly and painfully. Poor baby. Poor Melinda. She blew out an unhappy breath. She hated the idea of the coming stress for the young mum. And maybe for a lot of the women in the town as they cheered Melinda on.

He continued. 'If you could discuss this with your patient and arrange further tests next week, the diagnostic centre in Moree will see her again. Or, even better, Sydney or Newcastle for a Level Five or Six service, if you can arrange that.'

'I see. I'll read the reports as soon as I get off the phone. Thank you.' The call ended.

'Problem?' Which reminded her that she wasn't alone dealing with this. A tiny fraction of her distress eased as she looked into Konrad's concerned gaze.

Voice low she said, 'Melinda's scan. Possibly gastroschisis or omphalocele. I'll shower and meet you in half an hour.'

He winced and nodded, and she unlocked her unit.

Well, that sucked. She thought about the happy, bubbly Melinda of five minutes ago and how this would change the next few weeks, if not months and years, of the young mum's life. Hopefully, the health issue was a standalone mechanical problem that could be surgically repaired – fast – at the birth or days later. That was the best-case scenario. Then Melinda and her baby could come home as soon as the baby healed. Fingers crossed.

But at the back of her mind were the other problems that could sometimes accompany the hole in the abdominal wall already seen. Hopefully, this was a simple gastroschisis existing as an isolated defect and not part of a chromosomal syndrome.

For now, she'd shower, read the emailed report and discuss it with Konrad. Then she would have to break the news to Melinda.

By the time she stepped, dressed in fresh linen trousers and a sleeveless cream top, into the common room, Konrad had made a huge pot of Earl Grey tea and pulled some chocolate biscuits from somewhere. If-in-doubt comfort food. She appreciated that. A lot.

'Feel better?' His eyes travelled the length of her and suggested that externally she looked mighty fine. Surprisingly, or not, that did lift her spirits.

'Do I smell better?'

His eyes crinkled. 'I didn't have any complaints.' Just because they didn't launch into the topic on both of their minds didn't mean they weren't thinking of Melinda. She knew it with a certainty that amazed her.

'Yes, I feel better, thank you.' She gestured with her head to the table. 'Thanks for the tea, and the chocolate. I assume it's for sharing?'

He nodded. 'Comfort food.' He poured her a cup and didn't offer milk or sugar, so he must've noticed that she had hers black, unsweetened and not too strong. He nursed his own cup. 'So, Melinda has to go back for further tests?'

She nodded. 'This will rain on her happy parade.'

He huffed out his worry. 'How much more does she have to take? And alone.' He pulled his hand through his hair, making the damp ends stand up. She wanted to pat it down, but finding amusement in his odd hairstyle wasn't to be knocked back today. Not much else was funny.

'She's not alone. She has us and Greta and her friends.' She sipped – the tea was hot and perfect – and felt her shoulders drop a little more. 'She's not a kid. She showed that today, and I think she'll take this on the chin and move forward. I think your Mel is going to be a fierce little mother.'

'Why do you call her Mel?'

'She said she prefers Mel. Didn't you know that?'

'Did you ask her?' By the look on his face he hadn't.

'Yes.'

Konrad looked down at his cup. 'I'm just glad she got to have some excitement and joy before it all caves,' he said.

'I suspect she'll be fine. I'm not sure about you. I never picked you were such a softy.'

'Not soft.' His head jerked up. Offended. 'Normal, concerned, typical adult response.'

'Really? From the man who gets all embarrassed and cringes from gratitude?'

She watched him shift in his seat and she shook her head. 'Thanks for the smile, Dr Grey.'

'Shut up,' he muttered and she smiled again.

'Anyway, from where I'm sitting, it's actually nice to be able to talk to you about this. Have you read the report?' She'd forwarded it to him as soon as she'd finished her read, before the shower.

'Yes, thanks for sending it through.'

'Melinda's technically your patient, not mine. I'll be gone in three weeks.'

The words hung strangely in the air between them, and oddly she wasn't looking forward to driving out of town as much as she'd thought she would. But that was a problem to pick over later.

Back to details. 'For now, it looks like a small defect. Still, you never know how much of the bowel will slip through the hernia before birth. Or how difficult it will be to push it back inside and close the defect that's letting it escape.'

He gave her the side eye. 'I don't have any experience in this. Where do you recommend she delivers?'

'Unless Melinda has relatives in Brisbane or Newcastle, I'd go for the Children's Hospital in Sydney. I'll check with her first and then contact a friend of mine who consults for the surgical unit there.'

'So, again we're lucky you came to the Ridge, as it turns out.'

Now it was her turn to not want gratitude. It did feel a little uncomfortable. 'You would've managed. Someone would've known where to refer. I'm glad we've got time to work everything out.'

Chapter Thirty-eight

Melinda

Melinda sat in her small unit holding two black-and-white photos of her baby. He or she would be here soon. Her child. She'd be a mum. Without her own mother as a role model, how the heck was she supposed to know what to do? But there were people helping generously. She knew she was blessed.

'We can do this, baby.' She tucked the ultrasound snapshots carefully into the two corners of a picture frame until she decided how she was going to mount them. 'Your mum is going to get a car. Dr Konrad has painted us our new unit. When you arrive, we'll go back to work as soon as possible and start saving again. Because, one day, we'll have our own house here.'

Showered and dressed in a cool cotton pregnancy frock that Greta had secretly bought at the department store and given to her as they unloaded the boot, Melinda poured herself a glass of cold milk. She sat down with a pen and paper and tried to work out how much of her savings she could spare for a car while still leaving a safety nest egg.

Her gaze strayed to where all the shopping bags were lined up along the wall. She'd spent money, but sensibly on wonderful, essential things. Baby things. There was no need to put anything away if she was gonna be moving soon. She thought of the lovely peppermint unit three doors down and her heart swelled with delight.

It was such an exciting day. So many unexpected windfalls had happened. She patted her belly gently. 'You brought all these good things to me, baby. Mummy loves you very, very much.'

Someone knocked on her door. Nobody except Dr Konrad knocked on her door. Ever. She frowned.

As she crossed the room, she noticed that she actually waddled like a duck now when she walked, and the frown slipped away to be replaced by a small hiccupping giggle. When she opened the door, Dr Brand stood there.

'Oh. Hello, Dr Brand.' She noticed the kind but careful expression on the doctor's face and fear sliced through her. 'Is something wrong?' she managed.

'Mel. You can call me Riley, at least when we're not at work, please. Toby does now and you should too.'

Melinda nodded. 'Would you like to come in?'

'I won't come in, thank you. I was hoping if you weren't busy, you'd come through to the common room. Konrad's in there. We're offering a cup of tea so we can have a chat about your pregnancy. I have some new results.'

'Oh?' Melinda's heart stuttered. But then Riley – that would take some getting used to – smiled, and some of Melinda's trepidation eased. Maybe everything was fine? 'Oh. Okay.' She glanced back at the room. She didn't need anything and pulled the door shut behind her, before following Riley into the room next door.

Konrad stood up from the table when she came in and gestured to a huge teapot she hadn't seen before on the table. His lips curved too, but his eyes looked strained. The dread came back.

'Would you like a cup of tea?' His voice sounded kind. Too kind.

She saw the two half-filled cups and one for her. Unease crawled along her shoulders. Was this bad news coming? Had they been sitting here talking about her until they came and got her? Just when everything had seemed to be finally going right. No. She needed to stop guessing and listen. She lifted her chin.

'Yes. Thank you.' She sat down, which wasn't easy as her belly seemed to be growing so fast now she couldn't get close to the table.

Konrad pushed the milk and sugar towards her and Riley sat too. Then Konrad took his seat. Silence fell and Melinda lifted her chin and said, 'Do you have something to tell me?'

Riley nodded, as if Melinda had done something clever when she'd done nothing but ask the question. 'Yes, Mel, and I have great faith in your good sense. It's about your ultrasound. I had a phone call from the chief radiologist from the health service.'

Melinda broke in, as if she could stop something she didn't want to hear. 'The sonographer man said everything was fine at Moree.'

'I know. He rang me, as well, and said the same. It seems he thought it was, but every ultrasound and X-ray is checked by a specialist radiologist as a second assurance that they haven't missed anything.' She let her words settle.

Melinda felt anything but settled. Alarm jangled along her nerves and in her throat. Her hand moved down and she cupped underneath the bulge of her belly, as if to hold her stomach safely away from any bad news.

Riley said, 'They've detected a small hole in your baby's abdominal wall that didn't close as it should during the baby's growth. The skin across the baby's tummy near the umbilicus has an opening.'

'Like a hernia?' Melinda nodded, her mouth parched and she felt as stiff and jagged and dry as one of the white mullock heaps outside a mine. Her heart pounded in her ears, her fingers tightening on her stomach. Konrad pushed her tea closer and she lifted it with one hand and sipped. It wasn't too hot and she took a second one to settle herself. Riley waited until she put the cup down again.

'Sort of. Hernias have skin on them, whereas this is a hole. A part of your baby's intestine has wiggled out through the hole. It's called gastroschisis or omphalocele when it does that, depending on whether the bowel is covered by a membrane or not.'

'But my baby will be fine?'

'Your baby is well now. For the safest outcome, your baby needs to be born in a tertiary hospital where they can do the operation to fix the hole as soon as possible. It's good that they've picked it up now and not when the baby is born because it's safer for the baby if everyone is prepared.' She paused, but Melinda waved her on. 'I'd like you to have a consultation and further tests in Sydney. Though, if you prefer you could go to Brisbane or Newcastle?'

'Sydney is fine.' It didn't matter where. Her baby was not going to die. 'Is it a dangerous operation?' She couldn't imagine a tiny new baby – *her* tiny baby – being operated on. Her throat closed.

'The operation itself is not usually dangerous.'

Not usually – what sort of answer was that? Melinda's eyes narrowed and Riley must have noticed because she lifted her hand and launched into an explanation.

'The surgeon will ease the bowel back inside the baby's tummy, then stitch the hole closed. It depends how much bowel has eased out as to how long it takes. Sometimes it takes more than one operation but not usually. It can be over in days. If you and your baby are unlucky, it can take weeks or even months. Next week, you'll have tests with higher-powered ultrasounds and the surgeon will be able to tell you more.'

She didn't understand. 'Why didn't the man see it today?'

Dr Konrad said, 'It's not an easy thing to see on the scan and can be missed.'

'And after the operation?' she asked. 'Will my baby be fine?'

'The operation should be straightforward, but I can't give you that answer because I don't know.'

Melinda nodded. She appreciated that honesty.

Riley said, 'Sometimes a problem like this can be associated with other problems. When you have more tests back from the pathology company, we'll be able to eliminate some of those things. For the moment, we know your baby is moving easily and is active. Today showed that. He or she is safe inside you and the heart rate was good.'

Melinda replayed that information. Yes, she'd heard the heartbeat and her baby's movements were definitely there. 'So, what you're saying is, I have to go to Sydney to have the tests, come back for a week or two and then go to Sydney for the birth. But a week or two after the birth, hopefully we'll be able to just come home and live normally.'

'Yes,' Riley said. 'That's what I hope will happen. Best-case scenario.'

Oh. 'There are other possibilities, then?' Melinda knew her voice sounded horrified. 'And what's the worst-case scenario?'

'I have to leave that answer until we can know for sure what's really happening. Would you like me to arrange transport and accommodation at the hospital in Sydney early next week? The hostel is free for remote patients.'

'You'd do that? Then, yes. Thank you.' She hadn't even thought of that. She'd have to stay in the city. She'd never been to the city. She'd be alone, she realised, and panic fluttered in her throat, spread to her belly and her baby kicked. Deep, deep inside, Melinda quaked at the possibilities of danger for her baby and her own lack of experience outside her home town. But she'd manage, because she had to.

She took a calming breath. No, she wasn't alone. She'd have her baby and they'd do this together. Her baby shifted and kicked again, as though saying yes, they were a team.

Chapter Thirty-nine

Riley

Riley watched the emotions play across Melinda's face and savoured the young mum's determination to get through this crisis for her baby. 'In Sydney, you'll have tests and see the paediatric surgeon to discuss the results. If there is a problem, they will also arrange a visit to the neonatal intensive care to see where your baby will be admitted after the birth.'

'Can I stay with my baby?' Clear as daylight, Mel didn't want her baby to be alone. Such a sweetheart. She'd be a wonderful mum.

Riley said, 'You can sit beside the baby for as long as you like in the neonatal intensive care. Your accommodation will be walking distance from there.'

Riley suspected where Mel would be spending most of the time. It wouldn't be lying on a bed in a lonely room.

'Thank you.' Mel pursed her lips. 'Will I be back in time for the baby shower next Saturday?'

'I have heard about that.' Riley had forgotten. Mel hadn't. But something to look forward to was good. 'I'll know more on

Monday morning, but I should be able to arrange everything for travel on Tuesday, tests and results on Wednesday and Thursday, and you should be able to come home on Friday.'

'I'll be in Sydney for three nights, plus the travelling.' Melinda looked at Konrad. 'I'll let you down as receptionist.'

He shook his head. 'We'll sort something out. You and your baby are much more important than work.'

Riley spared a glance at him. His square jaw had pulled rigid but his eyes held only concern and kindness.

'Thank you, both.' Mel glanced at the door. 'I think I'll go back to my room and think about all this. And I might phone Greta.'

She and Konrad stood when Mel did. 'That sounds like a very sensible idea,' Riley replied. 'Remember, you're not alone, Mel. We're all here for you.'

The young woman ducked her head. Konrad opened the door for her, and Melinda left with her head high and her chin up. Riley wanted to cheer. Or weep. Or hug Konrad.

The door shut and very shortly later, another door closed in the distance. Konrad said, 'You handled that better than I could have.'

It had gone well but that was almost entirely because Melinda was such a champion. Riley closed her eyes. 'I've had more practice with unexpected results.'

When she opened them, his gaze rested quizzically on her face and those too-darned-attractive crinkles were back at the corner of his eyes. Two deep blue irises darkened more as he said, 'Can I tell you how much I admire you? You're an impressive woman, Dr Brand.' And then more softly, 'On so many levels.'

Her gaze tangled in his and surely someone had turned the heat up in the room. She resisted the urge to glance at the aircon control.

She moistened her lips and felt his gaze shift. 'You're not trying to sweet talk me, are you, Dr Grey?' Because it was working, and she couldn't help the infinitesimal sway of her body towards him.

He widened his eyes and those wicked lips curved. 'The thought crossed my mind. And I'm not lying. Sweet talking sounds like a wonderful idea to me after the curveballs we've had today.' He stepped closer. Reached out one big, beautiful hand and snagged her fingers in his. She knew she could tug free, but she didn't – she didn't want to. Funny that. She had no desire to leave at all.

Slowly he drew her closer, until they were chest to chest. His masculine, sensual aroma so subtly swirling around her. His muscular pecs against her softness. 'Is it hot in here?' he asked innocently, and his finger slid down her warm cheek.

Riley tilted her head and stared into his face. 'Maybe you should kiss me, and find out?'

His mouth hovered suddenly, tantalisingly, teasingly close to hers. 'Have I shown you the connecting door between here and my room?' He said it softly, more of a promise than a question, and she reached up until her lips brushed his.

'Now's a good time.'

Chapter Forty

Adelaide

Adelaide woke to the gentle blush of first light painting the dark ceiling. She shifted her back, which was a little stiff from the hard surface under her, and turned her head on her pillow. She and Tyler both had ended up on the floor and she'd slept the night spooned and satisfied and softly pleased that he'd stayed.

Her lips curved. Last night he'd whispered in the dark, 'I can't believe you're an opal miner now.' She'd said, 'If you're good I'll let you play.'

They'd played all right.

But it was nice he was captivated by the idea of the mine at the moment. Riley had been impressed too, the first time she'd come to visit.

As she lay there, she mulled over their daughter's absence last night. She'd half expected her to turn up for dinner or at least phone to arrange something for today, but she hadn't heard from her. Probably giving them time and privacy. She'd give her a ring after breakfast and see if she wanted to come out today, or perhaps she and Tyler could go in to town.

'You awake?' Tyler's breath tickled her shoulder as his fingers curved over her hip and he pulled her in closer. She snuggled, teasing him. She hadn't thought she'd missed this intimacy, but as desire heated her belly, she remembered how much fun it could be in bed with Tyler.

Riley still hadn't rung by the time they finished breakfast, so Adelaide tapped her daughter's speed dial. When the phone picked up and Riley spoke, she sounded sleepy and muffled. Adelaide tilted her head. Was she sick? She rarely slept in.

'Hello, darling. Just wondering if you were coming out today to see your dad and me for Sunday brunch?'

'Oh, yes, of course.' Riley's voice sounded more awake, then she spoke to someone in the background and Adelaide's brows rose along with the corner of her mouth.

'I'll come out for lunch if that's okay.' A pause. 'Konrad might come,' she said in an attempt at nonchalance that did not fool her mother.

Was he sleepy too? How delightful. 'That sounds wonderful,' Adelaide said, ensuring her voice lacked any inflections while her mind worked overtime. 'Did you have a nice run this morning?' she asked wickedly.

'I didn't run this morning.'

'Ah. Everyone deserves a lie-in on Sunday. We'll see you later, then. Don't bring anything. Your father brought a carload of food.' Which she had no idea how to keep cool as she didn't have room in her off-grid fridge.

She hung up, but the snicker that escaped attracted her husband's attention. 'What's the evil grin about?'

'I do not have an evil grin. And nothing. Riley's coming for lunch and bringing Konrad Grey, the local GP she's working for.'

Tyler paused in wiping as he dried a plate. 'She sees him socially?'

'Not much else to do around here,' Adelaide said, and then could've bitten the words back. 'Well, not for a young woman like Riley.' Or a city husband. There was lots for her to do, though. Like emptying all the old crockery and refilling the shelves with her favourite set from home. She couldn't wait to do that.

Tyler finished drying the old crockery and picked up the blanket that had ended up on a chair. He'd never been much help around the house, but maybe living on his own had broadened his skillset. She liked that idea and wondered how she'd never thought of it before. She'd assumed he would have hired a housekeeper when she didn't come back.

Already he'd moved their bed from the floor while she was in the shower. Pointedly, neither of them had discussed where he would sleep tonight.

'What do you do on a Sunday around here?'

'Normally, the same as I do Monday to Friday – clean tools and polish stone. Pottering, digging, noodling.'

'What's noodling?' He pretended to be jealous. 'Not canoodling, I hope?' He'd actually made a joke, an endearing trait he'd seemed to have lost over the years. He used to make her laugh every day when they'd first met.

She laughed. 'Noodling is fossicking. Sifting for small pieces of opal through the rock I bring up from the mine. The miners who owned this place before were after extra-special opals, not the fragments that lie everywhere. I'm finding some lovely pieces even if they're small. It's exciting when something shines under your fingers. Or a piece of chalky stone opens and shows colour that promises more. Sometimes it even hints at something spectacular.'

He was looking fondly at her, as if he'd missed her face. As if he'd missed *her*. 'I can see it would be.' He looked around. 'I know you don't have a TV, but do you have a radio?'

'No.' It had come quicker than she'd thought it would, but she shouldn't have been surprised. He was a news addict.

He frowned. 'How do you keep up with current events?'

'At the end of the week, we have a girls' night out. Friday-night ladies. If there's anything interesting, it'll come up in conversation. Otherwise,' she shrugged, 'I don't worry about it.'

Tyler's eyes almost crossed in horror and she laughed out loud. Still visibly appalled, he glanced to where his phone rested on the table. Then he blinked, as if remembering he'd prepared for this contingency. 'You do have internet.' There was strong relief in the words.

'It comes and goes but enough for you to notice if we go to war.' She shook her head at him. 'Would you like another cup of coffee?'

Riley and Konrad arrived at midday, and Adelaide twigged that her husband had been here for twenty-four hours without a television. That was a long time without visual media for him. There hadn't been one cross word between them. She hoped it stayed that way. She felt like a little fist pump might be in order.

They went out to meet their daughter and her escort. With luck, Josh had been replaced. There were lots of indications that Riley wouldn't continue that relationship if she'd been attracted so easily elsewhere. Her daughter had never been a two-timing woman and she must have been heart free to be with Konrad. Even short term, which was all it could be for now, this was excellent news.

He was such a good-looking young man, she didn't blame her daughter. 'It's so nice that you could come with Riley, Konrad.' She felt the presence at her shoulder. 'This is my husband, Tyler. Tyler, Dr Konrad Grey.'

The two men shook hands, Konrad towering over Tyler, which seemed to amuse Riley as she stepped forward and hugged her dad. 'Good to see you, Dad.'

All through the greetings outside, Adelaide couldn't help cataloguing the subtle differences in her daughter. Riley's cheeks were tinged pink and it wasn't make-up; there was just that trace of vulnerability she didn't usually see in her eyes, and her mouth seemed fuller, her eyes softer.

Konrad hovered at her elbow, vaguely protective in his stance, leaning just a little into Riley's space, and his eyes watched her face as if to ensure she was fine.

How unlike her daughter to allow a man that close. How delightful, and wonderful. Even if fleeting. Still, the last thing she wanted was to embarrass either of them, but yes indeedy, she suspected very strongly that they'd slept together.

Who would have thought, but she'd savour it all, later.

Chapter Forty-one

Konrad

Konrad watched the Brand family dynamics as those at the door began to file inside the little shack. The doting look Tyler Brand gave his daughter as he ushered her in front of him, as opposed to the slightly suspicious one he'd cast over his shoulder at Konrad, made his lips twitch. Daddy's little girl alright. He couldn't blame him. Princess Riley.

He remembered Adelaide's amusement when they'd come in the gate. He didn't doubt for a second that Riley's mother suspected there was something going on between her daughter and him. No flies on Adelaide. He doubted there'd ever been.

And his Riley – his, for the moment – hugging her dad, swinging her gaze between her dad and her mum, checking they were okay with each other. Like any daughter concerned about the parental relationship.

That was really why she was here in the Ridge, doing her thing. He'd figured that out. When she was sure they were fine, had reconnected, she'd head back to Sydney.

He wasn't sure if last night had been the best thing that had ever happened to him or the worst, because he knew it had imprinted on him in a permanent way. Tattooed onto his soul by Riley. He guessed he'd just have to wait and find out.

All he knew was Riley had absolutely blown him away last night. Through the night. And waking with her this morning had been incredible. Earth-shaking. Dangerously addictive.

Yesterday had been filled with cameos. Riley's paint brush racing him around the floor edges. Riley treating the burns at the pub. Riley using such delicate skill to break the news to Melinda. Many moments of drama packed into one day, but even that day finally ended. Through the door.

They'd suddenly found themselves rammed up against the wall in his room. Glued together. Starving. He closed his eyes at that memory and almost groaned.

Riley's totally unexpected hungry response and playfulness, along with something that was close to innocence in her lovemaking, had slid silver shackles into his soul and pulled on something that made him want to shield her from life. Protect her from pain. Hold her forever. A woman he'd known for a week. Which was insane because the woman was tough and ballsy and fiercely intelligent, all traits he decided he really, really admired but had never actually looked for in somebody he lusted after before.

That was the problem, of course. She was out of his league. The Sydney socialite specialist consultant, and he was a country doctor living in a remote town. They were absolute polar opposites.

'Are you coming in, Konrad?' Adelaide's kind, all-seeing eyes were focused on his face. He nodded, forced himself to grimace more than smile back and wondered what her family thought of him. He'd doubted he'd ever find that out, but that was for another day.

Inside, his eyes met Riley's across the room and she raised her brows in question. He flicked a finger to dismiss his wool-gathering and she nodded. She studied him and then inclined her head before looking away to answer something her father said.

How bizarre. They'd just had a silent conversation across the room with other people present. This was nuts for one night of connection, because basically they'd been bickering since she'd arrived.

'Would you like a cup of coffee?'

Adelaide's voice pulled him back to where he needed to be present. 'That would be great. Thanks.'

'Riley said your parents live in Port Macquarie?' Tyler had turned his way. He couldn't see much of Riley in him, not so for Adelaide. He saw so much of Riley in her mother – eyes, build and fine features – but Tyler was a confident and fit man in his late sixties, who had that aura of intellect that shone out of Riley.

'Yes, Dad's a GP and had a practice there. My sister works there now, instead.'

'So, he's retired?'

'Except for the occasional locum if it's somewhere he and Mum want to travel to. They're in Broome at the moment. He finds it hard to not work.'

'I get that. My wife's like that, but she has no problem deciding what to do.' Tyler's voice had come down a level, but there was pride in it, and the man glanced to where the two women were looking at a chalky rock, holding it to the light at the window.

Konrad said, 'It's easier for some to break the mould. We see a lot of people out here changing direction, discovering new adventures, or spiralling down when things don't go their way. It's a great place for fresh starts.'

'Is that what you're doing?'

No, he was doing the opposite, actually. Wallowing in guilt. 'I'm expanding my remote medical skills.'

'And are you? Expanding your skills, here?'

'This week I'm learning all about infertility and neonatal abnormalities.'

Riley must have heard his comment because she looked across at him, then touched her mother's arm. She said, 'Mum. You know how I asked if there was any chance of you working at the surgery after Mel leaves for her baby?'

Riley mentioned the concept last night and he'd jumped on the idea. Neither of them had any desire to be answering phones and making appointments while doing consultations.

Without her mother having time to answer, she went on. 'It turns out that Melinda has to go to Sydney for tests for her baby and I'm hoping to get her in on Tuesday.' She glanced at her father. 'I know Dad's here, but I don't suppose there's any chance of you doing four full days this week until Melinda comes back? I imagine she'll return here until she's thirty-eight weeks and then go to Sydney to wait for labour.'

'Pretty easy job interview.' Adelaide looked at Konrad. 'You're okay with that?'

'I'd be eternally grateful. Your daughter has the afternoons double-booked for the next three weeks.' It wasn't far from the truth. As the word had spread through the bush telegraph, more women had phoned to see Riley and she was fitting them in as best she could in the time that she had.

Adelaide looked at her husband and he shrugged. *Oops, Dad's not happy*, Konrad thought. Tyler shook his head with resignation and waved a hand. Not his decision, the hand said. The silent communication of an old married couple. He and Riley had just done that. Was that significant or not?

Adelaide had come to a decision. 'What would I need to do?'

Score. He wasn't letting the possibility pass if he could help it. 'Take the phone calls, enter patients in the medical software program and put in the appointments.'

'No practice nurse stuff?'

Riley laughed. 'We wish. We'd love you to, but you won't have time.'

Chapter Forty-two

Riley

As they drove away from the Wayfarers Inn, Riley checked her phone for messages and missed calls. They were out of service. It came and went. Today was a 'went' day. God she was full of food and tea . . . and guilt.

'I hope I didn't ruin everything by putting Mum in our secretary position as soon as Dad arrived.'

'Can't be helped. And it's not till Tuesday and it's short term.' Konrad glanced at her quickly. 'Hopefully, Melinda will be back before the end of the week. By the time she goes on maternity leave, your dad will have returned to Sydney or be settled here.'

'Yes, I get that. I hope so.' Konrad was certainly getting a heavy dose of her family in his face. He'd been wonderful. Sweet to Mum, not at all uncomfortable with her dad and so calm and confident. It had made things easy for her. 'What did you think of my dad?'

'He's a good guy,' he said carefully, then paused. 'You're a lot like your mother – determined, kind – but your dad I can't read as easily. But I do think he's as proud of your mum's choices as he is of you, which says a lot for him.'

Riley felt pleasure at his praise of the people she loved. And why? She'd never been needy like that. This place was getting to her. Turning her into something she wasn't – or maybe turning her into something she'd been hiding from. 'I'm proud of Mum, too. I think she's amazing for following her dreams.'

'I think *you're* amazing,' he said and his tone said he wasn't joking. A frisson of disquiet hit her. This was a fling – she'd told herself that. She shouldn't care so much what he thought.

She played it down. 'Thank you, kind sir.'

He turned his head her way as if picking something in her voice he wasn't sure about. Well, that made two of them. He returned his gaze to the road. 'Do you want to do a tourist run? See the artesian baths or opal fields?'

She wanted his bed, but no way was she saying that. Not out loud, at any rate. 'Not today. Though I'm keen to see the hot pools as I read an interesting article about the benefits for arthritis in artesian water. Maybe next weekend.'

'So, you want to just go back and take it easy?'

Something in his voice made her lips twitch. 'What's your definition of easy, Dr Grey?'

He shrugged those glorious shoulders and she felt instantly motivated to have him do that again. Stretch his shirt tight across his chest so she could imagine the play of skin under the fabric. Imagine her hands there. Her mouth.

This time when he turned his head, their eyes met. His were smoky and very, very interested. 'Oh, I don't know. A Sunday nap. Lying down. Tousled sheets.' He slanted her a wicked grin. 'I'm not presuming anything.'

'Nor am I,' she said primly, but her mouth felt dry. She

checked her phone again. One bar of service and four messages came in.

'Looks like when we get back there's no chance of naps.' Or anything else. 'The Friday-night ladies are coming in force before Melinda goes to Sydney. Greta wants to know if it's okay to hold the baby shower tonight? In the space between the units and the back of the surgery.'

Konrad's phone pinged four times as well.

Riley read more. 'Five o'clock okay for you, for the baby shower that is suddenly front and centre of our lives?'

'Can't think of anything I'd rather be doing,' he lied. She laughed. It really was funny but a little frustrating. Which was funny as well. 'Me either.'

By five-thirty, everyone had arrived, including Adelaide and Tyler. The ladies had created a whimsical streamer courtyard outside the door of Melinda's new unit with balloons and bunting, even if the underwire of the bunting looked like electric fence tape.

The balloons were blue and pink, and Gerry and Elsa were setting a long picnic table on the grass. Down one end were brightly wrapped presents, and down the other stood a punch-bowl, glasses and plates of finger food.

Konrad had opened up the empty unit as the visitor bathroom, and he and Tyler had moved the dining chairs and table outside, with a dozen chairs from the other units. They'd achieved a lot in a short amount of time, and the afternoon temperature had dropped to make a pleasant dusk.

As Riley stood with her mother, both shaking their heads

fondly at the determination of the ladies, she said, 'Goodness knows where they got the presents from.'

'Maybe someone dashed into Walgett, but surely nothing would be open on the weekend.' Adelaide shrugged. 'Gerry and Elsa's shop probably took a hammering. Elsa was there today to take Sunday sales for tonight. She had my baby travel bag already wrapped, and your father and I picked it up on the way. I'll buy more later when the baby is born.'

Riley was buying the bathroom bag and nighties. She'd have to order it online and get it posted out for next week. 'This place is crazy. And Mel looks remarkably calm considering she's the centre of attention.'

Melinda had been settled into one of the chairs. She looked pretty and very pregnant in the dress she'd had on yesterday. Her face held such a look of determination and she kept patting her belly like she was burping a baby.

'Greta's sitting beside her. That might help.'

'And Toby's here. He's probably responsible for the inflated balloons.'

Adelaide laughed. 'Unless Desiree blew them all up with her air hose at the service station.'

'And told anybody who wanted to pay for their petrol that they'd have to wait.' The thought made them both chuckle.

Chapter Forty-three

Melinda

Melinda stared out at the people surrounding her, women and men, some she barely knew. Why were they all here? For her? She didn't understand, but inside, in that cold, lonely place that had been ripped and torn by her mother's disinterest and her grand-father's loss and then later almost destroyed when she'd been held up, she could feel that place of belonging wriggling, regrow-ing, very slowly renewing. Becoming a restored and healthy place with hope again. Hope that she could be happy. Hope that she could do this. Hope that she and her baby could have a home and friends surrounding them.

These were things she hadn't expected to feel again. Maybe she'd been depressed and this was coming out of it. Healing. Or knowing about the baby, seeing her baby on the screen, was creating this change in her, which made a lot of sense with the maternal side she'd just discovered. The side that shouted she would do anything for her baby. She was someone who never shouted. Ever. But she would if needed. She still didn't understand why all these people cared. She'd done nothing for them.

'You okay?' Toby asked.

She realised she'd been staring, and felt the heat creep up her cheeks and her throat dry with embarrassment. 'Just a bit thirsty.' She had no idea why she said that out loud.

Toby shot out of the seat beside her and almost ran to the end of the table to pour her a glass of punch. He brought it back and handed it to her. 'It's non-alcoholic. You can't have alcohol with the baby, Mum said when she stirred the ingredients.'

'The things you know, Toby.' She felt more tension ease and suddenly it was easy to do. 'I'm not a drinker. I saw too much of that at the pub to want a part of it.'

He nodded sagely, thoughtfully, as he stared at the ground between his feet. 'Sometimes I drink too much because I'm scared. But it doesn't fix anything, it just makes it worse.' He looked up. 'You'll have your baby soon. Are you scared?'

She narrowed her eyes at him. Was he asking because her baby would look funny with its belly everywhere? Because her baby wasn't 'normal'? 'Scared of what?'

'Of the labour.' Toby's eyes were wide. 'Of pushing it out.' He shook his head in horror at the thought. 'Women are so brave.'

Melinda laughed. It wasn't about the baby's problem, then. She should have known that wasn't Toby. 'No. Half of the women here have done it. That's the least of my problems. I'm scared for my baby. That they can't fix its belly, and we have to have multiple operations instead of one. That we can't come home quickly.' She twisted the glass in her fingers. 'And I'm scared of going to Sydney on my own.' She lifted her chin. 'But I know I have to.'

'It's a big place,' Toby said, his head down as if remembering his time there. 'I went with Mum.'

She would manage. 'Riley had her secretary in Sydney email me the train and bus tickets and travel connections. Tomorrow I'll get a schedule for all the appointments. When I get there I'm to take taxis and pay with special vouchers.' She straightened her shoulders. 'I'm just going to believe everything will be fine.'

She glanced at Toby. He'd never appeared bored with her like the other boys had. It was always comfortable around him. 'Did you know they were going to do this tonight?'

'I heard Mum on the phone as soon as you told her about the tests.'

There were a lot of people here. A lot of noise and shifting of furniture. All for her. 'I hope Konrad doesn't mind.'

Toby snorted. 'He seems happy. I think he fancies Riley.' He peered back at her, slightly embarrassed. 'She said to call her that, yesterday, when we were painting.'

'Yes, she said.' Yesterday. Despite the results for her baby, it was still one of the best days of her life. 'I can't believe what you all did. The units look so beautiful, Toby, thank you for being a part of that.'

His neck tinged red and the obvious sign of his embarrassment reminded her that he had always been awkward. Sweet. Reliable. But easily embarrassed. She'd never embarrass him.

'Mum said you drove her car really well. And that you want to get your own?'

'Yeah, well.' *That's crashed and burned*, Melinda thought. 'I did. Now I have to save my money until after we come back from Sydney. Just to make sure I don't need it for the baby, or accommodation, or transport or other things that might happen.'

He nodded, understanding. He looked . . . impressed? With her? She felt a little of the pressure of all the responsibility ease for a moment. At least Toby understood that she needed to think about these things now and not just what she wanted.

'I'll keep an eye out, anyway,' he said. 'There's a bloke out on the Grawin fields with a little Barina, who wants one of those tiny utes like mine, instead. He's going to Sydney next month to look around. I reckon he'll sell it cheap to me if he finds one. It's dirty and nobody would want it like it is. I could clean it up for you, clean it properly for the baby, and save you money.'

She liked small cars. She liked Toby's kindness. She liked Toby. 'That sounds good. Let me know. I'll have more of an idea how much money I'll have left in a month's time. If it all works out, I can pay you an hourly rate to clean it.'

Toby frowned and opened his mouth, but she held up her hand. 'No argument.'

Chapter Forty-four

Adelaide

Monday afternoon came around quickly. Adelaide put on lipstick for her OPAL Medical Centre orientation. Melinda was leaving for Sydney tomorrow and would show her the computer programs for her new job as temporary receptionist.

Tyler had his arms crossed over his chest. 'Why on earth hadn't they been able to find someone else to do the job? Aren't you retired?' As if it was all about him, all comments that strangely made her more determined to help out her daughter.

'I'm still registered as a nurse, Tyler. Riley's only here for another few weeks. She needs clerical help to do her job.'

'You're not a receptionist.'

'No, but I'm sure I can be for a few weeks. Do you want to go and do it? You understand computer programs and customer relations.'

'No. Not likely.'

Now he just sounded grumpy. She hadn't missed this part at all, but she wasn't conciliatory Adelaide any more. 'You'll be fine. Take the pick down the mine. We can noodle the buckets tomorrow morning. You might make your fortune.'

'I already made my fortune with the company.' More huffing.

Adelaide smiled. 'Then find me an opal. I'd love to be rich from my claim. I'll bring home something delicious from Greta's café for dinner.'

She arrived in town before the afternoon clinic started at one and already there were two couples sitting in the waiting room. Even in the quick glance she gave them, she could see they were nervously hopeful. Her heart went out to them and she wondered how many outback couples had never asked for help because it meant leaving their stations unattended for days, even weeks.

Looking the surgery reception area over – it was peppermint like Melinda's new units – she decided the rooms looked friendly and unpretentious, much like Konrad, with space for ten chairs and a modern reception desk. Melinda already had a spare chair behind the desk, and the young woman stood and waved her towards another doorway.

'You can put your bag in here. It's the tearoom.'

She put her bag away and Melinda showed her the three-way bathroom with the sluice sink and the door leading into the observation room. 'The practice nurse did ECGs and dressings in there. It's used for emergencies.' She waved to the room next door to it. 'That's Konrad's consulting room.' The door stood open and appeared deserted. 'He's at lunch.' She gestured to the other side of the room. 'That's Riley's room. She doesn't usually have time for lunch.'

Her daughter's door was shut.

Melinda murmured quietly so the clients couldn't hear. 'I make her a cup of coffee and she drinks it around two while she's seeing the patients.'

Hmm. She'd bring her some food tomorrow. Protein that could be eaten easily.

'It's because she takes extras and hasn't turned anyone away.'

That sounded like Riley. Adelaide felt the swell of pride in the chest. 'She always said she wanted to make a difference to people's lives.' She sat down at the desk and looked at the computer. It had been a while since she'd touched a keyboard. 'Okay. Let's do this.'

Melinda settled awkwardly into the chair next to her, her big belly pushing her away from the desk so that she had to lean forward to touch things. Adelaide wondered that Melinda didn't have a sore neck or back. Or maybe she did and didn't complain. Yes, that seemed more likely.

'Have you used the software program for a doctor's surgery?' Melinda whispered.

'No,' she responded in a normal tone, letting her know it was okay to share that she was new at this. 'But I used the New South Wales Health software for the emergency department.'

Melinda nodded. 'It's probably similar. At least you'll under-stand all the medical terminology. I had to do an online course to learn that. Anyway, the program's pretty easy once you've done it a few times.' She ducked her head. 'I can do it.'

'Yes, but you're a smart, tech-savvy youngster,' Adelaide told her. 'And I bet you're a great teacher. What's this tab for?'

By the time they'd taken a few phone calls and Adelaide had entered the new data for each woman waiting to see Riley, she knew how to enter a name, check a date of birth and address for those just arriving and 'put them in the waiting room' on screen, so the doctors could see who was waiting.

Riley's door opened and she accompanied a large, hairy, tattooed man, who looked sheepish.

Riley said, 'Keep going with all you're doing, Cyrus. There is improvement. Your blood pressure will keep coming down.'

'Thanks, Doc.' He ducked his head in pleasure at the approval. 'I do feel better.'

'Good to hear. Make an appointment with my mother over there and Melinda, to see me in a week before I leave. I expect great things, Cyrus.' She turned to the couples waiting. 'I won't be long,' she told them, then disappeared into the bathroom.

Melinda heaved herself up faster than expected. 'I'll just make her a coffee.'

The man called Cyrus, a slightly hygiene-lacking behemoth, she noted as he came closer, gave Adelaide a friendly, tooth-deficient grin and put two brawny hands on the desk. 'I need an appointment.'

Adelaide was pleased at his enthusiasm to see her daughter again. 'She saved my life, you know,' the behemoth said. 'I didn't even know I had high blood pressure. The doc she sent me to said I was days away from a stroke.' He shook his head. 'You her mum? You must be proud.'

'I am.' Adelaide nodded as she found the screen for future appointments and searched for a morning one with Riley – there weren't many left – and added the man into the dialogue box.

'So,' he drawled, looking around the room, 'you livin' here?' As if she had a bed under one of the chairs.

She suppressed a grin. 'I bought the old Cooper camp.' She could hear the coffee machine and wondered if her daughter had brought her own. Somehow, she didn't think Konrad was the type to care if his instant coffee came from a tin.

'Cooper's, eh? Good little mine, that,' Cyrus said. 'Still got promise. Just watch that ladder. It's always been a bit dodgy.'

Adelaide wrote the appointment on the card and gave it to him, then gave him her full attention. 'Dodgy ladder?' And she'd sent Tyler down there this afternoon to dig. 'That's a bit of a worry.'

Cyrus waved his hand. 'Should be fine. Cooper didn't believe me and never had trouble, but I could go out and look at it if you like? See what it's up to?'

'My husband's out there at the moment.' It was good to get across the point that she wasn't alone. 'Maybe you could show him?'

'Sure. I'll do it on the way home. It's the least I can do for my doc's parents.' He took his appointment card and disappeared just as Riley came out of the ladies' room. In that time, Melinda had prepared a coffee and slipped into her office and put it on the desk.

Looking as fresh as an outback wildflower, Riley stopped at the door and looked at those waiting. 'Mr and Mrs Lawson?' A jeans-clad couple stood up. 'Come through, please.'

Melinda sat down again. 'How'd you go?'

Adelaide raised her brows in amazement. 'Okay, I think. You are a good teacher.' The phone rang and to her delight she managed to enter a woman without mucking up any of the details, then created an appointment despite the fact that there were none. She'd been shown how to shorten Riley's lunch hour until it was non-existent. She needed to talk to her daughter about that. But yes, she could do this.

Melinda said seriously, 'Don't enjoy it too much. I want my job back.'

Adelaide smothered a laugh. 'Retirement really is all it's cracked up to be. I'll be happy to stop as soon as you're ready.'

Melinda blushed. 'Sorry, that didn't sound polite.'

'Honesty has its own manners.'

The outside door opened and Konrad came in carrying a small brown paper bag. 'Hello, Adelaide.' He looked delighted to see her. That was nice. 'How's it going?'

'Fine. Melinda's a wonderful teacher.'

'Of course,' he said, as if he had no doubt. He inclined his head towards the other consulting room. 'Riley had lunch?'

Melinda said, 'No, but I've just taken her coffee.'

'Okay.' He nodded approvingly at his employee. 'Next time she comes out, hand her the sandwich. Tell her the boss said she has to eat,' he said to Adelaide before he disappeared into his room, and two seconds later he came out again and called a middle-aged man into his office and shut the door.

So, he cared if Riley ate. And actually did something about it. Now that was interesting.

Five pm seemed to come around fast, but she saw little of Riley. Apart from several brief appearances to farewell the last and invite in a new couple, her daughter spent the entire time locked in her rooms.

Konrad finished before Riley and left for a home visit to an older man who couldn't get out. He said he'd be back to see Riley.

Melinda showed Adelaide how to shut down the computer and close up for the night, and still Riley wasn't finished. There was no exchange of money because everyone was bulk-billed, including Riley's fertility clinic clients, and Adelaide applauded the service they provided, along with being impressed with the work ethics involved.

The phone seemed to never stop ringing. For a town of less than twenty-three hundred – though lots of people were not registered as they camped out of town and prospected – there seemed to be a need for both doctors, which made her wonder how Konrad managed when he was here alone.

The mornings looked especially busy, judging by the lack of appointment slots she had available for callers. Yet Riley seemed twice as busy in the afternoon.

As she finally drove home, Adelaide's shoulder ached just a little from the stress of working out new systems and working in a new role. Maybe Tyler was right. Perhaps she'd retired for a reason. Was she too old to work? She didn't think so. Just out of practice.

Odd how the idea of returning to permanent employment didn't seem so attractive now that she'd tried a day. She liked the idea of being free to come and go, work or rest as she wanted, and not having a boss other than herself. Working played havoc with that. Still. She'd said she'd do it for the next couple of weeks and she could manage that, but doubted she'd be looking for something long term.

She'd picked up a glorious-smelling risotto from Greta's that she'd ordered earlier and a bottle of white wine, but she suspected half a glass and she'd be asleep. That wouldn't make Tyler happy because he leaned towards night-owl body clock and there was nothing to do unless he'd changed his tune and would try reading a book.

Tyler looked in better spirits than when she'd left. He kissed her cheek and took the bottle from her. 'You have a shower and I'll set the table.'

'Who are you? And what have you done with my husband?' Tyler rolled his eyes. He'd never said that in Sydney, but she just grinned at him and went to stand in her bucket and relax under the hot water, for as long as the heat lasted. She was catching the wastewater for her few plants. And she felt she needed to revive herself so that she was ready for managing the reception desk all by herself tomorrow.

By the time she came out, she did feel more relaxed.

'That bloke you sent around . . . Cyrus. He was a card.'

'Ah, he came to check the ladder in the shaft. Is it okay?'

'It's fine. He put another bolt into the wood it hangs onto and used some wire at the bottom as well. He could talk under water, I reckon.'

'He seemed like a man's man.'

Tyler nodded, puffing up a little at her words as he dished out the risotto, which still steamed thanks to the insulated bag she'd brought it home in. Life was interesting without a microwave to reheat food. 'You know what he said?'

'No.' She sipped her wine and then took a forkful of the moist and flavoursome rice. 'What?'

'I dig in the ground, I get dirty, and I love it.' He laughed. 'He was full of fascinating stuff about the history of the opal fields and the characters who lived here.'

Adelaide stuffed her mouth with risotto to stop it yawning. She chewed, clenched her jaw and nodded with a plastered curve to her mouth. Tyler frowned but went on. 'He told me how he picked up his first bit of opal and was hooked. His stories were hilarious.'

And, she'd bet, risqué. She finished the last bite, sipped her wine and sat back, pleasantly relaxed. She couldn't help the yawn that followed.

Tyler sighed. 'You're tired.'

'I didn't sleep well last night.' She knew he had. He'd snored for most of it, though it wasn't quite as bad now that they had a little more room on the mattress. They'd bought an inflatable queen bed from the hardware store for while Tyler was here, and it was actually very comfortable. 'Would you mind if I lie down while you talk?' Maybe close her eyes. She could tell he was dying to tell her all about Cyrus, and she couldn't help another yawn as she climbed into their bed.

Tyler finished his meal and put the dishes in the sink. 'It's fine. We'll talk tomorrow. You crash and I'll go for a walk down the road before it gets too dark.'

He was jogging early in the morning and walking after dinner in the evenings when the weather was cooler. He had to stay fit, he said. She should get him shovelling the tailings.

She waved him off as her head hit the pillow and she barely felt the pressure on her cheek as she dropped into sleep.

Chapter Forty-five

Riley

Today had been a huge day in the clinic. Riley managed to avoid a conversation with Konrad by not stopping her patient stream. She couldn't help the avoidance tactics. Her mind was still grappling with the magnitude of the attraction between them and she needed to draw back to get a breath. To understand what had happened, she needed time.

Konrad wasn't going to give her time. She had the feeling he was going to pounce on her as soon as the office was empty, then he'd want to talk about all the things she didn't know what to say to, and she couldn't do it. The idea made her freeze in fear of what she'd agree to.

As soon as Melinda and her mother left, she eased open her consulting-room door, heart pounding ridiculously fast as she listened, and heard him on the phone in his office.

Yes, now. Quietly. She slipped out and half closed her door silently, so it looked like she was still in there without a patient, and she eased out of the back door like a wraith. She hoped like a wraith and not like a baby elephant.

But he didn't call after her. She eased her key into her unit, wriggled in and shut the door. This was ridiculous. But she couldn't help it. He'd done this to her.

The earth had moved on Saturday night and she was still quaking with the aftershocks. What she really needed was a fast, full-out run. It wasn't a metaphor for her state of mind needing to escape. Not at all. She just needed a release of her built-up tension.

After a rapid change of clothes, she headed for the carpark door and out the back. She glanced at her watch – it had taken her three minutes to escape.

She started with a slow jog, but her legs itched to move faster, so she increased her speed long before she had warmed up and broke into a run. And what was she running from? Lust. Want. Desire. She knew she'd fallen for the outback doc. She might even love Konrad.

Riley sped along Harlequin Street, crossed Opal Street and headed all the way to Gem Street, where she turned towards the racecourse out of town at a fast clip. He didn't run this way that she knew of. Neither did she, really, except she'd driven down here once to see the outside of the cactus nursery and the walk-in mine. She didn't need to see a mine because she could just go to her mum's. Some of the tension eased at the thought. She could talk to her mum about all this.

The houses disappeared and she was back to dirt and gravel and realised she'd come a couple of kilometres and it would be a fair way back into town. A small rise beckoned ahead to the left and promised a possible view which would be nice to see, then she'd turn around.

As she cut across the corner of one of the mining fields, some-thing caught her shoe, something solid – a brick or a lip – and it pitched her off balance. Her other foot tangled in a wire square which shifted sideways, and she knew she was going to fall. And that it was going to hurt.

She put her hands out, expecting to faceplant. Except she only touched the edge of something that crumbled under her hand and then she was falling, cool air against her face as she tumbled, scraping a wall as she fell, and her mind screamed, *A mine shaft!*

She was going to die.

Riley woke in the dark, knowing that something was wrong. Something had happened. She groaned at the pain in her body, and oddly, the moaning sound that escaped her lips seemed to echo.

Her pounding head fought with the throbbing in her leg and shoulder, and her whole body ached as she lay in an awkward frog-like position on what felt like sharp and shattered rocks.

Nothing was familiar. She couldn't think clearly. She could barely think at all.

Darkness pushed in at her like tar, but she slitted her eyes open. She forced them wider, but still there was no light. Her tongue caught fine gravel on her lips and her mouth clogged stickily as small, jagged rocks dropped from her cheek when she dragged her hand across the roughness to her mouth.

Gravel on her cheek didn't make sense and she tried to figure out the situation.

She eased herself to a sitting position and her head spun as nausea rose. She retched but nothing came up. Concussion?

Had she been knocked out? Her head was pounding, so that made sense. Had she fallen somewhere?

Once semi-upright, a feat achieved in micro increments over a long period, she slid her hand behind her hip and felt a rough wall against her aching back. Easing her pained ankle straight, she carefully pushed her legs across more rough gravel until her running shoes touched another wall. The wall was curved, a circle maybe, narrow. She tilted her head to look up.

Nausea swirled and she hurriedly closed her eyes. Resting her head back against the rough wall, she breathed noisily in and out through her mouth until she didn't want to gag. When she could open her eyes again and look up, through a tunnel of blackness, stars twinkled and dotted the dark sky. A long way away.

Ah. Idiot. She closed her eyes as the memories rushed in like a broken pipe washing through her, sweeping in clarity.

She'd gone for a run, avoiding Konrad. Not ready to face him, she'd taken herself for an evening run without food or drink. And stupidly cut across the corner of one of the mining fields.

Now she remembered tripping on a brick, or something solid – maybe a concrete lip? – then her foot catching on a sheet of reinforced wire and pushing it sideways, then falling forward down a shaft.

Holy heck, I'm at the bottom of a mine shaft.

Nobody knew she'd gone for a run. And she had no idea how long she'd been here. More than a couple of hours knocked out, anyway, because it was dark, which wasn't good. It was lucky she'd woken up at all.

She felt for her phone in her tight pocket, but when she slid her hand in, the crunch and stab of glass made her pull hastily out. She hitched her long sleeve over her fingers and eased the mangled metal and glass out in pieces, trying not to cut herself. Gingerly running her fingers over the damage in the dark, she tried the side of the screen left of her phone, but no light came on. There was no screen. It was completely smashed. Her head swam and the desire to do anything faded away. She'd look again when morning arrived.

Her mouth was so dry she had to be dehydrated, and her head pounded as if chisels were being hammered into it. But she was alive, which was good. But she'd be here for a while unless someone found her. Why hadn't she told anyone she was running? That was incredibly dumb.

Tentatively, she began a careful pat and finger slide of her extremities. Her shoulder felt wrenched, and she vaguely remembered grabbing onto something as she fell, so maybe she'd broken her fall a bit with that. She'd obviously hit her head on the way down, which was making it hard to focus.

Perhaps it was a good thing it was dark because she had the feeling that light would hurt her eyes. She gently dabbed at the bump on her temple where she must have hit. *Ouch*. Her fingers pulled away, then skittered back to feel again. It was a bump indeed but not bleeding. More slow, deep breathing was required. Eventually, the pain settled as she stayed still.

She established that her knees were scraped. Her lower leg on the right side was fine, but the left ankle . . . painful. Her hand skimmed and searched but couldn't feel any deformity. Then again, she hadn't moved anywhere much. If she hadn't broken anything she was very, very lucky.

She remembered reading about a young, local woman who'd fallen down a shaft somewhere out of town a few years ago, who hadn't been found for seventy-two hours. That girl hadn't broken anything either, so Riley wasn't special. But she wasn't planning on spending that long down here. And she had read about the dead man.

Her huffing groan sounded like a raspy croak and she thought again how dry her mouth was. She'd been here for more than a few hours and it was unlikely that anyone would look for her until morning when she didn't turn up for work.

What if she had a slow-leaking brain injury? She could be dead by morning.

No sounds filtered down here. Nobody worked the opal fields in the dark, which she guessed was lucky as she couldn't have called out to save herself. Well, she could, but it would hurt in a hundred ways.

At least Konrad had a key to her unit, so hopefully he'd see that she hadn't slept there and start looking for her. He was an efficient guy. Smart. Perhaps invested in finding her. Which was what had got her into this position in the first place. She closed her eyes and sleep was easy to find. Too easy.

Chapter Forty-six

Konrad

Konrad came back from a home visit and fiddled with odd jobs in his office, waiting for Riley to finish her last patient, but he must've looked away because she'd slipped out before he noticed her door was open.

She hadn't said anything, which was odd. Almost as if she was avoiding him. Very like that. And why?

Adelaide and Melinda had already left, so he locked the back door after checking there was no one in the building and pushed open the common-unit door – the lounge and kitchen were empty of noise and movement, except for the humming of the refrigerator.

He pulled the door shut and stared at Riley's closed door. He'd thought a few times that she'd been avoiding him today, but he'd told himself not to be ridiculous, that she was just busy. Crazy busy. The problem was, they hadn't exchanged a word since Sunday night when she'd laughingly said, 'Thanks for the incredible weekend. Back to business tomorrow.' He'd thought she was joking, but maybe she wasn't? Irritation and something else, surely not hurt, slid along his nerves and he pushed it away and rapped on her door.

When she didn't answer, he glared at the door in lieu of glaring at Riley. He wasn't used to this awkwardness, this itchiness, this inability to settle.

He didn't like it.

He checked out the front. Her car was there, so he decided she must've gone for a run. Maybe her parents had arranged dinner and he'd missed it. Not that he had any right to be included in family conversations, but it would have been nice to have been included.

On that thought, he took his stupid self off to Greta's for dinner and went to bed early.

The next morning, Konrad headed across to the surgery early so she couldn't slip into the rooms without him seeing. He made himself a coffee with her coffee machine, and once he got to the sipping part, admitted it was much, much better than his usual.

By the time he'd rinsed out the milk container and cleaned the tamping plate, Adelaide was there. Not Riley.

He forced a welcome. 'Good morning.' He saw again the likeness of Riley to her mother. They were both striking women, and resourceful. 'All ready for a big day?'

'I'll be fine.' She laughed. 'But I went to sleep as soon as I got home last night. Must be getting old.'

'Never.' But his thoughts zeroed in on the words. Riley didn't visit her parents as he'd thought. So where did she go? Where was there to go?

'Riley not here yet?'

'It's not often I beat her in.' He held up his cup. 'Want one of Riley's coffees?'

At eight-thirty am, Konrad called in his first patient, but his attention stayed fixed on the open door across from him.

Riley wasn't in yet. She should be. There were already two women waiting for her.

His patient shuffled past where he stood at the open door and sat on the client chair, and reluctantly, Konrad shut the door. Riley hadn't been late once since she'd arrived. Was he was over-reacting? She could be stuck on a phone call.

'Hello, good to see you, Jim,' he said to his elderly client, but he couldn't carry on. 'Can you just give me a second?' At the man's nod he said, 'Thanks,' and picked up his phone.

'Adelaide? Can you give Riley a ring and ask if she's okay?' At his new receptionist's fervent yes, he thanked her and hung up.

He forced his attention to Jim and listened while his old mate talked about the aches in his bones and the flare-up of arthritis in his fingers. He thought about Riley's interest in the hot pools down the road and the medicinal benefits. 'Tell me, Jim, when was the last time you took yourself across to the artesian baths?'

Jim snorted. 'That's for tourists.'

'Come on, that's not true. Lots of locals go.'

Jim harrumphed.

'Mineral springs are really, really good for arthritis, mate. They're good for a lot of things. It might even bring your blood pressure down. You should give it a go.'

Jim screwed up his face. 'Get away, Doc. I'll catch a disease from there.'

You have a disease – arthritis, he told him silently. 'I haven't heard of catching things, the water changes all the time,' he said mildly. 'But,' he leaned forward, 'as your doctor, I suggest you try it. You came here for help, so I'm giving you my doctor's advice. Take yourself across to the pools. Every morning or evening, whichever one suits you, or both. Climb in, stay for ten to fifteen minutes. You know the baths are open twenty-two hours a day. It's free entry.'

Jim grumbled a curse. 'I'd look like an idiot in me budgie smugglers.'

Konrad held back the grin and tried to block the mental picture of Jim's skinny legs and his no doubt perished Speedo-style bathers with the budgie-shaped bulge at the front. *Crikey, no.*

'Give it the rest of the week and the weekend. You make another appointment next Monday and I want to hear how you went. I think you'll be surprised.' And why hadn't he suggested this before? Maybe, after she'd turned up to work, he'd ask Riley if she'd like to go across tonight and they could try it together. Then his disquiet crashed in and he looked at the phone, willing it to ring and say she was here.

Jim wrinkled his nose. 'So, you haven't got a different pill for me to try?'

Konrad blinked at him and then looked at the open medical file document on his screen, which listed all the medications he'd trialled with Jim to give him some comfort. 'Just give the hot pools a go for a week. There are lots of minerals and the heat will certainly help. If you have breakthrough pain after your dip, take one of those last pills that I gave you. And less red wine might help.'

'Jeez, Doc, you're turning into a goody-goody.'

'Do you want to get rid of the pain, Jim?'

The grizzly man nodded, groaned, then pulled another face.

'A week of soaking and I'll see you Monday.' Konrad stood up.

Jim heaved himself to his feet with a long-suffering sigh. 'Okay, but if I get one of them vulnerable diseases on me old fella it'll be your fault.'

Vulnerable? Ah, *venereal*. 'It won't happen.' It was extremely unlikely, he reassured himself, and opened the door.

The entry across from him stood open into Riley's rooms and the same women were still waiting. His eyes met Adelaide's worried ones and he touched his pocket for his keys. Pulling them out, he showed her and she nodded. Jim walked to the desk and Konrad slipped out the back door. He strode fast across the short open area to the units and knocked on her door. As he'd almost expected, there was no answer, so he unlocked the door and pushed it open slowly.

'Riley?' He put his head around the crack. 'You there, Riley?' He could tell it was empty – that it had been empty for a while – because there was no smell of soap or shampoo or Riley.

He looked to the wardrobe in the corner, crossed the room and did a quick search for her joggers under the bed and around the room. They weren't there. Had she gone for a run early and was sitting somewhere with a twisted ankle? Though why wouldn't she ring?

Unease spiralled down his neck and he saw the phone charger but the phone was gone. She had her phone. He pulled out his own mobile and tried her number, only to get the answering machine.

When had he seen her last? When had anyone seen her last? What time?

He glanced back at the bed. Did she remake her bed every day? He didn't know. She'd helped him make his.

Pain sliced through him. What if she hadn't slept in it and had been out all night. Hurt. Alone. Waiting for someone to find her.

Waiting for him to find her.

He hadn't found his brother in time.

Konrad spun and headed next door to knock on Melinda's room until he remembered she'd caught the five-fifty am bus to Walgett, connecting with the train to Sydney, and wouldn't be back for three days.

He spun back to the rooms and took a big breath before he touched the flat surface between him and the few patients inside. Pushing open the door, he looked directly at Adelaide.

'She's not there,' he said. 'Her sneakers and phone are gone. I'm thinking she might have twisted her ankle somewhere and maybe broken her phone.' His voice sounded calm, in control, capable of sorting out this little problem, which was remarkable and a total lie. He turned to the patients waiting for them both and forced a smile.

'I'm so sorry. We seem to have misplaced Dr Brand, who is normally on time. I'll be tied up this morning while we find her. Can you phone back after lunch and we'll prioritise your new appointment as soon as we can?' Sensible, stable, but he was far from calm inside.

'Of course.' Both women waiting for Riley stood, looked at each other and then at Adelaide. 'We'll go have coffee and if you don't ring us by the time we're finished, we'll call again this afternoon.'

'Perfect.' Konrad opened the door for them. 'Adelaide will make appointments for you then.'

They hurried away, no doubt to share the news that the doctor was missing with the patrons of the coffee shop, but he couldn't help that. It could be a good thing. Maybe someone would remember seeing Riley.

The other two patients he'd been going to see stood also. 'Sorry,' he said to them, but they waved that away.

'Hope you find the doc soon.'

So did he.

The moment the door was shut on them all, Konrad asked, 'Have you got any ideas where she could possibly go?'

'I'll get my husband to drive around the streets in case she's had a fall. Between here and my place, I suppose, is as good a trail to start as any.'

'Great idea.' His eyes met Adelaide's. 'She doesn't usually go off road, does she?'

'Not that I know of. He'll find her. There's nowhere else. You're right. She must've broken her phone.' Adelaide's tone sounded as worried as the thoughts that skittered inside his head.

'I'll get some people looking and we'll start driving around. With your husband as well, we can cover the town fairly fast.'

'Yes. It shouldn't be hard to find her.' Familiar green eyes searched his. 'But shouldn't somebody have come across her by now, if she's hurt?'

They both glanced at the clock. Eight forty-five. 'School mothers are out and about,' he said. 'Most of the tourists are up. Someone will come across her soon.' He didn't want to think about the similarities to when he'd lost his brother. 'If we haven't found her in the next fifteen minutes, I'll ring the police for help.'

'I agree.' Adelaide lifted her own mobile. 'I'll ring Tyler, and then all the other patients.'

He thought about the logistics. 'Close the surgery until after lunch. In fact, cancel all of Riley's outreach patients for this afternoon. Try to get them before they leave home. The most distant ones first.'

'I'll do that.' She lifted the phone to her ear and he heard her speaking as he went to his own room to make calls. 'Tyler. I need you to drive around and look for Riley.' He heard her explaining the situation, giving Tyler the absolute best-case scenario. Anything else didn't bear thinking about. He needed to stop comparing her with William.

Konrad shuddered and decided to ask the miners for help. He'd get Cyrus to round up some men. He'd be motivated and persuasive. Konrad knew in his gut they'd have to start looking in mine shafts because that's where people disappeared to.

Some had even died.

There were hundreds of shafts, but all of them should be covered by mesh or fences. Except, it wasn't until the 1980s that the law said old, unused shafts had to be filled in. There were miles of them, scattered everywhere.

Chapter Forty-seven

Adelaide

Adelaide's heart thumped in her chest as she made each call to cancel appointments, forcing herself to sound calm. A calm she didn't feel. A calm that shuddered and shook even while her voice remained level. 'The doctor is unwell today. I'll reschedule the appointment sometime this afternoon or tomorrow morning as soon as we know when she can come back. Thank you. We apologise for the inconvenience.'

Konrad swept out of his room jiggling his keys. 'I'm leaving. You can shut the surgery.' He waved his hand in that direction. 'When you've contacted everyone, put the CLOSED sign up. I'm happy for you to make a short recording for the answering machine to say the clinic is temporarily unattended. They can leave a number for you to get back to them when we've found Riley.'

He stopped and met her eyes. 'I will find her, Adelaide.'

Some of the horrid fear did ease a fraction. She believed he'd do everything in his power to do so. 'Good. Let me know when you do.' She'd stay here anyway. In case Riley came back.

Unsmiling, he nodded and left.

Adelaide phoned the next patient, time and again. Twelve times, to be exact. Everybody was extremely easy to get along with, which was lucky, not something she expected but was very grateful for.

Tyler had phoned after driving around town and had nothing positive to add. He was still driving. Konrad had notified the police, who were spreading the search wider. It wasn't like Riley to be careless, and worry gnawed at her throat. She wanted to be in the car driving, searching. Be there when they found her. But she couldn't go. She had to stay here and man the phones and prepare for later. When they found her – not if!

What had happened to Riley? What could've happened? She couldn't have been attacked and hurt. Abducted. Killed. *No.* She closed her eyes and prayed.

This panic was silly. She had to believe that Riley was fine, slightly hurt somewhere. They'd only been sure she was missing for less than an hour, so surely she'd turn up soon. The clock said nine forty-five.

An hour of worry. She couldn't imagine how families with missing loved ones did this for days, weeks, years. She suspected today could be the longest day of her life until her daughter came home.

Chapter Forty-eight

Riley

When Riley woke up again, she'd ended up lying concertinaed, knees sideways, on her back, staring upwards. She must have slid down the wall and shifted in her sleep. Sleep. Right. Semi-comatose state was more like it.

At least from here she could see there was a circle of light at the top of the shaft. It was morning. She hoped it wasn't the afternoon. So much for all the rushing around she'd done all her life, always on a mission. There was no mission down here. Nothing here at all. Not even a ladder.

Enough of that light was shining down to show her the broken pole leading out of the shaft, near the top. It was too far to reach.

So. This wasn't like her mum's shaft, and there was no steel ladder secured to the wall like a swimming-pool exit. Not that she felt strong enough to pull herself out of here just yet, even if her brain had woken clearer. But there was something reassuring about the small, lighted window to the outside world above her head.

She eased herself back up into a sitting position, taking time out to wait for the head spins to stop at each part of the journey, like a rock climber with vertigo. The shaft had been made in a narrow circle, about a metre across, with horizontal lines etched in the rock and what looked like some footholds chipped into the walls. Unfortunately, they weren't footholds she fancied using. Not when they were more likely to send her straight back down again.

It was as if someone had drawn a circle on the ground and dug six inches through all the rocks, looking for opals in the tailings. Then they'd dug another six inches, looked through all the rocks, and dug another six inches until they decided to dig somewhere else. The shaft seemed at least ten metres deep, maybe fifteen if she was unlucky. But it was time to be proactive, even if she wanted to just curl up and go to 'sleep' again.

It was daylight, prime rescuer time. The only chance that someone could hear if she called out. Riley forced her drooping head to lift. She should be panicked and screaming to get out, but the strange lethargy that held her sucked away all her energy.

No. She had to get out now. She pursed her lips and called as loudly as she could. The soft cheep of her voice calling for help sounded like a gentle . . . 'elp'. Great. She was so dry she could barely make any noise at all. She tried again, and this time the full word came out. 'Help.' But she doubted it would have risen a metre above her head, let alone ten.

She turned her gaze to the shattered screen of the electronic lifeline that was her phone, and in the dim light she doubted any jiggling, wiggling or pushing parts was going to make a call happen. Assuming there was a signal ten metres down in a hole. *Note to self: buy a shockproof phone case for the future.*

'Okay. Stop being defeatist,' she muttered. She couldn't type a message – she had no idea where the keyboard keys were without a screen – but she could hold the side buttons together and an emergency noise would happen. She hoped.

With trembling fingers, she squeezed both the volume key and the on-off buttons on the sides of the phone. Five times. On the fifth squeeze the phone made three spaced, wailing-siren screams that made her jump and then smile.

It was way louder than her tiny cheep of help. She'd always understood that if she didn't cancel the warning wails, then it would automatically send a distress signal to emergency services. She'd actually done something useful to save herself. About time.

'Help,' she croaked. With the pounding in her head, it would be incredibly easy just to close her eyes and wait for a miracle, but even miracles needed effort. She pulled herself to a wobbly stand and held up her arm, which took the noise closer to the surface. 'Help.'

Riley pressed the buttons again, five times. After the third wail, she sank back against the walls and slid down to a crouch, keeping her weight off her ankle, and waited. What a shame she hadn't thought of this last night.

Chapter Forty-nine

Konrad

By lunchtime, Konrad's frustration and dread threatened to swallow him like one of those empty shafts out here. Adelaide's hopeful look tore at his heart every time he came back to check that Riley hadn't returned. Tyler's gruff, 'Anything?' when he spoke to him made him wince.

His last call to the police had said there were close to fifty searchers and the search dogs would arrive this afternoon. He needed to do something more physical than driving. He'd driven slowly and thoroughly all over town, searching for an injured runner, driven all the streets a dozen times – more than a dozen – and the police had brought in a drone which would fly until night, circling and checking the opal fields in widening loops looking for someone injured and helpless.

He'd slipped into running shoes and shorts, and for the last hour he'd been jogging down the back streets on the outskirts of town, peering into backyards, leaning over fences and checking behind vehicles. His eyes were constantly scanning for a figure low to the ground, injured, ill, unconscious.

Had she had a stroke, aneurysm, or had some unknown congenital time bomb in her body silently taken her down? Could she have been attacked? Kidnapped? Neither were something that commonly happened in the town, but they were still possible.

No. Not Riley, his mind screamed.

He ran on, further out of town, towards the wide stretches of old workings, the more deserted sections, his trainer soles slapping the dirt now, off the tar. Would she run down here?

He took the edge of the fields at a slow jog when he heard the noise. Strange, like a distant siren wail. Three short blasts that made him stop and try to figure out which direction it came from.

The breeze brushed hair into his eyes and he swiped it away urgently, unblinking as he turned slowly. And waited, his heart pounding.

Then it came again. Distant, yet not. *Wail. Wail. Wail.* He realised what it was. The emergency alert from a phone.

Riley.

He spun in the direction of the noise, searching out over the white heaps of podge, men in the distance, and the whine of the drone somewhere behind him in the sky. His eyes scanned as he began walking carefully through the deserted field. They'd checked all this earlier, when he'd been with Cyrus, and they'd heard nothing. And they had called out repeatedly.

Every twenty feet or so, another deserted shaft lay fenced or covered or half filled. Some shallow, some deeper, all with piles of discarded white rocks like a moonscape in mounds.

The muffled alert came again and this time he followed it to the source. A shaft with the reinforced net half pushed aside, barely covering the concrete lip above it. Was it coming from there?

He eased down on his knees and leaned over the lip of white concrete that protected the edges of the shaft and peered down. It was dark, but the sun was high and shining almost directly inside.

'Riley?'

Something shifted slightly and his breath caught. 'Riley?' he called again.

'Konrad?' The voice was weak, barely a whisper, but he heard her. In the distance, he could hear sirens.

'Thank God,' his voice almost growled with the relief. 'You okay?'

'You're late.' Two words, scolding in a thin, cracked voice.

His throat closed and he wanted to climb down and hug her. 'Hey, I found you. The emergency SOS worked. It would've been good if you'd used it earlier.'

She made a noise. He wasn't sure if it was a laugh or a sob. A police car, ambulance and of all things, a fire truck, were racing towards him. At least they'd have ladders.

Chapter Fifty

Adelaide

Adelaide sat at the reception desk with Tyler at her side, the heat of his body jammed up against her. His chair couldn't get any closer and at least he made her feel less cold, but his presence didn't take away the fear or trepidation.

He'd brought her lunch but really he wanted to check that she was okay, and she was so glad he had. This was what forty years of sharing time was about. In tough situations, partners in life understood each other, understood without words. They shared the pain and the worry, and comprehended because they pooled the moments that changed a person.

On the desk, her mobile phone rang. She almost dropped it in her haste to pick it up and Tyler steadied her fingers with his. She used both hands to hold the phone to her ear. 'Hello? Konrad? Have you found her?'

'Yes. She's alive.'

'Thank God.' The words were a whisper from her dry lips, and her own relief was mirrored in Tyler's gaze, which was fixed on hers. She pressed the loudspeaker so Tyler could hear. 'Where?'

'She fell down a deserted shaft out of town. Hit her head. She's woozy, but she was able to press the emergency SOS buttons on her phone.'

Not unconscious, then. 'Thank God,' she said again as her shoulders sagged and Tyler's arm went around her. She leaned back against him and closed her eyes.

Konrad went on. 'I'm taking her to the emergency centre and we'll check her out there. To see if she needs to be transferred anywhere.'

'I'll meet you there,' she said, thankful she'd made the recording earlier for the surgery. She doubted she could make sense now if she had to do it again. She switched the surgery phone over to the answering machine before anyone else could call.

'I'll tell them you're coming.' He hung up.

She disentangled Tyler and her freed hand stretched blindly for her bag. It wasn't there.

'Here,' Tyler said, passing her bag across. 'You put it in the drawer.'

Adelaide huffed out a breath. She needed to calm down. 'Thank you.' Her voice sounded strange, and together they locked up and climbed into Tyler's car. Adelaide was thankful she didn't have to drive. It seemed when her own daughter was the one involved in a medical emergency, she wasn't collected and professional at all.

When they arrived outside the small building, parking was limited, what with the ambulance, half-a-dozen private cars, a police vehicle and even a fire engine outside.

'Fire in the hole?' Tyler's poor attempt at a joke made her grimace, but she patted his arm.

He shrugged. 'Sorry. Stupid comment.'

She could see the strain etched in his face like someone had taken a biro to the lines of his forehead and the sides of his mouth. Deep, dark lines of dreadful worry standing out.

'Funny man. Let's get inside and see our daughter.'

He took her hand and his fingers squeezed hers, warm and strong, but with an almost imperceptible shake. They walked in hand in hand, united in concern and love for their grown woman child.

She passed Cyrus, who said, 'We found her,' and she could see his relief. Sweet, smelly man.

She passed the policeman who had pulled her over once when she'd first come to town to check the width of her tyres. She'd thought him a pain then, but if he'd been out looking for her daughter, he was a saint now. She smiled at him, and the fire-brigade officer talking to a paramedic. All these people were here to help. They all earned a smile from this grateful mother.

The receptionist stood up and directed them through a closed door without asking – Konrad must have passed on the message – and into a room that seemed full of people.

On second glance, there were only four. And Riley.

It wasn't a big room, only a little larger than the observation room at the doctor's surgery, and Riley lay in the centre on an examination table with blankets pulled up around her. An efficient-looking woman, who nodded when they came in, returned to unobtrusively placing cardiac monitor leads to Riley's chest under the blanket.

Riley turned her head and their eyes met. Hers were a little unfocused. 'Hi, Mum. Dad. Sorry for the worry.'

Adelaide, calm Adelaide, turned her face into her husband's broad chest and silently wept.

Chapter Fifty-one

Riley

The nurse finished clipping the last lead onto the dots on her skin and Riley tried to focus on the concerned people in the room. She'd caused a major incident and she cringed at the attention, wishing she could crawl away and lick her wounds in private. But she knew she couldn't.

She'd be infamous in town now. 'The Doctor That Fell Down the Hole'. It sounded like a children's book warning kiddies to be careful. Warning *her* to be more careful. Squirm.

Her parents were hugging. At least that was one good thing out of it. Better than none.

Konrad hovered, his hip against the bed, studying her vital signs on the monitor. He hadn't been more than a foot away from her since they'd winched her up from the shaft.

The first glint of that ladder easing down beside her had been a wonderful sight. Konrad climbing down had been so much better, even if it had been very tight quarters in the shaft. His big hands had cradled her face gently when he whispered, 'Thank God you're safe.' Then he'd given her a quick visual assessment and looked up. 'Pull out the ladder. We'll need the winch.'

She'd whispered, 'You can tell that just by looking at me?'

His voice had been grim. 'Yes.'

She knew then she'd been lucky to get out alive.

At least now she felt a lot better than when she'd first been wheeled in, but the thumping head still felt like a pick-axe sledge-hammering away at her brain.

Konrad was saying to her parents, 'We don't think her ankle is broken, but we'll X-ray it soon. She needs to be transferred to Moree for a brain CT. I want the computerised topography to rule out a cerebral haemorrhage. She had a prolonged blackout, which is never a good thing. They might want to keep her in. With that, and her spending the night in the shaft, she needs observation, but she's not keen.'

The nurse said, 'Doctors make the worst patients.' She winked when she said it, then inclined her head at Konrad. 'He said he's going with her.' Her tone said doctors make the worst concerned friends, as well.

The last thing Riley wanted to do was spend three hours swaying in the back of an ambulance, but she didn't want to end up with a subdural haematoma, either. Tiredly, she said, 'When do I go?'

'As soon as the next ambulance is free. I'll go with you.'

She thought of all the infertile couples who had driven hours to get to her. 'What about the clinic?'

'Your mother's contacted everyone. She's doing a splendid job. We'll sort it all out next week with your ladies when you're up to it.'

She closed her eyes again, hoping that the persistent opal miner in her head would stop with the pick-axe. She wanted to just leave it all in Konrad's hands, or her parents', which was so unlike her. Maybe she did have a brain injury. Normally, she wouldn't let anybody do anything for her, but she was too tired to worry about it now.

The trip to Moree in the ambulance passed more quickly than she expected it would. Konrad held her hand, checked her pulse and her pupils. She slept between the observation checks, feeling safe. If it had been Josh cosseting her, she'd probably have been annoyed by his solicitous attention, but no-nonsense Konrad made her think the babysitting was fine.

He'd said her parents were following the ambulance, Mum in her dad's car, Dad in Konrad's, so he could get home once the ambulance left. Everything would be sorted.

An hour after arrival, the CT of her brain suggested she had marked swelling of the brain but not bleeding. In other words, a severe concussion.

Four hours later, with her ankle bandaged and her shoulder strapped, she limped out of the hospital with Konrad holding her good arm as he directed her to his car.

He drove silently for too long, after he pulled away from the hospital.

Riley prompted him. 'Sooo. I guess I was pretty lucky,' she said.

His knuckles whitened on the wheel, but he didn't say anything.

She poked his shoulder. 'You there?'

Eventually, he said, 'Yes.'

'You okay?'

His breath hissed out and he stretched his fingers as if they were cramped and then regripped the wheel. She suspected he'd been somewhere not good in his head. 'A lot better than I would be if we hadn't found you.'

Ah. A bad place. Worst-case scenario. 'I need to say thanks for that. You found me.'

He shook his head. 'You spent the night there and could have died. And in the daylight, you saved yourself with the emergency tracker.'

'But, my dear, dear friend Konrad, you were out jogging the streets looking for me. You found me first.'

He smiled at that, but it didn't look like he found it an easy thing to do. 'Lots of people were out and about looking for you.'

'Hearing your voice was the best part of my day.'

'Ditto,' he said. 'I've been pretty bossy since we found you. Sorry about that.'

She waved that away. 'You're always bossy.'

He laughed. 'I can see you're feeling better.'

'I am. The guy, I called him Cyrus, who's thumping in my head has receded to a mild tap with his pick.'

'Good to hear. I won't be offering you any wine for a few days.'

'Fine by me. Are you sure I can't work tomorrow?'

'Are you asking me to be bossy again?' His tone was amused. 'Because I can be.' He flicked her a look. 'And no. You've had a severe concussion. Let's leave it till Monday. Then gradually increasing activity through next week until we both agree you're ready to take on your patients. Then half days. We can shift all your morning GP appointments to me. Just do your patients. I'll be fine.'

'That makes you too busy.'

'I can still take the urgent ones. The patients who can be will be put back a bit. They'll still be seen.'

She knew she wasn't up to working for a few days. Her brain wasn't clear enough and the last thing she needed to do was to make mistakes. Her clients needed a doctor with sharp focus. 'Okay. Monday sounds good. Full-day clinics. Though I might do Friday afternoon in my office so I don't get lost in the pathology. Maybe see a couple of locals.'

He was still frowning. 'Hmm.'

'What?'

'I'm not happy about you sleeping alone tonight in your unit.'

She raised her brows, which pulled the painful side of her head and made her wince and spoiled the effect she was going for. 'Dr Grey? Are you propositioning me?'

This time it was a real smile, one that made him so handsome she had to close her eyes. 'I wish. I was thinking if you slept in my bed, I could sleep on the floor.' He shrugged, slanting a glance her way to see how she was taking it. 'There's no room at your mother's shack. And I'd feel better if I could hear you breathing in the night.'

The man was so sweet, but she didn't need a minder. He'd already given her a new phone to use. 'I'll be fine in my room. You can text me to check. And I can phone if I need you.' It was her turn to smile. 'Or I can just press the emergency alarm. You know I can do that.'

'And you know I'll come running.'

Chapter Fifty-two

Melinda

On Friday morning, Melinda caught the seven am train from Central Station in Sydney to Dubbo. That took six and a half hours. Two hours later, she boarded the coach for Lightning Ridge, and at seven o'clock that night she climbed wearily down off the bus with relief. Twelve hours of travelling and her back was killing her.

It wasn't quite dark, but she was too tired to hurry the short distance to the units at the back of the doctor's surgery, so she hoped no one jumped out at her.

The door to Konrad's unit was open and he rose at the sound of her suitcase trundling past his door. 'Mel. Welcome back.' His swift glance made her push the hair out of her eyes with a limp hand. 'You must be exhausted. Can I make you a cup of tea?'

She hadn't been so tired in a long time, and she needed her bed, but tea did sound like heaven. She sagged a little and her hand loosened on the small pull-along case. 'I'll just get rid of the bag and freshen up.' She was dying for the toilet. 'But yes. That would be wonderful. Thank you.'

She relaxed more, feeling the familiar aura of safety she always felt with Konrad. He asked, 'Okay if I tell Riley you're here?'

'That would be great, too,' she said over her shoulder. She had stuff to share, but first she dragged her little case the last fifteen feet to her door. Not the new room, the old one. She hadn't moved in there yet. A small spurt of excitement thrilled through her, though. She'd move in tomorrow.

By the time she'd washed her face and cleaned her teeth, she felt almost human and headed back to the common room. Riley and Konrad were sitting at the table with that big teapot between them. Konrad pointed to the sandwich press. 'Have you eaten? These build muscles.'

Her stomach rumbled as if it could already taste Konrad's cheesy treats. He'd made them for her just after she'd moved in and had been still jumping at every sound. He'd said they were superpowered. She hadn't believed him then, or now, but the thought made her smile. 'Not since Dubbo.'

'Cheese on toast?'

Melinda lowered herself into the chair, her butt protesting that it didn't want to sit down again, but at the idea of food she didn't have to make for herself her mood lifted. 'Sounds awesome.'

Konrad stood up. 'Riley?'

'No, thanks.' Her eyes twinkled at him and Melinda wondered what they'd got up to while she'd been away. 'You look pale and sore,' Riley said.

Melinda cast a glance at Riley. She did too, actually, Melinda thought, as Riley said, 'Long day on the bus?'

Gawd, the bus. 'Too long. Five hours. But the train was fine, 'cause I could walk when I needed to. It's a big trip to a big place. I wish I didn't have to do it again.'

'You've done well to do two big trips in four days. When's the labour induction?'

'Two weeks.' At least she knew what was happening now. And she was fairly calm about it. 'Caesarean at thirty-eight weeks. They said the latest scans show they should be able to replace the herniated bowel and repair the tummy hole in the same operation. And do it fairly soon if the baby is well after the birth.'

Riley's face lit up. She really cared and Melinda felt warmth push away some of her exhaustion. 'That's great news. How was the social worker?'

She thought about Chris, who'd introduced her to Janey, and what a lifesaver she'd been. 'Amazing. She had a social worker student from the uni with her and Janey came to all the appointments with me. It made such a difference because she knew where she was going and did all the introductions for me. She said she'd be there for the operation as well if I wanted her to be.' She looked at Riley. 'I do.'

'Good for you. There's no reason you can't have her there.'

That was a relief. They'd talked about it after they'd seen the obstetrician. Melinda thought about Janey's big smile and confident air. 'Could you check that for me, please. I haven't asked the obstetrician. Janey comes from Dubbo, her parents farm there, and we got on like a house on fire.'

'Of course. I'll be ringing him on Monday, anyway.' Another look passed between the two doctors, like they were both thinking the same thing and knew what the other thought. They definitely had something going on.

Konrad said, 'That's wonderful, Melinda. I'm really pleased you found someone to be there with you.'

Riley asked, 'How was the consultant?'

'The doctors were great. The anaesthetist saw me at the same time – we had a group meeting in the clinic – and I'll be awake during the operation.' She thought about that but also the reasons why. 'That way the baby doesn't have to go to sleep when I go to sleep and it's safer for him. They promised I wouldn't feel anything, but they'll be watching my face the whole time to make sure.'

'Excellent. And the nursery?'

The nursery. That was one scary place with the tiniest babies. She'd had to wear a gown and mask and wash her hands. 'Janey came with me to the neonatal intensive care. The staff showed me a cot like he's going to go into.'

'You've said "he" twice,' Konrad teased. 'Did they tell you the sex?'

Melinda rolled her eyes. 'Not until after I saw a penis that was as plain as day on the ultrasound,' she huffed. 'Like a spare finger sticking up. I asked and we all laughed about it.'

She relaxed back into the chair. She was surrounded by kind people and Sydney hadn't been too bad once Janey was on the scene.

'We need to find someone who's driving to Sydney next week,' Riley said. 'To make it easier for you instead of going back on the bus. IPTAAS, that's the Isolated Patient's Travel and Accommodation Assistance Scheme, would pay their petrol.' She looked at Konrad. 'I'll ask the Friday ladies and you could keep an ear out with your patients.'

'Great idea.' He nodded.

Riley's hair fell away from her forehead and a dark-purple lumpy bruise came into view. Melinda gasped. 'What happened to your head?'

Riley looked at Konrad. He said, 'We've had adventures here, too. Riley fell down an old mine shaft on her run and knocked herself out.'

Melinda shuddered, remembering one man fairly recently who'd died just like that. 'Crikey. That's terrible. I hope it was a short shaft.'

'Thirteen metres,' Konrad said. 'She was in big trouble with us for scaring everybody, but she's been lazing around taking the rest of the week off since then.'

It sounded like there was more to it, Melinda thought, but she didn't want to be nosy. 'Are you okay?'

Riley nodded. 'Yes, thanks. I'm much more rested. We cancelled Tuesday and all of this week for me, but I should be fine to work half days next week. If it's okay with you, then the following week I'll do morning and afternoon to catch up.'

She'd be there for that. Her last week of work. Melinda looked at Konrad. 'You'll be busy.'

Riley agreed with amusement. 'That's what I said. He's doing a weekend clinic tomorrow morning.'

'Oh.' Her shoulders drooped. 'Did you need me?'

'No.' Konrad shook his head. 'You rest tomorrow.'

'Well . . .' She wouldn't be resting. Guilt twinged. 'On the bus today, I phoned Greta to tell her about Sydney and the tests. She and Toby are coming over to help me move into the new unit tomorrow morning, if that's okay.'

He gave her a big happy grin and she relaxed. 'I'm glad. That works out fine. Adelaide's coming for reception because we thought you'd be too tired, just for the half-day, and Riley can sit on a chair and watch the toing and froing you people do.'

'Gee, thanks,' Riley said, but she didn't look upset about it. These two were surely acting strange.

Melinda woke up on Saturday morning refreshed from a good night's sleep in her own bed. Thank goodness she was home. The baby shifted and poked her and excitement bubbled in her chest that soon the worries would be over and she'd be able to bring her baby home. Today, Greta said they'd go to the second-hand shop and look for a cradle or something for the baby to sleep in. Tonight, she'd be sleeping in the new unit.

She dressed and walked to the IGA and bought fresh cream, strawberry jam, proper butter and three packets of already made pikelets for morning tea. People who were doing you a favour deserved to have refreshments.

Toby and his mother arrived at nine and Riley came out to see if she could help. Greta shooed her back to the chair. 'We've got this piddly little job. You rest.'

It seemed the town was looking after Riley now. Riley grimaced and pulled out an e-reader, giving Greta a glare.

They were looking after her, too. The biggest surprise was when Desiree appeared at nine-thirty pushing a huge, silent-moving ancient stroller that had been polished within an inch of its life. The reflective wheels were the size of dinner plates and the sides were shiny black. It had a curved black hood to shade the baby's face and a new mattress and beautiful sheets. Like an old English nanny's pram in a movie.

Tears pricked her eyes. 'Oh, Desiree,' she breathed. 'It's gorgeous.' Greta clapped her hands and she knew then this was planned.

'This'll give your baby somewhere to sleep until you get a cot,' Desiree said. 'Cots are too big for a tiny baby, anyway. You can push the stroller over next to your bed or take it out for a walk if you want.'

Melinda hesitantly hugged the gruff woman and Desiree patted her back awkwardly. 'Glad you like it.'

'I love it.'

'Good,' Desiree said, 'I've gotta go back to work.' And she hurried away.

Toby said, 'When you go back to work, Mel, you'll be able to push the stroller in there, too.'

She could. It would take up a mountain of room, but she didn't think Konrad would mind. 'Everything will work out once this baby is home and healthy.'

'I think so, too,' Toby said.

The whole move-in working party had everything shifted and packed away by lunchtime. Greta said she'd come back tomorrow and do the cleaning for the empty unit. This came with a big warning for Melinda not to touch it.

Melinda laughed. 'Okay, thank you. Thank you both. Have another pikelet.'

Greta had bossed Toby around all morning, but he'd taken it with unending good humour, raising his brows at Melinda when his mum shooed him from place to place. There'd been lots of jokes and, well, happiness the like of which she couldn't remember. They were all so good to her, like the family she didn't have.

Now it was done. She clasped her hands in delight. 'I'm so glad to have everything tucked away.'

It looked like a home! The new peppermint curtains Greta made let light in but didn't let people on the outside see her. The drawers were full of baby clothes. There was a change mat on the old side bench that ran along the wall and a baby bath on a stand to make bathing easier. It was so unbelievable having all this room in the lounge room and practically a full kitchen all to herself. She couldn't have been luckier.

Chapter Fifty-three

Konrad

Konrad spent the Saturday morning catching up on patients who were a touch more unwell than normal, because he and Adelaide had cherry-picked those who needed earlier appointments.

The diagnosis and treatment challenges had been satisfying, though, as if he'd rediscovered the reason he'd gone into medicine in the first place. From today's vantage, he could see a lot of that joy had slipped away after his brother's death and somehow, with Riley, he'd rediscovered it.

Except that when he'd opened his door to usher a patient out and looked across at the open door of Riley's room, reality kept slamming home to him that she'd be gone in one week.

Just what was he gonna do about that?

'Riley's coming out for afternoon tea today,' Adelaide said as she packed up her handbag and locked the front door. 'Like to come with her, Konrad?'

Yes. The thought was instant and he frowned at himself. It screamed *needy*. 'If you're sure I'm not intruding. Family time and all that.'

Adelaide stepped across, looked up at him and poked him in the chest, just like her daughter would've done, and held up the offending finger. 'You, sir, have been outstanding and I thank you for the care you took of our whole family during Riley's disappearance. You're like family and welcome at my hearth any time.'

She meant it. Assertively even. He almost blushed. 'Thank you. Maybe we'll drive out together if Riley wants.'

'Do that.' She waved and slipped out the back door, leaving him comforted from her sincerity. Of course, dropping in to see Riley's mother once her daughter went back to Sydney would be more awkward.

When Riley went back to Sydney.

In one week.

Six days.

He walked into his room and stared blindly at the computer screen, knowing he was edging towards a conclusion that could change his life. If he could figure out how to convince her they needed to be together. Forever.

Whoa – there it was. That decision. So much for working towards it bit by bit.

If she'd have him. She could never move here, but with Riley by his side, he could go elsewhere. Anywhere.

The people here were great, but he couldn't see Riley growing old at the Ridge. He could see himself and Riley on the coast. If not with kids, then growing settled. That's right, she didn't want kids. His mum would be disappointed, but they'd all love Riley. And he could deal with not having children. They could deal with it together.

It didn't have to be Sydney, though he imagined she'd prefer that, but that was something they could talk about if there was a future. All he knew was that he wanted that future with Riley. Together. Wherever it may be.

He closed the screens, turned off his room light and followed in Riley's mother's footsteps to the back door. That's when he saw Riley waving to her mother, a little bowed from protecting her shoulder. Seeing her discomfort made his heart clench like a fist. He'd been so close to losing her, it still woke him up in the night in a cold sweat.

He picked up the chair he'd put outside for Riley this morning and carried it back to the common room. By the time she was at the door, he was waiting for her.

Her smile lit her beautiful face. 'You gate-crashing my mum's place again?'

He wanted to cradle her cheek, but she was just too far away to reach. 'Doctor's orders.' He stepped closer, leaned in and brushed her cheek with his hand. *And*, he thought, *we'll stop somewhere along the way and have that discussion we need to have about our future.*

Chapter Fifty-four

Adelaide

On the drive home, Adelaide thought about Tyler waiting for her at the old inn. The man had been bitten by the opal bug, and while she'd been nibbled on herself, she wasn't at it twelve hours a day like he'd been the last two days.

Suddenly, Tyler had to be down the shaft digging or up the top poring over the tailings in the sunlight. It was amusing and fun to share the enthusiasm that she'd found when she'd come here. They were closer than ever. Maybe drawn together as well by their worry for Riley.

It was hard to believe that their relationship could change so much in so short a time. It was almost as if their marriage had needed this break, this shake-up. The new Tyler helped around the house, cooked, pored over her reference books, and they talked all the time about different challenges for finding opals and mining the gemstones. There was excitement in admiring each other's finds, wondering where the next find would come from, and best of all . . .

No freaking television or Netflix. Or Netflix discussions. Win, win, win!

It made her wish that she didn't have a day job, but that was short term. In fact, she had the next week off before she returned to the computer. Melinda had said again that she wanted her job back after the baby was born, and Adelaide had reassured her, very heartily, that it was all hers.

Not that she didn't enjoy working with Konrad. The man was a dream employer. The idea of seeing more of Riley was a huge bonus, too, and the main reason she was there. At least she could check that her daughter had breaks and ate when she went back, though she suspected Konrad would be on Riley's case as well.

Adelaide also suspected that Konrad had fallen hard for her daughter, and with the tyranny of distance looming, she just hoped he wouldn't get hurt. There was no way Riley could settle in Lightning Ridge and maintain her professional status as an expert in her field. She needed to practise in a major centre with her skills and experience in Sydney's assisted-fertility arena. It would be too easy to fall behind on the latest treatments and lose access to the network of professionals she needed, and that's what she was so proud of, providing a top-notch cutting-edge service.

Adelaide wondered where Konrad thought the relationship could possibly go. Unless he was thinking about following Riley. Would he leave the Ridge? For Riley?

Riley had seemed pretty uninterested in marriage with any man, which her mother agreed with as none of them had been inspiring, until now. And the idea of settling down to motherhood also had been mooted, which Adelaide did not agree with but had the wisdom not to say anything about.

She wondered if Konrad knew all that, but it was Riley and Konrad's business, not hers, and so she turned into her own driveway and closed down those incursions into nosiness.

Instead, she looked at her crazy little house and imagined possibilities where it might just work if she and Tyler shared their time between Sydney and Lightning Ridge until they were both too old to travel.

Chapter Fifty-five

Riley

Riley slipped into Konrad's roomy vehicle and inhaled the subtle scent of the man next to her. He didn't drive off until she'd secured her seatbelt, not like the first time she'd ridden in his car. He was acting strangely. In fact, he had been since he'd pulled her out of the shaft.

She got that he'd been scared for her, along with her mum and dad, and she felt unexpected delight that so many people in town had felt the same. Some had even dropped off flowers and cards, which was out there when she'd barely been here a couple of weeks. Though, of course, she'd met some pretty colourful characters in that time, but still, Konrad was acting weird.

'Not long till you get peace from me,' she mused with apparent nonchalance and saw his head turn her way from the corner of her eye.

'Hmm,' he said. 'How do you feel about that?'

The words popped like a paper bag in her face. She hadn't expected he'd bounce the question back to her.

She blinked. How did she feel about that? Fine, of course. Though she hadn't given her real home much thought in the last couple of weeks. And she didn't really want to think about it now, if she was honest. 'I'm keen to check out my flat,' she said. 'Make sure it's fine. And having a bit more room to swing that cat.' That was all true, even if she didn't mention that she was missing home.

After a long pause he said, 'Important thing, that cat-swinging.'

She nodded, but he wasn't looking. *Okay. Awkward.*

Suddenly, she felt compelled to fill the gap in conversation. 'The professor says she's looking forward to my return. Apparently, there's a backlog she wants me to clear. It seems that since I've been away, a bevy of my previous patients have come back for help with their second babies.' She should feel more enthusiastic about that.

He inclined his head, eyes still on the road. 'You do an important job.'

Was he patronising her? 'And you don't?'

This time he shot her a glance. 'I do, but I don't plan on staying in Lightning Ridge forever.'

That was interesting. She leaned towards him slightly. 'Where would you go?'

'Eventually, I think I'd like to settle on the coast. I love the ocean and I miss the surf.'

She could imagine him, tall and strong and brown, his blond hair blowing as he rode a long board into the sand like some surf-lifesaving champion. 'The chickie babes will like that,' she said lightly, but the words tasted unpleasant.

'I'm not really interested in chickie babes,' he said.

Who was he trying to kid? 'Not the impression I got when you seduced me.'

'Ha.' A sceptical noise if she'd ever heard one. 'I thought you seduced me.' This time he gave her his attention for a whole three seconds. Thankfully, he'd slowed the car to almost a crawl. 'And you're not a chickie babe.'

He turned back to the road and sped up. What did that mean? She wasn't sexy like a little beach bird? She asked, 'What am I? Chopped liver?'

'Way better.'

That made her smile. She couldn't help it. This conversation was crazy. 'I'm way better than chopped liver?'

He pulled over and left the car running so the aircon kept them cool. They were on the road to her mother's, so there was no traffic. 'I don't really like liver, so let's drop that.'

He turned in his seat and faced her, his ocean-blue eyes searching hers. His mouth tilted sexily at the corner, as if he was amused at both of them. 'Riley Brand, you're a stunning, sexy woman. A kind, fiercely intelligent champion of women. You're also someone I'd like to spend a lot more time with. But time is running out and I don't know what to do about that.'

'Oh.' It wasn't the most intelligent answer she'd ever given, but she was still replaying what he'd said in her mind. 'You barely know me.'

'In time spent together, true.'

'I barely know you.'

'True.'

'Stop being so damn agreeable. Just because we slept together for twelve hours doesn't mean anything.'

'Doesn't it?' He raised his brows and the deeper lines around his mouth widened. 'I think it does. I think it means we're attracted to each other. Mightily. Neither of us is the type to jump in and out of beds for one-night stands. Something'—he lifted his hands off the steering wheel as if asking a question—'must've connected us to make it so imperative we fall into bed and not get out for a long, long time.'

Words failed her and he knew it. Damn him.

'Because,' he said and his voice had gone deeper, rougher, causing a thrill to run through her like the hot wind that ran through the opal fields, 'when I had the chance to climb in, I couldn't have stayed out of your bed if someone had chained me to a wall.'

A vision of Konrad chained to a wall pulling the shackles out of concrete and coming to her swam before her. A hot, hot thought. Her cheeks heated up, as did her belly. What did she say to that? Thank you?

'So, that's what you're thinking? About me?'

'I'm always thinking about you.'

She blushed like a schoolgirl. How did she feel about leaving here, leaving him? She didn't know. It should have been cut and dried, mission accomplished, time to go home. It was anything but.

'I don't want you to go,' he said, reading her mind, putting his feelings in no doubt. He was braver than she was. Far braver. 'When you go, I want to follow you.'

'Follow me . . . where?' she asked, slightly stunned.

'Sydney. Anywhere.' He shrugged. 'But these are all big decisions we need to think and then talk about.' He put the car back in gear. 'I want you to think about it. I'm gonna chain myself to that wall and give you some space. No hassling you for sex. And sometime in the next few days, we should have a talk about the future.'

And what if she wanted sex? Was she supposed to ask? Holy heck, how had things gone this far, this quickly and this intensely? She remembered her hazy time trapped down the shaft, waiting for Konrad to find her, wanting him to be the one who found her. *Knowing* that Konrad would find her. Then she thought about having him there to rely on all the time. But he was an equal-opportunity guy. He'd rely on her, too.

Them bouncing medical conversations off each other, like she hadn't been able to do with Josh. The way he didn't give in to her unless he was sure her way was better, and even pulled her down when she was getting too cocky, as she did to him. The way he made her laugh, and she did to him.

All these things were things worth thinking about. 'Okay,' she said. 'I can think about that.'

Chapter Fifty-six

Melinda

On Sunday, Melinda felt twitchy. Not itchy on her skin or her belly, just her nerves, irritated and crawling-insects twitchy.

Toby had phoned and asked if she wanted to get out. He'd suggested they go out for a drive in his ute. Surprised by the unexpected invitation, she'd said no. It was a stupid, knee-jerk, shy-mouse reaction, which was dumb, because she wanted to get out, to go somewhere and enjoy her last day before the next five working days, after which she was leaving for Sydney.

Not that she wasn't waiting desperately for her baby, but she knew when he was coming now, which was Monday week, and she knew that she'd be back in Sydney next Sunday night. Tomorrow would be the start of her last week at work until after her baby's operation. Until after she'd sorted out being a mother.

A mother. Greta said she'd be fine, that Melinda would be a natural – though she had no idea how, when her own mother was far from natural. Her mum had left her with her grandfather when she was only six. But Greta said she'd help Melinda figure it out.

She paced the room. Toby had said to let him know if she changed her mind about the drive. She looked at the short list of contacts in her phone – Greta, Konrad, Toby and four others – and decided that a text would be easier.

Hi Toby, it's Mel. If you're not busy, a drive sounds great. No worries if you're busy now, though. M.

Toby arrived within fifteen minutes swinging the keys to his little ute. He offered her a small bottle of orange juice. 'Mum dropped me off. She said don't get dehydrated or low in sugar.'

Sweet Greta, Melinda thought.

He grimaced. 'She gave me one, too. And she said we're not allowed to drive over bumps.'

'I don't think a few bumps are gonna hurt me. There were plenty of those on the bus the other day.'

He laughed at that. 'Good. I thought I could show you where Riley fell down the shaft and then maybe we can drive out to the site of the old church that blew down, out past Riley's mum's house. Then I can show you where Adelaide lives.'

Melinda had wanted to see both of those places. Perfect. 'Ooh, I'd like that. I just needed to get out, which is terrible of me after everyone did such great work making my place so beautiful. I just feel twitchy.'

'That's okay. I'm fine if you drive. I'm terrified they'll take my licence off me permanently if my epilepsy becomes uncontrolled.' He looked away and his ears went pink. 'You don't have to worry that I'll miss a fit coming on. I always know. I get this funny smell and taste in my mouth, so you can stop the car.'

Melinda had been with Konrad when Toby seized once, before Riley came. She remembered the first aid – she would just keep him safe and wait for the seizure to stop. It never lasted long. And she could drive when he woke up because he'd be dopey for a little while.

'I'm not worried.' And strangely, she wasn't. Some things were scary, but Toby's epilepsy was just unfair on Toby. 'I know what to do.'

Toby's expression was hard to read, but it made her blush. He said, 'You're marvellous. You know that, right?'

She laughed, awkward again, and embarrassed by the praise. 'No, I'm boring.'

They drove the back streets and looked at the houses and yards and the signs, the car doors stuck on trees or posts, painted red, blue and yellow – the car-door tours for tourists so they could find the route to the next attraction.

Toby showed her where Riley fell down the shaft; it was closer to the road than she'd realised. Melinda looked across the deserted mounds in the afternoon light and thought about how frightening it would've been at night down the shaft alone. In pain from hitting her head, trapped, with nobody hearing her call.

'I would have been terrified.'

'Me too,' Toby said.

Melinda laughed. Toby made her laugh. Toby said, 'She and Konrad are like superheroes. Larger than life. Don't you reckon?'

Her big, confident boss was so kind, and Riley was like an Amazon woman, tall and unafraid of anything, and so smart

Melinda could only shake her head. 'You're right. They are.' She looked across at her friend. 'We'll just have to turn into super-heroes, too. There's no reason we can't.'

'Yeah right,' he scoffed. 'Captain Epilepsy, like in the comic.' He was looking at her with that expression again, his eyes wide and a smile kinking his mouth. 'You could be a hero, Mel, but not me.'

But the idea grew on her. 'Superheroes come from odd places. I have a feeling that maybe everything will work out.' She glanced his way. 'Riley said you were gonna look for kids with epilepsy in the school? Did you ever do that?'

'Yeah. We're gonna meet on the first day of every month. I turn up at the school and we talk about what's happened in the last month. I might be able to use that superhero stuff like those comics the Epilepsy Foundation creates for kids. Riley told me about them and they're cool, and maybe we can make up our own stories with the real kids' names and set them in the Ridge.'

Nice. And he sounded excited. 'I remember at school that you wrote good stories in English.'

'Maybe. We'll see.' She could almost see his brain working, like he just needed encouragement. Encouragement like she'd been given by Konrad for the last months. She'd just been taking, not giving back, staying a mouse. That was finished now. Her baby was coming and a baby needed a superhero lioness for a mother. Not a mouse.

Chapter Fifty-seven

Konrad

On Monday morning, Konrad looked across the reception area in the surgery at Riley's closed door and wondered how an occupied room could make him happy.

He had it bad. His crazy feelings for Riley had come out of nowhere like a wild tornado, sucked him up and spun him around from the day she'd arrived. Was it the improbable love at first sight he'd never believed in? Certainly, the fierce attraction had hit him that first day.

Then he'd thought he'd lost her. Since Saturday, after that talk on the way to her mother's, he'd seen Riley watching him. Thinking. Assessing. She hadn't said much, but she hadn't pushed him away, either.

And he'd been holding back. Despite the fact that he'd wanted nothing more than to carry her to his bed again and reassure himself she was alive – and sleep with her in his arms – he'd put a safe distance between them. And she was observing that distance. Often with narrowed eyes that made him hold in a smile, but she hadn't pushed for more.

Someone cleared their throat. Melinda. *Next patient*, her look prodded. That was another turn of events. Melinda, acting like the new boss. He glanced around the room and all the patients' eyes were on him. 'Jim. Come on in.'

Jim stood. The old bloke seemed to be moving easier. Maybe the artesian baths had worked their magic. He definitely looked more cheerful than usual.

Konrad pushed the door shut after him and gestured. 'Take a seat, Jim.' He watched the man lower himself less carefully. 'How'd it go?'

Jim harrumphed. 'Well . . . I reckon you could probably say you told me so.'

Score. 'Good, then. How many days did it take?'

Jim glanced at him from under his bushy brows. 'Me fingers were better after the first time, and they just kept getting better.' He shrugged without wincing. 'I haven't taken a pill for the pain for two days.'

Konrad felt the delight expand inside him. 'You little beauty,' he said as he typed the results into Jim's file. 'I hope you're gonna tell your mates, Jim?'

'We started meeting there twice a week just after twelve when they re-open after cleaning, instead of at the pub. Then we go to the pub after.' Jim snorted. 'Gotta say thanks, Doc. Good idea.'

'I couldn't be happier.' Konrad finished documenting and sat back to study his patient. 'Anything else bothering you?'

'Just wanted to say I cut down the red wine a bit.'

Go Jim. 'All good news, mate. You've started my day in a good way.' He leaned forward. 'Can I check your blood pressure?' He pumped the bulb and the belt of the sphygmomanometer tightened around Jim's scrawny arm. Well, well. His blood pressure had dropped by twenty since his last check. Systolic and diastolic.

While he was there, Konrad noted the occasional sunspot that was looking inflamed on the forearm, redder than normal. 'We probably need to do a skin check, too, Jim. Maybe get a couple of those spots burned off next time you come, before they turn into something nasty.'

'Can I go in the pool if you do that?'

'Not for a week or so.'

'Yeah, well, probably not yet, then.'

Konrad grinned. 'We'll leave it for a couple of weeks. But Melinda will make an appointment for the skin check.' He stood. 'I'll see you then.'

Jim looked at him hard and Konrad thought he was going to decline, but instead, he actually smiled. Konrad couldn't remember when he'd last seen that. Jim put his hand out to shake. 'I'll do that. Just wanted to say, thanks, Doc.'

The rest of the morning followed the great start. Konrad's last patient before lunch was Cyrus, with Konrad as second choice because he couldn't get in to see Riley. Konrad held back a snort of amusement at being runner-up. Melinda had told him that it was only for a BP check and to confirm the new pills the specialist had started Cyrus on were working well.

The usually florid-faced Cyrus presented as a healthier colour, with more spring in his step as he came in. 'Looking good, Cyrus.' And even better, he'd showered. There were some great changes happening.

'Yeah. I'm taking more care of myself. Scared myself with what that specialist said.' He sat in the chair and leaned forward, lowering his voice. 'How's the doc? She okay after her ordeal?'

'Nearly all healed up. We really appreciate your help in that search, Cyrus. You're a good man for organising the blokes.'

'Couldn't have anything happen to her.' He shook his big head. 'It'd be a terrible loss.'

Konrad shuddered inside at the remembered fear. 'You're right there. But she's good now.' Time for a subject change. 'How about I check your blood pressure?' He took Cyrus's beefy arm in his and wrapped the cuff around it. 'Any side-effects from the pills?'

'Nope.'

He completed the check – another patient's BP that was improving. 'It's coming down, Cyrus. Hold your hands out palm up.' There wasn't as much tremor as usual, either. 'Turn them over.' He tapped the bottom of Cyrus's palms with the top of his hands. 'Can you squeeze my fingers.' He held his fingers still, waiting for Cyrus to grip them. 'Both together?'

Cyrus pulled back. 'I won't tell anyone you held my hand,' Konrad teased.

Cyrus shot him a look and then huffed out a laugh. 'Bloody stirrer.'

Cyrus squeezed hard and Konrad held in the wince. 'Got your strength back, I see. There's still some loss of strength on the left, but not much. Are you noticing it at work?'

'Not now.'

'Good. It's getting better. Did you hear that Jim's going to the pool every day for his arthritis?' Konrad asked.

'I did hear that. The blokes were laughing about it at the pub.'
He shook his head. 'Now half the clowns are going.'

'You should join them. It could bring your blood pressure down
more, and if you exercised your hand in the hot water it might help
the circulation to make it stronger.'

Cyrus looked thoughtful, which wasn't his usual expression.
'I'll consider it. That all?'

'If you don't have any other concerns. How's the rash?'

'Better since I started showering daily like the doc suggested.'

Konrad jammed his lips together and managed to say, 'That'll
do it.'

Cyrus leaned in. 'You make sure that our lady doc stays safe.'

There was sincerity in the words, and a barely veiled threat. 'I'll
do that, mate.'

It seemed that every patient who came in wanted to know how
Riley was. Konrad couldn't believe how much of an impression she'd
made. Actually, he could. She'd certainly made an impression on
him. Plus, he guessed, with a few daughters of the town who thought
they'd never conceive, everybody was pretty invested.

He showed Cyrus out. It was twelve-thirty. He raised his brows
at Melinda.

Melinda glanced at her watch. 'She should be finished soon.
I kept the lunchbreak free like you said.'

'Good work. I'll put the kettle on.'

Chapter Fifty-eight

Riley

The last patients for the morning. Riley could admit she'd been slightly annoyed at Konrad's highhandedness when he'd said the lunchtime slot had been made non-negotiable. But, with a vague headache starting from the concentration required, she'd be glad to take a break.

A headache despite the absolute pleasure she'd gained from this consultation with Olivia and Aiden, Desiree's daughter and son-in-law. They'd each lost four kilos in three weeks and had increased their nightly walks to eight kilometres. Most useful to them, they'd not touched alcohol since she'd seen them last, and their faces were positively buoyant. Their eyes sparkled, their skin glowed and they smiled openly at each other and at her.

'We feel better,' Olivia said.

'We're sleeping better,' Aiden added with a grin. 'And we're practising making love without going all the way to boost my sperm count like you suggested.'

'And that's certainly spiced up the evenings.'

Olivia actually blushed and Riley may have felt the tiniest smidge of jealousy because Konrad hadn't touched her since before she fell down that stupid shaft. What was with that? 'Well done,' she said like a good doctor who wasn't jealous at all.

Aiden said, 'We've been following our apps.'

Olivia's head bobbed. 'Since you told us last week that our tests had come back with no huge barriers to contraception, we've been feeling calmer about it all.'

Riley had commenced Olivia on medication to encourage ovulation. She'd also broached the subject of spacing intercourse to reduce actual ejaculation to boost Aiden's sperm count. They were ready for the next ovulation cycle with all the minor adjustments they could do to maximise fertility without major intervention. Fingers crossed.

She discussed the rest of the results that had come in, cautioning them against impatience, and finally they all stood. 'Fantastic results on your lifestyle changes. Good luck, you guys.'

When she opened the door to usher them towards Melinda, she found Konrad standing long and lean outside the tearoom, waiting for her. He held up her 'I like my eggs fertilised' cup and she could smell the coffee from across the room. *My hero.*

The couple waved and she moved to him. Possibly, her hips may have shimmied just a bit. She couldn't help herself. 'Sustenance for the invalid? Thank you.'

Voice low, he said, 'You look very sexy.' He'd noticed. 'But tired around the eyes. Headache?'

He'd noticed that, too. 'A little. Coffee will help.'

'And food.' He'd made a standing order for sandwiches to be delivered every day this week to ensure she ate. More coddling. 'You'll need it for your recovery.'

She could see the sense of it. He'd laid them out on the bench in the tearoom, and because they'd come from Greta, they looked like a feast, not a plate of bread and fillings.

In the background, Olivia sang her praises to Melinda and she inclined her head back towards the couple. 'They're a beautiful team. And amusing, like so many people out here. I hope they have success in their dreams.'

His look said he approved of her and was proud of her work. 'If anyone can make that happen, you will.'

The way his attention was so focused on her made her wonder what it would be like to wake up next to Konrad every morning – and that made her think about the blush on Olivia's cheeks five minutes ago.

She narrowed her eyes at him. He was playing with her with this no-sex-until-we-talk-again thing. 'Thanks for the care.' She poked him in the chest. Not too hard, but hard enough for him to notice. 'But when are you gonna take me to bed?' she whispered.

He gaped. She could almost feel the sudden heat in the fast perusal that scorched her body with those now pitch-dark blue eyes. It took one second for him to turn from carer to voyeur. He sucked in a breath and looked back to her face and saw her satisfied smirk. She thought, *Good, you rat. I've been pining away and you've been holding out. Stew on that for the next five hours.*

'As soon as we have our talk,' he said in a voice that betrayed only a hint of the intense heat she'd just seen. Great control. Too great. Not great.

'It better be shortly because I'm leaving soon.'

'I know. I'd say tonight, but I think you might wilt after your first day back. Let's leave it till tomorrow night. I'll order an early dinner from Greta and we'll talk.'

That didn't sound too hopeful as far as the body-contact business went, but she wasn't asking again. No siree.

But the way he was looking at her, she couldn't feel bad. Just sad and disappointed.

By the time she'd shown her last patient out, Riley needed to lean against the doorframe.

'I'll sort your next appointment,' Konrad said to the couple. He sat in Melinda's seat at the computer and put her patients at ease as receptionist. He must've been waiting for her to open the door. When her clients had left for the street, he stood and backed against the wall next to her. 'Do you want Melinda to cancel tomorrow's patients?'

'No, I'll be fine. Where is Melinda?'

'Toby had a seizure this afternoon waiting for his visit to me. She did well. She took him into the observation room when he said he had an aura and called me in. We left him safe on the floor until it was over and she's driven him home. The fit was mild, but he was dopey afterwards.'

'Should we go and pick her up?'

'She's waiting for Greta to close the café and I think she's staying for dinner. Greta said she'd bring her back.'

'You closing up?'

He nodded, watching her face, not saying the obvious: that she looked like crap. She assumed she did. She felt it, anyway.

'I'm heading for a shower and bed. You were right.'

'I'm having scrambled eggs. You want some?'

She remembered her mum making that when she was sick. She guessed his mum must've too. The man was seriously sweet. 'Toast soldiers?'

He laughed. 'How did you know.'

'We both have mothers.'

'I'll bring it to you in half an hour. Tea in bed.'

'Now he says bed.'

He laughed again, but it was a soft, sexy and seriously swoon-worthy chuckle. 'I'm a doctor. I can do a no-touch technique.'

Damn. For a minute there, she'd thought she might get that cuddle, after all.

Thirty minutes later, a knock sounded at her door. Restored by hot water and a five-minute power nap, she sat up in bed in her favourite nightie and adjusted the sheets to cover at least some of her cleavage. Stupid, but she couldn't help it.

'Come in.'

Konrad, also showered, judging by the damp hair curling on his collar and the waft of shampoo and soap, carried a tray with short legs. Goodness knew where he'd found it, but there was a pink bougainvillea flower from the bush outside across one corner, and a plate of steaming eggs and toast. He'd cut the toast into fingers and her mouth curled up. Who knew toast soldiers could be so soothing?

'Dinner in bed, my lady.'

'Service with a smile.' Oops, she felt her cheeks heat up, but she was feeling better. Even more since Konrad had come in with the flower.

'Tomorrow night,' he promised and settled the tray over her knees.

Chapter Fifty-nine

Melinda

Melinda stood in Greta's kitchen, which had obviously been hit by the white tornado of bleach. Everywhere she looked surfaces sparkled. Windows, floors, benches and sink all reflecting the light in a blinding statement of cleanliness. She put on the pot of suggested tea while she waited for Greta to come home.

Toby was lying in a recliner rocker, feet up, eyes flicking open as he grew more alert and the dopiness from the seizure passed. He'd refused to go to bed, so they'd sat companionably in the lounge with the sound of the wind chime pinging outside until she put the kettle on.

Baby names were such fun. She'd been tossing them around and Toby had suggested a few, mostly footballers' names. She turned back to look at him. 'But mostly, I was thinking of Edward, after my grandfather. Little Teddy. What do you think?'

She felt remarkably relaxed, which showed she'd grown accustomed to visits with Toby and his mother. And curiously happy. A feeling she'd almost forgotten from some long-ago afternoon swing on the porch with her pop before he'd got sick.

Greta had said she'd bring dinner and that Melinda should stay with them to eat. Melinda was happy with that because she didn't feel like making something for herself when she got home, and it was cosy here.

'Your back's sore,' Toby said, not a question, and she stopped unconsciously rubbing the ache low in her back. It was almost as uncomfortable as when she'd come home on the bus. She hadn't realised she'd been doing it.

The jug clicked off and she poured the water into the teapot. 'Most likely from sitting in the chair all day at work.'

'Do you think you should take it easy this week instead of working?'

'No.' She chose a cup from the regiment of mugs standing in the cupboard equally spaced. 'There's no way I'm giving up my job early. This last money's going into the nest egg for my baby and me.'

'I did see a small van that was cheap, yesterday,' Toby said. 'Reckon you could get some little ramps and push the big pram in the back if you wanted to take it somewhere. It'd be easier than a car.'

'A van? How could you put a baby seat in that?' But before she could expand on the thought a yawning, aching pull speared deep inside her. Between her legs, something twanged and sudden warm, gushing wetness saturated her underpants and flooded down her legs to pool on the floor. And it kept coming.

She'd wet herself. No. Worse. 'Tobyyyy.'

'Yeah.' She heard Toby click back the footrest of the chair as it creaked forward to sit him up.

'You have to ring Konrad.'

Toby appeared beside her, then took a hasty step back when he saw the puddle on the floor. 'You okay?'

'No. I think my waters just broke.' Her hands pushed into the kitchen bench as a prolonged shaft of pain twisted from her back to the front, down low and nasty. *What are you doing, Baby?* 'Now!'

'I'm doing it. I'm doing it.' Toby must have put the phone on loudspeaker because she could hear it ringing. Someone answered. 'Konrad.'

'It's Toby. Melinda's at my place. Her waters just broke.'

'Right. Ring the ambulance.' His voice sounded so calm that Melinda felt her fear ease a fraction. 'We'll be there in five minutes. If the ambulance is faster we'll meet you at the Multi-purpose Health Centre. Ring if you need us before then.'

The line dropped out. Toby rang the ambulance, but while he was talking Melinda had another pain that seemed to pull her apart and she didn't listen. By the time the contraction had eased, Toby had completed the call. 'Okay, the ambulance is coming too.'

She would not panic. A mantra she began to repeat. *I will not panic.* 'You better ring your mum.'

He didn't need the speaker because he didn't give his mum a chance to speak. 'Mel's just broken her waters at the kitchen sink. The ambulance, Konrad and Riley are on the way. Come home.'

The sound of a car accelerating their way floated through the window, and in the distance was the sound of a far-off siren. The car pulled up and a door slammed.

Toby took off for the front entrance and she heard them all stride in across Greta's polished floors, but she couldn't turn away from the sink as her fingernails dug into the laminate of the bench.

Riley appeared beside her, her manner serene as if it was an ordinary day at the surgery, and Melinda felt the tension ease another fraction. 'So, your baby decided today was the day.'

323

'So it seems . . .' But before she could finish the thought another contraction, like a huge vice of tightness, gripped her front and back and she leaned into the sink.

Riley's hand slid down her shoulder to the top of her arm, just resting with the tiniest bit of pressure, lending strength, so she knew she wasn't alone.

'Keep breathing. You're doing beautifully.'

She shifted her feet as she unconsciously rocked her hips.

'Don't slip.' As the contraction eased, she realised Konrad had sent Toby for a towel to put on the floor, so she stepped onto the dry spot.

Embarrassment flooded her. 'I made a mess.'

'It's not your fault,' Konrad said. 'We'll talk to the baby about it later.'

Fear slammed into her. 'Am I gonna get to Sydney in time?'

Riley squeezed her shoulder again. 'We'll try. It depends how fast your labour is. Your job is to believe you and your baby are safe.'

'We're here.' Konrad was on her other side. 'Whatever happens, we'll all manage. You just have to come along for the ride.'

'I wasn't gonna ride. I wasn't gonna feel a thing.' She sucked in a breath past a tearful throat. 'My baby . . .' But she had to stop as the next contraction crashed into her.

Riley said, 'We're going to take you to the Multi-purpose Centre. Until the air ambulance can arrive.'

By the time that maelstrom of squeezing eased, Greta had skidded up next to her and the paramedics were at the door. Toby let them in and they pushed a stretcher across to the kitchen.

She heard Riley ask Greta, 'Do you have a new roll of cling wrap?'

That was an odd thing to ask. When she'd been looking for the cups she'd seen the store of neatly stacked kitchen wraps. All types and all sizes lined in rows.

'What size? Short or wide?' Greta sounded so businesslike amongst all the craziness that more tension eased from Melinda. She was surrounded by sensible people who cared.

Riley said, 'Both. Just in case we need to wrap up the baby.'

And that stole any amusement away. In other words, just in case her baby arrived in Lightning Ridge, with his bowel outside his body. Babies weren't born here, especially not sick ones. 'I should have stayed in Sydney,' she moaned. She'd put her baby at risk because she wanted to come home.

'The obstetrician said Monday was fine. It wasn't your call.' Konrad touched her cheek and she looked at him. 'The trolley is behind you, Mel. Just sit down and I'll lift your feet. Lie sideways.'

She tried to move her feet, but the start of another spearing pain travelled all the way down her buttocks, between her legs and down her thighs. Suddenly, she needed to push. 'I can't move. It's coming.'

'Not here it's not,' Konrad muttered.

Riley said, 'You don't have to move, Mel. Konrad will do it. Pick her up.'

It all happened quickly. One minute she was standing and the next she was lying on her side with a blanket over her. The paramedic put a strap above her belly so she wouldn't fall off. 'Time to go,' he said. 'Next stop the Multi-purpose Centre.'

'Can Toby and Greta come?'

Konrad was pushing one end of the trolley. 'Yes. They can meet us there. Greta said she'll go to pick up your hospital bag from the flat. She has a key.'

Chapter Sixty

Konrad

Konrad wanted Melinda in the mini-hospital, and when Riley had said to pick her up he'd been indescribably relieved that the decision had been made. They needed to get somewhere where neonatal equipment and medical supplies were available. Not that there was a place more sterile than Greta's house, but they needed to keep Melinda and her baby as safe as they could, and that wasn't here.

They had to be able to deal with resuscitation or obstetric complications. Thank God Riley was here. He'd delivered half-a-dozen babies in his medical life, but he'd had no opportunity for refreshers since coming to Lightning Ridge. And certainly none with major abnormalities.

In the rapid drive after Toby's phone call, Riley had said, 'It's unlikely Mel will have the baby fast. First-time mum.' Ha. That had gone out the window if he wasn't mistaken. But Riley had also said, 'If she does, treat it as a normal birth and we just wrap the baby in cling wrap. Keep him warm and sweet until NETS arrive to fly him to Sydney.'

So that's what they'd do.

'Warm and sweet and his belly wrapped in cling wrap.' He said the words under his breath as they secured Melinda in the back of the ambulance. 'I'll climb in here. You meet us there,' he said to Riley. It was silly to risk Riley jumping in and out of the ambulance when he wanted her primed and ready for birth-attendant duties.

She was already opening the door to his car, cling-wrap boxes under her arm. She'd rung the Multi-purpose Health Centre on the way over, so the nurses would have prepared everything by now and called in some help.

He climbed in after Melinda for the two-minute ride, and when he looked down her big green eyes stared into his filled with dread. 'It's okay, Mel. Riley said we just treat this as a normal birth and if he gets here to wrap him in cling wrap.'

Her eyes widened and then slowly, she nodded. 'Let's do that,' she whispered.

When they pulled up, the main entrance stood open and a nurse held the door. The emergency treatment rooms were clipped back for the trolley and they zipped past like some amusement ride going through a tunnel.

Thankfully, the centre was out of hours, so no waiting patients milled around and he could see the staff – not experienced in babies but well-practised in emergencies and they'd manage fine – waiting. He could see flickering faces on the big screen in the corner, so they'd already logged on to the virtual care team online.

They'd made it here before the baby came. *Phew.* His neck eased the rigid tightness he'd been holding. They could do this. It was telling how he needed to be in a medical environment to feel secure.

He squeezed Melinda's shoulder. 'You're doing brilliantly. You've got this.'

'I've got this?' Melinda squeaked.

'Everyone is here for you. But yes, you've got this,' he said.

As soon as he helped Melinda off the stretcher and onto the bed, the nurses moved in to start her observations and he eased away to check the equipment they had ready. A neonatal resuscitation open cot for the baby, with the new Neopuff they'd fundraised for, and a hastily assembled trolley with the few things needed for a birthing mother.

By the time he turned around, Riley was already talking to the screen, giving Melinda's background and names of the referral doctors for medical notes and scans they could access. She looked calm and confident, stating her plan of action and what she wanted from them. This was a part of Riley he hadn't seen. His girl was high-powered and crisply authoritarian and wasn't wasting time. He knew she wanted to get over to Melinda but had timed her discussion well while the patient was getting settled.

'I'll be back with an update in a couple of minutes.' She turned to face the room. Now that Melinda had her initial stats recorded, Konrad had the feeling Riley would take over. He wasn't wrong.

'Melinda. What's happening with you, honey?'

'I feel like I need to go to the toilet.'

Riley scanned the room. 'Do we have a privacy screen? No? Then everyone except one nurse and Konrad, who can face that way in case I need him, can slip out. Just while I feel her tummy and establish how far Melinda's labour has progressed.'

He ducked his head to hide his amusement at that and obedi-ently went to the corner and opened a screen on the MPC laptop.

Two nurses slipped out, the ambulance paramedic departed with his trolley, and Konrad kept his eyes averted. 'I won't look, Mel,' he said, a silly attempt to lighten the moment. 'You're a champion, Mel. And your baby will be too.'

The sharp inhalation of breath as the next contraction arrived, the rustle of sheets and the murmur of voices told him what was happening behind him. He made himself focus on writing medical notes, using the observations handed to him, accessing Melinda's old file and adding a new entry.

Finally, Riley said, 'You can turn around. It looks like we're having a Ridge baby. NETS will have to come in and scoop up him and Mum after he's born.'

Damn, Konrad thought. *Thank God for Riley.*

'Okay, everybody, we need some help,' Riley said.

The door opened and people came in. 'Let's get ready for a baby. Mel's nine centimetres dilated. Let's get organised.'

Melinda's voice sounded timid after Riley. 'I need to stand up.'

Lord no, he thought. *The last thing we need is a baby with its guts falling everywhere*, but he bit back the words with clamped teeth.

'I think that's a good idea,' Riley said. Konrad's eyes widened in shock. 'It's easier to push in an upright position, but once the head is nearly out, a quick lie-down is in order, okay?'

Melinda nodded and he stepped forward to help her ease from the bed. The way Melinda's face cleared as she took her weight on her feet made him reconsider his disagreement. 'Oh my.' She blew out a big breath. 'That is so much better.'

Riley turned to the nurse. 'Can you pass me that ultrasound

doppler, please.' The nurse did and then squirted clear jelly onto the handheld probe.

Riley pointed. 'The foetal back is here,' she said to the nurse, then she put the doppler over Melinda's pelvis halfway between the hip and the groin.

The sound of a baby's heartbeat filled the air and everybody in the room stopped. A stillness unexpected in the busy area.

'Oh my,' Melinda said again, her face softening. She blew out another of those gale-force breaths. 'That's good to hear.'

Everyone listened through the next contraction, and after that for another thirty seconds as the baby's heart rate stayed happily galloping along.

Riley took the doppler away and wiped the jelly off Melinda with a tissue. She pulled a pen from her pocket and drew an X on Melinda's skin. 'Listen there every fifteen minutes and after every contraction when she's pushing. You right with that?' The nurse nodded. 'Then record it for me, please.'

'Is Greta here?' Melinda whispered and Konrad lifted his head. 'Outside, I think.'

'Can she come in? Hold my hand?'

'Sure,' Riley said, before he could decide.

Melinda nodded. 'Tell Toby he can come in after the baby is born.'

'Okay.' Konrad shook his head at the stream of possible answers he'd already got wrong. He opened the door and slipped through, and found Greta and Toby in the waiting room, with the paramedic sitting next to them. 'Greta, she wants you.' Greta stood instantly.

'Toby.' The young man's eyes widened. 'She said after the baby is born.' There was absolutely no doubt that Toby looked mightily relieved.

Chapter Sixty-one

Melinda

Melinda pushed, inside herself, down, the way her body wanted her to direct the force, but it felt like she was pushing against a brick wall. Now that it was almost time for her baby to arrive, a sudden landslide of fear hit her like a slurry of rocks washing her into panic.

She couldn't do it.

She wanted out of here. Away from these people.

She wanted it all to stop.

At that moment Greta came in, took her hand, and squeezed. Melinda looked desperately into the kind eyes of the older woman and Greta squeezed her hand again. 'It's okay.'

The fear settled for a moment, then came back. It wasn't. She remembered how fragile her baby would be when it arrived. She'd seen the pictures of other babies that had their abdominal contents on the outside. They'd shown her at the hospital in Sydney. She understood there was no protection over her baby's bowel and any damage she did by pushing him out could cause an infection. He could die.

She should have had a caesarean, where they could do all this carefully. Not this. Not here. Not now.

The power in her pushes faltered, and her control wavered. Her mouth opened and she screamed in fear and denial.

'Melinda.' Riley's voice. 'What's wrong?'

'I don't want to do this.'

'Nobody wants to do this.' Riley remained calm, reasonable. 'Especially at this stage. It's hard work and scary. We understand you must be more scared than most, but you need to push.'

Maybe she did understand, but Melinda couldn't push. She couldn't be the one to kill her baby. She met Riley's eyes.

'I'm scared.' Then very, very softly she said, 'If I push my baby out, he'll die.'

'No, he won't. We're here for your baby. Konrad is here. All these people are here.'

The contraction came and she screamed again out of pure fear. Fear for her baby. She tried to push when Riley said so, but she couldn't.

Somewhere she heard Greta's voice. 'Toby told me, "You and your baby are superheroes." Superheroes know who to trust, Melinda. Trust Riley.'

She tried, but she still screamed the head out more than pushed. But at least she pushed. And pushed. And when almost all of the head was out . . .

'The forehead, nose and mouth are here,' Riley said. 'Sit back on the bed. Lie back.' Riley's voice was firm, no-nonsense.

That felt all wrong, but Melinda understood why. They didn't want a rush of the baby's body that might tear his intestines. She sat back. It was too late now to stop the birth. She'd have to put up with lying flat.

Except she didn't have to lie flat. They'd put the pillows in a big pile so she was almost sitting up. She could probably even see what was happening if she dared.

Burning stinging. Burning stinging. Burning stinging.

Instead, she looked at Greta's fingers, which she'd squeezed terribly white. She loosened her hold, allowing Greta to carefully wiggle her damaged hand.

'Sorry,' she whispered and snuck a look down her own body. She could see her baby's head between her legs. *Oh my goodness.* She froze, not daring to move because it felt horrible.

'Little panting breaths, now,' Riley said. 'Just little breaths.'

She did the little breaths and then Riley said, 'The baby's head is out.'

She put her own head back and closed her eyes. This was too much. Too much sensation. Too much pressure. It should have been too much that everyone was watching, but strangely she didn't care about that.

The contraction came again and she pushed. There was no scream this time because there was nothing to fight against. It was too late. Too late for fear, too late to stop. She had to do this. Everything was stretched and hot and burning down below, and she could feel the shifting of the baby.

'He's coming,' Riley said. 'Nice and gentle, now.'

She couldn't even hear anyone breathing. As if everyone in the whole room was holding their breath. The silence continued as her baby was pushed into the world.

Everyone breathed out. A gush of relief and emotion, and maybe, exhilaration.

She blew out the breath she'd been holding too. It held all those things. And more. Incredibly, she heard a mewling cough.

Riley said, 'Well done, Melinda. You have a son.' And then he cried once and then twice and the tension flooded from her. She hadn't killed him.

Tears stung her eyes. The pain was gone, and she felt strangely empty.

Riley said, 'Great. You did well.'

She didn't want to see, so instead she peered around at the faces. There was something like sympathy and softness on the faces but not pity. If it wasn't horrible then maybe she could look.

Except she had another pain. Panicked, she looked at Riley. 'Pain?'

'Afterbirth,' Riley said, and she remembered. And then that too was over.

Melinda leaned forward just a fraction and saw baby feet. Then a little further up Riley clamping the umbilical cord, then cutting it. It looked really long where she'd cut it. Konrad was leaning over her baby with a stethoscope.

Her baby lay on his back, his head near her feet, a purply mass of coils on his tummy about the size of an adult hand, but everything else looked perfect. Feet. Hands. Face. He screwed his mouth and nose and eyes and let out a bellow that made Konrad laugh. He was noisy!

A tsunami of need to protect and touch and hold her baby washed over Melinda, her fingers clenching with the need to caress his skin, to press him to her. But she couldn't. They'd told her that. Not yet.

She saw that he was lying on a messy towel as Riley slid her hands under his back and lifted him so the nurse could take out the towel and roll a new one under him. When she unrolled it, the cling wrap was there stretched under his back.

Konrad lifted Greta's cling-wrap roll across the baby's belly over the top of the coils and Riley lifted him again. Konrad passed the cling-wrap roll under him and Riley put him down. They rolled it over the top again until he was wearing a singlet of filmy plastic wrap with his arms and hands on the inside.

'It'll keep the moisture in until NETS arrive. It'll also keep his arms warm if they want to put cannulas in. They just make a little hole in the plastic to get to him.' Riley was smiling. 'He looks great. Konrad said his vital signs are good. We'll move him to the open cot because the overhead radiant heater is on. Would you like to touch him before we move?'

She couldn't touch his hands, which were wrapped in plastic. Melinda's throat closed and she couldn't answer, but she nodded. Riley must have seen because she lifted him the same way she had before and took a step towards Melinda.

Melinda reached out and stroked her son's precious face in his little plastic raincoat. His teeny, tiny fragile toes were pale and cold. 'He's blue.'

'Just his hands and feet. That's normal for a while until he gets used to living outside your tummy.'

Oh, she remembered that now. In the books the midwives at Moree had given her, she'd read about acrocyanosis – blueish hands and feet at birth. It was all perfectly normal.

Chapter Sixty-two

Riley

It was done. The baby had arrived safely and was wrapped in plastic.

Exhaustion crept down Riley's neck, but she kept her shoulders straight, pretending she didn't want to hunch and lean against something as she checked that her patient was stable.

Melinda looked good. She remembered Melinda screaming the baby out. Riley understood it wasn't the pain she'd been screaming about. Melinda had been terrified she'd damage her baby by pushing. But the young mum had trusted Riley and fought her instincts. Riley couldn't imagine doing that, despite knowing her baby was at risk if she pushed, and at risk if she didn't. She was damned both ways.

Mothers always blew her away with their strength and power. She'd seen the moment Melinda had shifted from a woman pregnant to a mother. That instant protective maternal beam that had changed her eyes.

Riley watched for it now when babies were born. Every now and then, she didn't see that glowing ignition of love, she saw disinterest, or fear, or even distaste for the newborn of their body. She always felt such sorrow for that mother and baby. She'd always been terrified that she would have been one of those who didn't feel that connection. She wondered if maybe Melinda's mother had been one of those. A non-maternal mater.

Right there, that's why she wasn't having children. Because she didn't think she could live with herself unless she gave her child one hundred and ten per cent. Like her own mother had.

It was a skewed rationale that could have come from all those desperate women over the last ten years, women willing to do anything to have a child, while she could quite easily consider not having a family as she built her professional life around being childless. Ergo, accumulative guilt that she didn't deserve a child, so she wasn't going to risk a maternal failure.

Her gaze shifted briefly to Konrad, the blue of his gaze soft-eyed and mushy as his eyes tracked between Melinda and her baby. A man who needed children. Which was why she'd be heading back to Sydney without him. Then he looked across at her and there was so much admiration and warmth in his gaze that she almost flinched.

She swung her attention to Melinda. 'Everything looks good on your side, Melinda. We'll wait half an hour to see you're not going to bleed after the birth or anything dramatic, then you can get up and shower. After that, you can sit and stare at your beautiful boy while we wait for NETS. I'll go talk to them.'

As she turned away she heard Konrad explain to Melinda, 'NETS is the Neonatal Emergency Transport Service. A specialist neonatal team who will fly with you both to Sydney.' Riley nodded her thanks to him and went to talk to the online consultants.

NETS arrived in under two hours from the birth, which was brilliant considering the flying time from Sydney and the equipment and staff they needed to bring. Basically, their aircraft held a neonatal intensive-care module, transportable on a trolley that bolted down for flight. A consultant paediatrician and two neonatal specialist nurses took over the scene and stabilised their tiny patient, or patients if there was a multiple birth, before they took off for their destination hospital. Sometimes they couldn't take the mother due to space issues, but today wasn't one of those days.

Riley watched as baby Edward in his hi-tech crib and new mum in a wheelchair were pushed to the helicopter pad. Melinda would have a whole pile of new experiences to add to this pregnancy.

Riley glanced around the wreckage of the room, open packets of sterile instruments and empty medication vials, plus the detritus of birth. 'Great job, guys,' she told the nurses, glad she didn't have to clean up, order new stock and restore order to the chaos before she could have a cup of tea. 'You've been amazing. Thanks for making it easy for Melinda and us.'

They all wore matching expressions: adrenaline dregs and excitement. 'Big day. Not one we'll forget in a hurry.'

She wanted to go home. 'Konrad?' He looked up. 'I'll wait in the car.'

'Coming. Thanks, everyone.' His smile had them all calling goodbyes as he followed her out, his big, brawny presence at her shoulder.

'You okay?' he asked, opening her car door. When had he started doing that?

'I'm fine.'

He shut the door when she was settled before he climbed in and steered the car away from the kerb. 'Nice work in there.'

'Teamwork,' she said.

He slanted a look at her. 'So much for your quiet evening.'

'It's worth it,' she said.

'You love it, the drama of birth.' He sounded pleased for her. 'Do you miss it with most of your time being taken up by consults?'

'It's not like I don't get to see births. I do my part when needed.'

'I saw the consultant in there.'

Yes, she'd run the show, but still it had been a team effort. 'It's what I do.' It was all she was good at. She flopped her head back against the leather headrest.

His face crinkled up in amusement. 'I'd forgotten how noisy birth can be.'

Riley closed her eyes, remembering. 'She wasn't screaming from the pain. She was scared for her baby. You could see it in her eyes.'

'I know,' he said seriously, so she knew he got it. 'You were both champions.'

'She was.' They'd pulled up and she opened her door the minute the car stopped. 'As soon as I ring Mum and ask her to work tomorrow, I'm going to bed.' She needed to phone that social worker, too, and make sure Melinda's new friend would meet her at the hospital. Without looking at him, because for some reason she wanted to reach back and touch Konrad for comfort, to have him hold her, carry her to bed and wrap himself around her, she said, 'I'll see you in the morning.'

'Don't forget dinner tomorrow night.' His voice was deep and rough, as if he wanted to say more.

'I won't.' She didn't look back. She wouldn't forget because that was when she was going to tell him that there was no future for them as a couple.

In the cool of the morning, Riley still wasn't up to running, but a brisk walk would clear her head. She left the unit before six am with that dusting of pink and blue to the west over the sparsely bushed scrub out of town and that hint of orange glow to the east through the maze of telegraph wires and single-storey rooftops.

The breeze on her cheeks blew cool and refreshing, unlike the furnace at midday would be. Desiree had said it was to do with the iron in the soil that made the ground hold the heat. The pink-and-white gravel crunched underfoot as she passed the old mine site only yards from the surgery with its rusted skeletons of vehicles and mine equipment hidden in weeds, all shadowed and silent in the early-morning light. The birds weren't silent, however, calling and trilling and chirping as the sun drew nearer.

At the deserted crossroads she pivoted, so unlike her usual focus, not sure which way to walk until some compulsion drew her left towards the Castlereagh Highway as if practising. Practising for when she turned her car this way to head back to Sydney. Practising to leave.

The town retreated at her back as she crunched over uneven stones, and it was hard to imagine she'd grown attached to a small, colourful outback mining town so far from the city. A crazy idea. Ridiculous.

Tonight, she'd be telling Konrad that there was no future for them, that there was no use digging a bigger hole for themselves.

She'd already fallen down one painful mine shaft and didn't want to fall again. Escape to her normal world was the way to the light.

Two and a half hours later, Riley pushed open the rear door to the surgery, showered, serene – at least externally – and ready for new people to help before she left.

Her mother sat with composure in Melinda's seat. Wearing a crisp white shirt and blue slacks, Adelaide projected confidence and professionalism as the new receptionist typing away. *Go Mum.*

Seeing Riley, she stood, stepped around the desk and held her arms open, her face beaming. 'So, Melinda's okay? And the baby?' They hugged briefly.

'I spoke to Melinda this morning. Edward goes into surgery at nine tomorrow. She sounds strong and has her student friend with her.'

'I'm so pleased she has support.'

'The social worker was waiting for her last night when she arrived.' She hugged Adelaide again and stepped back. 'Thanks for coming in, Mum.'

'That's easy, darling, I'm pleased to help. Especially after your exciting day yesterday.'

The street door opened and a couple peered inside.

Adelaide turned to them and Riley stepped into her consulting room to put down her bag. At a sound she looked to where Konrad leaned against the door.

'I'm making a coffee. Do you want one?' The white of his teeth showed, lips curved and wicked. 'There's this clever machine in the kitchen and I've got the hang of it.'

'Ah, that machine,' she said. 'Might have to leave it with you when I go?'

His smile didn't slip, but his eyes lost the crinkle. Guilt prickled because she'd been fickle. She'd led him on. She hadn't meant to, but . . .

'Yes, please. Coffee would be great.'

'I've made a booking for six pm at the Italian restaurant.'

She'd thought they were having takeaway in the shared unit? This was unexpected. 'There's an Italian restaurant in town?'

'Two. Both are great. This one I usually eat at once a week.'

The man had been here eighteen months. That was a lot of pasta. Or pizza.

Nine hours later, she was dressing for dinner out. She hoped she didn't spoil his favourite restaurant for him with her decision. She wriggled under mixed feelings of loss, stern decision, regret and maybe a little nervous anticipation, as she showered and put on a strappy, floaty sundress to combat the heat and the heated evening breeze that fluttered her dark curtains. If this was going to be their only real *date*, then the least she could do was make an effort.

He came to her door in a white button-down shirt and blue knee-length canvas shorts that showed off his strong calves and sexy feet in sandals. He looked like the surfer dude she'd imagined when he'd spoken about Port Macquarie. A well-heeled surfer dude, and casually relaxed. The tilt of his lips reminded her of strong sheltering arms, sunshine and sex.

He looked good enough to stay home and snuggle up to. It was a shame that she was going to dampen that shining light. 'Let's go, then.' The words blurted out quickly and his brows creased in question. She waved her hand. 'You look great.'

He shook his head. 'You look beautiful.' He took her hand and lifted it to his lips. 'I'd like to walk if that's okay?'

Stretching her legs after a day in the office sounded way better than climbing into a hot car. 'Perfect.'

And it was perfect as his fingers curled around hers. She noticed his other hand swung a wine bag that clinked softly.

He shrugged when she raised a brow. 'It's BYO. I didn't know if we'd go for red or white wine, so I brought both. A glass to complement the meal.'

As they walked, he gently squeezed her hand, as if checking she was okay, and her heart broke a little more as she savoured him beside her, caring for her. Riley savoured the warmth and the strength of his fingers, a warmth that she wouldn't feel when she went back to Sydney. She savoured the height and breadth of him as his shoulder brushed hers. She savoured the fall of his gold hair as it flicked in the evening breeze across his brow, highlighted by the late-afternoon sun.

Konrad Grey the Viking. Going. Going. Gone.

Oblivious to her thoughts, he pointed out houses of people he knew as they walked. He talked about how opals had changed people's lives, swinging their hands between them.

'The opals keep them here, keep them with promise and delight and being elusive, but always in their eyes you see that passion of the search and the thrill of the cut of the stone shaping their lives.'

'It sounds insane.'

He shook his head. 'A passion. Addictive. It's exciting, they say.'

'What do you say?'

'I like opals, but I'm not a miner.' He shrugged. 'Miners are a tough mob.' He spread his hands as if to encompass the town. 'Year round, there are only about fifty full-time miners here. Some are generations of the same family, some are passing through, but there are a thousand or more regulars who have camps and come part of the year, every year, to comb through the ground in search of a find.'

She could imagine the diversity. She'd seen some of it.

'Add to that,' he said, 'there are grey nomads who fall in love with the place and stay.'

'Plus, there are tourists like me.'

He stopped, turned, lifted his hand and touched her cheek. 'You're not really a tourist. More a treasure to appreciate for those who need your services.' His hand dropped and they started walking again, their other hands still clasped.

'Smooth, Dr Grey,' she said, but her eyes stung a little with his admiration. Thankfully, she didn't have to add to the conversation as they'd reached the end of the road and the restaurant on the corner.

He touched her elbow to usher her in through the glass door in front of him. Two wait staff and a cook came to welcome them, Konrad's long-lost friends obviously, and inside was not what she expected for an outback restaurant. White tablecloths, formally dressed staff, candles on the tables and big windows letting in the last of the afternoon light. Air-conditioned and redolent of garlic, breads, herbs and browning onions.

Their table butted up against the wall and faced two windows, with a large free space between them and the nearest couple, which ensured their privacy. She doubted that was by accident.

Konrad waited for her to settle before he took his own seat and handed his two bottles to the waiter. 'They'll keep the second bottle here for me for next time. Let's look at the menu before we decide.'

The menus looked extensive and intriguing. 'What do you recommend?'

He'd already put his menu down. She suspected he'd eaten everything on it by now. 'I always enjoy the steak, although the duck's great.'

She wondered about a duck, out here, in the outback. She guessed they had them. She knew for a fact that the prawns wouldn't swim here, so she decided on steak and he agreed. So, they called for the red wine. The waiter arrived, took their orders and returned with the bottle of red, which he opened and placed on the table.

She could approach the subject soon. They weren't really here for the food, right?

He leaned back in his chair, a small glint in his eyes. 'What have you enjoyed the most since you've been here?'

She blinked. Was this a red herring? 'It's been an action-packed month.' She thought about the word 'enjoy'. 'Apart from my work, which I always enjoy, the cool, fresh breeze in the morning for my run is wonderful. No people. No cars. No fumes or odours. Totally different to Sydney. There's complete silence except for the birds and crunching gravel.' She met his gaze ruefully. 'Not so much the evening run where I fell down a shaft.'

He winced. 'Nobody enjoyed that one.'

She shrugged. She'd lived. She'd barely been hurt, really, considering what could have happened. 'I do like the people very much, even Cyrus,' she conceded, 'who was a little daunting that first day, but has a heart the size of the biggest boulders out there.' She glanced out the window at the closed shops. 'The women in town awe me, like Desiree and co. More big hearts in tough exteriors.'

'And the area. The opals. The underlying town?'

'The town is fun with murals and humour and messy white mounds everywhere. But opals. Everyone has so much knowledge of opals. I've never really been an opal fan. I love the blues more than the expensive reds they're all looking for, but'—she thought about some of the many thousand-dollar opals she'd seen on her walk through the shops—'oh my goodness, the colours are incredible.'

'You're saying you found lots of things you enjoy?'

'The people I work with are nice,' she teased, then she sobered up. She needed to, to deliver her next words. 'But I'm not staying here.'

The words were there on the table in front of her and she stared as if she could see the invisible jumble of letters, refusing to look at him.

'I never expected you to stay.' His voice was low, calm and unsurprised.

Her gaze lifted.

'I expected you to leave. Maybe come back and visit your mum sometimes, when she's here. But your work is in Sydney. I get that.'

'Oh.' She pulled her knees together under the table. How embarrassing. Her hand tightened on her glass stem. Then she pushed it away.

His hand reached out and touched her fingers, slid over hers until she had her hand wrapped in his safe grip. Comforting. Peaceful. Soothing.

346

'Of course, I did wonder what would happen if I followed you? Courted you? Flew to you a few times before I asked for more. May I?'

She lifted her other hand, spreading the fingers to cover her breastbone. She tilted her head and a tentative joy built as the surprise sank in. Court her? 'You'd think about leaving the Ridge? You love it here.'

'I never expected to stay either. I stayed because of my brother and then because of Toby. Finally, because of the place and the people. And yes, I do enjoy my life here, though more since you came. But I don't want to lose you. I love you.'

She sucked in a breath at the word.

He shrugged. 'I love you more than this town.'

He said it again, in a restaurant, with people around. Freaking fearless man.

Words dried in her throat as her eyes widened. She opened her lips to say something, anything, closed them, and then tucked her bottom lip between her teeth. *Oh my goodness. Love?*

'We haven't mentioned the "L" word, but I'm putting it out there.'

She spluttered, 'You certainly are.'

His gorgeous blue eyes twinkled. 'I'm an old-fashioned guy. I've seen what I want. I know I want you, but I get that you haven't made your mind up about me.'

No, she hadn't. Because she'd been hiding behind going back to Sydney, still rushing from task to task, even when the Ridge had made her slow down a little. She'd never been someone to smell the roses, but there had been times when she'd soaked in the colour of the bougainvillea everywhere here.

Which made her think about what he was saying. She had dived into bed with him. Stupendously stellar as that was, there'd been fewer men in her bed than the fingers of one hand and she'd never felt what she had with Konrad. Not with anyone else. Ever. What else did she feel?

She felt sad to leave him. Concerned that she might hurt him. Sorry for herself at putting distance between them. So why was she leaving? Why? Because she always rushed somewhere. She lived in the fast lane of cutting-edge medicine. Had a harbour apartment. Drove a fast car and rode her fast career arc.

Could she be just as honest as he was? She moistened her lips, measuring the words. 'I have feelings for you. Complicated ones. But if you come visit, I'd like that.'

Chapter Sixty-three

Konrad

Konrad watched her green eyes widen across the table when he'd spoken of love. He hadn't intended to put it out there quite so boldly, but once said he meant it with every atom in his body. If she ran because of that, then it was better to know now.

She hadn't run, though, she'd looked skittish, but 'come visit' was what he'd hoped for. 'It's a long distance between Lightning Ridge and Sydney, but I'd like to try.'

She dipped her head to hide her face. She wasn't terrified at the thought, then. *Phew.*

The waiter approached with their meals – he had the feeling they'd held off while he talked – and Konrad sat back and let his fingers reluctantly slide from hers.

Once the plates were set and they were eating, head tilted, eyes gently amused, she rested her cheek on her hand. 'You knew I wouldn't stay. Did you have some sort of a plan?'

'Of wooing you? Nebulous at the moment.' He pretended to chew thoughtfully. 'I needed you to know I wasn't a stalker, though. No uninvited visits.'

She spluttered again at that. 'Not a stalker,' she said. 'Got that.'

'I'll come next weekend.' He watched her eyes widen. She hadn't expected that. 'It's a start I can be happy with. What about you?'

Her eyes met his and he could see the amusement but also her truth. 'That sounds good.'

The steak looked and smelled fabulous, but he didn't taste any of it as he ate. It might have been because he was watching her mouth, and the way her eyes kept skittering to his and back to her food again. She didn't look like the high-powered consultant now – she looked like a woman unsure of her feelings.

At least she had feelings. Even if they were 'complicated'.

'What about your dream of moving to Port Macquarie? Surfer Konrad? Your parents?'

'All for the future. Too distant and secondary.'

'Secondary to what?'

'To you.'

'You're mad. You barely know me. I'm a city girl. Then there's the issue of kids. I may never have kids. You should have kids.'

But his intent didn't change. Would never. 'I remember.'

She didn't look convinced, and something inside him, maybe that burst of hope, shrank just a little. Almost as if he could see her building back the wall he'd knocked a hole through with his unexpected declaration.

They'd finished and the waiter came for the plates. She sipped the last of her wine in the glass.

'Tiramisu? They do a to-die-for dessert here,' Konrad said.

'No, thank you. But you go ahead.'

He studied her, could see the distance growing between them, and he needed to stop the downwards plunge. He signalled for the bill and stood. It would be ready at the door for him. He stepped around to stand behind her chair. 'I'd rather go for a walk in the dark with you.'

She pushed out and rose. 'Let's do that.'

So they walked in the dark the long way around, past the closed shops on Opal Street, onto Morilla Street, past the club and the closed opal shops until they came to Desiree's service station, and then turned up their street to the accommodation behind the surgery.

'Have you been to the hot pools yet?'

'I've run past but not actually gone in. There are always cars there.'

'It's popular with tourists.'

'And now the old blokes in town?'

He grinned. 'You heard about that? Did you bring your swimmers?'

'Melinda told me. And yes.'

'How about we have a dip. You can't stay long in the water with the heat, and we'd be back in half an hour. It's nice at night.'

She looked dubious and then amused. 'Sure. It sounds great.'

'Meet you back at my car in ten?'

'I can do that,' she said.

He was there in five and she was there before him. 'How? I've never met a woman who could change clothes so fast.'

She raised her brows at him. 'Know a lot of women getting in and out of clothes, do you?'

'None that I'd follow to Sydney.' He opened the door for her.

She paused before climbing in. 'When did the door-opening thing happen?'

'Since you fell down a mineshaft. It made me strangely protective. And I did tell you I was old-fashioned.'

She slipped into the car past his arm. 'You did.'

Less than five minutes later, they were pulling up in the gravel parking area in front of the arched entrance and he wished he'd thought of this earlier. They could have done this on more nights after work.

When he switched off the engine she said, 'I've passed this on my morning runs over the last couple of weeks but always there've been cars here.'

'There are none tonight. You're safe.'

She looked at him from under her brows and muttered what might have been, 'Too safe,' but he couldn't be sure, though he hoped so.

As the safety gate clanged shut behind them, the large and small round pools were silent and steamy in the night with orange lights illuminating the area. A few damp footprints were drying, so it hadn't been long since people had left.

'It's warm tonight. Not so popular, thankfully. It's open all day, seven days a week, and closed for two hours in the middle of the day for cleaning.'

'It looks magical.'

She made it magical. 'Yes.' He took her hand and walked between the pools to the amenities block, stopping off to leave their towel bags on the picnic table on the way. He let go of her hand outside the ladies' showers. 'Just shower over your swimmers in the change rooms, it's a rule before entering, and I'll meet you at these steps when you come out.' He pointed to the handrails at the bigger pool. 'We'll sit on the steps and ease in.

You can't see much of them with the lights on, but we'll know the stars are above us.'

She sped into the change rooms, her voice floating back with, 'Race you.' She'd probably beat him, so he took off. He knew she was quick and he wanted to be waiting for her this time.

Two minutes later, they both walked fast and wet from the shower block and grinned at each other as they met at the rail at the exact same time. 'A tie,' she said.

Chapter Sixty-four

Riley

Riley stopped and turned slowly to take in the pools in the enclosed area. Despite the lights, to the south she could see the billions of stars that weren't visible in the city, and to the north the bright-orange lights on the shower block roof made her blink.

Inside the fenced area, the glow of the spotlights mounted high on the amenities turned everything a weird red like a smoky bar as they shone down and highlighted the steam rising above the pools. The odd light gave an almost sultry feel in the haze, despite the slightly off odour of eggs from the sulphur. The smell wasn't over-powering as it bubbled from the bottom of the pool, but it was there.

More delightfully, light bronzed the man beside her, who was waiting for her to stop checking out the surroundings, and high-lighted the rivulets of shower water into glistening beads on his bare chest.

Dressed only in his plastered shorts, he stood lean and powerful with water drips chasing each other down strong pecs and abs, and she wanted to follow one glistening runner with her finger as it disappeared into his shorts.

She looked up, and mischief must have been in her face because he pulled her wet swimsuit-clad body against him with a barely audible growl.

'A reward for our race to the pool.' He leaned down, curled his fingers around her neck and pulled her gently to him, until their lips met.

Somewhere in her mind, she could imagine her wet swimsuit drinking his droplets into her, like the heat of him soaking into her skin until she wanted to stay fused like this forever. Heat, hotter than the scalding artesian shower water, steamier than the mist above the pools, consumed her thoughts until only sensation remained.

She pushed her mouth against his and the sultry caress turned into a heat-soaked demand that made her gasp with need. She opened her mouth, answering, inviting, and his tongue slid in a slow, potent dance with hers, like the tendrils of vapour that danced on top of the water behind her.

With her eyes closed she sighed closer, pushing into him, loving the feel of his arms as they tightened around her body, jamming her against the hardness of him.

They kissed. Mouths melded. Time passed. Until the sound of the gate opening intruded and a voice called out, 'Enough of that.'

They broke apart, gasping, and then laughing.

It was Cyrus.

'Of all people,' Konrad muttered ruefully.

As if he heard him, Cyrus said, 'You told me to come here.'

'Not now, I didn't.'

Cyrus laughed. 'There are more mates coming.' His big, hairy belly bounced as he chuckled his way across the concrete towards them. 'Don't worry. We'll sit in the kiddies' pool. We won't watch you.'

'That'll be good,' Konrad said, 'you just make sure you keep your eyes away.'

Still laughing, Cyrus disappeared into the shower.

Konrad took her hand again. 'Quick. Let's get in before he comes back.'

'He said he'd sit on the other side.'

'I wouldn't put it past him to sit on the step next to you. He's got a bit of a crush on you, you know.'

She shrugged, teasing as she dipped a toe, 'Anyone who can fix an itch deserves a crush.' But she wondered what would've happened if Cyrus hadn't turned up.

Konrad kept her hand and led her onto the first step, showing her how to slide her fingers down the rail with her other hand so she didn't slip. The water enveloped her toes and then ankles. It was hot but bearable, like easing into a steaming bath. No way could anyone dive in. It would be like putting your head under the hot tap at home.

They went down the second slightly slimy concrete step, the third, and when their feet were on the fourth step, they sat and eased their bodies into the liquid heat. *Oh my goodness.* 'Glorious.' The word sighed out of her as the water slid over her upper chest and arms.

'Indeed, you are,' he said and she turned her head to see him admiring the view. 'Beautiful.'

She squeezed his fingers. 'As are you.' As was Konrad's strong hand in hers. Beautiful. Glorious. Sexy. 'It was a great idea, Dr Grey, to come here.' But with her eyes shut, she was thinking of that smorgasbord of kisses they'd just indulged in. Her whole body still thrummed beneath the heated water.

She leaned her upper arm against his and her head against his shoulder. Peace flowed over her along with the water. Peace like she couldn't remember feeling. Maybe she didn't do peace? Or at least she hadn't done peace, until now.

She could hear the shower in the amenities block running, so the holistic harmony of her heart and Konrad's would be gone soon, but she savoured it now. Maybe they'd get another chance to come here at night before she went home. Alone.

'I guess we're lucky there's only Cyrus here for now,' she murmured with her eyes still shut.

'It's walking distance from the caravan park across the road. So, yes, we are fortunate. Lots of locals use the place, too. Sometimes at night, the bore bath's a huge gossip group, mostly of men. But let's not waste time talking of others.'

He touched her cheek and she opened her eyes. 'I wanted to talk to you in the dark,' he said, 'even though it's not really dark and Cyrus will reappear shortly. It's important.'

She snuggled closer but tilted her head to watch his face. His profile had shadows and strong lines and was too dear to think sad thoughts about leaving, now. 'Sure.'

'In the restaurant, you changed. Like you left me when you mentioned children.'

Her stomach dropped, sliding somewhere into the pool below the steps, down where the sulphury smell bubbled up from, as sadness that made her mood flatten and her good humour die took over. She said the words again, 'You need to know that with me there's no happy, boisterous brood to come.'

He leaned the side of his head into hers and said softly, 'Why do you think no children is a problem for our future?'

Riley sighed out her reluctance to answer. However, Konrad deserved to know why she couldn't commit when they obviously fitted so well together, in other wonderful ways. Still leaning against his shoulder, she closed her eyes again and allowed the words to whisper out into the steamy night. Her deepest fears shared with a man, something she'd never wanted to do before. Something she wasn't so sure she wanted to do, even now.

'I think I'd make a terrible mother.' There it was, the stark reality. She was just too selfish with her time.

His fingers tightened on hers. 'How can you say that?'

She ran the heat of the water through her free hand, swaying it back and forth under the surface to create ripples of heat. 'I don't have time for kids. Despite my expert knowledge that the longer a woman waits to fall pregnant the harder it is, I still have no desire to beat the ticking clock.'

'Many women have no urgency.'

And now the guilt. She sat up to look at him. 'But it isn't fair when you consider all the women I see who would give their right arm to hold a child in their left.'

'Do you like children?' His eyes roamed her face with what looked like tenderness, and she did not understand that.

'Of course I do. Just other people's. I have no burning desire for one of my own.'

'That's valid, of course it is. And you don't need me to say so. But what has that got to do with you and me?'

Was he kidding? 'You should have kids. And I won't give them to you.'

His brows drew together mockingly. 'You're telling me I have to do something that you don't have to do?'

She frowned at him. 'You're laughing at me.'

'Never. Or not about this, anyway.' His arm crushed her to him. 'I love you. I want you to be happy, and I think you'll be happiest with me. The concept of children, like the decision of where we live and what we do with our lives, all depends on the core foundation. You and me together. The rest we work out as we go along.'

He still needed kids. 'But what if one day you desperately want a child and I say yes, then I make a terrible mother?'

He leaned down and whispered, 'What's your definition of a terrible mother?'

She knew the answer to this. She'd listed it so many times in her brain when a relationship edged towards the next stage. 'Not being there for them. Not being my mother. My mother always waited at home for me after school. She never missed my school events, sports carnivals, awards nights, plays and concerts. She came to every single one. She even did tuckshop. My dad came to none of them. I'd be like him. I'd be the mother who missed all those things that my mother made time for. Things I took for granted but relied on.' Like a verbal dump, suddenly it was pouring out. 'I won't have time to do that with my research and my clinics and my obstetric call-outs.'

'I hear you. And that you've thought about this. And maybe I'm hearing a fear of failure, foreseeing you'd let a family down.'

Was that what it was? A fear of failure. God, she was pathetic. And would be a terrible role model. But he wasn't going to let her wallow.

'Times have changed,' he said. 'Women aren't responsible or expected to fulfil all the nurturing. Men can nurture too. Men *should* nurture. Most love it. Maybe your dad didn't get the chance because he lived in a different time. I'd nurture you and our child if we had one, or our pets if we go that way, or just you, if you'd let me.'

'You're not coddling me.'

He chuckled, a low masculine rumble of sound that made her quiver with want. 'You won't let me coddle, but I can share.'

No, he wouldn't get to share, because he'd just confirmed everything she'd thought. He had so much to give, too much for her. He needed kids and she might never give him any. There was no future for them. But at least she'd told him so he could understand when she left.

'I'm getting hot.'

Suddenly, it was good that the conversation had paused because Cyrus stepped out of the showers with a splatter of flat wet feet.

'You sure you want me to go into the kiddies' pool?'

Riley patted the rail next to her. 'You should sit over here, Cyrus. We're nearly ready to leave. It's boiling in here.'

He guffawed. 'I thought you two were pretty heated before you got in.'

Riley felt her pink face grow hot. Yes, they had been, and she wanted more. And she didn't want to talk any more about having children, or not having them. Or making Konrad live without them. Or her future life without Konrad. Very low, as the slap of Cyrus's wet feet drew closer, she whispered in his ear, 'How about you take us home and me to bed.'

Chapter Sixty-five

Konrad

Konrad stood while he could without showing just how excited he was about that idea. The woman could blindside him with a whisper. It seemed he wouldn't have to worry about their sex life, just the briefness of their relationship. He needed to find a solution to her obsession over his future fatherhood. And that cooled his ardour.

She smiled, but now it didn't reach her eyes. That wall he'd seen earlier was back up and was gathering substance as he watched. There was a huge possibility of having a life without Riley if he couldn't figure out how to make it clear it was her – not her ovaries – he wanted to spend his life with.

He took her hand and helped her from the pool, thinking maybe he needed advice from someone who said he'd be welcome at her hearth any time. Adelaide Brand. Then again, Riley's mum worked for him now, so they'd have a chance to talk. For now, he'd take Riley to his home and show her just how much he loved her, and hopefully he could pull down that wall before it was too late and the concrete set and he was locked out of her life forever.

*

The next morning, Riley had gone for her run and Konrad thought of Melinda so far away in Sydney, alone and worried. He knew today would be as busy as the beginning of the week, but over everything they were all on tenterhooks for the news of baby Edward's operation. If Edward came through fine, then mother and baby would be home the following week. They'd find out by lunchtime.

If he wasn't mistaken, Riley was disappointed that she'd miss seeing the newest family settle into the community at the Ridge. He expected she'd call in at Edward's neonatal unit in Sydney when she returned. But that wouldn't be as good as the welcome committee when Melinda came home. He didn't want her to miss that. But then he didn't want her to miss anything. Basically, he didn't want her to go.

This Friday, when her contract ended, she'd be driving away and he had no expectation that she'd change her mind. Although she hadn't rescinded her permission for him to visit her in Sydney, she'd still be driving away, for good.

She had spent last night in his unit, and they'd filled the hours with achingly sweet lovemaking and a sort of panicked tenderness, but with very little conversation. This morning, for the first time in his career, he'd been tempted to call in sick for his surgery when the sun came up. He would have played hooky if he thought he could keep her in beside him, but of course she was gone by six am, kissing him and telling him to stay in bed. Establishing boundaries again.

And so she went for her first run since the accident, and although he'd hinted that he'd like to go with her, she'd declined and asked him not to. And he'd seen she needed the time alone.

*

So when he stepped into the surgery at eight-fifteen, after his own much-needed run in the opposite direction, he found only Adelaide there. Riley's door stood shut, so she was back safe.

'She's on the phone,' her mother said when he inclined his head towards the closed door. 'To her professor in Sydney about one of her Sydney clients.'

He nodded. She had women who needed her in Sydney, too. A life. An apartment. Her career.

As if she'd read his thoughts, Adelaide said, 'You two are lovely together. Riley needs to get over the idea that she can only have one thing in her life. Either a family or a career.'

'Nowadays you can have both,' he agreed, with a wash of hope that Adelaide at least thought he had a chance and was cheering for them.

'Hang in there,' she said. 'I did my one thing, being a mother and wife,' she said. 'I threw my whole soul into it, but one day, Riley was at boarding school and Tyler didn't see me as a thinking person.'

'That must have been hard.'

She tilted her head, her eyes on him. 'I realised I'd excluded my own happiness and fulfilment. I always wanted to be a nurse, and when I finally became one,' she paused and sighed, 'well, there were too few years to savour the career. Last year, it felt as if the health system changed to computer-focused cost analysis of modelled health care. A young person's game. I was outdated, hated the loss of patient focus and wanted out. It wasn't what I signed up for. It felt a bit like my daughter leaving home all over again.'

'She said you were a brilliant mother.'

'Oh, I was.' She laughed. 'Awesome. I might have scarred my daughter with the awesomeness.'

His eyes crinkled. She was such a sensible, wonderful woman, this mother of his love.

'I fear I did my "good mothering" at the expense of my own happiness. I don't want my daughter to do her "good doctoring" at the expense of her happiness. She's choosing career as her one thing, like I chose being the best wife and mother. She's making that same mistake of being the best to the exclusion of everything else.'

Adelaide scrutinised his face and she must have seen something that reassured her because she said, 'You love her.'

It wasn't a question. 'Yes.'

'Lucky Riley to have found a man prepared to be her equal from the beginning. I suspect you'll support her in whatever she wants to do.'

'Always.'

'Then don't give up.'

The door opened and a couple came in. 'We're here to see Dr Brand?' the man said. And the day started.

He didn't see her till lunchtime. But he was waiting.

'So, I've arranged to come to Sydney next weekend. It'd give you a week to find your feet again and unpack your bag. Is that okay?' Konrad watched his love's eyes widen. Oh yes, hadn't she believed him? He'd surprised her. 'Can I stay at yours?'

Riley blinked, took the cup of coffee he'd made for her lunch-break and perused the sandwiches laid out as she sipped. He saw when she noticed that her mother had left and they were alone. She moved the cup away from her mouth and nodded. 'Sure. I stayed in your house.'

'Not just my house.'

She narrowed her eyes at him. 'Are you suggesting you share my bed when you visit?'

But the wobble of humour gave her away and his tension eased. 'I am indeed. Because I'm not giving up on us. I see a whole future of your visits to the outback and mine to the city. Maybe me with a pilot's licence to cart you back and forth.'

'Carting?'

'I'm saying why restrict yourself to the city? And me to the outback.' He raised his brows and one finger. 'What has your time in Lightning Ridge taught you?'

She crinkled her eyes at him. 'The Friday-night ladies are to be feared?'

He smiled. 'Yes. But most importantly, that you can have more.' He spread his arms. 'While you've been out here, you've helped women who were losing hope of ever being mothers – that's your core business. But, you've also enjoyed the GP work – you've saved Cyrus from certain death, just ask him.'

She laughed, but he was serious and not finished. 'You've become a part of the community, this community, you've reconnected your parents and established a stronger relationship with your mother.'

She nodded at that. 'True. Not benefits I expected, but definitely added bonuses.'

'So, I don't think you should sell yourself short by deciding on one aspect of your life – your career. You can do more. And with me you can do it all.'

She leaned back, taking her coffee cup with her, as if he was suddenly contagious. 'You sure your father wasn't a preacher rather than a doctor?'

'What can I say. You inspire me.'

She laughed again, but he still wasn't finished. 'If you were to consider doing all those things you've enjoyed, the best of the last four weeks, what would you include? How could you see the future?'

He saw the moment she understood. Saw where he was leading her. Hopefully, she also saw the love in his eyes.

'You're saying do outreach as well as time in the city? And fit you in between?'

'Of course. I've enrolled in my first flying lesson. What we have is an opal-in-the-rough relationship. It needs rubbing and cutting and polishing. But there's a rare and valuable beauty in what we have together. It has a great intensity of colour. I'm going to fight for that. For you. Will you fight for us, too?'

He stopped. That was it. His best argument.

She stared at him, silently shaking her head. Until he saw something he'd never seen before. Not when she was down the shaft, broken and alone when he reached out for her. Not when Melinda's baby was born safely. Not even in their most tender moments.

She put down her cup and reached out her hand to his. His heart clenched as Riley's eyes filled with tears and she nodded. 'Yes.' Her head lifted higher and held his gaze. Hers softened and grew tender, her beautiful lips trembling as she repeated, 'Yes. I will fight for us, too. Come visit me and we'll talk about it. Make it happen.'

Chapter Sixty-six

Riley

Almost a year later, the harbourside wedding of Dr Riley Brand to Dr Konrad Grey was held in Mosman, Sydney, but that didn't mean the locals from Lightning Ridge didn't attend. Riley was their adopted daughter who came every six weeks to spend a week in town doing outreach clinics. This time, they'd go to her.

Travelling in a coaster bus, reminiscent of someone called Priscilla on her way to Broken Hill, this bus held Olivia and her husband, Aiden, who was driving because he wasn't trusting anyone else at the wheel with his pregnant wife onboard, singing about a road trip off key. The trip began raucously, with the group entertaining each other with jokes and songs. Desiree and Greta brought food, and Toby handed it around. Silvia and Selena brought alcohol. Elsa and Gerry took turns helping Melinda by amusing toddler Edward as they trundled past Ozzie the Emu as the bus drew away from the outback opal fields, past wheat-fields and small towns. Little Teddy grew sleepier through boulder country and over mountains, and woke again to the wilds of Sydney and the hotel two kilometres from the wedding venue.

An accommodation deal brokered by Riley's father, Tyler, at an upscale hotel in Mosman saw them all settled in harbour-view rooms to rest and recover before the next day's nuptials.

For those who hadn't spent much time in the state's capital, the wedding came with the opportunity to enjoy the harbour at its best. To savour a place away from their normal world without heavy traffic and multitudes of people. To see ships and sailboats on the harbour, planes soaring past the bridge, and to use free passes to the zoo before the late-afternoon wedding.

Adelaide and Riley had come up with the idea of hiring the Gili Rooftop, a top-floor space above the landscaped gardens and enclosures of Taronga Zoo, for the reception. The doors pulled back and the space embraced a glass-balconied terrace that was open to the skies and later the stars, with a view that expanded across to the Sydney Harbour Bridge in the distance, and the sounds of animals in the foreground.

Riley wanted to share the best of the city she loved with her friends from the Ridge.

An hour before sunset, after an afternoon of being styled, dressed and coifed with her mother and Konrad's sister, Bella, her brides-maid, it was time to meet her husband-to-be on the open deck overlooking the harbour.

Riley heard the wedding music as they came out of the lifts. It wasn't the march. Yet. Her father's hand tightened on her arm. 'You can change your mind,' he teased.

She laughed, blew out a nervous breath and felt her shoulders sink in relief. It was stupid being nervous. 'Thanks.' She met her dad's eyes. 'I love him.'

'I know. I'm very, very happy for you.'

They stopped in front of the open doors, still out of sight. Bella tweaked Riley's veil straight and fluffed her train so it spread in a circle. The photographer took a final photo then scooted past them into the room to capture their entrance.

Bella winked. 'You right?' Her bridesmaid had known she was nervous. They'd become fast friends and confidants, with Bella set to take over her brother's practice at the Ridge as principal doctor.

'Can't wait.'

'Then I'm gone.' Her new sister-in-law straightened her shoulders, and as the wedding march began she moved into the doorway and took one measured tread away. Riley and her father took one step forward.

And then she saw him. Tall and powerful in a grey tuxedo, his height and breadth and beauty suddenly fading into a blur when she saw the love in his eyes. He smiled. Saying *Come to me* with his gaze as he stared at her. Telling her she looked beautiful. That he couldn't wait. And suddenly, neither could she.

This novel contains themes of suicide and mental health. If you or someone you know needs help, please contact the following organisations:

Lifeline: 13 11 14
Beyond Blue: 1300 22 46 36

Acknowledgements

Thank you, dear reader, for spending time with my opal miner's daughter. I hope you were swept along with Riley's story in Lightning Ridge, because it was such a joy to write.

There is warmth and welcome in Lightning Ridge, which for me started with booking accommodation through Jo and Andrew at the Fossickers Cottages – such a great place to stay – and whose position in town I turned into the OPAL Medical Centre in my story. If you've been to the Ridge before, then I hope you recognised things that made you smile and feel the need to revisit. If you've never been, then I wish you smiles and fun when you travel to this wonderful outback mining town.

I need to thank fellow author Kelly Hunter for being my travel buddy in that brief window of opportunity that popped up to visit the illusive Lightning Ridge amid Covid-19 restrictions. You're a fabulous companion and co-driver in the nine hours it took us to get there.

Huge thanks to Diane Kearl – Di – the manager at Lightning Ridge Visitors Information Centre, who gave me maps, stories, recommendations and, best of all, introductions to fabulous people that I could talk to about all things Lightning Ridge.

Theresa Smith at the Australian Opal Centre has such passion and knowledge about fossils and gems and geology. Do not miss out on chatting with her. I'll be back to Lightning Ridge when their fabulous new Glen Murcutt-designed building opens and they have the space to truly shine a light on all their treasures.

Thanks to Vicki Bokros and Andrew from Down To Earth Opals for their passion and an incredibly fun and informative night at the Lightning Ridge Bowling Club. Such fabulous discussions on opal discovery, buying and selling and so much more inspiration for the next book, too.

Kelly Tishler – The Opal Queen with an open heart – you rock. Thank you for taking me around the opal fields, to places only miners go, and sharing your passion for opal hunting. Also, a huge thank you for knowing exactly where I meant and taking me to the place that inspired it all – an opal miner's camp that had been for sale two years ago. That's what started Adelaide's story in my head.

Dear readers, may I suggest you call into Piccolo Italian Restaurant for a great dinner, the place where Konrad took Riley – remember, Konrad eats there once a week!

The ruins from the church where Riley and Konrad found Toby are real, but it was actually built as a prop for a movie set that blew down in a storm. So if you're looking for the church, all that is left is a pile of pieces that nobody else has a use for.

To the Sheepyard Inn, Club in the Scrub, and all the other quirky and fun places at the Ridge and Grawin – thank you for being you.

ACKNOWLEDGEMENTS

On a less happy note, the charitable organisation Rural and Remote Medical Services (RARMS) announced with heavy hearts that it had to close its medical practices in Lightning Ridge and Walgett in May 2022. The escalating costs of primary health care and the historic underfunding of rural and remote health have made it increasingly difficult to attract and retain permanent doctors in remote communities. Huge kudos to all isolated doctors and nurses who carry the weight of being first and second responders to the health of our outback population. If one GP reads this book and considers remote medicine, I'd be thrilled, and I know the communities would be grateful. Our rural communities deserve the passion and commitment of Konrad and those many heroes I have met in real life.

As always, I would love to thank the team at Penguin Random House. My awesome publisher, Ali Watts, my wonderful editor, Amanda Martin, who follows up all my questions, designer Louisa Maggio and the super Connor Parissis in publicity, who works so hard to let readers know my book is out in the world and waiting to be found. Thanks also to Alex Nahlous and Sarah Fletcher for your insight and polish.

Special appreciation to my first reader and super-savvy writer friend Bronwyn Jameson for your amazing input with that first draft. I do love your sense of humour in dealing with me. You are a great mate. And all the amazing reviewers who do such an amazing job of sharing their thoughts on my fiction.

I also would like to thank my agent, Clare Forster, who is never too busy for me and is the person I turn to for career advice and as my sounding board. Thanks, Clare, and I've missed seeing you in person over the last two years!

ACKNOWLEDGEMENTS

Thank you to my writing friends in RWAus and RWNZ, where I found our lovely Maytone group – special mention to Trish Morey, who always provides forward motion when I lose my way. To Annie Seaton, who so generously provided a lovely quote for the front cover – you are an inspiration. To Jaye Ford/Janette Paul, for being my writer buddy and sounding board when we're at retreat, and all the WWOW writers at lunches for motivation.

Then there's my hero: my husband. No acknowledgement would be complete without the man who is, as the song goes, the wind beneath my wings. Dearest Ian, my love, my best friend and my biggest fan – I am *your* biggest fan. Thank you.

As always, it takes a village to write a book. And that's what I love about writing – we give, we learn and we share so that we can create books that touch our readers, experience magic moments and inspire the joy and satisfaction that comes from reading a story we love. I hope, dear readers, that you'll love *The Opal Miner's Daughter*. Thank you for your wonderful support. xx Fi

Book Club Notes

1. Have you ever wanted to pack up and take a break from your life for a little while? Where would you go?

2. Riley thinks a committed relationship will interfere with her career ambitions. How does her attitude towards this change throughout the novel?

3. Several of the characters, like Melinda, Konrad and Toby have experienced trauma and are still dealing with its consequences. How do these characters start to put their lives back together and heal?

4. Adelaide finds a sense of belonging among the eccentric and wonderful people of Lightning Ridge. Why do you think this is?

5. Riley tells Toby, 'One life, that's all you get. Up to you.' What do you think she means by this? Do you think this is good advice?

6. Adelaide decides to learn about mining opals later in life. What's a hobby or interest you've always dreamed of pursuing and why?

7. 'Mothers always blew her away with their strength and power.' How does meeting Melinda help change Riley's ideas about motherhood?

8. What is the role of community in the novel? Which characters are helped the most by the community of Lightning Ridge?

9. Adelaide's relationship with Tyler has changed by the end of the novel for the better. Do you think it is a case of 'absence makes the heart grow fonder' or another reason?

10. If you have read any of Fiona McArthur's other books, what similarities and differences do you notice between them and *The Opal Miner's Daughter*?